the STORM and the ROSE

T.L. Johnson

Contents

THE STORM AND THE ROSE

Copyright © 2025 T.L. Johnson

www.tljohnsonauthor.com

Published by Midnight Haven Books

www.MidnightHavenBooks.com

First Print Edition, 2025

Library of Congress Control Number: **2025906627**

ISBNs:

Paperback: 979-8-9923666-1-7

Hardcover: 979-8-9923666-2-4

Ebook (Kindle): 979-8-9923666-0-0

Cover design by **Jacie Neher**

Lyrics excerpted with permission:

"Take Me Home, Country Roads"

Words and music by John Denver, Bill Danoff, and Taffy Nivert

Copyright © 1971 BMG Ruby Songs, My Pop's Songs, Dino Park Publishing, JD Legacy Publishing, and Reservoir Media Music

Reprinted by permission of Hal Leonard LLC. All rights reserved.

For the survivors:
For those who have found the light,
and those still fighting through the dark.
Your strength is not just survival.
It is power. It is fire. It is yours.
Your story matters. Your journey is your own.
And no one can take that from you.

"Out of suffering have emerged the strongest souls;
    the most massive characters are seared with scars."
Kahlil Gibran

Preface

Every storm begins with a whisper. The first breeze against your skin. The faint scent of rain in the air. The subtle shift that tells you something is coming.

This story began the same way—a whisper, quiet and persistent, that grew into a storm I couldn't ignore.

I've always been drawn to tales of resilience. To characters who weather life's fiercest tempests and emerge stronger, sharper, undeniably changed. Maybe that's because I've lived through storms of my own—the kind that strip you bare and demand you stand even when it feels impossible.

Arden and Gideon's story was born from that same resilience. Arden's strength in the face of her past. Gideon's struggle to break free from a legacy that threatens to consume him. These aren't only fictional conflicts. They're reflections of the battles we all fight, the scars we carry, and the hope we cling to when the world feels too heavy.

As I wrote, I found myself returning not just to love, but to the kind of connection that challenges us—forces us to grow, to heal, to remember our worth.

It's about finding light in the darkest corners. It's about discovering that even the most battered souls deserve the chance to bloom.

I hope *The Storm and the Rose* pulls you in the way it pulled me: as something unexpected, inevitable, and impossible to ignore.

This is a story of tension. Of passion. Of the courage it takes to face the storms that threaten to define us. But most of all, it's a story of hope—the kind that lingers, even when the rain won't stop falling.

To you, the reader: thank you for taking a chance on this book.

Whether you're here for the romance, the suspense, or the storm itself, I hope you find something that stays with you long after the last page.

Let the storm begin.
—T.L. Johnson

Prologue

Arden Rivers didn't look back.

Some shadows followed her anyway.

Morgantown had once been her escape—not only from her past, but from the weight of a name she had never wanted to carry. Nursing school became the plan, then the lifeline; a path carved through sheer will, distance, and exhaustion. She buried herself in trauma nursing because there was mercy in being useful, in learning how to stop bleeding she could see.

For a while, it worked.

She thought she could outwork the loneliness. Outlast the exhaustion. Outrun the feeling of being watched.

The first note appeared in her locker, folded with careful precision and tucked into the metal slats as if it had always belonged there.

You deserve to know how special you are.

The handwriting was looped and deliberate, the kind of script that looked rehearsed. Like someone had written the words a hundred times before committing them to paper. At the bottom, he had signed it simply:

Your secret admirer.

She laughed it off at first. A prank, maybe. Some awkward, harmless attempt at romance from someone who had mistaken discomfort for intrigue.

But the notes kept coming.

Each one more personal than the last. More precise. Each one knowing her in ways she had never offered.

Then came the flowers.

The first was a single red rose slipped into her locker with a note signed J.T. After that, they started arriving at her apartment, always pristine, always silent, always without a card.

A friend joked that Arden had a secret Romeo.

Arden didn't laugh.

The precision rattled her. Every petal was immaculate. Every delivery arrived without witness or explanation, and somehow, despite everything she had done to disappear into the ordinary rhythm of her life, someone had found her.

Chad didn't even look up when she told him. He only rolled his eyes, fork hovering midair.

"Probably some loser with no game," he said with a shrug. "You're reading way too much into it."

Then the calls started—late at night, breath against the line, no voice behind it.

That was when she told him she was scared.

He smiled.

"You worry too much. No one's actually going to hurt you."

That was Chad's answer to everything. Don't worry.

She had known the relationship was over long before it ended, but she had held on out of habit. He was comfortable. Predictable. Safe, at least on the surface. When he mentioned moving back to Silverbranch, his hometown, she brushed it off at first.

Arden had sworn she would never end up in another nowhere town—the kind with gossip for gospel and quiet that crept beneath your skin.

But the night J.T. found her in the parking garage, breathing wasn't the only thing that became a fight. She packed her life in the dark and drove until her hands stopped shaking.

She wasn't running toward Chad. She knew better than that. He wouldn't follow through on any of his vague promises, but Silverbranch offered what she needed.

Distance.

She told herself it would be safe.

A sanctuary. A reset.

The wind sliced across her face as she pulled her scarf higher and turned the lock behind her.

The streets were quiet, wrapped in the heavy tranquility that only existed in small towns after dark. She told herself she preferred it—the calm, the predictability, the way nothing ever seemed to happen where everyone could see.

But tonight, the silence pressed too tightly.

Her keys jingled as she walked toward the lot, breath curling into the cold air in quick, uneven bursts. She had stayed late to clean up after a busy shift. Normally, she didn't mind, but something was off. An itch beneath her skin. A wrongness she couldn't name.

She glanced back toward the rear entrance of Dot's.

A faint flicker of movement.

Her pace faltered halfway across the lot. One step, then another. Slower now, her body understanding before her mind caught up.

A rose waited on the windshield.

Centered. Crimson. Placed with intention.

Arden stopped cold.

Her breath caught, and something twisted low in her stomach.

She didn't need to read the signature... *JT*.

The air thinned around her. She fought to breathe, to think, to make sense of the impossible thing in front of her. She had been careful. She had changed her number, deleted her socials, avoided old friends who might give her away.

How had he found her here?

Her fingers shook as she reached for the lock.

Too slow. Too uncertain.

A rustle sounded behind her.

Her head snapped up, eyes sweeping the shadows. Streetlights flickered across the pavement. Nothing moved.

But the feeling remained.

A presence.

Watching.

Waiting.

She yanked the rose from the windshield and let it fall. The note fluttered down behind it, landing faceup against the pavement, but she didn't read it.

Not tonight.

She slid behind the wheel and slammed the door hard enough to rattle the glass, as if noise could frighten fear away. Her hands fumbled for the lock, muscle memory moving faster than thought.

Too slow.

Too late.

Her breath stuttered against the window, each exhale ghosting the glass. Outside, the shadows blurred and multiplied until the night itself seemed to have noticed her.

Then came movement at the edge of her sight.

A figure stepped from the dark.

Her chest thudded with each beat—loud, uneven, frantic—as if her body had been trying to warn her all along.

The handle jolted once.

Then again.

Harder.

The door ripped open.

Her scream split the quiet.

Fingers seized her wrist, tight and sudden, too real to be imagined. Iron-cold. Unrelenting.

"You can't keep running," he said.

Calm. Certain. Like the outcome had already been decided.

Arden clawed at him, panic blazing hot beneath her skin, but his grip didn't budge. It was bone-deep, bruising, meant to own.

"You don't get it," he said, dragging her closer. "I've given you time. I've watched you. Waited. For you to see me."

Her stomach lurched.

"Let go of me!"

"You smile at everyone," he whispered. "But not me. Never me."

His other hand moved.

Arden's gaze dropped.

A knife gleamed in his grip, thin and reflective and waiting.

His fingers flexed.

She flinched.

"God, the way you smell," he murmured. "I searched everywhere for it. Jasmine, lavender... vanilla. It stays with me, you know. Your scent. Like it wants me to remember."

Her pulse roared, drowning everything but the need to move. Her thoughts fractured into panic, survival, escape.

"You don't have to fight me." His hold tightened—measured, smug, certain. "I'm trying to give you something real. Why are you fighting it? If you'd just let me—"

That was when it hit her.

The burn of old wounds. The memory of hands that didn't ask. Words she had never wanted to hear again.

The fire came fast, rage eclipsing fear.

"No," she snarled, her voice trembling but unbroken.

Then she moved.

Fast enough to catch him off guard.

Her free hand wrapped around the steel blade before he could pull away. It slashed through her skin, sharp and hot, but she didn't let go. She wrenched it back, desperate and raw, and drove her elbow into his ribs.

A sharp grunt tore from him.

His grip faltered.

Her hand bled, warm and slick around the knife, but she held on because she had to. That half second of hesitation was all she needed.

Arden tore free and stumbled back, legs unsteady, breath ragged.

But she didn't stop.

She didn't look back.

She didn't realize she was crying until she saw her reflection in the windshield: eyes wide, cheeks streaked, blood trailing down her arm.

Her hand throbbed. The pain tethered her.

She blinked, fogging the glass.

In the glow of the streetlight, something red caught her eye.

The rose.

It lay where it had fallen, broken open like a wound.

This time, she picked it up.

Blood smeared the petals as she closed her fingers around it. The thorns bit deep, but she didn't let go.

Her vision blurred.

Still, she stared.

A terrible truth rooted itself.

Some shadows didn't fade.

CHAPTER 1

Static & Smoke

Arden Rivers slipped behind the bar, her hands moving on muscle memory: cleaning glasses, straightening bottles, resetting for the next rush. The din of laughter, clinking drinks, and heavy boots on tired floorboards filled Dot's; a racket she'd long since learned to tune out.

She glanced at the clock. Two more hours. Then she could swap the noise and fluorescent haze for the hush of her apartment—where quiet wasn't a preference. It was survival.

Dot's was a dive, plain, unapologetic.

The place reeked of old wood, fryer grease, and beer gone flat. Secrets lived in the walls, soaked into the floorboards like spilled whiskey and older regrets.

In the corner, the jukebox crooned something slow. Ache and smoke in every note. The song hung in the air, clinging to her skin like ashtray ghosts and sins no one paid for. It suited the regulars—men who drank to forget things they never admitted, not even to themselves.

This place never pretended to be more than it was. She respected that, even when she hated it.

"You gonna stand there gawking, or you gonna earn that paycheck?" Dot grumbled from his usual corner, nursing the world's most bitter cup of coffee.

Arden didn't miss a beat. "Only basking in your warmth and charm, Dot. It's... overwhelming."

"Smartass," he muttered, the twitch of his mouth giving him away. "Keep it up and I'll start docking your pay for sarcasm."

She tossed the bar towel over her shoulder. "I could start charging by the comeback. Might actually turn a profit."

Dot shook his head, chuckling into his mug. "Better not leave me stuck babysitting the regulars when the next shift bails."

She grabbed a clean rag and let her hands take over: wipe, rinse, repeat.

Anything to mute the jukebox, the half-spoken apologies, the noise gnawing at the back of her skull.

Overhead, the fan stuttered through another lazy turn, stirring nothing but the stale haze curling toward the rafters. In a bar like this, no smoking was more decorative suggestion than rule.

But something was off about tonight.

It wasn't loud or obvious; it moved through the room like static before a storm, raising the hair at the back of her neck before she knew what had changed.

The door hinges groaned.

She looked up on instinct. Years of tending bar and avoiding trouble had trained her to sense the shift before the sound.

The regulars hadn't moved.

But the room had.

He walked in, and the air rebalanced around him.

GIDEON BLACKWELL ENTERED like the first drop before the downpour: sharp, inevitable.

The room didn't go silent, but it shifted. Conversations dipped. Heads turned. Everyone felt it.

He didn't announce himself. He didn't have to. Power followed him like a shadow—quiet, but unmistakable.

Arden straightened. Not alarmed. Aware.

His suit was charcoal and clearly tailored, clean-lined without being flashy. The man wearing it was the same. Tall, but not in that lean, forgettable way; he carried his height with the quiet confidence of someone who understood exactly how much space he took up. Broad shoulders. A fighter's build honed beneath restraint.

His dark brown hair was cropped short at the sides, the top left just long enough to tousle—a quiet rebellion even discipline hadn't managed to crush. His jaw looked sharp enough to wound, and his gaze hadn't softened for anyone in years.

But it wasn't the looks that made her stop.

She didn't pause for pretty. Pretty smiled while hiding the lie, and she'd had her fill of liars.

This man wasn't simply watching the room. He was reading it. Calculating. Every step measured, efficient, controlled.

And still, something wild flickered underneath.

Then his gaze found hers.

Eyes like smoke and steel. Clear, unreadable, cool as winter air. They didn't merely look at her; they saw her. Cut straight through.

The room tilted.

The moment passed in a breath, unspoken and electric.

But it didn't vanish.

It settled.

Marked her.

He didn't get distracted.

Gideon had trained himself not to react to appearances. He didn't scan for style or symmetry; he studied motive, intent, survival. Not seduction.

But this woman cracked through discipline like a match struck against dry kindling.

God, she was stunning.

Her eyes cut through the bar's haze, that impossible shade of blue—more ocean than postcard, more storm than sky. Cool. Unbothered.

Her hair fell in loose, wild waves, dark brown touched with auburn where the low light caught it. It framed her face with a kind of reckless grace, as if the world had tried to tame her and failed.

The kind of hair that made a man wonder how it would feel wrapped around his fingers, and whether he would ever earn the chance.

Nothing about her looked arranged for anyone else's approval; she seemed unpolished in the most dangerous way, alive down to the smallest movement.

She wasn't shy, and she wasn't sweet. She moved like a woman who didn't ask for space; she took it, then made a man grateful she had decided to stay.

The black V-neck clung just enough to look understated and intentional. Black jeans, worn soft in all the right places. Scuffed boots. Every detail said she wasn't asking for approval. There was no polish in it, no posing, only the disarming reality of a woman who seemed uninterested in being softened for the room.

A dark goddess in denim and leather.

Not the kind a man worshipped from a distance. The kind you didn't think you'd survive.

And damn if that didn't make her dangerous.

He should have looked away.

His pulse answered first.

The bar faded beneath the noise of his attention.

His stare found her, and there was no curiosity in it. Only challenge.

Her spine stiffened—not from resistance, exactly, but recognition. He was reading her, and she hated how quickly it made her feel exposed.

A barstool scraped.

The spell broke.

Then he was there, too close and too quiet, still as a loaded gun.

"Bourbon," he said, his voice smooth. "Neat."

Arden didn't react. Not visibly.

She scanned him the way instinct had taught her to scan anything that might become a threat: suit, stillness, watchful eyes. Trouble, without question.

God help her, though. Beautiful trouble. The kind that left bruises a woman might hate herself for wanting to remember.

Arden didn't have to think. Muscle memory guided the pour, clean and unhurried, and she slid the glass toward him.

Their fingers met.

A brush. Nothing more.

But the contact struck through them both, brief and bright and impossible to dismiss. Intentional or not, it held.

His grip tightened for half a second.

Her skin was too warm. Softer than he expected, in a way that contradicted everything else about her.

But it wasn't the touch that unsettled him.

It was the look in her eyes.

She didn't flinch, didn't soften, didn't offer him the satisfaction of being impressed. She only watched him, steady and unsparing, measuring him with the same quiet precision he had turned on her.

The background noise of the bar thinned until everything else slipped out of focus. The moment stretched between them, taut and electric, thick with the air before a lightning strike.

Destruction, if either of them blinked first.

"TELL ME SOMETHING," he said, holding her gaze a second too long. Whatever passed between them wasn't quite a smile. "What do you do for fun around here?"

Arden arched a brow, cutting him clean with a glance.

"That's your opener?"

Her voice moved like smoke, cool and unimpressed.

"The guy at the tire shop has better lines, and he once told me my chassis looked 'well-maintained.'"

Gideon's laugh came low and real, rough around the edges.

He liked that she didn't soften for him. Liked the way she threw his words back with enough precision to make it clear she expected him to keep up.

"Figured honesty was safer than charm," he said. "Subtle doesn't seem to play well here."

She didn't argue. Her gaze drifted over the tailored lines of his suit, slow enough to make a point.

"Neither does that."

The line hung between them, taunting and amused, sharper than it needed to be.

Then she leaned in with sudden, elegant mockery, close enough for him to catch the faint warmth of her perfume beneath the bourbon and smoke.

"So, tell me..." Her mouth curved. "What's a woman like you doing in a place like this?"

"Careful," he said. "You're stealing all my best material."

She folded her arms, chin lifting as if she had already found him guilty and was only waiting to see whether he would make sentencing interesting.

"Let me guess," she said. "You think being mysterious makes you more interesting?"

It shouldn't have landed.

It did.

Every word from her felt like a wall and a test, and nothing about her asked to be won over.

"You tell me," he said, his voice dipping low. "Is it working?"

THE DOOR CREAKED OPEN AGAIN.

The air snapped.

Chad Dawson strolled in with his swagger on autopilot, his mouth curled into the same tired sneer Arden knew too well.

"Well, well," he drawled. "Entertaining the masses, Arden?"

The change in her expression could have stopped traffic: cold, immediate, complete.

"What do you want, Chad?"

Gideon didn't flinch. He only watched, quiet and assessing.

Chad's eyes flicked to him, taking in the suit, the posture, the kind of presence that didn't need an introduction. His lips twitched.

"Didn't know Dot's was taking reservations from the GQ crowd."

Gideon didn't blink or budge.

The silence stretched long enough to become deliberate.

"Arden was giving me a crash course in local customs," he said, his voice smooth as poured bourbon. "I'm beginning to think your version might be more dramatic."

Chad's jaw ticked.

Arden's smile didn't reach her eyes.

Just like that, the game changed.

RAISED voices cracked through the noise, sharp and escalating.

Near the dartboard, Donny and Travis squared off, already halfway to stupid. Shoulders braced. Fists twitching.

Then glass shattered.

Arden moved before the sound finished breaking.

Dot started to rise, but she cut him off with a quick shake of her head. "I've got it."

The bar stilled around her, the air pulling tight.

"Enough!"

Her voice split the tension cleanly, sharp enough to stop the room where it stood. There was no panic in it, no pleading, only command.

For a moment, even the smoke seemed to hold its breath.

FROM THE BAR, Gideon watched her move through the room—commanding, unflinching, built for moments like this.

Donny turned, but his gaze flicked sideways.

Right to Chad.

Of course.

"What, we got a problem in my bar?" Chad stepped forward, his grin slick as oil.

Arden's spine locked. "It's not your bar."

But Chad had never known when to quit.

"Gonna let her treat you like that, Donny?" he said, loud enough for the room to hear. "She's real good at sticking her nose where it don't belong."

Her fists curled at her sides.

"Chad," she said, each syllable sharpened by restraint. "Sit down."

Too late. The spiral had already begun.

A barstool screeched against the floor.

Gideon rose.

Steady. Quiet.

"Maybe it's time we dial it back," he said, his voice low. "She had it under control right up until you opened your mouth."

Chad turned, sizing him up. "And who the hell are you s'posed to be?"

Gideon didn't flinch.

"Someone smart enough to stay out of her way."

For a split second, nothing moved.

Then Chad blinked.

Wavered.

And stepped back.

THE BAR EXHALED AROUND HER.

The pressure broke. Voices returned in murmurs, glass clinked, and life resumed in the uneven way it always did after men remembered themselves.

But when Arden turned, Gideon was watching her.

His gaze hadn't drifted once.

"You handled that well," he said quietly.

No grin. No teasing. Pure fact.

She let out a low, controlled breath and tossed the rag over her shoulder. "Don't get impressed too fast. It's just a Tuesday."

He didn't laugh, and he didn't look away.

Arden narrowed her eyes as she dropped the broken glass into the bin. "What? You waiting for the part where I hand out gold stars?"

He tilted his glass with the barest movement. "No. Just admiring the execution."

Something in his tone settled beneath her skin, quiet but deliberate.

She shrugged it off. "Not my first bar fight. Won't be my last."

His gaze held. "You don't strike me as someone who lets her guard down."

She paused for half a second, just long enough to hate that he'd noticed.

Then she said, coolly, "Maybe I just know where the boundaries are."

"And who's allowed to cross them," he added, his voice low.

The space between them dared her to answer.

Her chest tightened—not because of the flirtation, but because of the precision.

"I don't believe in blurred lines."

"Neither do I."

The air stretched taut between them.

Then—

"Arden! Table four!"

Dot's bark cracked through the moment.

She exhaled, relief and frustration tangling in the same breath.

One last glance.

Gideon hadn't moved. Worse, he still looked as though he understood exactly why she needed to.

That unnerved her more than anything else tonight.

She pulled herself upright, recentering. "Duty calls." Her tone lightened by a careful degree. "Try not to scare off the locals while I'm gone."

His answer came easily. "No promises."

She turned.

His presence followed her anyway—quiet, focused, unrelenting.

WHEN SHE CAME BACK, tray steady in her hands, he hadn't moved.

Same seat. Same glass. As if he had settled into the space and quietly dared it to reject him.

His fingers rested near the bourbon, his gaze locked on her with an attention that felt too deliberate to be casual and too focused to be simple curiosity.

He looked at her as if there were lines missing from the page, and he meant to find them.

A ripple passed through her—discomfort, curiosity, and something lower, more primal.

She paused.

Too long.

Then she stepped behind the bar and let routine anchor her. Glasses clinked. Her hands found their rhythm. The familiar motions steadied what his silence had unsettled.

Still, he didn't look away.

His attention pressed heavier than any pickup line.

She flicked a towel over her shoulder. "Planning to sit there all night, or just waiting for round two?"

The question came out casual, but her pulse betrayed her.

His mouth curved, slow and sure, as if he heard everything she had buried beneath the surface.

He had noticed her voice immediately. Smooth. Measured. Textured with something that lingered after the words were gone. It wasn't smoky, wasn't sweet, and it sure as hell wasn't designed to please. It was the kind of voice a man remembered after a single word and resented himself for wanting to hear again.

"Didn't plan to leave just yet," he said, his tone easy. "Unless I've worn out my welcome."

Her breath caught, subtle but real.

The challenge in his voice should have raised a wall. Instead, it drew her closer to the edge of one.

His gaze dropped briefly, not with hunger exactly, but with perception; the kind of attention that noticed details and gave them weight.

She didn't match this place. Not exactly. But maybe that was why she caught the light the way she did.

"Most people come here to drink," she said, folding her arms. "You don't look like most people."

"Neither do you."

He didn't say it like a compliment. More like a fact he had already tested and found true.

She tilted her head, studying him. "You never answered my question. What are you really doing here?"

He leaned back slightly, calm as ever. "If I said I was just passing through, would you believe me?"

"Not for a second."

His laugh came low and warm, surprising enough to slip beneath her guard before she could stop it.

"You're good," he said.

She lifted a brow. "At seeing through bullshit?"

He took another sip. "At making me want to keep talking."

THE SILENCE STRETCHED AGAIN, but this time, it had lost its edge.

Something gathered in the quiet between them, unsaid and impossible to mistake.

They talked.

Nothing earth-shattering. Nothing rehearsed. Stories traded in careful fragments, a few guarded truths offered with the kind of restraint that made them feel heavier than confessions. At some point, he said something dry enough to make her laugh before she remembered she didn't do that easily.

And he watched her like a man who noticed things.

Not the surface. Everyone noticed that.

Gideon saw what lived beneath it.

When she reached for his glass as he set it down, their fingers nearly touched again, and the almost-contact moved through her with the same bright, unwelcome current.

That was when he said, "I have a proposition for you."

Her hand paused mid-reach, fingers curled around the glass. She looked up, brows raised. "That sounds suspiciously like an invitation."

He didn't deny it.

Instead, he reached into his jacket and slid a card across the bar, smooth and intentional.

Black. Matte. No nonsense. Clean lettering without embellishment.

Gideon Blackwell.

The Blackwell Room. New York City.

"Consider it an opportunity," he said. "Not everyone gets one."

She didn't touch the card.

Not yet.

"Why me?" she asked, her voice quieter than before.

His expression shifted, something thoughtful edging out the charm. "Because you don't belong here."

She didn't flinch.

"I'm guessing you already knew that," he added. "So did I."

Their eyes locked again, and this time there was no posturing between them. No clever line to hide behind. The charge was still there, but it had changed shape, settling into something that felt less like attraction and more like recognition.

A pull toward someone who saw her clearly: sharp edges, shadows, and all.

"You ever take a leap," he asked, "just to see where you land?"

His voice had dropped, low and measured.

A quiet dare.

THEN HE STOOD, straightened his cuffs, and turned toward the door.

She still hadn't picked up the card, but she felt the weight of it as if it had already marked her.

At the door, he paused and looked back.

Their eyes met one last time.

The faintest lift of his mouth.

Then he was gone.

The door eased shut behind him, quiet and deliberate, but the storm he left in his wake was anything but.

Thunder rolled somewhere in the distance, low and approaching.

Arden slipped the card into her pocket.

Her pulse was steady.

Her thoughts were not.

For a long moment, she didn't move.

The quiet in the bar wasn't real silence; it never was. Ice clinked in a glass across the room. Someone muttered near the jukebox. Overhead, the dim lights hummed low and grating, prickling at her skin.

But inside her, something had gone still.

Not calm.

Waiting.

She ran her thumb along the edge of the card in her pocket, the matte finish snagging faintly against her skin. All friction and memory. Clean. Unmistakable. As deliberate as the man who had left it behind.

She didn't believe in fate. Not really.

But timing had teeth.

Arden exhaled and reached for the rag on the counter, choosing routine, motion, anything to ground herself before her mind pulled her somewhere she wasn't ready to go.

Gideon Blackwell.

She hadn't known his name thirty seconds ago. Now it moved through her like a warning.

Or a promise.

He hadn't said much, but he hadn't needed to. She had met men who talked too much—men who bragged, overshared, filled every inch of silence because they were terrified of what might appear inside it.

Gideon hadn't filled the silence.

He had used it.

And that unsettled her more than anything he'd said.

He watched. He listened. Somewhere between the two, he had seen straight through her armor, and Arden wasn't used to being seen that cleanly. It unsettled her. Worse, it intrigued her.

She shook it off.

Or tried to.

The door creaked open again, and she tensed, but it was only a couple of locals stumbling in, laughing too loud and tracking in wet leaves.

"Last call's in fifteen," she called out, voice steady.

Neutral.

Her hands moved automatically: bottles, glasses, cleanup. But her mind hadn't left the card. The city. The offer. The fact that Gideon hadn't asked for anything, not exactly, and yet she still felt the weight of his question.

You ever take a leap?

She had leapt before. Out of obligation. Out of desperation. Out of the kind of fear that dressed itself up as practicality because that was easier to survive.

Never just to see where she might land.

Arden glanced at the clock: 12:46 a.m.

Dot had already slipped into the back room, the usual end-of-night shuffle beginning around them. Chairs turned up. Lights dimming. The bar settling into itself one tired sound at a time.

Her fingers brushed the edge of the card again.

There.

Real.

The possibilities were forming behind her eyes faster than she could stop them.

She didn't trust easily, and she sure as hell didn't chase men in tailored suits who whispered about leaps and left storms in their wake. But tonight, there had been a shift. She felt it in her bones.

Arden wiped the final glass clean, locked the cash drawer, and turned toward the door.

The wind howled as she stepped outside. Low storm clouds clung to the horizon, swollen and electric.

And beneath them, something unnamed.

Unshaped.

Pulling her forward, just the same.

CHAPTER 2

Bloodlines & Boundaries

Sunlight flared against glass and steel as Gideon Blackwell stepped out of the sleek black sedan. Hawthorne Holdings loomed above him: sleek, imposing, unapologetically modern. A monolith built on ambition and legacy. His grandfather's vision. His inheritance.

It was the backbone of an empire. A source of pride. And a weight he could never put down.

Gideon held the majority shares, but none of the ego required for the CEO title. Let someone else handle the press, the reports, the boardroom parade. His place was at the helm, but behind the curtain.

Quiet power suited him. He didn't chase credit. He controlled outcomes. While others postured, Gideon played the long game. He selected the sharpest minds and steadiest hands, then gave them room to operate. Micromanagement reeked of insecurity. Real control moved in silence, shaping decisions without ever clamoring for attention.

The title wasn't the power. He was. And everyone in the building knew it.

He moved through the marble-lined lobby with unhurried precision, his polished oxfords striking a steady beat. The receptionist nodded, smile taut with professionalism. But beneath it, a flicker of nerves he was used to provoking.

He didn't demand presence. He simply had it.

The elevator whispered closed behind him, sealing him in with only his reflection and the rising hum of memory. This space had carried countless negotiations, victories, betrayals. He preferred the view from above, where the whole field lay visible—every move calculated before it was made.

His grandfather, Richard Blackwell II, had built the company on integrity and a ruthless vision for legacy.

His father, Richard III, had corrupted both. He had smoothed the edges into something polished and hollow, the family name remade as charismatic rot wrapped in charm.

Gideon was neither of them.

And he was both.

Their ghosts lived inside every decision he made: brilliance and burden, instinct and restraint, the old hunger to build something worthy tangled with the newer knowledge of how easily power could be dressed up and sold as virtue.

The elevator chimed.

The doors opened to a floor humming with quiet intensity.

Staff moved with the kind of purpose born from something deeper than routine. Fear, maybe. Reverence. More likely, the uneasy place where the two became difficult to separate. Voices dropped as he passed.

He walked past the CEO's office without slowing.

That chair could have been his once, but titles were for people who needed to be seen.

The boardroom waited ahead, all glass walls and steel trim, power woven into every clean line. Conversation halted mid-sentence when he entered, not from fear entirely, but from the quiet awareness that the stakes had changed.

Gideon took his place at the head of the table.

Not because the seat was designated.

Because no one else would dare sit there.

His gaze swept the room and landed briefly on Daniel Cole, already seated with a tablet in hand and the unmistakable expression of a man suppressing a grin.

Dan.

Chief Financial Strategist. Unbothered genius. Gideon's closest ally.

"Let's begin," Gideon said, his voice smooth as glass and sharp enough to cut.

Around the table, the air shifted. Focus tightened. Whatever anyone had thought they were walking into, it was no longer merely business.

It was legacy.

By late afternoon, the boardroom's heat had cooled.

The spectacle was over, replaced by something quieter: a private room tucked out of view, where the real strategy unfolded.

Mahogany. Leather. A skyline knifing across floor-to-ceiling windows.

Dan leaned back, the glow from his tablet throwing faint light across his open collar. His blazer looked effortless, his demeanor even more so.

He lived in numbers the way Gideon lived in control.

Where Gideon wielded force like a scalpel, Dan moved with the inevitability of gravity. Together, they were a study in calibrated tension—order and precision, pressure and restraint.

Gideon didn't trust easily.

Dan had earned it anyway.

"You're late," Dan said, adjusting figures with a flick of his stylus.

"I'm exact," Gideon replied, smoothing his cufflinks as he took the seat across from him.

Dan slid a folder across the table. "Parker's playing games. New terms came in."

Gideon opened it and flipped through the pages with quiet intensity, his instincts already three steps ahead of the language on the page.

"They're bluffing," he said. "Offer a minor concession. Let them think they're winning. They'll sign by morning."

Dan tilted his head, faint amusement sparking. "Classic. Let them feel clever while you walk away with the kingdom."

Gideon didn't react. He didn't need to. Dan wasn't wrong.

"It's leverage," he said simply. "Let them keep their pride. We keep the deal."

Dan's expression sobered as he passed over a second sheet. "Thorpe's circling. Nothing concrete yet, but they're sniffing."

Gideon's jaw tightened.

Thorpe.

He hated their kind: ruthless without precision, all appetite and no discipline.

"They won't get their foot in," he said. "Accelerate the close. Forty-eight hours, max."

Dan nodded, though his attention remained on the tablet. "Evelyn's been asking questions again."

The room cooled.

Gideon's grip tightened slightly on the folder. "She's always watching," he said, his voice flat. "I'll handle it."

Dan didn't press. He knew where to push and where to fall back, which was part of what made him invaluable.

"I'll loop in Andrew," Dan said. "Get it wrapped."

Gideon nodded, his focus already shifting again. Strategy. Reputation. Damage control.

He hadn't thought of West Virginia in days.

Not until now.

✻

Later, in his office above The Blackwell Room, the city stretched beneath him like a promise he had already conquered.

The low hum of the club bled through the walls: muffled bass, laughter, movement, the restless pulse of people trying to become someone else for a few hours.

This space usually gave him clarity. Dark wood. Glass. Bourbon. Everything chosen with intention, designed to quiet the noise and give his thoughts clean edges.

But tonight, his thoughts were loud.

Arden Rivers.

She surfaced again—not as memory, but sensation.

Sharp wit. Controlled fire. A voice like velvet and smoke, unrushed and grounded and real. Nothing about her felt flashy or performed. She was simply herself, and somehow that had been the most dangerous thing in the room.

She hadn't tried to charm him.

She hadn't needed to.

She hadn't pretended to be impressed, either. She had looked straight through him as if charm were just another language men used when they wanted something badly enough to lie for it.

He hadn't been able to stop thinking about her voice, the way it dipped when she warned him not to play favorites. The way she had stepped into chaos like familiar ground, as though she had learned long ago how to survive inside it without letting anyone see where it had touched her.

His grip tightened around the glass in his hand.

She shouldn't have been in his head.

One night. One bar. One conversation.

Still, she had unsettled something.

It wasn't lust. Lust, he knew how to ignore.

This was more dangerous because it had found its way beneath discipline and stayed there.

She challenged him, and he didn't yet know what to do with that.

His phone buzzed.

Evelyn.

He answered.

"Mother."

"Gideon." Her voice was smooth. Detached. "I hear you've been revisiting old ghosts."

"I've been working," he said coolly.

"Oh, I'm sure. And West Virginia... such a curious destination for business, considering how much we've buried there."

She paused, giving the words room to do what she had sent them to do.

"You forget I know your moves before you make them."

He said nothing.

"Don't be naïve, Gideon. You may think you've built your own kingdom, but you're still a Blackwell. That comes with consequences. Obligations."

"I'm aware."

"Then act like it."

Another pause. Measured. Sharp.

"You've always had a blind spot when it comes to complications. Be careful where you place your trust."

Then silence.

The line went dead.

He didn't move. He only stared out over the city, the glass warming slowly in his hand.

Arden came back to him again: her voice, her defiance, her composure. The way she had looked at him without asking permission to see too much.

"She's trouble," he muttered.

But the truth answered before the lie could settle.

Arden wasn't the trouble.

He was.

The knowledge landed with the weight of inevitability, quiet and absolute.

Because some part of him already knew that if she ever walked into his world, he would not let her go.

CHAPTER 3

Farewell Echoes

Weeks of research. Sleepless nights. Too many hours spent scrolling, searching, mapping out a life she wasn't sure she had any business entering. But no matter how deep she dug, one name remained stubbornly elusive.

The Blackwell Room.

Arden leaned against the counter, the stove clock's faint glow splintering across the worn linoleum and casting long, uneven shadows through the quiet.

The name surfaced in articles about elite gatherings and whispered business deals, always present enough to prove it existed and vague enough to feel intentional.

No website. No menu. No photos.

Only a name, spoken in certain circles as if it were less a place than a secret not meant for outsiders.

Her fingers hovered over the edge of the card before tracing it absently, as if the matte texture might unlock answers she couldn't seem to find in herself.

Could she uproot everything for a man who might only be toying with her?

Gideon Blackwell wasn't merely enigmatic. He was unnerving. Magnetic. Danger dressed as a dare. Her first instinct had been to walk away, which should have made the decision simple.

It didn't.

Silverbranch was familiar, but familiarity had never been the same thing as home. She knew its edges and silences, the tired rhythm of a place that never asked her to become anything more than what it already understood.

New York City was uncertainty on a scale she couldn't soften into something manageable. A storm with no shape. A life she couldn't rehearse before stepping into it.

And Arden had never been the kind of woman who thrived on uncertainty.

Then again, when had she ever truly belonged anywhere?

Her jaw tightened. She folded her arms across her chest, holding herself together out of habit more than comfort.

Comfort had never belonged to her.

Not as a child. Not as a woman who had learned too young how easily safety could be mistaken for a locked door. Not even now, standing in a kitchen she could navigate in the dark, staring down a choice that felt too much like want.

What she'd called her comfort zone wasn't comfort at all; it was necessity. A cocoon she'd spun for survival. Maybe that was the problem. Maybe she'd learned to survive too well. The thought scraped against something raw as her focus drifted back to the card. Temptation moved through her, smoke-soft and suffocating.

She should throw it away—cut the tether before it pulled tighter.

But that quieter voice, the one that always asked the harder questions, whispered the one she hadn't dared say aloud: *What if this isn't reckless? What if it's exactly what I've been waiting for?* She exhaled, more groan than sigh.

"It's just a business card," she muttered, as if the words could strip it of its weight. "Just a man. One conversation. Nothing more."

But even she didn't believe that. A card shouldn't be this heavy. A man shouldn't have this much power, not after everything she'd survived. And here she was, heart unsteady, breath shallow as if the ground itself had shifted.

This felt different—a door she wasn't sure she was brave enough to open.

❦

The card burned in Arden's pocket as she left Dot's a few nights later.

She hadn't fully decided, but the pull had grown stronger with every passing hour, every quiet, restless flicker of what might come next.

Overhead, gray skies pressed low, brimming with static and unspoken tension.

What if this was her moment?

A chance to start again.

She had reached the edge of the lot when a voice cracked the quiet.

"Arden."

Chad.

He materialized like a regret with a name, hands jammed in his pockets, his posture wound too tight to sell indifference. The second she saw him, her stomach coiled.

"Heard you're leaving," he said, bitterness dragging at every syllable. "Figures. Some guy shows up, and suddenly this place isn't good enough for you."

She didn't answer. Didn't flinch.

Her silence had always bothered him. Tonight, she let it.

Chad took a step closer, his voice brittle. "So that's it? You think going to the city's gonna fix something? You think a guy in a suit makes everything better?"

Her expression didn't change.

Her tone did.

"This isn't about him," she said, clean and controlled. "It never was."

His mouth twisted.

"This is about me," she continued. "It always has been. You just never wanted to see that."

He laughed, hollow and sharp. "Right. You, doing what? Slinging cocktails for fancier assholes?"

The jab found old bruises.

She didn't break.

"You think that's all I'm capable of?"

He shrugged, and the nothing of it said plenty.

"You're just running," he said. "That's all you've ever done."

"No," she said quietly. "That's what you've done."

He blinked.

"You sat still and called it loyalty. Waited for everyone else to fail so you wouldn't have to feel small."

Something in his face shifted.

Arden stepped forward before he could hide it.

"You always wanted me to shrink, Chad. Because if I outgrew this town, if I outgrew you, then you'd have to face what you wasted."

His face cracked.

She didn't give him time to gather the pieces.

"You don't dream," she said. "You resent people who do."

Silence snapped between them, sharp as a slap.

Then he sneered. "You think you're getting a clean slate? You're making yourself a bigger target."

Her eyes narrowed.

"You never cared about that," she said, quieter now. "Not really."

His posture stiffened.

"When I told you I was scared, you laughed. You didn't believe me until he showed up, and even then, it wasn't concern." Her voice held steady, every word placed with care. "It was control."

He looked away.

But Arden didn't.

"You hated the idea of someone else getting close enough to challenge your grip."

"Don't flatter yourself."

"I'm not." She took a breath, and for the first time, it felt clean all the way down. "That's what makes this easy."

His jaw worked, but no answer came.

"You don't get to pretend it was concern," she said. "Not when it never looked like protection."

He opened his mouth, but whatever he meant to say fell apart before it could become language. A curse left him instead, sharp and bitter, and then he turned and disappeared into the dark.

She didn't watch him go.

Her shoulders eased with every step forward.

This wasn't only goodbye to Chad. It was the end of a story she had never agreed to be written into.

For once, her choices didn't settle over her like burdens.

They settled beneath her like ground.

❦

The laptop screen glowed faintly as Arden sank into the couch, Dot's still clinging to her like a film: grease, smoke, and the sour-sweet trace of old bourbon.

The apartment wasn't much, but it had been hers.

For a while, that had been enough.

She scrolled past another overpriced, undersized listing and hovered over the browser's close button, frustration creeping in at the edges.

Then one headline caught her eye.

**ROOMMATE WANTED:
FUN, FRIENDLY & NO SERIAL KILLERS, PLEASE!**

Arden blinked.

Despite herself, amusement cracked through.

She clicked.

———

Hi there!
Are you tired of scouring the city for a place that doesn't feel like it's plotting against you? Look no further!

My name's Penny, and I'm looking for a roommate who loves good vibes, bad movies, and the occasional wine-fueled 🍷 karaoke night (no talent required, just commitment).

The Apartment: 2 bedrooms, 1 bathroom, sunlight galore (perfect for plants or existential crises). Located in a safe, weirdly charming neighborhood. Cats own the sidewalks. 🐈‍⬛
Rent: Not terrifying.
Bonus: I'm a graphic designer, so the place is always changing. Cookies show up mysteriously. 🍪 And yes, I own too many throw pillows.
What I'm Looking For: Someone reliable, semi-chaotic in a fun way, and down for glitter emergencies. 🌐 Must tolerate loud playlists 🎶 and strong opinions about cereal brands. 😊

If this is your vibe, message me with your go-to karaoke song. Mine is Total Eclipse of the Heart. No shame.

———

Arden stared at the screen.

Then she smiled.

The expression came slowly, surprising her with how little effort it took.

It wasn't the rent that hooked her.

It was the voice.

Whoever Penny was, she wasn't simply renting out a room. She was making space for a life.

And maybe Arden wanted in.

> Hi, Penny. Your ad made me laugh, and that felt rare. I don't usually sing for anyone but my steering wheel, but I'll clap for Total Eclipse and pretend Zombie is in my range.

> Penny: OMG. Yes. Anyone who respects Zombie and karaoke gets full roommate points. 🎸 Tell me you're okay with glitter and cats and you're basically approved.

> Glitter is fine as long as I'm not part of the cleanup crew. Cats are negotiable. But I'm more sarcasm than sparkle.

Got it. Glitter containment crew: Activated.

Sarcasm is sparkle in black.

Also I don't actually have a cat, but I'd like to keep my options open.

Oh! Warning: our nosy neighbor's cat Midnight could come prowling, but he's harmless. 🐱

Arden laughed. A real laugh, sharp and sudden.
Her reply came easy.

I think this might work. Let's set up a video tour.

Saturday. Prepare yourself. There's a disco ball involved. 🪩

Arden closed her laptop and leaned back, a small smile lingering.
Maybe this was the start of something new.
Something that was *hers*.

❦

The night before she left, Dot slid a bottle across the counter.
Top shelf. No label. No comment.
"For the road," he muttered.
Arden took it with a nod, because anything more would have made them both uncomfortable.
Jim pressed cash into her hand.
Tommy offered a solemn, "New York won't know what hit it."
Her last box fit snugly in the backseat. The old sedan hummed low beneath her, thick with the ghosts of every mile she had survived.
As she pulled away, Dot's neon sign flickered once—a farewell it didn't quite want to give.
But Arden didn't look back.
She couldn't.
This wasn't only goodbye to a place. It was goodbye to the version of herself who kept making room for people who had never deserved the space.
The road ahead was wide, jagged, and unforgiving.
But it was hers.
For the first time in a long time, she wasn't chasing safety.
She was choosing the life beyond it.

CHAPTER 4

Concrete Dreams

The road stretched ahead, winding through the last miles through Appalachia. Trees lined both sides, their branches thinning as autumn edged closer to winter. Maple leaves tumbled across the pavement, catching in the slipstream before vanishing behind her.

In the rearview mirror, the mountains shrank. No longer the unmoving sentinels they once were.

Only distant silhouettes now, dissolving into fog.

Once, they had been her shelter. Her prison. A history carved in ridgelines, long winters, humid summers. Silent roads that kept secrets better than people ever did.

Now, they were just something she was leaving behind.

Static crackled through the speakers. Then, soft and familiar, the first chords rang out.

"Almost heaven, West Virginia..."

She hadn't touched the dial or searched for the song.

It found her anyway.

A quiet laugh pressed against her throat: ironic, maybe, or inevitable. She reached for the dial. But didn't touch it.

"Take me home, Country Roads..."

The timing felt cruel. Or maybe perfect.

The road lay ahead, but her gaze stayed on the curve of mountains behind her, standing as they always had. Not guiding her. Not protecting her. Just there.

No longer towering. No longer inescapable. Just a jagged silhouette against the sky, growing fainter with every mile.

She hadn't expected to feel anything. Not now. Not after all the goodbyes.

She whispered the next line under her breath, soft, off-key. A voice she hadn't trusted in years, softening.

"To the place I belong..."

For the first time, the words didn't ache.

They didn't mock.

They simply existed.

A thread in the fabric of memory.

It wasn't just a song. It was a tether to every backroad she'd ever driven, every night spent staring at the stars from the bed of an old truck, every unspoken dream she'd tucked beneath the weight of survival.

Her eyes flicked to the mirror again, watching the peaks blur into fog.

"West Virginia... Mountain Mama," she murmured, this time without bitterness. Just remembering.

The final notes faded, and she reached down, turning the volume to silence.

Silence filled the car in its place: not hollow, just quiet. Stillness that wasn't absence, but release.

❦

The landscape shifted gradually: mountains flattening into hills, the hard lines of Appalachia softening without fanfare. Fences appeared. Fields. The kind of open space that made her feel like she was somewhere else, even if she wasn't there yet.

And though she wouldn't call herself sentimental, something in her chest stirred with every mile.

The morning light stretched golden across the hills. White church spires broke the horizon like watchtowers. Fields stretched wide beneath a pale sky, broken only by farmhouses and lonely steeples rising sharp against the horizon, silent promises written in stone.

Rusty fruit stands and festival signs flickered past her window. Pumpkins sat in bright orange rows, apples gleaming beneath hand-painted signs. Smoke curled from food trucks parked along gravel shoulders. Wool blankets flapped in the breeze.

The air, even through the glass, felt crisp. Smelled like woodsmoke and fallen leaves.

Lovely. Romantic, even.

She thought about stopping. Letting the moment settle. Maybe picking up a paper cup of cider from a roadside stand, letting the warmth of it wrap around her for a minute.

In another life, she might've slowed down, let herself breathe in the change of season, sip something warm for the sake of it.

Not today.

She didn't need nostalgia. She needed distance. She drove as if forward was the only option.

By early afternoon, her body protested. Stiff knees. Aching back. A gnawing hunger she hadn't noticed until it drowned out her thoughts.

She hadn't planned to stop. Hadn't even noticed how long it had been since she'd last eaten. But when she spotted a roadside diner, its silver frame gleaming beside a quiet lake, her hands turned the wheel before she could second-guess.

The neon OPEN sign buzzed faintly against the window.

Arden slid into a corner booth where the vinyl groaned beneath her, the table sticky but warm from the sun cutting through the glass.

The waitress poured her coffee without asking. Bitter. Strong. A jolt to the system. She took another sip. Then another. It grounded her anyway.

"Long drive?" the waitress asked, eyes kind but unreadable.

Arden nodded. "Heading north."

She drank slowly, eyes fixed on the lake beyond the glass. The surface shifted in lazy pulses, the wind dragging across the water like a passing thought.

Before getting back on the road She rested against the hood, steam curling from the cup between her hands. The heat bled into her fingers, slow and steady, chasing off the chill one joint at a time. The cold nipped at her cheeks, sharp but clean. Steam curled upward in slow, silver spirals before vanishing into the open air.

The lake glinted in the pale light, reflecting a sky bruised by oncoming weather. Wind moved through the trees with a whisper, almost enough to make her believe they were speaking.

Warning her, encouraging her. Maybe both—she couldn't tell.

The water met the sky at the far edge of her vision, soft and seamless; the boundary seemed to vanish.

Her thoughts stretched with the horizon, her gaze fixed on the place where sky and water blurred.

She didn't see an ending there.

And for a moment, Arden let her eyes close, just for a breath.

The road waited, and so, she drove on.

Arden's first glimpse of the city rose like a challenge: steel and glass catching the sun, towering without apology.

Overpasses twisted overhead. Lanes split and tangled, feeding into the gridlock ahead like veins pumping toward a restless heart. The enormity of it stole her breath.

New York was nothing like the version she had built in her head during those late, sleepless nights. Her imagination had given it edges, landmarks, a shape she could study from a distance. Reality moved differently. It pressed close, electric and alive, refusing to become small enough for her to understand all at once.

Cabs cut across traffic. Horns slashed through the air. Engines rumbled beneath the rise and fall of sirens, while pedestrians surged into crosswalks with practiced defiance, fluid and fast, as if the chaos had rules only they could hear.

She rolled down the window.

The city poured in, warm air thick with roasted nuts, exhaust, concrete after rain, and the bitter drift of coffee from a cart somewhere nearby. Beneath it all was something harder to place, a scent that felt almost familiar without feeling safe.

Arden let it in without flinching.

The weight of it—the noise, the movement, the sheer scale—wrapped around her like static. Too much and not enough and everything at once.

And she leaned in.

Let it settle on her skin.

In her breath.

Alive.

That was the word.

She hadn't felt that in a long time.

"So," she murmured, her voice nearly lost beneath the chaos, "this is New York."

Here, she felt small, but not the way she had in Silverbranch. There, smallness had meant invisibility, a quiet erasure of self that happened so gradually a person could mistake it for peace.

This was different.

Here, being small meant becoming part of something vast. A single, fierce note in a wild, unending symphony.

For the first time, being one among many didn't feel like isolation.

It felt like room.

Like possibility.

And for once, Arden didn't pull back.

PARKING NEAR PENNY'S place felt like threading a needle, equal parts luck and stubbornness.

Arden slid into a narrow space along a street humming with contrast: graffiti curled across old brick walls, jazz drifted out from a café, and something warm—cinnamon or clove—hung in the air like a promise.

She stepped out slowly, rolled her shoulders, and shook off the ache of too many miles. The weight of the drive began to loosen first, then something beneath it, something older and harder to name.

Cold air filled her lungs.

Sharper. Cleaner.

She stood with one hand on the car door, letting the moment take shape around her.

Letting go had never come easily.

For the first time, it felt possible.

She exhaled, long and slow, and the old memories shifted with it. They didn't vanish. Nothing that deep ever left cleanly. But they loosened their grip enough for calm to settle in the space they'd occupied.

Ahead of her, the building waited.

Not a promise.

An opening.

Arden closed the car door and looked toward it, steadying herself beneath the unfamiliar sky.

Whatever waited on the other side, she had come this far to meet it.

ARDEN RAISED A FIST TO KNOCK, and the door opened before she could.

And there was Penny, wild curls framing her face, her outfit a kaleidoscope of clashing colors in constant motion.

Constellations danced across her leggings. A neon-pink sweater radiated its own kind of energy.

"Look who's here!" Penny practically bounced forward, arms flung wide as if she'd been waiting her whole life for this exact moment.

"Come in already! Your new life starts here or, like, two steps inside. Either way, don't just stand there."

Arden froze, momentarily caught off guard by the sheer force of Penny's exuberance.

But then like rays of light breaking through clouds, she stepped into the hug, letting Penny's infectious warmth pull her forward. Her defenses didn't stand a chance.

Weeks of late-night calls and endless texts hadn't prepared her for Penny in real time. This was something rare. Something real. The start of a friendship that felt like home.

Penny didn't just comfort. She woke something up as if she stepped into the sunlight after years of shadow.

When Penny finally pulled back, her green eyes sparkled with mischief as she gave Arden a quick once-over. "Oh my God, you're even cooler in person! And taller than I imagined. Well, not tall-tall, but taller than me, which is basically everyone."

Her gaze landed on Arden's shirt: a black tee with equally black words that read, *little ray of pitch black.*

Penny's laugh burst out, quick and bright. "Oh, we're gonna have fun. I knew we'd get along, but that? That graphic seals it."

Arden gave a half-smile, brushing wind-tossed hair from her cheek. She hadn't planned the outfit: black tee, worn jeans, scuffed boots. Just what was easy to grab. Clothes for traveling, not arriving.

But Penny made her feel seen, as though she had dressed with intention. Like she belonged here. Like this was exactly where she was supposed to be.

Penny threw the door open wider, revealing an apartment that was equal parts art gallery and thrift-store jackpot. A work of art, but also pure chaos. Vintage posters whispered from the walls. Plants sprawled in mismatched pots. Crystal prisms scattered rainbows across the sunlit room. It felt lived-in. Loved.

An extension of Penny herself: warm and wild. Compared to the spaces Arden had left behind, this one didn't just exist.

Arden's past spaces seemed... temporary.

Books leaned in uneven stacks on every surface, competing for attention with quirky figurines and jars filled with who-knew-what. At its heart, a deep blue couch was drowning in pillows, each one clashing magnificently with its neighbors. The whole place seemed alive, vibrating with vitality and charm.

Arden stepped inside, suitcase catching on the threshold as if it, too, hesitated before crossing into something new.

She paused, hyper-aware of herself in her travel-worn clothes, feeling like a faded photograph in a gallery of vibrant portraits.

Penny twirled to face her, reading the hesitation with surprising grace. "I know it's... a lot," she said, her grin softening a fraction. "But it has a way of becoming home. And if it doesn't? No worries. We'll remake it until it does. I practically have a PhD in space transformation and self-reinvention."

Arden shook her head quickly, her attention returning to the room. "No... ," she said, her voice softer now. "It feels... alive."

Penny's grin returned full force, lighting up her face. "Come on, let me show you to your room. It's not as colorful yet, but that's intentional. A blank canvas for you."

Penny waved her down the hall to a small bedroom tucked in back.

The walls were a soft, unremarkable cream. Blank, not cold. One window overlooked the street, where fire escapes carved crooked paths across brick façades. Muffled voices rose from the street, blending into the hum of the city, present but indistinct.

Sunlight cut across the floor in golden bands, warming the worn wood beneath her feet. A desk sat beneath it. Nothing fancy. Just smooth wood and rounded edges, softened by time. It felt used. As if it had been waiting. Welcoming private thoughts and untold stories.

Penny's usual sparkle faded a notch when she spoke. "I didn't know exactly what you'd need, but the desk felt right. I thought... maybe you'd need a place to think. To create. To just... exist."

Her gaze caught on the desk, and something shifted, quiet and tentative. Not quite hope, but close enough to hurt.

Penny clapped her hands, eyes gleaming with mischief. "So, I have an idea... no unpacking tonight."

Arden arched a brow. "No unpacking?"

"Nope," Penny confirmed. "Tonight is for celebrating, and I take my celebrations very seriously. Chocolate cake, bubbles, and a lineup of gloriously bad TV. Trust me, I've curated only the best."

The absurdity tugged a laugh from her. Small, but real.

"Cake and champagne for... not unpacking?"

"For new beginnings," Penny corrected, giving her a conspiratorial wink. She leaned in, voice dropping to a faux-serious whisper. "Now, crucial intel needed: cake or cookies? This is a friendship-defining moment."

Arden barely had to think about it. "Cake. Definitely cake."

Penny gasped, clutching her chest as if she'd been personally blessed. "I knew we'd get along, but this? This confirms it."

Arden let out a sharp laugh, half protest, half surrender, as Penny grabbed her wrist and started dragging her kitchen-ward like the night had an agenda.

"Alright, before anything else," Penny said, smacking the light switch with all the flair of someone making an entrance. "We're toasting to fresh starts, terrible reality TV, and the long-overdue arrival of you."

The cork launched with a sharp pop, pinging off the fridge before hitting the floor. Penny didn't even flinch. She filled two mismatched glasses and slid a plate of cake across the counter toward Arden with the effortless precision of someone who had done this a hundred times before.

"Eat," she instructed. "Drink. Surrender to the madness."

Arden picked up her glass, the fizz whispering against her lips before the first sip. Then came the cake: dense and dark, the kind that cut the sweet with just enough bite. She wasn't sure when she last enjoyed something without bracing for the cost.

LATER, once Penny was asleep, the apartment settled into a quiet that didn't quite feel like hers. Arden stood by the window, watching the city pulse below. She wasn't planning. She wasn't bracing. She was just here, and that felt like enough.

Behind her, the desk waited: patient, unfinished, full of half-formed thoughts—words she hadn't expected to write.

She turned from the window, bare feet whispering across the worn hardwood, and crossed the room, drawn not by obligation but by the quiet pull of possibility.

CHAPTER 5

A World Away

The air was thick with cinnamon and fresh coffee, Penny's signature welcome. Arden had spent the afternoon methodically unpacking, grounding herself in this new reality. Suitcase by the closet. Mission complete.

Her room gradually became something more. Not just a place to sleep, but hers.

Music filtered through the walls, indie beats pulsing with Penny's irrepressible energy. The apartment thrived on motion.

After aligning the last book's spine with quiet satisfaction, Arden stepped out, curious to see her new roommate in her natural habitat.

Penny sprawled on the floor amid a riot of sketches and design mockups, her tablet casting a cool blue glow across her face. The stylus swept across the screen in time with the music, her focus absolute.

"If you're hungry, there's a killer charcuterie board on the counter," she called, without looking up. "And by killer, I mean I spent exactly ten minutes pretending to be a food influencer."

Arden arched a brow. "Charcuterie?"

Penny grinned, unrepentant. "Every day should feel celebratory, right?"

In the kitchen, Arden found the board laid out with suspicious precision: salami slices folded into neat roses, cheese arranged like dominoes mid-topple. A crystal pitcher of iced tea sparkled beside it, studded with mint leaves and translucent lemon wheels.

She hadn't expected this level of effort, or flair.

"Do you always live this way?" she asked, reaching for a glass, amused.

"What way?"

"As if you're auditioning for a lifestyle magazine."

Penny laughed, light but laced with conviction. "What can I say? Life's too short to be boring."

She grabbed a piece of cheese, popped it into her mouth, and shot Arden a grin that could've closed a tab or started a bar fight. "If you're going to exist, might as well make it fabulous."

Arden leaned her hip into the counter, her glass cool in her palm. "Your brain never stops, does it?"

"Story of my life." Penny twirled the stylus like a conductor guiding chaos. "Between impossible clients who think 'concept' means 'copy Pinterest,' soul-crushing deadlines, and the three side projects I definitely shouldn't have taken on."

She finally set the tablet aside, eyes shining with that brand of energy that could either light up a city or spark an existential crisis.

"But mediocrity is the enemy, right?"

A wicked grin. "Besides, now I've got you, my perfectly brooding counterweight. We're going to be legendary. Trust me."

Arden wasn't sure about legendary. But she didn't feel entirely alone.

❦

The city's noise washed over Arden in layers—horns cutting through traffic, voices blurring at the edges, footsteps gathering into a relentless cacophony that somehow moved with purpose.

By midweek, she had carved out small routines. Grocery runs at off-hours. Meandering walks to map her new territory. Quick conversations with Penny that anchored the day more than Arden wanted to admit.

New York moved around her with sharp, restless force. It should have overwhelmed her, all that sound and motion, but the city's unpredictability had begun to feel strangely steadying.

She had made peace with chaos years ago, learned how to carry it without flinching.

The coffee shop sat wedged between a boutique and a used bookstore, as if it had slipped through the cracks and stayed hidden on purpose. A little battered. A little overlooked. The kind of place that didn't mind being alone and didn't mind if you were, too.

A chalkboard easel by the door listed the drinks in playful, uneven script: *Lavender Latte. Rose Cardamom Cold Brew. Honey Cinnamon Latte.*

Arden's hand hovered on the door before she pushed inside.

Light poured through tall windows, pooling across mismatched chairs and uneven tables. Books slouched in stacks around the room, some abandoned mid-thought, others aligned with quiet intent, waiting for someone to return. The air was thick with coffee and sweet lavender, and despite herself, Arden felt the tension in her shoulders loosen by a careful degree.

At the counter, she studied the ornate menu while the barista paused her work, ink-covered fingers resting lightly against the edge of the register.

"What can I get you?"

Black coffee felt like a surrender in a place like this.

Arden glanced at the menu again. "What's worth trying?"

The barista's mouth curved into a knowing smile. "Depends. Are we fighting demons today, or making peace with them?"

A laugh slipped out before Arden could stop it. "Peace. For now."

"Lavender Latte it is. Trust me. It's our claim to fame."

"Perfect," Arden said. "I've always had a thing for lavender."

The barista returned with a wide ceramic mug, the foam sculpted into delicate petals that caught the light before softening at the edges.

Arden claimed a corner table with her back to the wall and both exits in view, then set her laptop beside the steaming drink.

The first sip surprised her. Lavender threaded through dark espresso like twilight through storm clouds, unexpected and gentle enough to make her pause.

Peace had never come to her without conditions.

That was what made this moment feel dangerous. The warmth of the mug beneath her hands. The quiet corner. The scent of lavender rising with the steam. The unsettling proof that even with shadows trailing her steps, thin as a veil, she could still find something soft and let herself want it.

Her fingers flew across the keyboard: deliberate, precise. She didn't need to look. Perfection lived in muscle memory.

tactical defense training near me

Search results populated the screen in a scattered barrage: glowing reviews, cautionary tales about cash-grab dojos, red flags dressed as certifications.

She filtered them methodically, saving only what met her standards, mentally organizing next steps. The shop's gentle hum receded, fading into the background as her focus narrowed to the task ahead.

Penny burst in, a confetti bomb in motion, shopping bag swinging from her wrist. Her arrival obliterated the quiet in a way that was both predictable and jarring.

"Found you!" she declared, dropping into the chair across from Arden with theatrical flair. "And here I thought you were off orchestrating world domination."

Arden's lips curved. "I'm researching classes."

Penny eyed the artisanal latte with mock suspicion. "Well, look at you going full hipster. Never figured you for the fancy coffee type."

"Neither did I," she murmured, wrapping both hands around the mug like it might keep her from saying too much.

Penny leaned in, unabashed as ever, eyes scanning the screen. Her brow furrowed. "Krav Maga? Should I be worried about your secret identity?"

Arden shook her head, closing the laptop. "I like being prepared."

Something flickered behind Penny's bright expression. The spark dimmed into something softer.

"Fair enough."

She grabbed a sugar packet and quickly tore it open. "But don't forget to make time for this too, okay?" She nodded at the coffee, the low buzz of conversation, the simple act of being here. "Even badasses need coffee breaks with their friends."

Arden arched a brow. "And you've nominated yourself for the position?"

"Obviously." Penny beamed with certainty.

Arden let that warmth settle, Penny's conviction wrapping around her like sunlight through glass. Just for a moment.

❦

The boutique assaulted the senses: a riot of texture and gleaming fabric that set Penny free.

She became an unleashed force of nature, darting between racks with her arms loaded in a geology of fashion—sequined blazers, crystalline sunglasses, scarves that rippled like metallic waves.

Arden drifted in her wake, hands in her pockets, cataloging exits and sightlines without thinking. She hadn't planned to buy anything. She wasn't entirely sure why she had said yes.

Until she saw the coat.

Jet-black leather trench. Understated, but impossible to overlook. The kind of piece that didn't follow trends so much as outlast them.

Before she could think better of it, her steps carried her closer.

Her fingers skimmed the details like braille: the modest Burberry lining, quiet with class; the lapels cut with deliberate drama; the stitching precise enough to pass inspection under a microscope.

A worthwhile investment.

Not flashy. Not impractical.

Just...right.

"This isn't just a coat," she murmured.

"No," Penny breathed, appearing at her shoulder, her haul of color and chaos thrown into sharp contrast against the trench's elegant restraint. "It's a weapon. Put it on."

Arden shot her a look, part surrender and part skepticism, but Penny had already removed the trench from the mannequin before Arden could form a protest.

"Stop overthinking," Penny said, handing it over. "Certain things demand wearing, not admiring."

The leather settled over Arden's shoulders with perfect weight, solid and grounding without stiffness. The lapels framed her collarbones. The clean lines sharpened everything they touched. No excess. No pretense. Armor, if armor knew how to move like luxury.

In the mirror, she didn't see a statement.

She saw alignment.

Unnervingly precise.

"Oh, hell," Penny muttered, propping herself against a rack. "You're not just dangerous in that. You're criminal."

Arden glanced at her reflection again.

Penny's grin spread, delight brightening her whole face. "It's your essence in leather. Timeless. Unapologetic. Exactly the right amount of terrifying."

A quiet thrill stirred beneath Arden's skin as her fingers skimmed the flawless stitching.

"You're not wrong."

Penny tilted her head, studying her. "I get the feeling you don't make impulse buys."

"No," Arden said, voice flat and matter-of-fact. "I don't."

She had grown up knowing what it meant to have nothing. New clothes were rare. Saving money had been a fantasy her father made sure stayed out of reach. Every purchase had to matter, because waste had consequences, and wanting things had never been as simple as wanting them.

Maybe that was why she had built a safety net sturdy enough to survive almost anything.

If the floor gave way tomorrow, Arden wouldn't simply survive the fall. She would rise. The job at The Blackwell Room wasn't survival; it was strategy. And if it didn't work out, she would land on her feet. She always did.

Penny hummed thoughtfully, tucking that truth away to revisit later. Then her bright smile returned, triumphant.

"If you're still standing here with it on, it's already yours."

The thought dropped and stayed.

Arden reached into her bag before she could talk herself out of it, already halfway to the counter.

No hesitation. No second-guessing.

A practical investment.

Nothing more.

Nothing less.

❦

Back in her room, the coat hung from the closet door, supple black leather catching faint streaks of light as they filtered through the window.

Arden sat on the edge of the bed, eyes fixed on it while her mind drifted elsewhere.

She reached for the laptop with the same certainty that had guided the purchase.

One click.

Session booked.

Krav Maga.

Another layer of defense. Another form of control.

Later, Penny's music wove through the walls, a restless counterpoint to Arden's racing thoughts. She folded herself into the couch, shadows flickering across her face as she tried to focus.

Training schedules blurred. Logistics faded.

Her fingers found the black card tucked in her wallet.

That damn card.

Even tucked away, it felt heavy.

Who the hell made their business card black?

Mysterious. Exclusive. Dangerous.

Maybe pretentious.

But God help her, it worked.

A traitorous smile tugged at her mouth as Gideon Blackwell threaded through her thoughts.

Devastating.

That was the word.

The kind of sexy that should come with warning labels and liability waivers.

And his voice? Warm whiskey. Smooth. Rich. The kind that slipped past defenses and burned slow.

A voice built to dismantle every boundary she had constructed.

Literally fuck me now, she had thought, and immediately hated herself for becoming every bad cliché she had ever sworn she wasn't.

Yet here she was.

Still thinking about it.

About him.

She scrubbed a hand down her face, frustration rough and restless, and shoved the laptop aside.

Jesus. Get it together.

One meeting. One stupidly intense, chemistry-drenched interaction. And she was spiraling?

The black card pulled her attention again, practically taunting her from inside the wallet.

She had tried digging into The Blackwell Room—articles, forums, social threads. Nothing turned up the way it should have. Only curated mentions in business columns and social gossip, always vague enough to feel intentional.

According to Penny, you didn't apply to work there; you were chosen, which made Gideon's offer even more suspect.

Arden didn't belong in his world of old money and power plays. That should have settled the matter. It didn't.

Penny's door hinges whined, slicing through Arden's thoughts.

Penny wandered into the living room barefoot, her hair twisted into a loose, haphazard bun. She clutched her oversized sketchpad like a security blanket, holding it tight against her petite frame. With a practiced sprawl, she dropped into the armchair, radiating that uncanny awareness that made Arden brace for impact.

"So," she said, her tone casual. But Arden caught the intent beneath it. "When exactly are you going to the club?"

Arden's spine went stiff, shoulders ticking up slightly.

"I'm not sure yet."

Penny stared. Blinked. Then did that rapid-fire flutter that said oh, we're definitely talking about this.

She leaned in, brows raised. "Not sure? You've got the look, the chops, and me, your personal hype woman. What gives?"

Arden wrapped both hands around the mug. The heat helped. Solid. Steady. But it didn't loosen the tension coiled low in her gut.

"It's not like applying anywhere else. A place like that..." Her voice thinned. "It plays by different rules."

Cue Penny, loading a comeback. "Exactly. Which is why you need to walk in like you invented it. You're smart, capable, and let's be honest, you're more likely to intimidate than be intimidated. They won't know what hit them."

Arden stared into her drink. Steam curled upward, and she let out a long breath.

That club wasn't just exclusive; it was prestige—polished, veiled, stitched into the tapestry of the city.

Power didn't need an introduction. It passed in posture, in silence. Murmured in the way the walls breathed around you.

And men like Gideon didn't just belong; they built it. They *were* it.

"It's complicated."

Quiet. An afterthought.

Penny flipped her sketchpad open, eyes gleaming. She landed on a blank page with a theatrical flick.

"Okay, picture this. You, Arden Rivers, are the kind of woman who rattles the room just by walking into it. And that smoky eye? Absolutely fatal. Gideon Blackwell won't stand a chance."

A reluctant flush crept up Arden's neck. "You've got too much faith in me."

"Nope. Just enough." Penny grinned, sketching. "But can I ask one thing?"

Arden gave her a look. "Since when has that stopped you?"

"Why is everything you own in grayscale?" Penny gestured with the pencil. "Color exists, you know."

"Black and gray are timeless," Arden said with a shrug. "They speak without shouting."

"They whisper 'I'm plotting your demise,' which is on-brand, I'll give you that. But a little color could throw them off their game. Add some mystery."

Arden chuckled, genuine and rare. "I'll consider it."

"You'd better," Penny said, flicking her pencil. "Because when you show up with that look, that attitude? They'll hand you the keys just to keep you from burning it all down."

Arden tilted her head, catching something softer beneath Penny's smile. Joking aside, she meant every word.

"I'll figure it out," Arden murmured, her voice low but steady.

"I know," Penny replied, settling back like the scene was unfolding in her mind. "And I can't wait to see it happen."

Arden let the weight of those words sink in. Penny's confidence was a kind of pressure: a lit match handed to someone made of dry tinder.

She reached for her wallet, knowing the black card lay inside, sleek and quiet, but dense with implication.

The Blackwell Room.

Even the name felt like a dare.

And Gideon.

His name *was* temptation, waiting to be answered.

Her gaze flicked to the window. A sliver of her reflection stared back—sharper, steadier, and hard to ignore. The kind of woman who didn't just survive—she planned, then struck.

Music filtered through the walls again, low and pulsating; the tempo threaded possibility into the silence.

Outside, streetlights shimmered across the leather curve of her new coat.

Maybe caution had overstayed its welcome. Maybe it was time to walk into fire and see who flinched first.

CHAPTER 6

First Impressions

City life murmured through the cracked window, a low rhythm beneath the hush of her room. Arden faced the mirror, outwardly calm, though a quiet tension stirred beneath her skin. Her black cigarette pants fit perfectly to her curves. The clean angles of her boots grounded her. She'd chosen the blouse carefully. Tailored enough to say she belonged, without trying too hard to prove it. A delicate silver watch rested on her wrist, quietly elegant, the kind meant to be worn, subtle rather than showy.

She reached for the silver hoops, twisting them gently until they caught the light. One last detail. Subtle. Intentional.

Earlier that week, Penny had dragged her on a marathon shopping spree, determined to inject color into Arden's wardrobe. To Penny's horror, Arden had bought black in every texture known to mankind. Silk? Naturally. Leather? Without question. Soft knits, tailored blazers, a whisper of lace? Yes, yes, and obviously.

You can never have too much black.

Penny had groaned, throwing her hands skyward. "Why do I even try?"

Arden had shrugged. "As if you expected anything different."

Now, she flicked a stray piece of lint from her sleeve and turned to the business card perched on the dresser. The Blackwell Room. The silver embossing caught the light: clean, deliberate, like it had something to hide. It felt unreal, like stepping into a story made of shadows and velvet, where everything important happened just out of sight.

The woman in the mirror looked too composed, or that she belonged. Arden wasn't sure she did. She wasn't reckless. Not usually. She wasn't the kind of woman who walked into Manhattan's most exclusive club just because a stranger handed her a card.

But the card said otherwise. Said maybe she wanted more. More than safety. More than routine. More than the small, careful life she'd built in Silverbranch.

"Damn, girl. If that's not a 'take-no-prisoners' look, I might need to step up my game." Penny's voice cut through the quiet as she swept into the doorway, a joyful mix of wild curls, floral layers, and striped tights that somehow worked in her chaotic magic.

Arden fought a grin. "It's basically a go-see, Pen. Not the Met Gala."

"Oh, please," Penny scoffed, stepping in to adjust Arden's collar. "When it's the Blackwell empire, same thing." Her eyes glimmered, playful, but protective too. "Remember: eye contact. Steel spine. And don't let anyone, no matter how important, rattle you."

Arden exhaled slowly. "I think I can handle one night with Manhattan's elite."

Penny's brow arched. "But babe, this isn't just any boss. We're talking Gideon Blackwell, the city's most eligible billionaire slash enigmatic club owner slash brooding mystery man."

Arden rolled her eyes. "Let me guess. He rescues kittens and funds orphanages?"

"I mean, probably," Penny shot back. "But more importantly, he's a walking thirst trap, and you're about to walk straight into his lair. I'm living for it."

Arden laughed, soft and unwilling. Amusement edged in anyway. She slung her bag over her shoulder, Penny's words still ringing. Less a joke, more a challenge.

Her boots struck pavement, steady as her pulse. The city unfolded ahead like a challenge. Maybe tonight wasn't about playing it safe. Maybe it was time to find out what happened when she rewrote the story herself.

❦

The Blackwell Room didn't loom. It waited.

Unmarked. Unassuming. A sleek black façade without signage or invitation, as if power had no need to announce itself when the right people already knew where to look.

Arden paused on the sidewalk, chin lifted slightly as she took it in. Calculating. Noting what most people wouldn't.

A brass plaque bore a solitary B.

A symbol, not a name.

Recognition wasn't offered here; it was assumed.

Two men flanked the door, their posture too still to mistake for hospitality. They weren't greeters. They were gatekeepers, and the threshold itself felt like a test.

Tonight, she was the one being evaluated.

Arden smoothed the line of her blouse, squared her shoulders, and exhaled as if drawing a blade.

Confidence wasn't flair.

It was armor.

She reached for the handle.

The door opened before she touched it.

A man stood in the threshold, tall and motionless, his expression unreadable beneath eyes sharp enough to make stillness feel deliberate. He wasn't in uniform. He wasn't expected. He had the quiet, watchful air of someone who had been waiting long before anyone noticed.

Arden didn't flinch.

"Thank you," she said evenly, moving past him without a second glance.

Inside, luxury unfolded in low tones and subtle textures, an elegance that didn't beg for attention because it had never needed to. The chandeliers glowed warm overhead, casting quiet halos across polished wood, marble, and velvet trim.

No grand gestures.

Only atmosphere, thick with intention.

The scent reached her first: woodsmoke and citrus, curated to linger in memory. Marble gleamed beneath her boots, each step echoing with quiet defiance.

Her gaze moved over velvet chairs and dark wood tables arranged less for comfort than strategy. This was the kind of place where deals weren't made so much as sealed.

No windows. No phones. No distractions.

Only whispers, dark liquor, and leverage dressed in couture.

But Arden hadn't come to disappear into all that careful elegance. She had come to be seen.

She approached the bar with purpose while curious eyes followed her, gauging, assessing, deciding whether she belonged before she had given them permission to wonder.

Let them look.

Let them wonder.

"Arden Rivers," she said. "I'm here to see Gideon Blackwell."

The bartender stilled mid-pour, his eyes sliding from Arden to a narrow, unmarked door behind the bar.

"I don't believe Mr. Blackwell is expecting anyone."

Her smile sharpened.

"No," she said. "But he'll want to see me."

He hesitated, reading the challenge for exactly what it was, then vanished silently behind the door.

Arden exhaled.

She wasn't here for a meeting.

She was here to make noise.

HE MOVED through the room with gravity.

No urgency. No flash. Impossible to ignore.

Gideon Blackwell descended the staircase with the same focused intensity she remembered from Dot's. Only here, he didn't look out of place. Here, he was the axis around which the club turned.

His suit was expensive in the quietest possible way, the kind that whispered rather than shouted, but it was his eyes that stopped her. Steel-gray. Locked in. Already reading her. When their gazes met, something passed between them, fast and hot and undeniable.

He stopped in front of her, close enough to thin the air between them.

"Arden Rivers."

Her name sounded remembered, not discovered.

She didn't flinch.

"Gideon Blackwell."

His name carried weight here, danger wrapped in elegance. Up close, she could see the tension in his shoulders, the faint exhaustion beneath his eyes. None of it dulled his presence. If anything, it made him sharper.

"I have to admit—" she started, hesitating just long enough for her teeth to catch her lip before she lifted her chin. "I wasn't sure you'd remember—"

"I could never forget you."

Not flirtation.

Truth.

A breath caught in her throat, but she hid it beneath the edge of a smirk. "Good. Because I didn't come here to be forgettable."

A real flicker sparked in his eyes: amusement, approval, something darker.

"No," he murmured. "You're not."

"You've seen what I can do," she said, tipping her head toward the polished bar. "But this place isn't Dot's."

His mouth curved faintly. "No, it's not."

A pause settled between them, no more than a breath.

"Show me."

Not a request.

A challenge.

And Arden answered.

She moved behind the bar smoothly, cool and confident, letting the familiar shape of work settle into her hands. "This place isn't really about the drinks. It's about control."

She poured without hesitation.

"Your regulars want to feel curated. Chosen. Known." She glanced at him. "They come to be served before they ask. To feel powerful."

He watched her with a calm that demanded attention, the space between them charged enough to make the room feel smaller.

"You think you can give them that?"

She slid the glass toward him. "I don't need to think. I know."

His gaze held hers.

"But this isn't about them," she said. "It's about you."

He lifted the glass without breaking eye contact, assessing her rather than the drink. "What makes you think I need convincing?"

Her smirk deepened. "You gave me that card. You wanted me here."

"This was never about answering to you," she added. "This was about flipping the script."

He leaned in slightly, his voice dropping. "The card was a door. What you choose to walk through is yours."

She didn't flinch. "Then consider this my entrance."

Something shifted between them.

The test had become recognition.

"You want the job," he said.

"I want the opportunity. The job's how I prove I earned it."

His fingers tapped a sharp rhythm against the marble. "Most people would've called first."

She smiled. "I'm not most people."

He laughed, low and genuine. "I'm starting to believe that." Then his expression settled back into something more measured. "The standards here are high."

"So are mine."

"The clientele are demanding."

"Good. I do my best under pressure."

"The rules aren't flexible."

"Neither am I."

He exhaled, unreadable.

"Tomorrow night," he said. "Eight sharp."

"I'll be here."

He slid a folder toward her, sleek and black, like everything else in this place. Her fingers brushed his as she took it, the contact intentional enough to be a question and grounded enough to be an answer.

"You knew I'd come," she said.

"I trusted you'd make the right choice."

"And if I hadn't?"

His eyes darkened. "Then I'd have been wrong about you. But I'm not wrong often."

She didn't blink. "What if I'm not easy to manage?"

He smiled. "That's why I'm hiring you."

A wink of silence passed between them.

Then he said, "Welcome to The Blackwell Room."

"Thank you, Mr. Blackwell."

She let the title hang between them, then twisted it.

"Gideon," he said, his brow lifting almost imperceptibly.

Her smile turned deliberate.

"Gideon."

His expression shifted. Subtle. Dangerous.

He nodded once, a silent cue, and Marco appeared beside her as if summoned by tension and inevitability.

"Until tomorrow," Gideon said.

Arden turned, folder in hand, pulse steady.

She didn't look back.

She didn't have to.

He was still watching.

And for the first time in far too long, she had landed somewhere that felt less like escape and more like arrival.

The night air slid beneath Arden's collar, sharp and cool against her skin.

Inside, she had been polished. Controlled. Out here, the façade thinned.

She shoved restless hands into her pockets and willed the tremor to stop. The folder rested against her hip like a test, but it wasn't ambition tightening her chest.

It was him.

A quiet laugh slipped out, brittle at the edges. This was supposed to be progress. A step into something bigger. Instead, she had walked into something charged and complex, something that refused to offer its name before it took up space inside her.

Some part of her wasn't ready to walk away.

❦

The second Arden walked in, she was hit with a wall of sugar, spice, and pure Penny.

Vanilla. Cinnamon. A thick cloud of determination masquerading as baked goods.

"Surprise!" Penny beamed from the kitchen, holding a tray of cupcakes like she had just defused a bomb with frosting. Flour streaked her apron, and her curls bounced with every movement. "I had a feeling tonight called for a celebration."

Arden blinked, startled, but a laugh escaped anyway—light, unguarded, and out before she could stop it.

"Pen... I haven't even told you how it went."

"Please," Penny said, popping the cork on a bottle she must have had chilling for hours. "I saw that walk. That was not an 'I hope it works out' walk. That was a 'bow before me, peasants' walk."

She twirled dramatically, eyes gleaming. "Now spill. Tell me everything. What was he like?"

Arden unwound her scarf, fingers careful as she bought herself time.

"He was…"

The words stalled in her throat.

Complicated felt too easy.

Intense wasn't wrong, but it wasn't enough either.

"Actually… not so different from the first time I met him."

Penny froze mid-pour. Her head snapped around.

"I'm sorry… what."

Arden winced. "I said—"

"I heard you." Penny's voice jumped an octave. "You've met Gideon Blackwell? And this is the first I'm hearing of it?"

"It wasn't relevant!" Arden tossed the scarf onto a chair.

Penny looked personally offended on behalf of gossips everywhere. "Not relevant? You met Manhattan's brooding monarch of mystery and forgot to mention it? Sit down. You're not getting out of this with vague hand gestures and a cupcake."

Arden rolled her eyes, but let herself be herded toward the couch. Two flutes were waiting.

She grabbed a cupcake and peeled back the wrapper. "He came into Dot's one night. Ordered bourbon. Said I was wasting my talent. Left a card."

Penny narrowed her eyes, her voice dropping low and sultry. "'He came into Dot's' is the first line of a romance novel, and you're telling me it wasn't a big deal?"

"It wasn't," Arden muttered, though the heat in her ears betrayed her.

The memory resurfaced anyway, clearer now than she wanted it to be.

That stare. The way he watched, calm and sharp all at once, as if he saw straight through her and still suspected she was two moves ahead.

"So?" Penny prompted, smirk firmly in place. "Is he all broody billionaire and panty-dropping charm?"

Arden picked at the edge of the wrapper. "Well, you could say that."

"But?" Penny's voice dropped, curious now. Expectant.

Arden paused. "There's… something in his eyes. The way he looks at you. Like he's studying you, but not in the obvious way. Like he's sizing you up, deciding if he wants to tear you apart or let you keep your secrets."

Penny made a noise that was part gasp, part gleeful screech.

"Oh my God. You are so gone."

"I'm not," Arden said quickly. Too quickly.

"You absolutely are," Penny declared, raising her glass like a toast to fate. "To Mr. Blackwell and the spicy subplot I didn't see coming."

Arden groaned, but tapped her flute against Penny's anyway.

"To new beginnings," she muttered.

Penny's grin softened. "And to that glow you're pretending isn't there. Whatever this is? I have a feeling it's just getting started."

——

SHE ENTERED LIKE WILDFIRE.

Uncontainable. Inevitable. Fierce.

She had no idea—someone had felt her presence before she even brushed past. Felt the subtle ripple that moved through the air, invisible, electric, altering everything in its wake.

The club was a carefully controlled sanctuary. A private stage crafted for the powerful.

She didn't enter as an observer. She was a force. A tempest wrapped in silk, every motion a statement without words.

He'd noticed her first. Outside, beneath the muted lights of Manhattan's secret streets. She'd paused—not hesitant, but assessing. Measuring the club's unmarked façade, its dark, polished walls masking secrets within secrets. No sign, just a single brass letter etched sharp: B. A hidden symbol, its meaning known only to those who mattered.

Most would rush inside, eager to belong. But not her. She chose to pause. To claim the moment on her own terms, owning space that didn't yet know.

He stayed quiet, deep within the shadows, heart pulsing steadily, breaths matching the calm, precise beat of her footsteps.

She moved with rhythm. Purposeful. Alive. He watched her lift her chin, saw the quiet defiance etched in the elegant line of her throat, the proud set of shoulders beneath perfectly tailored fabric.

Her hair caught the glow of hidden lights, a dark river against the pale canvas of her skin. Beautiful, yes, but it wasn't beauty that drew him; it was the subtle power beneath her surface.

The intelligence in her eyes, alert and wary. The careful elegance in every gesture: natural, unpretentious, yet commanding all the same.

He remained perfectly still as Gideon Blackwell appeared. Watched as the energy in the room shifted, turning subtly toward the man who owned this hidden empire. But Gideon didn't claim her; he couldn't. Not entirely. Not yet.

Even Blackwell couldn't contain her.

She didn't move. Didn't blink. Just stood there, quiet and unmoved. Looked like she'd seen too many tempests to be shaken by this one. She belonged to no one, not even this billionaire who'd laid claim to everything around him.

Gideon moved closer. Too close. A challenge.

His fingers flexed instinctively, an unconscious echo of possessiveness he had no right to feel.

But he felt it anyway.

She didn't flinch, didn't yield. The space between them crackled, an invisible storm forming silently, inevitably. And when she smiled, it wasn't surrender, but a *subtle reclaiming of territory, a promise that she was the one deciding how close Gideon got to stand.*

A dangerous game, but she played well.

He exhaled quietly, eyes never leaving her, even as Gideon spoke, as she responded, as they exchanged words he couldn't hear but somehow already knew. He didn't need their dialogue. Their bodies told a clearer story. A negotiation in posture, in silence, in the heated language of controlled breathing and careful glances.

When she finally turned away, he read relief in the line of her spine, victory in her easy, unhurried step.

His pulse quickened subtly, watching her leave. Not because of Blackwell or the power games woven through the night.

But because tonight he'd glimpsed something rare. Something that mattered.

Her true strength. Her subtle grace. Her quiet fire.

She'd walked away untouched, still her own.

But something had shifted between all of them.

The game had changed.

He felt it deep in his bones—a new clarity, sharper edges around his careful plans.

Because now he knew exactly who he was playing against, and what she was worth.

She was more than a fixation, more than a whisper in the darkness.

She was the flame he didn't realize he'd been waiting for. The perfect storm to challenge Gideon's cold authority. To challenge him.

He smiled softly, unseen, in the shadows.

Because he knew what Gideon didn't and what she hadn't realized.

This wasn't Gideon Blackwell's story.

Not anymore.

Tonight belonged to her.

And whether she knew it or not, he'd now been written into it.

CHAPTER 7

A Fine Line

I nside, Gideon remained motionless until the door clicked shut behind her.

Only then did he exhale, his fingers loosening from the bar. Weeks of anticipation had led to that moment. Weeks of wondering whether she would accept the challenge he had never quite put into words.

Arden Rivers wasn't merely stunning. She was fire held inside composure, defiance edged with skill.

Everything he had sensed that night at Dot's rang true the moment she stepped into his domain and claimed space without hesitation. Without apology.

"I take it the position that never existed has been filled?"

Marco Santiago, The Blackwell Room's head bartender since the days of Henry Hawthorne and Richard Blackwell II, spoke with the laid-back assurance of his Miami roots. Rolled-up sleeves revealed leather bracelets around his wrists, an appealing contradiction against the club's polished restraint.

Gideon turned and met the bartender's knowing gaze, the corner of his mouth curving. "Was there ever any doubt?"

Marco chuckled, brown eyes glinting. "None. But I've never seen you so... invested in a hiring decision."

Gideon should have dismissed it, but it was true.

Different.

She was different.

He made his way toward his office, needing space, or at least the illusion of it. He loosened his tie. It felt too much like a noose.

Beyond the glass, the city sprawled in a sea of shifting lights, but his mind wasn't with the view.

He was still at the bar, watching the way she had met his stare. Unflinching. Assessing. Turning every professional question into something else entirely.

A negotiation. A test. And she had played it too well.

The logical decision would be to place her at one of his other venues, somewhere she wouldn't remain in his periphery every night. Somewhere he wouldn't have to navigate the quiet pull of her presence or wonder whether she knew exactly what she was doing when she looked at him the way she did.

It would be easy—the simplest solution. But he knew he wouldn't do it because as dangerous as this was, the alternative felt worse. Not watching her work his bar. Not witnessing her in motion; her precision, her command of the space, the way she made skill look like instinct. Not feeling that pulse of something sharp and electric whenever she was close. That, he realized, was an entirely different kind of risk.

His phone buzzed.

Dan.

Gideon let it go unanswered, fingers curling instead around the glass of bourbon.

Not now.

He wasn't in the mood for the kind of silence Dan specialized in, the kind that didn't need words to call out your shit. Especially when his own thoughts were already doing the job.

The way she had held his stare and said, I think we understand each other well enough.

The memory settled into him like a dare.

And he knew this wasn't only about a job anymore.

"Sir?"

Marco's voice came from the doorway.

"The final contracts..."

Gideon didn't turn. "Leave them."

The door clicked shut.

For the first time in years, he wasn't sure whether he was steering or spiraling. Handling it meant something different now. This wasn't about bringing in new talent. This was about letting someone into his carefully controlled world who made him want to lose control.

He lifted the glass to his lips, the bourbon burning slow and deep, but not as fiercely as the memory of her parting glance.

That look like she knew. Like she had stripped away his professional distance and seen something far more dangerous underneath.

GIDEON DIDN'T READ the first text right away. But ignoring Dan only delayed the inevitable.

He was halfway through the message when the second one hit.

> Since I know you're in your office brooding like the world's richest gargoyle, I'll see you soon. We're drinking. Tonight. Don't even think about bailing.

Gideon sighed, setting the phone aside. Only for it to buzz again.

> And no, you don't get to pull the "too busy" card. This is an intervention. Your brooding quota has been exceeded.

A reluctant smirk tugged at his mouth.

Leave it to Dan to crash through the silence with all the grace of a wrecking ball, and enough truth to make retreat impossible.

> I'm not brooding.

The reply came instantly.

> You're right. Brooding doesn't cover it. Let's go.

> I have work to do.

> Wrong answer. Try again. I'm literally five minutes away.

Another vibration.

> Don't make me come in there. I'll drag you out like a toddler. Public shame included.

A breath of amusement slipped out. Not a laugh, but close.

> Fine. But if this is some dive bar, you're paying.

> That's the spirit, Blackwell. Meet me outside.

❦

The noise in the bar was steady: quiet conversations, the faint clatter of glass, a worn-out rock song barely holding a tune.

Nothing fancy. Just threadbare booths, scuffed floors, and a fried-food haze that seemed to cling to the walls.

It was a far cry from The Blackwell Room, and maybe that was exactly why Dan had picked it.

He slid a bourbon across the table with a grin that said he already knew the answer. "So, let me get this straight. You hired her?"

Gideon gripped the tumbler, the cool weight grounding in his hand. He took a slow sip and let the silence do the work.

Dan whistled under his breath, then leaned back, settling in like this conversation wasn't going anywhere anytime soon.

"You," he said. "Mr. No-Mistakes. Mr. Every-Move-Is-a-Twelve-Step-Chess-Game. You hired the woman who's been living rent-free in your head since the night you met her. At your own club. Where you'll see her every night."

He didn't need to raise his voice. That was never Dan's way. His tone dropped instead, calm and deliberate.

"Tell me you see the problem."

Gideon didn't respond. He only took another measured sip.

Dan leaned in again, elbows on the table, the edge creeping in now. "This isn't only about attraction, and you know it. You could've sent her across the city with a glowing reference and never looked back."

He paused, watching him.

"But you didn't."

Gideon's silence stretched thin.

"She was the most qualified candidate," he said finally, the words cleaner than the truth.

Dan gave a short laugh, low and unimpressed. "Yeah? And I'm a monk."

He shook his head once, the smile gone now. "Don't tell me this was strategy. You hired the one woman who rattles you. That's not business. That's something else."

Gideon's jaw worked, but he didn't reply.

"Didn't think so," Dan muttered, lifting his glass like a man toasting a mistake in real time.

He took a drink, then added, "You don't mix business with pleasure. That's your whole brand, man. But this? You just threw a match into your own damn oil reserve."

Gideon's voice dropped. "She can handle the job."

"That's not the question," Dan said. "The question is, can you handle her?"

The silence stretched between them.

Dan leaned back again, eyes glittering with amusement, and raised his glass once more.

"To chaos, then."

Perfect.

Gideon clinked his glass against Dan's out of reflex, but the words lodged deeper than expected.

Because this wasn't the kind of move he usually made. It wasn't clean. It wasn't tidy. It sure as hell wasn't smart.

It was something else entirely.

And for the first time in years, Gideon couldn't tell whether he was playing the game or being played by it.

Gideon left the bar, but the conversation didn't leave him.

Dan's words looped in his mind, needling at the edges of his control and pulling at something he had no interest in naming.

So instead of going home, instead of lying in bed while the tension chewed through him, he went to the one place that demanded more from his body than his thoughts ever could.

When his mind wouldn't quiet, he let his fists speak for him.

Not in words. Not through strategy. Through sweat, muscle, and the clean brutality of impact.

The gym was stripped down and functional. No mirrors placed for vanity. No luxury. Nothing designed to impress. It existed for one purpose: to break a man down and see what remained.

Scuffed floors. Chalk stains. The faint tang of metal and effort in the air.

The heavy bag hung in the center, waiting.

He wrapped his hands tight, the friction of the tape rough against his skin. Grounding. Familiar.

Then he hit.

Left. Right. Again.

The sound cracked through the room, each punch landing with clean precision. His breath found rhythm. Sweat slicked down his back.

But no matter how hard he hit, the flicker remained.

Her.

Not soft. Not sweet.

Striking.

Present.

Eyes steady and sure, as if she had decided intimidation was beneath her—not the club, not him, not the world he had built to make other people feel the weight of entering it.

Another punch.

Harder.

She hadn't adapted to the room. She had taken it.

Most people bent in unfamiliar territory. Arden Rivers had walked into The

Blackwell Room as though she had been there all along and made the space adjust around her.

Another punch landed. Then another.

His knuckles stung. His breath came rougher.

Gideon knew how to read people. He could map intention before most men had decided what face to wear.

But Arden remained maddeningly unreadable.

Composed and volatile. Polished, but dangerous beneath the finish. Controlled, but never contained.

She hadn't flinched.

Not then.

Not now.

She didn't back off in his head, either. Not even here.

His fist slammed into the bag with a final, punishing thud. The bag swung hard, and he caught it with both hands, steadying it as if anchoring himself through the weight.

Silence followed, thick and unforgiving.

He dragged a towel across his face, breath catching hard, then dropped onto the bench. The damp fabric hung around his neck, clinging to the back of his shirt.

Across the room, the mirror caught him from an angle he didn't like: drenched, hollow-eyed, wrecked in ways a workout couldn't explain.

Not the untouchable Blackwell figure people expected. Not the controlled man who made entire rooms recalibrate around him.

Just a man staring down something too large to get his hands around.

He leaned forward, elbows planted on his knees, jaw tight. The quiet pressed in from all sides, heavy and unbroken.

She came.

The thought kept circling, relentless.

Despite every alarm flashing in the back of his mind. Despite the part of him that knew better.

The card.

The offer.

Her.

He didn't regret any of it.

CHAPTER 8

Dangerous Ground

Gideon stood by the windows, tall and unreadable, the desk behind him scattered with open files and unopened questions.

His mind circled back to yesterday: the way Arden had walked into the club as if she already belonged, meeting every challenge with that quiet fire. Holding himself in check had felt like damming a storm.

Logic told him to regret it.

Bringing Arden Rivers into his world was a risk, and not only to his carefully curated existence. To her.

His family's world had a way of devouring the unprepared, twisting strength into weakness and calling the damage refinement.

But Arden was anything but weak.

The thought landed hard and refused to settle.

Beneath the caution, something darker stirred, quiet and unrelenting, untouched even by last night's workout. She had that rare combination of raw talent and fearless defiance that made the room feel electric.

She hadn't stumbled into this.

She had chosen it.

And he respected that more than he should.

More than he could afford.

The quiet creak of the door broke his reverie.

Without turning, he knew who it was. Only Dan would dare walk in without knocking.

"You know," Dan said, his voice easy with the weight of long history, "I haven't seen you this off-balance since your grandfather left you the company."

Gideon set his glass on the desk with measured care, his attention fixed on the city lights. "I'm not off-balance."

"No?" Dan crossed the room and braced a hand on the desk. His gaze flicked to the untouched bourbon—Henry's favorite—then back to Gideon. "Then why do you look like a man trying to outmaneuver his own heartbeat?"

When Gideon stayed silent, Dan's smirk tilted.

"Damn. Still thinking about her, then?"

"She starts tonight."

"And that's all it is?" Dan pressed. "I've known you since college. I've seen you pull off mergers with less hesitation."

Gideon didn't respond.

Dan dropped into the chair across from him. "You think hiring her was the smart move?"

"She earned it."

His voice held, though something beneath it frayed.

Dan studied him. "Okay. So we're pretending this is just business. Got it."

Silence stretched between them, not hostile, but full of everything neither of them had said yet.

"You want to tell me this isn't like Isabel?"

Gideon stiffened.

"That's different," he said, too quickly.

Dan held his gaze. "You were different."

"She was—" The words caught somewhere between his teeth and his regret. "Evelyn made sure Isabel didn't last."

"And you let her," Dan said evenly.

Not a jab.

Just truth.

"Because you thought that was the price of peace. Of control. And now look at you." He gestured toward the glass. "Standing here again, wondering what it's going to cost you."

Gideon exhaled, slow and hard. "My mother's already caught wind."

Dan blinked. "Of course she has."

A pause.

"How long before she circles like a shark?"

"She's circling."

Dan pressed his palms together. "Look, this world? Evelyn's world?" His voice dropped. "You've seen what happens to women who challenge it."

"She's not Isabel," Gideon said, low and sharpened.

"No," Dan agreed. "She's not."

Gideon turned away, back to the window.

"You've built your whole life around control," Dan continued. "But what happens when someone walks in who doesn't play by the rules you've written?"

"She starts tonight."

Quieter now.

Almost to himself.

Dan stood and adjusted his cuffs, slow enough to be deliberate. "Just make sure she's not walking into a fight she doesn't see coming."

He reached the hallway, then glanced back.

"And for what it's worth? I don't think you're worried about her breaking the rules."

A beat.

"I think you're worried she'll rewrite them."

The door shut behind him with an infuriatingly casual click.

Gideon remained still, fingers curled against the desk.

He should have let the words roll off his back. Should have dismissed them as noise.

But he didn't.

Because Dan was right.

This hadn't been a business move.

Not since the moment she met his eyes at Dot's, unblinking and unshaken.

And now she was in his world.

Working at his club.

Inside his domain.

Gideon set the glass down carefully, as if precision could rebuild what was slipping.

A SHARP KNOCK fractured the hush.

Then came the click of heels.

Precise. Clipped.

Gideon's jaw locked.

Evelyn Blackwell had a radar for disruption, especially when it came wrapped in female form. She had built a legacy on control and eliminated every woman who threatened it with the same polished efficiency she brought to everything else.

Gideon didn't have to wonder how she had found out.

She always found out.

She had sniffed out Isabel long before things could turn serious. One surgical conversation. One leaked rumor. After that, Isabel had disappeared.

He hadn't stopped her.

It had been cleaner that way.

But Arden wasn't Isabel.

And Evelyn had noticed.

She stepped into the office like she owned the oxygen.

Impeccable, icy, unyielding.

Her silver hair was twisted into something flawless and sharp, and the navy suit didn't soften her; it moved like sculpted armor. Every breath, every angle, every controlled pause claimed the room before she said a word.

Her gaze swept the office, cataloging and calculating, before it landed on him.

A pause.

Half acknowledgment.

Half warning.

"Arden Rivers."

She spoke the name as if reading an ingredient on a label: unfamiliar, suspicious, potentially contaminating.

"A rather... unconventional choice."

The pause before unconventional was purposeful.

Sleek disapproval disguised as poise.

"She's none of your concern," Gideon said.

Evelyn's smile cut with precision. "Isn't she?"

She approached his desk, one manicured nail trailing along the polished wood. "You involved me the moment you brought her in. The Blackwell Room isn't a passion project, Gideon."

She looked up, eyes gleaming.

"It's bloodlines. Legacy. And that means ours."

Silence followed, loaded and cold.

"She's off-limits."

His voice was flat. Iron wrapped in velvet.

Evelyn gave a soft hum, amused. "You've always been drawn to possibility."

It wasn't praise.

It was dissection.

"Just like your grandfather."

Henry Hawthorne.

Her father.

She didn't need to say his name. The weight of it filled the room anyway.

Gideon's jaw tightened.

Evelyn saw it and smiled as if she had struck exactly the nerve she had come to find.

"You think this is about a bartender?"

Her voice dipped, almost intimate.

Poison in silk.

"Do you know your grandfather's greatest mistake?"

She took a step closer.

"He believed in you. Enough to overlook his own daughter."

A beat.

Her eyes stayed on his, cold and gleaming.

"And now here you are. Repeating him."

The air shifted around them, colder and thinner than before.

"You've always had a weakness for strays," she said.

Another pause.

"For broken things."

Then, quieter:

"For potential."

The word hit like a stone.

Heavy. Final.

She tipped her head, studying him like a painting she had already sentenced to burn.

"And potential, when misplaced?"

A slow smile.

"Is almost always a disaster."

Then came the kill shot.

"Especially when the package is this... decorative."

His fingers clenched around the glass. The ice cracked softly.

He didn't speak.

She noticed, of course, but she didn't flinch. Evelyn always finished what she started. Turning toward the door, she adjusted her sleeve with a graceful, blade-sharp motion.

"Your grandfather believed in you," she said, voice smooth as lacquer. "Don't make him regret it."

The door closed behind her with surgical finality, but her words lingered, acrid and cloying.

Gideon turned back toward the city. The bourbon sat in his palm, useless as comfort.

The strings were tangled now, and not all of them belonged to him.

Worse, he wasn't sure he cared.

CHAPTER 9

Playing with Fire

The Blackwell Room exhaled elegance and control, but beneath the polish, something primal stirred.

Arden felt it the moment she stepped behind the bar: a pulse of power, secrets, and scrutiny.

She moved with intention. No wasted effort. No second-guessing.

Bottles in order. Glassware gleaming. Layout memorized like a trauma cart.

Different tools. Same urgency. Same pressure. New arena.

Everything in its place.

Every detail sharp.

Marco moved with the rhythm of someone who had done this for years, fluid and instinctive. He walked her through the club's signature cocktails like a quiet ritual, the weight of legacy tucked into every pour.

"It's all about reading the room," he said, watching her mirror his technique. "Skill is expected. Anticipation is everything. You need to know what they want before they even open their mouths."

Arden added a twist of citrus and slid the bottle back into place with smooth efficiency. "I pay attention."

Marco gave her a look, curious—maybe impressed—but said nothing. He nodded, then motioned subtly toward a suited man at the far table.

"Table twelve. Mr. Rochester. Macallan neat. Black napkin."

"Got it," she said without hesitation, already reaching for the bottle.

He chuckled. "You sure you haven't worked here before?"

Her grin was quick and cutting. "Careful. I've got a habit of spotting the cracks people think they're hiding."

Marco smirked. "Then you'll fit right in."

His tone shifted then, softening by a degree.
She didn't have to look to know what caused it.
The hum in the air changed first.
Then the attention.
He was here.
Her pulse kicked once in her throat.
Gideon.
He moved through the club like it belonged to him. It did, of course, but ownership wasn't what set him apart. It was the gravity.
His eyes locked onto hers.
She didn't flinch.
"I see Marco's showing you the ropes," he said, his voice low and smooth.
Testing.
"More like confirming I know how to use them."
The words landed with quiet confidence. No deference. No flirtation.
Only truth.
His mouth curved slightly. Not quite a smile. Something heavier. More dangerous.
"Confident as ever."
"Let's not act like that wasn't part of the job description." She reached for the Blanton's, pouring without looking away.
He hadn't asked.
She poured anyway.
The acknowledgment stirred something low in him. Not attraction alone, though God knew that was there. Something darker moved beneath it, possessive and primal enough to make caution feel like a language he had forgotten how to speak.
"Still trying to figure out what this is," she said, sliding the glass across the bar.
Gideon sat without a word, his gaze steady and calculating. Marco, always one step ahead, slipped away with a knowing nod and gave them space.
"And what do you think it's about?"
"I think it's what happens when someone stops pretending the rules apply."
His brow lifted, intrigued. "The usual rules don't apply here."
"Clearly," she said, folding a napkin with precision. "Otherwise, you wouldn't be testing my professionalism if you didn't already know I had it."
His laugh came low and surprised.
Unguarded.
A few patrons turned, startled by the sound. Arden didn't acknowledge it.
"Is that what I'm doing?"
"Among other things." She didn't look away, and she didn't soften the edge in her tone. "But we both know I don't rattle easily."

His gaze darkened, curiosity sharpening into heat beneath the surface of his composure.

"No," he said, his voice dipping into something dangerous. "You don't."

The air between them pulsed, electric and unspoken, tethered to something neither of them could name without giving it too much power.

Then someone at a nearby table laughed too loudly, and the spell broke.

Arden straightened, the bartender persona sliding back into place, though her eyes still carried the spark.

"You should mingle," she said coolly, nodding toward the VIPs. "Wouldn't want anyone to think you're playing favorites..."

His smirk deepened. "Wouldn't we?"

She rolled her eyes, turning back to the bar. "Some of us have a job to do."

He stood with deliberate grace, smoothing his cuffs. "Try not to dismantle the social hierarchy on your first night," he said, already moving. "Some of them aren't ready for your kind of honesty."

She arched a brow, amused. "No promises."

Her voice trailed him like slow smoke.

Thick. Lingering. Inevitable.

So did her presence.

From across the room, Gideon watched her handle the crowd. She commanded the bar with easy poise, deflected arrogance with sharp wit, and made even the most powerful men adjust to her rhythm.

When the rush finally slowed, their eyes met again across the space.

He lifted his glass slightly.

Not a toast.

A signal.

Of what, neither of them could have said.

But it landed like a vow neither of them had spoken.

GIDEON HAD SENSED her the moment she entered the club.

She moved through his domain like flame meeting oxygen, slipping into its shadows and illuminating corners he hadn't realized were dark. That same quick, decisive grace lived in her movements behind the bar: the faint tilt of her chin as she took everything in, the way she read the room's energy and adjusted before most people noticed anything had shifted. Her confidence wasn't performed; it had been earned, quiet and unwavering and real.

From his office above, he watched through the one-way glass as Marco walked her through the setup. Arden didn't miss a thing. Her focus was surgical, each glance precise enough to register more than most people noticed in an hour. It was the same sharp intelligence he remembered from Dot's, only now, standing in the middle of his world, it had sharpened into something far more dangerous.

But competence alone wasn't what held him. It was the way she occupied space, as if presence came naturally to her. She didn't demand attention; she commanded it, and she made no apologies for the room having to adjust.

The bourbon on his desk sat untouched. His focus was already gone.

From up here, he could watch her interactions unfold like strategy, except Arden didn't play games so much as dismantle them. When Harrison Palmer leaned in from table six, testing her as he always did with new staff, Gideon caught the twitch of her mouth. Not quite a smirk. Only a flicker of amusement, sharp enough to warn anyone paying attention.

"Having trouble deciding?" she asked, voice calm but edged with challenge. "I could suggest something more adventurous than your usual gin and tonic. Unless you're not up for it?"

Harrison barked a surprised laugh and waved her on.

Arden hadn't simply won. She had turned the provocation into performance and made him grateful for the privilege of losing.

Gideon felt the pull in his chest, unwelcome but undeniable.

She hadn't adapted to his world. She had rewritten its terms.

He told himself bringing her here had been a mistake, a risk to the club, to the distance he kept, to the control he had spent years mistaking for safety. Before the thought finished forming, he was already rising, already moving, drawn toward the bar by something he refused to name: the spark in her eyes as she worked, the rhythm in her movements, the way she met power not with reverence, but curiosity, as though she were sizing it up and deciding whether it deserved to stand.

He crossed the floor, and when she spotted him, her gaze didn't waver.

"Otherwise, you wouldn't be testing how professional I can be."

He hadn't expected her to say it out loud. He hadn't expected it to crack his composure, but it did. A low laugh escaped him, rare and real enough to make nearby patrons turn.

She had called it, named the energy humming between them with disarming ease. She didn't simply see him; she saw the test beneath the conversation, the control beneath the courtesy, the line he kept pretending neither of them had noticed.

In this world—his world—people wore masks. They smiled with teeth and spoke in subtext, but Arden met him without polish masquerading as softness. She matched him beat for beat.

He watched her too often. His gaze lingered when it should have moved on, and he knew it. Worse, he didn't care.

She didn't hold the room with money or pedigree. She held it with presence, with earned confidence, with that unsettling, razor-sharp knowing in her eyes. Even her voice posed a threat, smooth and teasing and always a second ahead of everyone else in the room.

He shouldn't have wanted to close the space between them or let her words land the way they did, but when she arched that brow and murmured, "Wouldn't want anyone to think you're playing favorites..."

It hit him square in the chest.

No touch. No invitation. Only precision.

She was playing with fire, and worse, so was he.

Gideon made his rounds, spoke with VIPs, shook hands, answered questions, and performed the role expected of him with the ease of long practice. But the whole time, part of him stayed with her: the tilt of her head when she laughed at something Marco said, the poised way she handled another demanding patron, the subtle shift in the atmosphere near her, electric and aware, as if the room had learned to listen when she moved.

When the rush finally slowed, their eyes met again across the space.

Something passed between them. He couldn't have named it if he tried. Her skill, her defiance, the unraveling of every line he had spent years drawing.

All he knew was that watching Arden Rivers behind his bar didn't feel disruptive.

It felt inevitable.

And he wasn't ready to look away.

His mother's voice echoed through him, caution and criticism wrapped in polished ice. Weakness. Sentiment. Distraction.

But Evelyn didn't understand.

Arden wasn't a weakness. She wasn't someone to control into safety or keep at a careful distance until she became manageable. She was a force—untamed, uncompromising, and impossible to mistake for anything he could own.

God help him, he wanted to follow where she led, even if it meant setting fire to the rules he had built his life around.

The night wasn't over, but Gideon knew one thing with a certainty that felt dangerously close to surrender: hiring Arden Rivers had never been only about talent. It had been an invitation, fire brought willingly into his world, and now he had to decide whether he meant to survive the burn or step closer.

———

SHE WAS unlike anything he'd ever seen. And he had watched her more than once.

She moved through the room with quiet certainty.

Every step, every gesture—fluid.

Not the polished ghosts that haunted the club, swirling aged whiskey and pretending wealth made them untouchable.

She was alive.

He stayed in the shadows, watching.

Consuming her. Every detail. Every breath.

The way her dark hair caught the low light.

The way those blue eyes swept the room: alert, assessing.
She wasn't playing their game.
She was studying it.
It seemed impossible she was real.
When he'd first seen her, it was just a flicker. A moment.
Something inside him had snapped awake.

NOW, *watching her move with quiet authority, the pull in his chest returned—tight, undeniable.*
She didn't belong here. That was obvious.
Yet... she did.
Not because she blended in.
Because she didn't.
She wasn't carved from the same cold marble as the elite.
She wasn't born to this place.
But she carried herself like someone who'd bled for every inch of ground she stood on.
She didn't demand attention.
She disrupted it.
And they noticed. The men with their curated charm, their expensive watches and hollow smiles.
They watched her.
Some with curiosity. Some with calculation.
Some with hunger.
Fools.
They didn't see it.
But he already did.
She was silk over steel. A blade beneath the curve of a smile.
He lingered, unseen, watching the tension in her shoulders.
The way she scanned the room. Not to be admired, but to understand.
To read the power lines. To find the cracks.
She wasn't pretending. She was preparing.
And he needed to learn her.

THEN GIDEON BLACKWELL APPEARED.
His chest tightened.
He recognized his power. Tailored. Weaponized.
Blackwell didn't just walk into a room. He took ownership of it.
But that wasn't what made his teeth clench.

It was the way Blackwell looked at her—a mystery worth solving. A prize worth keeping.

Worse, she looked back.

Not with awe or flirtation.

With challenge.

Gideon leaned in, said something too low to catch.

She answered. Steady. Unflinching. Unimpressed.

Blackwell thought he could have her. Claim her.

His hands curled into fists.

Another beautiful thing to tuck into his empire.

But she wasn't made to be owned.

Not by Blackwell.

Not by anyone.

THE REALIZATION HIT *like heat under the skin.*

He needed to understand her.

To see how she moved when no one was watching.

To hear her voice when it wasn't wrapped in performance.

To understand that look—the one that said nothing touched her unless she let it.

And he wondered. Had she ever let anyone in?

Because if she had, it sure as hell wouldn't be Gideon Blackwell.

Not if he had anything to say about it.

And he would.

FOR NOW, *he'd stay in the shadows.*

He would wait.

Watch.

Learn.

BUT SOON...

She'd see him, too.

CHAPTER 10

Behind the Velvet Curtain

The club thrived on money and secrets.

Jazz unfurled from the corner piano, curling through conversations that rose and fell in the hush between indulgence and intention. Crystal refracted light overhead, stolen stars flickering in every chandelier and casting gold across polished marble and velvet green.

It had been three weeks, and Arden knew the rhythms by heart.

Early evening belonged to sharpness: deals struck between sips of bourbon, ambition cloaked in silk and bespoke suits, every smile calibrated to reveal as little as possible. But past midnight, the edges blurred. Truth leaked in then, soft and sticky, staining everything by morning.

She had memorized the regulars and their patterns. Mr. Rochester always arrived at eight and always ordered Macallan neat on a black napkin. The hedge fund clique claimed the corner booth until ten, their laughter growing louder once international markets closed. Harrison Palmer came armed with cocktail riddles, still determined to catch her off guard, and the woman in sequins never ordered the same drink twice or gave the same name.

Nothing here resembled Dot's.

Everything was intentional: lighting designed to flatter, voices hushed to conceal more than they revealed, even the staff moving like part of an unspoken choreography Arden had learned beat by beat. Marco's subtle head tilt meant someone needed watching. Fatima's quiet double tap on the bar meant cut them off —with grace.

Arden hadn't always known what belonging felt like, but she had learned how to move as if she did. Confidence was armor here, and lately, it no longer felt borrowed.

This sliver of time between midnight and closing belonged to her.

The club shifted into something more intimate after midnight, still gleaming but gentled by the hour. Secrets came easier then, wrapped in laughter and masked by shadow.

Marco passed, his hand sweeping up empty glassware with practiced ease. "Another round for Palmer," he said, voice low. "Also, Arty's back. Third night this week."

Arden glanced toward his usual stool.

Arty Burnett watched the room with idle focus, a predator disguised as a patron. Unsettling, but not new.

Her phone buzzed.

She fished it from her pocket, expecting Penny's latest chaos.

Unknown: Starting over doesn't erase the past.

Arden's blood iced.

The towel slipped from her hand and hit the bar with a muted thud.

For one suspended second, she couldn't move.

Then instinct surged, dragging her gaze across the room. No one stood out. No clear threat announced itself. The familiar hum of the club continued around her, but it felt suddenly flimsy against the cold creeping beneath her skin.

Wrong number.

A coincidence.

Nothing.

Her phone burned in her pocket anyway. A text. A ghost from Silverbranch reaching through the cracks.

It was nothing.

She reached for a glass, but her grip tightened too hard around the stem, and it nearly slipped. Her rhythm wavered. Muscle memory, normally so reliable, stuttered beneath her hands.

A man two seats down arched a brow.

She didn't meet his eyes.

Another man appeared at the far edge of the bar, posture relaxed, suit flawless, expression unreadable. He raised his glass in silent acknowledgment, his smile tilted just this side of menace. Nothing overt. Nothing alarming.

Still, something about him twisted in her gut like a warning too quiet to explain.

She looked away quickly and wiped the counter even though it didn't need it.

The air shifted, denser now. Sharper. Even the light seemed to carry weight.

"Hey."

Marco's voice cut through the static in her mind, quiet and steady enough to ground her.

"You okay?"

Arden turned toward him and managed a nod. "Yeah. Just..." She gestured vaguely, the movement more reflex than explanation.

Marco didn't press. He slid a row of clean tumblers onto the shelf and started drying another, his presence a calm counterweight to the unease lodged beneath her skin.

"One of those nights?"

She huffed a breath that landed somewhere between a laugh and an exhale. "Something like that."

He tilted his head, watching her with the kind of patience a person couldn't fake. "You've got this."

Her throat tightened, just a little. She pushed it down. "You think?"

Marco gave a lazy shrug, his grin crooked. "I know. Few weeks in, and you're running circles around half the old guard. You read this place like you wrote the damn manual."

The compliment settled into her chest, unexpected and disarming.

She worked to prove herself, sure. But this was different. This wasn't about impressing anyone. It was about finally finding a place where being sharp didn't make her a threat.

It made her essential.

She offered him a small smile, though her eyes kept scanning the room. Still moving. Still watchful.

"Thanks, Marco."

His nod was subtle. "Anytime."

Then, as he walked past, he added quietly, "Whatever's got you off tonight—just remember who you are. You've got nothing to prove to these people."

She stood a little straighter after that.

Because he was right.

But as she poured a drink for a table of lawyers whispering behind raised glasses, the sense of being watched stayed with her. It wasn't Arty. Not tonight, not entirely. Another presence had crept in through the cracks, something she couldn't name but felt all the same.

Personal.

The text burned in her mind.

Starting over doesn't erase the past.

No threats or demands.

Only a reminder.

THE HEAVY OAK doors opened on a hush, letting in the soft spill of city sound and the flicker of passing headlights.

Sebastian Hawthorne stepped into the room like he owned it. His tailored suit caught the chandelier's glow, but it was the Hawthorne signet ring on his hand that caught the light—subtle, deliberate. A reminder. A claim. That detail wouldn't matter to most, but it did to Gideon.

Sebastian scanned the room with the lazy efficiency of someone cataloging wealth: rich fabrics, hushed power, old money folded into crystal tumblers.

But the dynamic had shifted. The room pulsed differently now, the rhythm off by a breath.

"Well," a smooth voice cut through the low swell of jazz, "if it isn't my favorite cousin. Here to inspect your little brother's latest... investment?"

Alex lounged against the bar with practiced ease, drink in hand, the curve of his mouth edged with something too pointed to be charm. Every detail about him was curated. Hair perfectly tousled. Suit pristine. But the faint sneer betrayed the performance.

Where Sebastian cut clean, Alex preferred finesse; his charm a velvet sheath hiding something far more dangerous underneath.

They were both dangerous, but in different ways.

Gideon stood a few feet behind them, posture unreadable, hands in his pockets like he didn't need them for leverage. He didn't.

The contrast between the brothers was stark. Alex wore his charm like armor: polished, practiced. Gideon didn't bother; his presence was quieter, heavier. Power that didn't need to posture, and right now, he focused on managing the rising tension in the room.

"Alex," Sebastian said smoothly, offering his cousin a brief nod. "Still here. I'd have thought you would have traded the city for the fresh Wyoming air."

The jab landed softly, wrapped in civility. But it hit its mark.

Alex's grin held, but something flickered behind his eyes, quick and sharp as a match catching flame.

"Can't let things fall apart because the wrong people are in charge," Alex said, his voice smooth as ever as his gaze drifted toward Gideon. "You know how Mother feels about legacy."

Family legacy.

A phrase Gideon had worn like a shackle his whole life: polished, rehearsed, hollow. But tonight, it landed differently, sharper and colder than before.

"The Blackwell Room is doing fine," Gideon said, his voice smooth but cold.

"And so is its newest hire." Sebastian's gaze drifted to the bar. To Arden.

She moved with quiet ownership, effortless and inevitable, though something about her seemed too bright for this place. Composed. Sharp. Watchful.

Too watchful.

Sebastian's mouth curved faintly. "Interesting addition. Doesn't quite blend in, does she?"

Gideon's jaw ticked. "She doesn't need to blend in."

Sebastian turned his head, studying his cousin more closely now. "No... I don't suppose she does. Still, one has to wonder what your mother thinks of such a... striking shift in ambiance."

There it was. The real game.

Gideon didn't flinch. "Mother doesn't run this club."

"No," Alex chimed in, sipping his drink. "But she knows how to clear a room when something—or someone—doesn't serve her vision."

Gideon's stare held steady. "She'll adjust."

Sebastian hummed, then looked back at Arden again, long enough for Gideon to notice. "She's handling it well, though. Surprising, really."

That word lingered too long in the air.

Surprising.

"Almost as if she was made for this world," Alex added, his tone laced with something smug and speculative. "Or maybe," he mused, voice too smooth, "she's smart enough to play the part."

Sebastian's tone dipped, quiet and precise. "Whichever it is, I have a feeling this will be interesting."

Gideon's voice dropped, low and cool. "Be careful who you watch too closely."

Sebastian's smile held, but something colder glinted beneath it, calculating and coiled. "Always."

Alex set his glass down, the sound soft but intentional.

"Don't worry, little brother. We're here to support you. Keep an eye on things. Isn't that what family does?"

No one moved as the implication settled between them, slow-blooming and unmistakable.

Then, as if nothing had passed, Sebastian straightened his cuffs. "Well. Do let us know if she lives up to your expectations."

"She already has," Gideon replied.

Alex smirked, almost indulgent. "Then we'll raise ours."

They turned and retreated into the velvet hush of the lounge, but their presence lingered behind them, heavy and unsettling.

Their interest had only begun.

Arden didn't catch their final words, but she didn't need to.

She saw enough in the subtle clench of Gideon's jaw, the way his fingers flexed once against the polished bar before he forced a slow, weighted exhale.

A storm held in check by sheer will.

And she wasn't the only one who noticed.

The room adjusted with elegant indifference around him. Conversations dipped, then resumed with careful precision, because even among the elite, instinct knew when gravity had shifted.

Marco, always tuned to the undercurrent, leaned slightly her way.

"You good?"

Arden offered him a small, practiced smile, the kind that had smoothed plenty of rough edges back at Dot's.

"Yeah."

But her gaze drifted inevitably toward the office door upstairs, left slightly ajar.

Like an unfinished sentence.

Whatever had unfolded tonight wasn't over.

Not even close.

———

SHE NAVIGATED THE ROOM, *fire wrapped in silk,*
measured, unaware of her own captivation.
He lingered at his usual vantage point, quiet in the dark, content to observe.

IN THE PAST FEW WEEKS, *she'd changed.*
More assured.
More attuned to the subtle currents of power beneath the club's opulence.
He'd memorized the way her hands moved behind the bar.

SHE DESTROYED *arrogance with a smile that never quite reached her eyes.*
The way she never let them see her flinch.
She belonged nowhere and everywhere.
A force the world mistook for decoration, unaware of the storm she carried.

THEY SAW HER.
But not like he did.
Never like he did
His fingers hovered over his phone, the message already typed.
"Starting over doesn't erase the past."
Not a threat or a warning.
A truth.

THE MOMENT IT REACHED HER, *he saw it.*
The subtle flicker behind her eyes, the breath caught just short.
The towel slipped from her hands.
She scanned the room.

But she wouldn't find him.
Not yet.
He wasn't hiding. He didn't need to.
He was already there. Watching the moment tighten beneath her skin.
Watching her steady herself.
And she didn't even know it.

SHE WASN'T *ready to face him.*
Not yet.

SHE DIDN'T KNOW *what he knew in his bones...*
That she was meant for more than this place.
More than this world built on whispers and glass.
More than these people who saw her only as something to possess.
Especially Gideon Blackwell.

HIS FINGERS TIGHTENED *around his glass at the sight of him: the entitlement in his posture, the hunger in his gaze.*

BLACKWELL WATCHED *her like he owned her.*
A new treasure. A captured flame.
But she wasn't an acquisition.
She wasn't a fucking prize.
She was a storm waiting to tear everything apart.

AND SHE DESERVED *someone who knew better than to contain her.*
Someone who knew her worth.
Someone like him.

SO HE'D WAIT.
Let her believe this place was hers.
Let her grow comfortable, convinced she'd found a sanctuary.

BECAUSE SOON, *the truth would find her.*

And when it did, he'd be there.
Watching.
Waiting.
Hers.

*

"You're here late."

That voice shouldn't have affected her, but it did.

Three weeks of carefully guarded distance, fleeting glances across the bar, and forced professionalism had only sharpened Arden's awareness of him. She turned to find Gideon emerging from the low light, sleeves rolled, tie loosened. The shadows sculpted hard lines beneath his cheekbones, giving him an edge that felt both too human and entirely unreal.

"New girl pulls the graveyard shift," she quipped, dropping a rag into the bin beneath the counter. Her blood betrayed the casual tone, pounding harder with each step he took. "Besides, isn't this your domain?"

His smile threatened her composure.

"I suppose I haunt these halls enough."

A pause followed, intentional and weighted.

"Have you seen the rest of the place yet?"

She folded her arms, hoping the gesture masked her nerves. "What, the kitchen? Supply closet? Riveting."

"Not exactly." The tilt of his mouth sent a quiet alarm through her chest. His voice dropped, coaxing. "Come on. You've earned the full tour."

Logic said no. It was late, the lounge stood empty, and Gideon Blackwell was as volatile as a lit match in a dry field. But curiosity, and something deeper—more feral —drew her forward anyway.

She trailed him up the narrow staircase to a door tucked so neatly into the wall most people would miss it. The lock gave way with a soft click, too sharp in the surrounding stillness.

Then he stepped back.

Not simply permission.

An invitation.

A line, crossed.

Arden stepped inside and forgot how to breathe.

The private lounge glowed with distilled opulence: green and gold velvet chairs arranged like whispered secrets, a marble bar gleaming beneath a low wash of light. Shelves lined with rare spirits cast golden shadows across polished wood.

It felt sacred. Heavy. A room that remembered.

She stopped just inside, taking it in slowly, letting the room settle around her like a second skin.

"Jesus," she murmured, the word escaping before she could catch it. "And here I thought the wine cellar was over the top."

"It's not pretentious," he said quickly, like he had answered that question before.

His presence eased through the space like a shadow returning home. Yet something in him had softened, the harder edges blunted by memory.

"It's exclusive."

She glanced back, the light turning his gray eyes nearly silver. "Because that makes it better?"

"I didn't say better."

She let her fingers drift across the velvet, plush and broken-in beneath her touch, like a secret kept in fabric. Her voice dropped, reverent despite herself. "What is this place?"

"It's the pulse," he said simply. "Where everything begins."

His voice pulled her around to face him, heavy with something deeper now.

"My grandfather's vision. He wanted more than business. He wanted connection. This is where he brought people who mattered."

The sharp polish of Gideon Blackwell had slipped. Something raw flickered beneath his surface, a rare flash of the man behind the name.

"He sounds... different."

"He was." Gideon stepped farther into the room, reverent. "Richard Blackwell II saw wealth as a way to build something lasting. Legacy, not power."

She trailed her fingers along the bar's edge until her hand paused on a small engraved plaque.

For the ones who matter.

The words settled deep, quiet as the thud of something familiar.

"It's... beautiful," she said.

Her eyes moved over the room, but the word landed elsewhere, aimed at something she hadn't named.

He tilted his head, gaze narrowing with interest. "Not what you thought I'd show you?"

She gave a breath of laughter, light but honest. "No. I expected... more gold-plated ego. A lot less soul."

What he gave in return wasn't a smirk.

It was something real.

"Gold-plated ego is the family specialty." His fingers skimmed an antique decanter, not in appraisal, but in memory. "But this room? My grandfather kept it untouched, even when the rest of them wanted another trophy."

"And now it's yours."

"Not without a fight." Steel underlined the softness. "They wanted the prestige. Not the responsibility. But it mattered to him. And he thought I'd make it matter too."

She understood that deeply.

Her gaze dropped to the marble bar, catching fractured reflections of them both. "He must've been proud."

A pause stretched between them.

When he finally spoke, his voice was quieter. "I hope so." He exhaled, bone-deep and unguarded. "But it's not just about him anymore. It's about what I do with it now. What I make it stand for."

Their eyes met, and for a moment there were no roles between them. No masks. Only truth.

It was too much.

She turned too fast, trying to escape the weight of it.

And—

"Shit—"

Her heel caught.

His hands found her waist, steady and sure.

Heat. Unyielding. Alive.

Her palms braced against his shoulders, solid muscle beneath crisp fabric, anchoring her before she could fall. His scent—wood, spice, something darker—wrapped around her like a pull she couldn't name.

Her pulse skipped.

"Easy."

Low. Rough. Dangerous.

She looked up, and everything in him had shifted. His eyes were darker now, holding something neither of them dared name.

Too close.

Too charged.

"Yeah."

The word left her like an exhale she hadn't known she was holding.

She eased back, brushing at her shirt as if she could remove the echo of his hands. "Guess I'm not used to floors this exclusive."

He nearly smiled, but his eyes stayed hot. "They can be treacherous."

"Noted." She reached for calm that wouldn't come. "Thanks for the save."

"Anytime."

Simple, but it landed with weight.

She should have walked away.

She didn't.

Instead, her eyes flicked to the plaque again.

For the ones who matter.

This place, and Gideon with it, felt carved from something deeper than she had expected.

As she stepped into the hall, cooler air greeted her, but her thoughts stayed lodged in that room: the soft reverence in his voice, the heat of his touch, the look in his eyes when every mask fell away.

Gideon Blackwell wasn't supposed to feel this real.
Tonight, he did.
And that made him infinitely more dangerous.

CHAPTER 11

Under the Surface

Laughter and jazz spilled from the lounge, bright and careless, but none of it reached the weight pressing against Arden's ribs.

She leaned against the breakroom counter, fingers curled around her phone, trying to focus on anything except the exhaustion coiling through her. Beside her, the espresso machine hissed in its low, familiar rhythm; usually comforting, tonight it barely registered.

Nearly a month in, she'd learned The Blackwell Room's choreography. She understood how power moved in glances, how wealth didn't speak so much as gesture, how entire conversations could happen in the careful lift of a brow or the precise pause before a smile. She had become fluent in its quiet language, its unspoken rules.

But something tonight was off.

She froze.

A rose.

Deep crimson. Flawless. Resting in the center of the counter.

The room tilted, nausea tugging low in her gut as memory opened beneath her: another rose, another night, a darkened parking garage, the windshield of her car.

No.

She hadn't seen it when she walked in. She was sure of it. The room had been empty.

Explanations scrambled for footing. A guest had left it behind. A prop from an event. Marco, being dramatic.

None of them held.

Her phone buzzed, and she jolted.

Unknown: Enjoying your new life?

Her skin prickled. Cold swept down her back like breath against the nape of her neck, and for a moment her fingers only hovered above the screen, torn between blocking the number and hurling the phone across the room.

Neither would change what she knew.

Her eyes flicked back to the rose. Too perfect, too precise, too familiar to be coincidence; not when it sat there wrapped in silk petals and shadows, offering beauty with a blade tucked underneath. The fluorescent light above her flickered once, then steadied, casting long, uncertain shadows beneath the lockers and along the baseboards, and the room sat too still around her. Silent. Watching.

No coat out of place. No forgotten coffee cup by the sink. Nothing human enough to explain it.

But the feeling lingered, slow and creeping, as memory struck like a match: the first rose, then another, then another. Petals blooming with slow, suffocating intent until the night it stopped being flowers and became something else.

Her stomach turned.

Not again.

Her hand gripped the counter's edge, cold and solid beneath her fingertips when nothing else felt certain. If she fell apart, she gave him power.

So Arden reached for the rose. Velvet petals brushed her fingertips, soft as breath.

Deceptive.

She didn't flinch.

She left it where it was.

If someone asked, she'd smirk and toss off a joke. Some guest thinks they're charming. Inside, her nerves pulled tight, stretching thin, straining for control.

The door clicked shut behind her, too loud and too final.

She didn't turn back. Couldn't.

But the sensation followed: breath at her shoulder, eyes just beyond reach, someone standing only a step behind her. A warning carried in fragrance and silence.

Arden stepped back into the gilded world of The Blackwell Room, where candlelight glinted off crystal and secrets softened in the shimmer of jazz. She lifted her chin. Set her shoulders.

She'd survived roses before.

She would again.

At least, that's what she told herself.

———

THE BREAK ROOM'S lights buzzed overhead, sterile and cold. A poor disguise for the heat blooming from the rose on the counter.

Crimson, flawless. Deliberate.

He watched from the shadows.

ARDEN RIVERS.

WITH TENSION in her shoulders and a quiet unease dimming her usual light, she moved with unconscious grace. Always aware, even when she thought she wasn't.

She froze at the sight of the rose.

Then the message.

THE HITCH IN HER BREATH. The way her lips caught and released—barely a flicker, but he saw it.

He always saw it.

A slow exhale left his lungs.

Not fear, never fear.

He didn't want her frightened.

THE ROSE WAS A GESTURE.

An acknowledgment.

Proof that someone had noticed her behind the mask.

That someone understood the armor she wore to navigate this temple of power and performance.

And more than that—someone admired it.

SHE'D FELT IT NOW, hadn't she? That pull.

Not fear.

Recognition.

HIS GLOVED FINGERS skimmed the edge of his phone, the screen aglow.

"Enjoying your new life?"

Clean. Intentional. Just enough to make her look over her shoulder—to wonder if the past had followed her into this gilded place.

HER GAZE RETURNED *to the rose.*
Perfect.
She hesitated again, just barely. That same unconscious tic. Lip caught, then released.
She's hiding something.
She always does that when she's hiding something.

HE SMILED.
It was happening. Slowly, inevitably, she was beginning to feel it.
Beginning to see the thread he'd woven for what it was: connection. Quiet and unbreakable.
She wasn't just a bartender.
She was everything.

ARDEN EXHALED AND TURNED, *her shoulders squaring as she walked toward the door. So strong.*
Little Fire.
Even in doubt, she carried herself like a storm wrapped in silk.
Unyielding. Luminous.

DIDN'T SHE KNOW?
She already ruled this world.
She believed polished glass and curated luxury could shield her.
Blackwell's kingdom couldn't keep her safe.

HE KNEW BETTER.
And he knew her better.

THE SOFT CLICK *of the door echoed as she left.*
But he didn't move. Didn't need to.

THE ROSE REMAINED, *a blood-red truth left in a sterile world built on appearances.*
It would speak for him.
A reminder.
That someone could still reach her.

Soon, *she'd stop searching for logic in the cracks.*
She'd stop fighting the unease and listen to what it was trying to tell her.
That someone saw her.
Not the version she presented.
Not the polished composure or practiced wit.
The fire underneath.
And he didn't want to tame it.
He wanted to worship it.
Not like Blackwell wrapped in suits, crowned by legacy, dripping with control.
Blackwell didn't see her—he saw a possession. But he would never try.

He would stand *in the center of her blaze and burn.*
Because fate hadn't simply brought her here.
It had delivered her to him.
The rose wasn't a threat.
It was a promise.
She was his.
She just didn't know it yet.

His fingers brushed *the petals before slipping away. The lights above flickered once—just enough to shift the shadows, but he didn't pause.*
There was more to come.
More to show her.
This rose was only the beginning.
Each message. Each whisper. Each reminder.
They would bring her closer. Strip away the walls until all that was left was truth.

And if anyone *tried to stand in the way, Blackwell included?*
Well.
Fire had a way of consuming everything.
Soon, she would understand.
Who truly saw her.
Who truly knew the heat behind her steel.
Who would never ask her to dim.
Not even to survive.

And when she did, *everything else would burn.*

The murmur of conversation drifted down the hall as Gideon closed the heavy door to his office, sealing off the curated world outside.

The club was thriving tonight, glimmering with wealth and whispered deals, indulgence polished to an art form. But here, in the dim quiet of leather and polished wood, different rules applied.

He leaned over his desk, papers scattered like fallen battleground maps, and one folder caught his eye.

WV.

The letters sat stamped in bold across the tab. Inside were deeds, legal filings, and a paper trail of quiet devastation.

His family's legacy, spelled out in partition sales and manipulated loopholes.

They called it strategy.

He called it what it was: theft.

Tension pulsed at his jaw as he skimmed the edge of a particularly incriminating page, the familiar anger settling low and sharp beneath his ribs.

A knock cut through the silence. Confident. Controlled.

Not Marco's polite tap. Not his brother's heavy pound.

"Come in," he said, voice level despite the weight spread across his desk.

The door eased open.

Arden stepped inside, leaning against the frame with her arms folded, a faint challenge tugging at the corner of her mouth. She didn't need to speak to shift the atmosphere; somehow, the room recalibrated around her anyway.

"Are we committing to maximum gloom in here," she asked, "or is this brooding aesthetic intentional?"

A small smile touched his mouth. "I prefer 'sanctuary.'"

She moved farther into the office, and something in the room tilted with her. Her gaze swept over the space in quick, quiet assessment, cataloging details, missing nothing. He watched her take in the late nights etched across his desk, the scattered evidence of purpose behind the power.

"I was beginning to think you were a myth," she said lightly. "Only appearing when summoned by emergencies or obscure whiskey requests."

"And yet, here you are," he murmured. "Daring to approach the cave."

"Someone's got to make sure you haven't turned to stone."

She dropped into the chair opposite him with that balance she carried so effortlessly—comfortable without ever fully relaxing, alert even in stillness.

Then her gaze shifted to the folder.

"What's that?"

His first instinct was to redirect. To close the file, redirect the conversation, lock the door on this part of himself the same way he locked down everything else.

But Arden's eyes held steady on his. Clear. Unafraid.

She didn't flinch from hard truths.

A breath. A choice.

"West Virginia."

Her brow arched slightly, no judgment in it. Just quiet interest.

"It's land," he said slowly. "Family land. Passed down through generations in rural Black communities. Land people fought to hold onto through Reconstruction, through Jim Crow, through every system designed to strip it away."

He shifted the folder toward her, an offering he hadn't planned to make.

"And now it's being stolen again. Legally."

Something tightened in her chest at the words, stirring memories she rarely touched unless forced. Not land her own family had lost, but neighbors and friends. Small plots tucked into the hills, passed down with handshakes and memory instead of paperwork, left vulnerable to anyone with a lawyer and enough ambition.

In West Virginia, it wasn't always history books and headlines.

Sometimes it was your cousin's place up the road sold out from under him for the promise of a new dollar store.

Her brow furrowed. "Heirs' property?"

He looked up sharply, something impressed flickering briefly across his face.

She gave a small shrug. "I read. It's a legal trap. Land handed down without a will. Dozens of heirs, no clear title. All it takes is one person selling their share and the rest are screwed."

"Exactly." His voice sharpened with the force of it. "It's classified as tenancy in common. One heir sells. A developer buys. Then they force a partition sale through the courts and the entire property goes on the block."

"And just like that," she murmured, "generations get erased."

He nodded once. "Most of the time, it's not even malicious. Just exhaustion. Families can't afford the legal work to clear titles. Half of them don't even realize they're vulnerable until it's already happening. In places like West Virginia, it goes back generations—no wills, no trust funds. Just land passed down through blood and faith until someone finds a way to take it."

A muscle jumped in his jaw.

"Land Black families held onto for a hundred years—gone in a court auction in ten minutes."

Arden leaned forward slightly, fingertips brushing the edge of the desk, close enough now for him to feel the tension gathering between them like a live current.

"And your family?"

His answer came without hesitation. "Not me."

Something shifted in her expression then. Not surprise. Something quieter. Deeper.

"I've been working quietly to undo some of the damage," he continued. "Helping clear titles where I can. Stopping new acquisitions. My grandfather's generation saw it as business."

His gaze dropped briefly to the folder before returning to hers.

"I see it for what it is."

She studied him for a long moment.

"Is that why you were in West Virginia? To help?"

"To try."

The words landed softly between them.

Her expression eased, though the faint pinch in her brow remained. "That's… rare."

"Rare?"

"Most people wouldn't bother," she said. "Too messy. Too hard."

A hollow smile ghosted across his mouth. "Most people don't even know it's happening. It's not the kind of injustice that makes headlines. It's quiet. Boring, if you don't know what you're looking at."

Her gaze dropped to the folder again, thoughtful.

"It's not boring," she said quietly. "It's survival."

Silence settled between them then—not awkward, not empty, but full of things neither of them quite knew how to name yet.

After a moment, she glanced back up at him.

"You could've said something."

He stilled. "What?"

"It might've made me trust you sooner."

Something in his expression darkened—not anger, but truth laid bare.

"Trust doesn't come from confessions," he said softly. "It comes with time."

The words hung there between them, weighty and unmistakably real.

Recognition.

Respect.

Maybe something far more dangerous.

She nodded once. "Thank you. For telling me."

He watched her carefully and felt something inside him loosen despite himself, some guarded part easing in ways he neither liked nor fully understood.

"Thank you," he said quietly, "for listening."

And the silence that followed wasn't silence at all.

It was the space where something real began to take root.

❦

After Arden slipped out, Gideon stared at the West Virginia folder for a long beat before closing it with measured care. The hush of his office pressed in around him, hollow and stark in the wake of the storm she left behind.

She unsettled him.

Not because she was intelligent; he'd expected that. Not because she grasped complexity with unsettling ease; he'd anticipated that, too. But because she looked past every carefully worded explanation and straight into the core of what drove him.

She stirred clarity he hadn't felt in years, laced with an ache he hadn't yet named.

Bringing her into his orbit had been a gamble, and the consequences were only beginning to take shape. The Blackwell Room wasn't merely a club; it was a battleground of legacy and bloodlines, power and pretense. Every hour she spent here pulled her deeper into that war.

His war.

Gideon rose and crossed to the window. His reflection hovered against the skyline, a ghost outlined in steel and glass, while the city stretched outward beyond him, glittering and untouchable. A monument to everything his family had built... and buried.

He couldn't rewrite what had already been carved into history, but perhaps he could chip away at the rot, one stolen piece at a time.

And perhaps he wasn't fighting alone anymore.

The thought should have rattled him. He had spent years keeping others at arm's length, shielding them from the ruin his name so often left behind. But Arden didn't need protection.

She needed truth.

He exhaled slowly, breath fogging the glass before vanishing almost as quickly as it appeared. Outside, the city glittered on, indifferent.

His gaze slid to the bourbon decanter, his grandfather's favorite, left untouched.

Some truths deserved to be faced with a clear head.

Whatever storm waited, he would meet it head-on. And if Arden stood beside him, perhaps the risk wasn't survival.

Perhaps it was living.

CHAPTER 12

Uninvited

The city buzzed beyond the apartment walls, a low, lively pulse threading through the quiet.

Arden lingered in the doorway with the weight of the night still pressing against her ribs. Her mind churned with stories buried in deeds and loopholes: Black families clinging to land through wars, through injustice, through every system built to take from them, only to lose it in courtrooms no one bothered to remember. Generations erased not with violence, but with signatures. With silence.

She thought of them now—their resilience, their stolen futures—and felt the familiar ache settle low in her chest.

So many had fought so hard to hold on.

So many had lost it anyway.

The apartment lay hushed before her. Too quiet.

Penny had texted hours ago, three margaritas deep and laughing somewhere across town, leaving Arden alone in the apartment. Normally, she welcomed solitude. Tonight, after the controlled chaos of The Blackwell Room, the hush clung too tightly. It pressed against her ribs, hollow and unnatural.

She fumbled with her keys. The lock resisted before giving with its stubborn click, and the door creaked open, its hinges murmuring in protest. Light spilled into the entry as her bag slipped from her shoulder and dropped to the floor with a muted thud.

For a moment, she only stood there.

The night hung heavy beneath her skin. She didn't want to name it, but the weight had settled behind her eyes, pulsing with every breath.

She stepped inside.

Everything appeared untouched at first. Penny's candles had left their usual trace, vanilla threaded soft and familiar through the air. The living room held its ordinary mess of color and comfort: scarves draped carelessly, sneakers peeking from under the couch, pillows tossed in defeat.

Then the latch settled into place behind her, and something shifted.

The air thickened, heavier than air had any right to be.

The thought barely finished forming before she noticed it.

A wrongness.

Small. Subtle. Sharpening with every heartbeat.

Her gaze caught on the coffee table.

The books.

Penny, chaotic as she was, kept that one stack squared. Always. It was her small concession to order.

Now they sat off-kilter.

And resting on top was Arden's journal.

Not tucked away.

No.

I put it away this morning.

The thought hit hard, undeniable. Her routine was meticulous, crafted from necessity rather than habit, and she never left it out. Never.

A chill crept up her neck as she hovered there, fingers inches from the cover.

But she didn't touch it.

Couldn't.

Something inside her pulled back, instinct running deeper than fear.

Nothing was broken. Nothing forced. But the room felt wrong in a way her body understood before her mind could explain it.

Her bedroom.

The thought struck like a flashbulb.

Had she left the door open? No. She would have remembered.

She moved closer, each breath shallow, each motion deliberate, then nudged the door wider.

At first glance, nothing.

Bed made. Closet closed. Everything where it belonged.

Except—

The bracelet.

The one she always kept in the small dish beside the jewelry box.

Unclasped.

She never left it that way.

But what would she even say? That her bracelet was undone? That her journal had moved? It sounded like paranoia.

But it wasn't.

She knew it wasn't.

Arden pressed her back to the wall and slid to the floor, knees drawn tight to her chest, her breathing jagged and uneven.

The journal. The bracelet.

Small things, but too exact. Too intimate.

Not a burglary. Not a break-in.

A message.

Her eyes swept the door again. The windows. The locks.

All secure.

And none of it mattered.

That hard-won feeling of safety splintered, quiet and absolute. She locked her arms around her knees, pulse hammering beneath her skin, and tried to think through the terror clawing up her throat.

Penny would panic. She'd call the cops. She'd drag Arden to a hotel, or worse, insist they stay somewhere else altogether.

Arden didn't want that.

She didn't want to be a victim again. She wanted this to be nothing. A mistake. A misstep. Some small domestic thing her tired mind had sharpened into threat.

But deep down, she knew.

Someone had been here.

And they wanted her to know it.

Surrounded by comfort and routine, by this fragile veil of safety, Arden understood with a coldness that stripped her bare: even here, they could find her.

———

THE LOCK GAVE beneath his hand like a whispered secret—soft, familiar.

He had studied her security the way he studied everything about her.

Every habit.

Every small defense she thought made her untouchable.

Devotion wasn't too strong a word.

Stepping into Arden's space felt like entering hallowed ground, a sanctuary built for something volatile. Almost holy.

His Little Fire.

But then—

His lip curled.

Penny.

A storm of clutter and chaos. Scarves tossed without care. Sneakers kicked beneath the couch. A half-drunk coffee mug abandoned like an afterthought.

Careless. Loud. Wrong.

Beneath it all, Arden's order tried to breathe.

He could see the contrast immediately, her signature in every quiet attempt to impose control. The neatly folded blanket among the disarray. Books aligned with careful precision. Small systems tucked inside a life that had learned not to trust the world to remain where she put it.

He approached the coffee table, fingers brushing the surface.

The journal.

Untouched.

A boundary line.

Sacred.

He didn't open it.

He wanted to.

But no.

He wouldn't violate her privacy. Not really. He respected her too much for that, just enough to leave a mark instead of a scar.

Instead, he shifted it. Only slightly.

A whisper she wouldn't miss.

A message only she would hear.

I see you.

He moved deeper into the apartment, reading the story she had written in textures and quiet cues. The way she organized her closet. The subtle repetition in how she arranged things. It wasn't perfection; it was survival, a woman layering order over the ruins of something shattered.

But she didn't need more walls.

She needed someone who understood how to walk through fire without flinching. Someone who wouldn't fear her flame.

Someone like him.

Then he saw it.

The bracelet.

Resting in its usual dish.

Waiting.

He unfastened the clasp and laid it back exactly as before. Except now, it was open.

A gentle nudge.

A subtle shift.

Not to scare her. Only to remind her that nothing was as secure as she believed.

His gaze landed on the perfume bottle.

Barely half full.

The scent he associated with her—floral, shadowed by warm vanilla. Delicate and defiant.

Like her.

He stepped closer, fingertips grazing the glass.

Soon, it would run out.

He would make sure she never noticed when it did.

One day, a new bottle would appear, wrapped in careful elegance. Identical in shape and label, except it would carry his signature too; a note in the base, a trace only he would recognize.

She would wear it without question.

And every time she did, she would carry him with her.

On her skin.

In her wake.

Marked.

Sliding into the hall again felt like stepping out of ritual.

But the message had been delivered.

The journal, tilted.

The bracelet, unclasped.

The fading bottle.

Threads unraveling, quiet and patient, from the fabric she thought would hold.

She would feel it. That subtle wrongness in the air. The prickle beneath the skin. The private, undeniable knowledge that someone had been there.

Seen her.

Chosen her.

She wasn't wrong to fear the shadows.

She was only wrong about the danger.

He wasn't here to hurt her.

He was here to complete her.

Soon, she would understand.

This wasn't surveillance.

It was devotion.

He wasn't watching.

He was waiting.

And when the truth landed—when she saw that he was the only one who could match her heat without burning—everything else would go up in smoke.

Especially Gideon Blackwell's carefully curated world.

He vanished into the dark, smiling to himself.

The ritual complete.

Let her wrap herself in that illusion of safety. Let her cling to locks and distractions and the deception of control. Let her keep reaching for that perfume, unaware of what it meant.

Because soon, his Little Fire would wake.

Nothing could keep him out.

Nothing could keep them apart.

Not even her.

Especially not her.

CHAPTER 13

Striking Distance

Each strike echoed through the studio, measured and relentless, a pound of effort Arden could claim, a kind of control no one else could steal.

She adjusted her stance, muscles taut and burning, and drove the next punch forward with pure intent.

"Again," her instructor called, stepping back and raising the pad higher.

Arden exhaled, reset, and threw another punch. The impact shuddered up her arm, grounding her in movement, in action, in the brutal relief of something she could control.

She'd been coming for weeks. She wasn't new to self-defense, but Krav Maga was different. No wasted motion. No excess. Only efficiency.

Get in. Get out. Survive.

She needed that more than she liked.

Because the more she thought about the club, about Gideon, about the tangled mess he was trying to unravel, the more she felt something dangerous stirring inside her. Something deeper. Quiet. Insistent. Impossible to outrun.

She threw another punch, harder this time, as if she could knock the thoughts from her head.

Gideon Blackwell.

The man was a contradiction wrapped in quiet intensity. His family had built an empire on exploitation, on taking, on generations of Blackwells bleeding others dry. But Gideon wasn't like them.

Not his father. Not his brother. Not any of the ghosts in his bloodline.

He was trying to undo what they had done.

She could still hear his voice, quiet but resolute, as he told her about the heirs' properties and the families his own had devastated. Afterward, she'd gone home and looked it up herself, reading story after story of land stolen not by force, but by silence. Families stripped of everything they'd built because they hadn't had the money, or the right last name, to protect it.

Some stories came out of the Deep South, where land promised after emancipation was gutted by courts and crooked deeds. Others hit closer to home: old farms in the hollers and ridges of Appalachia, where poverty, pride, and bad luck left families clinging to land by little more than memory.

It wasn't always the same history.

But it was the same grief.

That quiet theft stayed with her, because it wasn't history at all. It was still happening.

And Gideon wasn't only talking about change. He was fighting for it.

It shouldn't matter.

But it did.

A counterstrike came, and Arden dodged, breath steady, body moving on instinct, because she understood what it meant to have something stolen. Not land. Not wealth. Choices. Stability. A future that wasn't shaped by someone else's destruction.

Another strike. Another impact.

Sweat beaded along her temple.

She wanted to ask him if it ever felt like drowning, dragging the weight of sins he hadn't chosen, sinking slow and breathless beneath the ruin of a name. She wanted to know if he ever wondered whether he would claw his way out of it, or if it would swallow him whole.

She wanted to ask him a lot of things.

And that was becoming a problem.

"Alright, Rivers, let's wrap it up."

She dropped her hands and stepped back, breathing deep through the burn in her muscles.

Her instructor nodded in approval, tapping the pads together. "Good work. You come at it with a lot of focus."

Arden huffed a quiet breath and reached for her water bottle. "That's one word for it."

"Whatever's driving you, don't let it go," he said, watching her with a flicker of something unreadable. His glance shifted toward the entrance, where sunlight slanted in too bright and clean against the weight she carried in every movement. "Just make sure it doesn't burn you out from the inside."

She didn't answer.

Maybe she didn't know how to survive without burning.

❦

A muted clink of glass splintered the silence, a whisper against polished wood. The club rested in its pre-opening hush, its usual opulence holding still beneath the chandeliers, as if the room itself were waiting for night to give it back its pulse.

Behind the bar, Arden moved with steady focus, her cloth sweeping the counter in clean, unhurried strokes. It was more habit than necessity, an outlet for the tension still coiled in her shoulders from that morning's Krav Maga session. Her muscles remained charged with the clean, aching aftermath of effort, and that edge of energy was part of what she liked about this place: the focus it demanded, the rhythm, the ritual, the people.

Well.

Some of the people.

She wasn't aware she'd started humming at first. The melody eased from her lips without thought, low and instinctive, drawn from somewhere deep in her bones.

Almost heaven, West Virginia...

Her voice barely stirred the air, more breath than sound.

Blue Ridge Mountains, Shenandoah River...

The old song wove through the quiet like a loose thread, catching on the hush of footsteps and the soft clatter of glass.

Then—

Clink.

A sharper sound behind her. A glass set down with deliberate weight.

"Wait a damn second."

Arden turned to find Marco staring at her as if she'd confessed to a secret identity.

Fatima, on the other hand, looked thrilled one brow lifted, lips curved in anticipation, already leaning into the drama.

"What?" Arden asked, blinking.

Marco jabbed a finger at her as if she had committed high treason behind the bar. "Tell me I did not just hear our brooding, monochrome, jazz-shunning bartender humming John freaking Denver."

Arden paused. "I—what?"

"Don't play innocent." He eyed her with theatrical suspicion, like he was halfway through decoding a mystery and enjoying every second of it. "That was 'Country Roads.' I would bet my entire vinyl collection."

Fatima's grin widened. "Oh, this just keeps getting better."

Arden rolled her eyes, surrendering. "Fine. Yeah. I hummed it."

Marco reared back like this was revelation on a biblical scale. "You? Arden Rivers? Miss 'I don't sing along to the jazz trio' Arden Rivers? Just casually serenading us with West Virginia's unofficial state anthem?"

Fatima laughed, her bracelets catching the light. "Wait, hold on. You are from West Virginia, right?"

Arden hesitated. "...Yeah."

Fatima slapped the bar, bracelets jingling, delighted. "This is gold."

Marco's eyes lit up as if he'd been handed a sacred mission. "Oh, you know what this means."

"No," Arden said quickly, pointing a warning finger at him. "Absolutely not. Don't you even…"

He spread his arms wide in mock reverence. "Our mysterious, too-cool-for-this-place girl is now and forever—Mountain Mama."

Fatima cackled, nodding like it had been ordained.

Arden groaned. "I hate both of you."

"Yeah, yeah," Marco said, sliding a bottle into place like nothing monumental had just occurred. "But you're stuck with us now, Mountain Mama."

Arden turned back to the shelves, scowling. Almost convincingly. "Menaces," she muttered.

"Love you too, Mountain Mama," Marco called, all smug affection.

She rolled her eyes, but the grin broke through anyway—unruly, warm, and deeply inconvenient. A reminder that she wasn't quite as untouchable as she pretended.

And maybe she didn't mind being stuck with them.

❦

The apartment held traces of takeout and the faint ghost of citrus, likely the last breath of one of Penny's candles burned down to nothing.

Curled up on the couch with towel-dried hair damp against her neck and her skin still cooling from the shower, Arden felt exhaustion pulling at her edges, blurring the sharpness of her thoughts. She'd spent the afternoon at The Blackwell Room digging into the machinery beneath the glamour, learning how the place operated under all that polish. Ledger updates. Scheduling notes. The everyday minutiae tucked behind luxury.

She had kept her focus sharp.

But Gideon had been there.

And she had felt him.

The awareness crackled like static in the air—the way his eyes tracked her when he thought she wasn't looking, cataloging every movement with that maddening, disciplined stillness of his. She had done her best to maintain her composure, but the sense of him lingered beneath the surface like a current she could not quite step out of.

Her mind was still restless when Penny flopped onto the couch beside her, a technicolor blanket wrapped tight around her small frame. Arden had long since given up questioning where Penny found them. Against all odds, Penny made neon look like home.

"You've been weird today," Penny announced, stealing a piece of naan from Arden's plate.

Arden raised an eyebrow. "Thanks for that deep analysis."

"I'm serious." Penny tore the naan in half, waving it for emphasis. "You've been all broody and intense, and usually I would assume that means a certain brooding billionaire was involved, but since you're not glaring into the distance and sighing dramatically, I'm thinking this is something else."

Arden scoffed. "I do not sigh dramatically."

Penny just stared at her.

Arden rolled her eyes and leaned back into the couch. "I went to the Krav Maga studio this morning. That's probably why I'm quiet. I'm just tired."

Penny made a doubtful sound but didn't press. "I'm guessing you threw some people around?"

Arden shrugged. "It's not about that. It's about control. About knowing you can handle yourself."

Something in her voice must have given her away, because Penny shifted, her expression softening beneath the brightness.

"Yeah," she said, quieter now. "I get that."

A silence passed between them.

The kind that invited truth.

Penny hesitated, then asked, "Was that always something you worried about?"

Arden glanced down at her wine glass, fingers tapping lightly against the stem.

She knew where Penny was leading.

And she was too tired to sidestep it.

"You never talk about your family," Penny said carefully. Not pushing. Just offering the space.

Arden inhaled slowly.

She could keep deflecting. Keep burying it beneath sarcasm and carefully curated half-truths.

Or she could let someone see it.

Even a little.

"There's not much to say," Arden started, then stopped herself.

The same automatic response she always gave.

Penny made a sound somewhere between a scoff and a laugh. "Yeah, okay. Try again."

A slow breath left Arden as she tipped her head back against the couch. Studying the ceiling was easier than meeting Penny's eyes—keen and endlessly curious, entirely unwilling to let this go.

"I didn't have a great childhood," she admitted finally, keeping her voice level. "Money was... tight. What we did have, my dad spent on things that weren't keeping the fridge stocked. And my mom didn't work, so we relied on government assistance. Some months it was enough. Some months it wasn't."

Her thumb traced the rim of her glass in an absent circle, the motion grounding her.

"I learned young that food wasn't guaranteed," she continued, her tone measured in that careful way people spoke when they were trying not to feel the story while telling it. "We had stretches where dinner was whatever could be scraped together from the back of the pantry. And stretches where there was nothing to scrape together at all."

A pause.

"I knew real hunger."

The words settled quietly between them, heavy in their simplicity.

"Not the kind where you miss lunch and feel shaky after. The kind that sits in your stomach for days until eventually it stops feeling like hunger at all and just becomes normal."

Penny stayed silent, but Arden could feel the weight of her attention—not passive listening, but something gentler. Something deliberate.

A slow breath escaped Arden as memory tightened around her throat.

"My grandparents were good people," she said after a moment, steering toward something easier to hold. "They tried. But I wasn't allowed to go to their house. My dad made sure of that. So they came to me when they could. Sometimes when he was at work. Sometimes when..." She trailed off, her fingers circling the stem again. "When he wasn't around."

Penny didn't ask what that meant.

She just waited.

"They'd bring groceries. Tell stories. Try to make me feel safe in a house that never really was." Arden's gaze drifted toward the window, toward some distant version of herself she could still picture too clearly. "I used to beg my mom to leave him. I thought maybe, while he was gone, she'd finally see a way out. That we could start over without him."

The silence stretched softly between them.

"But she never did," Arden said quietly. "And by the time I hit my teens, my grandparents were already gone."

Gone.

The word felt too small for something that catastrophic.

Penny adjusted the blanket around herself, curling her legs underneath her with a sleepy sigh. "And after that?"

Arden managed a faint smile that barely reached the surface. "After that, I figured it out on my own."

Silence settled again.

But Penny didn't push. Didn't prod at the wound just because Arden had finally uncovered it. She simply sat with her in it—the way real friends did.

Then, after a moment, Penny sighed dramatically.

"Just so we're clear, if I ever get access to a time machine, I'm going back to throw hands."

A laugh slipped out of Arden before she could stop it, quick and startled.

Penny grinned immediately, like she'd been waiting for exactly that reaction. "I'm serious," she said, pointing at Arden with absolute conviction. "I'll come in swinging like a pint-sized gremlin and make everyone deeply uncomfortable."

Arden shook her head, smiling despite herself. "That, I would pay to see."

"You joke, but I'm scrappy."

"I believe you."

With a sweeping gesture worthy of community theater, Penny raised her glass. "Well, cheers to found family then. Because, for the record, you're stuck with me now."

Arden rolled her eyes, but something in her chest eased anyway.

She lifted her own glass. "Stuck with you, huh?"

"Absolutely. No take-backs."

Their glasses clinked softly together, and for the first time in a long time, Arden let herself believe it.

Maybe Penny was right.

Some family was chosen.

Maybe Arden wasn't quite as alone as she thought.

Penny shifted suddenly, reaching behind one of the throw pillows.

"Oh—by the way, a package came for you."

Arden blinked. "For me?"

"Yeah." Penny dug it out from behind the throw pillow and passed it over. "Didn't check the label. Figured it was something boring, but it's got your name on it. Came this afternoon."

Arden set down her glass, frowning as she took the small parcel. There was no return address. Just her name, neatly printed in a clean font.

She peeled the tape back, her heart ticking a little faster for no good reason.

Inside, nestled in pale tissue, sat a bottle of Mon Guerlain.

Her signature perfume.

A new bottle, sleek and familiar, identical to the one on her dresser—the one nearly empty now.

Arden stared at it.

"I didn't order this," she murmured.

Penny glanced up from the last bite of naan. "Maybe you did and forgot? You've been... elsewhere, lately."

"Maybe." Arden turned the package over, searching for an invoice, a card, some small ordinary thing that would explain it.

Nothing.

She studied the delicate etching across the glass, lingering longer than she meant to. The scent was right. The bottle was right. Everything about it was right, and that was what unsettled her most.

"I mean, it's your usual, right?" Penny asked, half-lounging again. "Could've been a freebie from somewhere you ordered before."

Arden nodded slowly and set the bottle on the coffee table with careful precision, as if it might shift or shatter if she looked away.

"Yeah," she said. "That's probably it."

But the lie clung to her skin, heavier than perfume.

———

He DIDN'T GET *to see her this time.*

That was the part he hated most.

Every other moment—every gift, every message—he'd been there.

Watching her breath hitch.

Watching the question bloom behind her eyes.

But now...

He could only imagine—her turning the box in her hands, searching for something. A receipt. A note.

Proof that this wasn't a mistake.

But there wasn't one.

That was the point.

It was perfect.

Almost.

Next time, he wouldn't settle for imagination.

This gift. Her perfume—Mon Guerlain.

Warm jasmine, wild lavender, smoldering vanilla.

A storm softened into something wearable.

Not sweet or innocent.

A scent like her—strength cloaked in softness, sharp where no one expected it.

The bottle itself was a tribute to everything she didn't realize she was.

Strong lines and curves. Elegance made physical.

Feminine, yes. But unyielding.

Like flame poured into glass.

He COULD SEE *the moment she hesitated.*

Her fingers slowing over the gold adornment, her gaze narrowing.

She didn't remember ordering it.

She would brush it off.

She would tell herself it was nothing.

But already, it was a part of her.

She would wear it.
She would move through the world wearing him. And no one would know.
No one but him.
That was the beauty of it.
She wouldn't see it as a message. Not yet.
But it was one.
Not a warning.
A promise.
She was his.
Not to own.
To understand.

He HADN'T TOUCHED HER. *He didn't need to.*
She was breathing him in.
She would think of him and not know why.
Feel watched and wonder.
Because he was there.
Moving through her life like breath through a flame. Gentle at first. Invisible. Patient.
His Little Fire.
Not fear or obsession.
Recognition.
She was rare.
And what was rare had to be protected—studied, cherished, claimed.
So he sent her the only thing worthy of her skin.
And soon, she would understand.
Not because he said it.
Because she'd feel it.
In the quiet.
In the dark.
In the way the world shifted when she moved through it.
She would come to see it for what it was. Not a gift. A bond.
She didn't know it yet.
But she would.
And when she finally saw what he saw—what he'd always seen—everything else would fall away.

CHAPTER 14

Into the Lion's Den

The days blurred into a rhythm of clinking crystal and measured smiles, a world bound by ritual and silence. Arden had grown fluent in its unspoken language. Here, power didn't boast; it whispered.

It lived in the subtle tilt of a wrist, in the murmured drop of a name over top-shelf bourbon. It moved through velvet shadows and gleamed in candlelight reflected off marble, and Arden moved through it as if it already belonged to her, even if it didn't.

She adapted. Learned the rules. The way patrons quietly staked territory without a word. How the most coveted tables weren't requested, but assumed. When a conversation meant nothing, and when it meant everything.

Here, even a flicker of attention could become currency. A glance was a gamble. A silence, a sentence.

She learned what mattered: Mr. Callahan's twenty-stir martini; the financier in navy Tom Ford, who never touched his glass until his date did; the woman with the choker and the Sancerre she never finished, her glass more prop than pleasure, the posture of someone who wanted to be seen rather than satisfied.

Every element of The Blackwell Room was deliberate. The absence of windows. The amber lighting engineered to obscure more than flatter. The grand piano sitting sleek and silent until Teddy brought it to life after midnight, lacing the air with jazz and suggestion, the kind that curled into the bloodstream and lingered.

But Gideon's tells were far less clear.

She sensed him before she saw him. Not looming. Not loud. Simply there, a presence at the edge of her awareness.

A bottle of water appearing at her elbow, small mercy offered without demand.

A difficult patron gone before she needed to intervene. The quiet choreography of a man who didn't ask for control because he already possessed it.

And sometimes, she caught him watching her.

Not like the others.

Not the hedge fund vultures scanning the room for leverage. Not the old-money sons of privilege who saw women as prizes or possessions.

Gideon's gaze held weight, but not ownership.

Something else.

Something that made her chest draw tight, her breath catch before she could stop it. Her hand would pause mid-wipe, or her eyes would flick away before she could fully mask the reaction.

The women here all seemed carved from the same elegant mold: tall, polished, styled to the point of sterility. Perfect on the outside. Empty on the inside.

Arden wasn't like them. She never would be. And from the way Gideon looked at her—steady, assessing, quiet—he didn't seem to want her to be.

There was a softness beneath his usual precision when his attention found her, a stillness that felt almost intimate.

And she had no idea what to do with that.

"You're getting good at this," Marco said one night, nodding toward the Old Fashioned she was pouring with a subtle twist, just the way Mr. Halloway liked it. "Barrett actually smiled when you remembered his obscure bourbon request."

Arden smirked and reached for a towel. "They're not as intimidating as they want to be. Once you learn their tells, they're easy."

Marco's mouth curved in agreement, but then his gaze flicked toward the entrance, expression sharpening.

"Incoming," he murmured.

She didn't have to look.

Sebastian Hawthorne and Alex Blackwell entered the room like men stepping onto a stage they believed they owned.

And maybe they did.

The air changed around them, dense and charged, conversations lowering as a ripple passed through the room. Sebastian wore his charm like tailored armor, all glint and polish, while Alex carried something colder: smug indifference honed into threat.

As they crossed the floor, Alex's gaze passed over Gideon and lingered a fraction too long. He offered a slight nod, nothing respectful in it.

Provocation, dressed as manners.

Arden's fingers curled around the edge of the bar.

"They've been around more lately," Marco said quietly, though something in his voice made her stomach tighten.

Arden didn't respond right away. She focused on straightening the whiskey bottles, ignoring Sebastian's gaze from across the room, slow and speculative.

"Family business," she said after a moment, the words brittle on her tongue.

Whatever had brought them here, it wasn't loyalty.

And it sure as hell wasn't family.

Her hand hovered near the Blanton's, Gideon's bourbon of choice. The bottle was nearly empty, which was strange. He hadn't ordered it in days.

But she had felt him.

Always nearby.

Watching.

Waiting.

A presence that unsettled the air without saying a word.

It should have unnerved her. Maybe it did. But it wasn't the same as roses left in break rooms, or a bracelet clasped wrong, or a journal nudged just enough to be noticed.

This wasn't threat dressed up as affection.

This was something worse.

Possibility.

Something she hadn't decided whether to fear or want.

LATER, as the night waned and the last patrons trickled out, Arden felt it again—that subtle shift in the air, the prickle along her skin that arrived before she ever looked up.

His gaze.

This time, when their eyes met across the dim expanse of The Blackwell Room, neither of them looked away.

The moment stretched, silent and charged, a held breath at the edge of something dangerous. The club had always felt like a set piece, a world Arden navigated with practiced precision, but tonight the scenery seemed altered somehow. The mask she wore felt thinner. The lights warmer. And the gaze following her from across the room no longer felt like a cue to perform.

It felt like an invitation to stop performing entirely.

And that...

That was dangerous.

Because she had been here before.

Not in this place. Not with him. But on this edge—the edge of surrender, of trust, of letting someone close enough to matter.

She had told herself it was different with Chad. Not love. Not trust. Just something close enough to mimic safety.

At first, it had seemed harmless. Gentle.

He always knew where she was, even when she hadn't told him. Always insisted on driving her home. Said it was chivalry. Said it was care.

And maybe she believed him.

At first.

She thought being wanted that fiercely meant being protected. That protection meant safety.

But affection had turned possessive. Concern sharpened quietly into control.

He never forbade her from going out, but he made her feel small when she did. He never raised a hand, but his voice could strip her bare. And his disappointment cut deepest of all.

It happened slowly. Quietly.

She stopped arguing. Started biting her tongue. Smoothed the sharper edges of herself down to something easier to hold, easier to love, easier to keep.

It's fine, she used to tell herself. He's just worried. He just loves me.

But it wasn't fine.

One day she looked in the mirror and didn't recognize herself anymore.

She had shrunk.

Made herself quieter.

More manageable.

More lovable.

More his.

And the truth hit her like glass shattering.

She had become the very thing she swore she never would.

She had become her mother.

Standing in the kitchen with her voice hushed and her hands folded, disappearing by degrees so slowly no one noticed until there was almost nothing left.

And the worst part?

No one had forced her.

She had handed over the pieces herself, believing that was the price of being chosen.

The realization shattered something in her, because she understood then that if she stayed—if she kept surrendering herself inch by inch—eventually there would be nothing left to reclaim.

So she walked away.

No explanation.

No dramatic scene.

Just a door closing behind her and a vow never to let anyone get that close again.

No one else got in.

Not until now.

She wasn't even sure when it had happened, when Gideon Blackwell had slipped past defenses she'd spent years sharpening. Maybe it was the way he listened. The way he never pressed. The way he saw things without demanding she expose them.

Now, as his gaze held hers across the nearly empty club, her throat tightened around something that felt dangerously close to fear.

Or maybe recognition.

Something deeper.

Something that frightened her more than control ever had.

Hope.

Her hand tightened around the bar rail, grounding herself in its cool solidity. She wasn't that girl anymore. She refused to be.

But trust was fragile.

And no matter how far she'd come, Arden wasn't sure she remembered how to hold it without breaking it in the process.

The Blackwell Room felt different tonight. The air heavier. The silence deeper. And somewhere in the charged space between her and Gideon sat a question she could not afford to answer.

Because trust wasn't a gift.

It was a risk.

Even after everything, a quiet voice inside her whispered.

Careful. Careful. Careful.

The air shifted, warning her before his voice followed.

"You don't have to stay late."

His voice broke the quiet, low and steady and far too aware.

Arden didn't turn immediately. Instead, she reached for another glass, her movements slow and deliberate, as if that sentence hadn't just brushed along her skin and settled somewhere warm.

"And here I thought billionaires appreciated hard work."

A quiet chuckle followed.

Then came the sound of footsteps, unhurried and steady, and the scent of his cologne drifted toward her, warm spice wrapped in shadow.

"I do," he said, calm but threaded with something sharper. "But I also know when someone's stalling."

She looked up at last, one brow lifting. "Stalling? You think I enjoy spending my nights scrubbing marble counters?"

His smirk deepened, lazy and dangerous. "I think you enjoy proving a point."

She tapped her chin thoughtfully. "That does sound like me."

His eyes caught hers, amusement flickering beneath something harder to name.

"Has no one ever told you? That mouth of yours could start wars."

"Hmm. Tragic oversight," she replied with mock sincerity. "Really appreciate the information. Changes everything."

A quiet laugh slipped from him as he braced one hand against the counter. "I'm here to enlighten."

"How generous of you." She tossed the bar rag over her shoulder and tilted her head. "I'll write that in my journal. Gideon Blackwell: dispenser of unsolicited wisdom."

"Please do. And while you're at it," he added, "you might note that sarcasm is usually a sign of deflection."

Arden leaned in just slightly, her smile turning sharper in response. "And here I thought it was a sign of intelligence."

"Maybe both," he allowed, studying her with exaggerated consideration. "I'm still deciding."

She shook her head and grabbed the last glass. "Take your time, Blackwell. I'll be waiting with bated breath."

"No doubt," he said softly, the words landing more like a thought than speech.

His gaze settled into her then, slow-burning and steady, something that thrummed low beneath the surface and refused to loosen its hold.

Arden turned away first, fingers finding a glass that didn't need straightening, using movement to disguise the pulse beating hard at the base of her throat.

The club sat dim and still around them, holding its breath.

But the tension didn't break.

It lingered between them, taut and unspoken—a quiet standoff edged with heat.

A slow-burn dare neither of them was ready to walk away from.

Tonight, the private lounge carried a different kind of stillness: softer, warmer, the usual noise of The Blackwell Room left behind and swallowed by velvet walls and low, deliberate light.

From somewhere overhead, Michael Bublé's "Feeling Good" slipped through the air, smoky and slow, folding itself around the room's polished edges as if it had been spun for moments exactly like this.

Arden hovered at the entrance, blinking against the dim glow. The weight behind her eyes hadn't disappeared entirely, but here, in this hush made of velvet and gold, it felt as if it might ease for a while.

A bottle of red sat open on the table, breathing. Gideon poured without a word and handed her a glass.

Their fingers barely brushed.

The touch lingered anyway, humming beneath her skin as she closed her hand around the glass and held on.

Neither of them broke the silence right away. The space between them was saying enough.

"Special occasion?" she asked, giving the wine a slow swirl.

"Something like that." He looked at her over his glass, his expression giving nothing away. "Figured we'd end the night on something slower."

She tasted the wine—deep and full-bodied, with a whisper of spice—and gave a small nod. "It's good."

Her voice had gone softer than she intended.

He didn't answer. He watched her instead, listening for something else entirely, and after a moment, he set his glass down and reached out.

"Dance with me."

She blinked.

It wasn't a question.

"Are you serious?"

"Do I seem like I'm not?"

No smirk. Just a flicker of something unguarded beneath his usual polish.

Arden hesitated, the base of her glass warm in her hand. Then she set it down.

He didn't push. He didn't plead. He only waited.

"I won't bite," he added, quieter now. Almost teasing. Almost not.

As the song deepened around them, she reached for his hand before she could talk herself out of it.

He took it and guided her forward, and the silence between them tightened, strung with all the things neither of them had said. His other hand found her waist, his fingers grazing the inside of her wrist in a way that felt both new and inexplicably familiar.

She became acutely aware of every detail: the way his palm settled at her hip, the pull of his cologne, the rhythm her pulse had taken on without her permission.

"Relax," he said, low and near her ear.

The word wasn't instruction.

It was invitation.

She wanted to say something sarcastic. Wanted to knock the moment off its axis before it could become dangerous.

But the words didn't come.

Instead, she fell into the rhythm of him, learning the language of his body through movement rather than explanation. Each step taught her how to speak without reaching for a defense.

He led with effortless control, but nothing about it felt forced.

He wasn't performing.

He was present.

"You're full of surprises, Blackwell."

The sentence came softer than she meant it to, her usual sharpness smoothed into something less defensive.

He didn't smile. His hand only flexed at her waist—intentional, barely there, impossible not to feel.

"And you don't like surprises."

Her fingers curled lightly against the fabric of his shirt. Reflex, not permission.

He felt it.

She knew he did.

"No," she said simply, because the word was a truth she couldn't dress up.

His thumb moved against her side, slow and thoughtless.

Except it wasn't.

She inhaled too quickly.

A shift.

Closer.

He leaned in, close enough for his breath to graze her skin, close enough to stir something unsteady beneath it.

"So why are you still here?"

The question settled in her chest, somewhere between a warning and a dare.

She didn't answer.

Not with words.

Instead, she moved with him slowly, carefully, like a flame she hadn't decided whether to touch or contain. Her hand gripped his shoulder tighter—not a decision, a reaction.

He didn't look at her mouth the way other men would have.

He looked at her throat, at the pulse fluttering beneath her skin.

His fingers pressed again, a fraction more pressure, enough to leave the shape of his touch behind.

She didn't pull away.

Neither did he.

What am I doing?

The thought came fast, uninvited. But she didn't step back. Didn't stop him.

Didn't stop herself.

Finally, he exhaled and pulled back enough to let air return to the room, but not enough to create true distance. Not yet. His hand slipped away slowly, as if breaking contact too quickly might startle her into disappearing.

Her skin burned where he had touched her.

Arden lifted her chin, masking the tension with a practiced smirk.

"Not bad for a broody billionaire. I assume you've rehearsed that in a mirror?"

A low laugh rumbled from him. "You're not so bad yourself, Rivers."

The use of her last name should have cooled things off.

Instead, it set something else smoldering.

Lines had been drawn.

Tonight, they blurred.

Tomorrow, they might regret it.

But right now, in the hush of the lounge and the echo of Bublé's croon, she wasn't ready to walk away.

And neither was he.

The music began to fade, but they didn't move. His hand rested at her waist, hers curled lightly at his shoulder, two people caught in a silence too full to break.

The last note lingered in the air, suspended like a breath neither of them had released.

Beneath her touch, his pulse beat steady, faint but unmistakably there. Not erratic. Not unsure. Just there, anchored and unwavering.

Neither of them spoke. The silence between them wasn't empty.

It pulsed.

It waited.

He looked at her as if he were trying to memorize this unguarded version of her: the warmth in her skin, the shape of her mouth, the quiet she rarely let anyone close enough to witness.

Arden swallowed, her throat dry. She held firm, torn between staying in the moment and stepping away, unsure which choice would say more.

Her hand didn't move.

Neither did his.

Then he shifted slightly, just enough to press a fraction closer, and his thumb moved again at her waist, a slow drag of pressure through fabric.

Not a tease.

Not a mistake.

A decision.

She should have stepped back.

She didn't.

When she finally did, her fingers skimmed the length of his arm—unintended, barely a brush.

But he felt it.

She felt the shift in him, the way something under his skin tensed, as if he'd caught himself wanting more.

Their eyes met, and this time there was no smile waiting to break the tension. No smirk to hide behind. Only the truth of two people standing in the aftershock of something they hadn't meant to start.

He let go slowly, like every inch mattered.

And maybe it did.

When her hand slipped from his, the absence felt like an ache.

Arden took a step back. Then another.

She was the first to look away.

Only then did the music finally fade into silence.

THE NIGHT AIR should have cleared her head.

It didn't.

Manhattan moved on around them, silver and shadow threading through the dark, the soft pulse of headlights cutting through the silence. The city remained indifferent, relentless, but here, on this narrow stretch of sidewalk, the world felt paused. As if time itself had taken a breath.

Their footsteps matched in quiet sync, falling into rhythm without conscious effort. Arden barely noticed the traffic, the chatter behind cab windows, the distant trill of horns. It all felt far away, muted, as if the city had lowered its voice to let her listen to something else entirely.

The thrum beneath her skin.

The echo of a dance that hadn't ended when the music stopped.

She didn't know why she let him walk her to her car.

Or she did, and didn't want to say it aloud.

Something had shifted. The balance that tethered them—professional distance, practiced restraint—had tipped in the quiet hum of the lounge. The dance was supposed to be harmless, a moment suspended in soft lighting and old jazz, but Gideon had a way of pressing pause on the world, of turning seconds into something weighted and intentional.

The memory of his hand at her waist lingered, firm and precise, never forceful. Each step they had shared felt instinctive, a rhythm neither of them had learned but somehow already knew.

And now she wasn't sure she could make herself forget it.

Her hand reached for the car door, fingers brushing the cool edge of the handle, searching for something solid. A tether. A clean end.

Then his fingers touched hers.

A soft press.

Measured.

Undeniable.

She stilled.

Turned.

He was there.

Close enough for the trace of spice in his cologne to catch her, warm and familiar as it threaded through the cool night. Her breath faltered before she could stop it. Close enough that stepping back did not feel like escape, but surrender.

The streetlight carved his face in silver and shadow, sculpting the quiet violence of him, but something softer lived beneath it. Something flickering in the space between them. Something that did not need to speak its name to be understood.

Gideon didn't move. Didn't speak. He only looked at her with that steady gaze of his, the one that never demanded and never pushed, but somehow made evasion feel like its own confession.

The air vibrated, charged with a quiet question neither of them had asked.

Not yet.

Her fingers rested against his.

Her heart beat like a drum inside a glass case.

Then his voice cut through the space between them.

Low. Intimate.

A dark thread of silk against the night.

"Goodnight, Arden."

Her name had weight in his mouth.

Like a secret.

Like a promise.

Her breath stuttered. Her chin lifted. Every instinct screamed at her to pull away before the moment deepened further, before it carved something permanent into her.

But she didn't move.

Instead, she met his gaze, unflinching and unresolved.

"Goodnight, Gideon."

The words came softly. Carefully. A breath wrapped in armor.

Arden slid into the driver's seat and shut the door behind her. The click of the latch landed sharp and final, but the quiet didn't empty the air.

It thickened it.

Filled it with the echo of him.

The ghost of his hand at her back.

The pull of a night that hadn't fully released her.

This wasn't a dance.

It was the beginning of something else.

And for the first time in years, she didn't want to run from it.

CHAPTER 15

Marked

Headlights skimmed the curb as Arden pulled into an open space—rare for this block, a small mercy after a night that had left her off-balance.

Her hands stayed tight on the wheel, as if she hadn't yet decided whether to stay or go. After a beat, she killed the engine and let out a slow breath through her nose, sharp at the edges, controlled only because she forced it to be.

Outside, the cold hit clean and sudden, peeling the last of the lounge's warmth from her skin.

The dance lingered anyway.

Gideon's hand at her waist. His breath near her ear. The way he had held her, solid and unyielding, as if restraint were something he could make feel intimate.

She should still have been thinking about that.

Then she saw it.

A rose.

It lay at the base of the steps, blood-red against the pale, weather-worn concrete. Too vibrant. Too precise.

No.

Her fingers tightened around her keys until the leather fob dug into her palm.

It wasn't. It couldn't be.

Coincidence.

Could it?

Her mind scrambled for ordinary explanations. It could have fallen from a bouquet. Someone could have dropped it. There might have been a wedding nearby, a florist's van, some careless romantic gesture meant for someone else.

Maybe.

But the rose wasn't crushed, windblown, or abandoned.

It had been placed.

Deliberate.

A cold ripple unfurled low in her gut. No note. No ribbon. Just the rose, perfect and intact, waiting.

Stop it.

I'm just tired. Overthinking. Stop making this into something it's not.

Except—

It had happened before.

The break room.

That rose.

The one she had convinced herself meant nothing.

This felt the same.

Arden pressed her tongue to the roof of her mouth, willing down the panic creeping up her spine. Then she moved. Not fast. Not frantic. Controlled. She stepped over the rose as if it were nothing, jaw set, shoulders squared, keys clenched so tightly in her fist her knuckles ached.

She wouldn't give in to fear.

Wouldn't flinch.

Wouldn't give whoever was doing this the satisfaction.

The night felt different now. The chill no longer belonged to the air. The light flickered overhead, its reach too weak, the shadows stretching farther than they should, and every sound around her landed sharper than it had before.

Coincidence, she told herself again.

Her mind repeated it like a charm, a shield against the truth pressing harder with each step.

The stairs seemed to lengthen beneath her feet, every footfall a drumbeat against her ribs. At the door, her hands moved on instinct—unlock, turn, latch, bolt.

Click. Click. Click.

She shut it tight and pressed her back against it.

The apartment was silent.

Penny wasn't home.

Everything looked untouched.

But nothing inside Arden was quiet.

Behind her closed eyes, she saw it again: the sharp red bloom, the eerie precision, the whisper of threat dressed as beauty. Her thoughts tumbled over themselves, colliding in the dark.

It's nothing.

It's something.

You're paranoid.

You're not paranoid enough.

A shiver moved through her.

Not from cold.

Memory.

Instinct.

She knew this feeling. She had worn it like armor once, back when the world had proven how quickly trust could become a weapon in someone else's hands.

The whiplash struck hard.

One moment, Gideon's hand at her waist. That steady weight. The impossible warmth.

The next, this.

A rose on concrete.

A threat without a name.

Her hand drifted to her waist, to the place he had touched. She could still feel the imprint of him there, the warmth she wanted badly enough to resent herself for wanting it.

But it wasn't enough to thaw the chill sinking beneath her skin.

Because no matter how far she'd come, some shadows didn't stay buried.

Some waited.

And tonight, they had followed her home.

———

HE STAYED HIDDEN beneath the dark, just beyond her reach.

The night pressed in around him—cold, unyielding.

He didn't feel it.

His focus tracked her every step.

Each movement. Each breath.

Reverence bleeding into hunger.

WHEN HER HEADLIGHTS swept the curb, they carved her from the dark. A figure of light.

Untouchable for a single, breathless heartbeat.

Then the shadows swallowed her again.

His chest tightened.

Longing.

And something darker.

Tonight had been a mistake.

She had stood too close to Gideon Blackwell.

Had let him take space that didn't belong to him.

Wrong.

The memory cut like glass—jagged, deliberate.

A*RDEN WASN'T LIKE the others.*
Ordinary. Predictable.
Easily claimed.
She was something else.
Something dangerous.
Something divine.
Her fire required patience. Precision.
She wasn't a thing to be possessed.
She had to be earned.
And he was willing to wait.
He had already given so much of himself,
and still, she didn't know.
She moved through the world with unconscious grace,
her rhythm at odds with the restless storm knotted inside his chest.
He had watched others.
Brief fascinations.
Women who sparked for a moment, then flickered out.
Too eager. Too soft.
Too easily shaped.
They stepped into his orbit with wide eyes and open hands.
He lost interest before they ever understood what they were supposed to mean
to him.
But Arden?
Arden resisted gravity.
She didn't bend.
She burned.
His Little Fire.
She was worth the wait.

W*HEN SHE STOPPED at the bottom of her steps—stared down at the rose,*
his pulse jumped.
Yes.
See it.
Feel it.
Placed with intention.
Every detail considered.
Not to frighten her.
Never to frighten her.
It was a gesture. A reminder.
A counterpoint to Blackwell's performance.
A thread woven from something truer.

Her expression shifted—something passed through her face in the glow of the streetlight.

Uncertainty?

Recognition?

A flicker of knowing?

It was enough.

He felt it strike through him like heat.

She didn't pick it up.

Didn't need to.

Seeing it. That was everything.

She walked past it.

Chin set.

Pace clipped.

Pretending.

Trying to outrun what she knew.

But she had seen it.

That was the point.

He smiled then—quiet, satisfied.

She could dismiss it.

For now.

But the connection was there.

Planted. Rooted.

Growing.

She didn't have to reach for it.

She belonged to it.

HE STEPPED BACK into the shadows, letting the wet pavement drink his silhouette.

Let Gideon think she was his to guard.

Let him posture with his brittle charm and borrowed power.

Arden didn't need someone to shield her.

She didn't need to be softened.

Didn't need silk and safety.

She needed space to rage.

To burn without apology.

And when the world tried to contain her—

he would be the one who let her be wildfire.

The rose wasn't a gift.

It was a vow.

A whispered truth curled beneath her skin: Someone sees you. Someone knows you. Someone won't let you fade.

That brief pause—that hitch in her breath when she saw it was the beginning.

Soon, she'd stop pretending.
Soon, she'd know.
That he had always been there.
Watching.
Waiting.
Waiting for her to come home.

LET *her lie to herself for now.*
Let her drink in Gideon's counterfeit warmth.
It would only make her awakening more cataclysmic.
More brutal.
Because when everything caught fire,
And it would,
She'd finally see:
Only he could match her flame.
Only he would set her free.

CHAPTER 16

In the Quiet Moments

The club thrummed with its usual subdued symphony: low voices, the soft clink of glassware, laughter pressed into polished edges. Every sound felt intentional, like a jazz riff played beneath a velvet curtain.

Behind the bar, Arden worked with efficient grace, slicing limes with rhythmic precision because it gave her hands something to do while her mind drifted. Across from her, Marco held court.

"I'm serious," he said, animated as ever, his hands carving dramatic punctuation through the air. "The guy swore up and down he invented the Negroni. Like, sure, buddy. You and some Italian bartender from 1919 are spirit twins."

Fatima leaned against the counter, her laugh effortless, bright enough to catch in the dim room like sunlight. "Maybe it's your hair, Marco. It screams, 'Tell me your worst ideas.'"

Arden's smile surfaced before she could stop it. She set the knife down with a sharp tap against the cutting board. "No doubt. Your hair's a beacon for weird drink orders and unsolicited therapy."

Marco pressed a hand to his chest in mock betrayal. "Et tu, Arden? I come to you vulnerable, and you cut me down like a bad vodka tonic."

"Maybe stop telling people you're a jazz musician in your spare time," she said, lifting an eyebrow.

"That's not a lie," Marco shot back, indignant. "I played triangle in elementary school band. That's jazz-adjacent."

Fatima nearly doubled over, laughter shaking her shoulders. "You're beyond help."

Arden shook her head, the grin tugging at her mouth impossible to suppress. It wasn't only amusement filling her chest; it was something steadier. Familiar. Safe.

Nights like this were rare. People like this, rarer. Marco's ridiculousness. Fatima's glow. The way they made the bar feel like something more than polished surfaces and curated playlists. A rhythm had formed between them, a fragile kind of comfort stitched together in jokes and side-eyes.

And then—

She reached for a coaster.

Her fingers paused.

Something was folded beneath it.

A receipt, its edges crisp, her name scrawled across the top.

Arden.

The warmth evaporated.

She froze.

The letters were rushed and uneven, as if written in a hurry, but deliberate enough to land right here, beneath her hand, folded just so.

Her chest clenched once.

With composure that felt paper-thin, she slipped the note into her apron pocket.

"What's that?" Marco asked casually, still riding the wave of their banter. He didn't feel the shift. Not yet.

"Nothing," she said.

Too fast. Too light. Too practiced.

She grabbed a glass to keep her hands busy. Poured. Polished. Played the part. But the lie had already begun to fray her calm.

Around her, the laughter continued, filling the room like white noise. She nodded along. Responded when expected. Kept moving because stillness would have betrayed her.

But her fingers drifted back to her pocket again and again, as if the paper might change, as if meaning were something she could soften by refusing to look too closely.

It hadn't been there before.

Someone had left it for her.

Someone knew exactly where to place it so she would find it.

And that was what made her skin prickle.

———

From the shadows, *he watched.*

Arden.

Little Fire.

Her laugh from earlier echoed in his mind—sharp and bright, cutting through the club's noise like a blade.

It had pulled every eye to her. With that faint crease of unease shadowing her features, she commanded attention.

He'd seen it the moment she found the receipt. The pause in her hand. The furrow in her brow. That split second when her confidence faltered—enough to let something else slip through.

Perfect.

He'd planned it that way.

The receipt wasn't just paper.

It was a message.

Precise. Deliberate.

Her name, scrawled in a neat line, unmistakable.

He'd placed it beneath the coaster with care.

Not hidden or obvious. Enough to catch her off guard.

And it had worked.

Now, she carried it.

He saw the way her fingers skimmed over it in her apron pocket when she thought no one was watching.

But he was always watching.

Her reaction had been everything he wanted.

Not fear.

Too blunt. Too crude.

Curiosity.

Laced with the faintest edge of doubt.

A question planted like a seed.

Who left this? Why?

He saw it in the way her smile wavered.

The slight hesitation in her hand as she wiped the bar.

Marco's chatter couldn't distract her.

Fatima's laugh couldn't shake what he'd left behind.

She carried it now—his mark, his connection.

Proof she felt it too. Even if she didn't realize it yet.

And it wasn't the first.

The rose had come before. Left in silence, not yet understood.

The receipt was simply the next breath in the conversation he was building.

Quiet. Intentional. Escalating.

Each gesture pulling her closer.

The others didn't see her. Not the way he did.

Marco, with his overeager gestures.

Fatima, with her soft charm.

They basked in her light without understanding it.

And Blackwell with his polished control and carefully measured attention, he only saw the surface.

They couldn't see what burned beneath her skin.

But he could.

He saw the fire.

The strength forged from whatever pain she kept buried.

The quiet defiance in how she carried herself.

She wasn't made for cages.

She wasn't made for pedestals.

She was meant to blaze.

To consume.

When she slipped the receipt into her pocket, his pulse quickened.

That was all he needed.

The knowledge that she was holding onto it.

Holding onto him.

He leaned back, the shadows wrapping around him.

The receipt was nothing.

A whisper in the noise.

A flicker of recognition.

But now, she'd remember.

Now, she'd wonder.

And when the time came—

When the fire finally caught—

She would understand:

She wasn't just his focus.

She was already his.

The club had settled into its late-night rhythm, conversation softening into a distant murmur beneath the quiet clink of glassware.

Arden braced an elbow against the bar, her fingers drifting absently toward the folded receipt tucked in her pocket. Her name—etched in rushed, uneven strokes—lingered in her mind like something half-forgotten and heavy, a shadow refusing to let go.

A sudden clink of glass pulled her back.

She glanced up.

Gideon.

Lingering at the edge of the bar.

The storm in his eyes sparked a tremor low in her chest.

His mouth curved, slight and unreadable. Not quite a smile. Not quite neutrality. Just enough to unsteady her.

"Didn't think you'd still be here."

Her tone was practiced. Steady. But tension hummed beneath it.

"I didn't realize you were watching." His voice was low and smooth, edged with something quieter as he gently swirled the bourbon in his glass.

She arched a brow. "Hard not to notice the guy nursing the same drink for an hour."

Her smirk flickered. "You know, they let you order a second."

"Maybe I'm savoring it." He lifted the glass slightly in mock acknowledgment. Then his eyes narrowed a fraction. "Or maybe you're the one stalling tonight."

Her tone turned playful, but her gaze stayed sharp. "And what exactly do you think I'm stalling for, Blackwell?"

He tilted his head as if considering it. "Could be the silence. Could be the company."

Her lips curved. "You think I'm lingering for your charming personality?"

"I think you're not in a rush to be alone with your thoughts."

That landed harder than she expected. Her gaze dropped for half a second before she looked back up, the same fire in place, still defiant.

"What about you?" she countered, softer now. "What are you hoping to find in the bottom of that bourbon?"

His smile thinned, then faded altogether.

"Maybe the same thing you are."

A beat passed.

Arden inhaled slowly, her fingers stilling against the counter. His answer hung between them, thick with something that felt honest in a way neither of them usually allowed.

"Sometimes," she said, her voice lower now, "keeping busy is easier than being still."

He nodded once. "Yeah."

"And what do you think about when you stop?"

His voice was gentle, but unrelenting.

Like he knew.

Like he already understood exactly what he was asking of her.

She gave a small smirk, more reflex than anything real. "How much time do you have?"

His mouth curved faintly, a rare softness moving through his expression. "How much time do you need?"

The care in his voice—open, unguarded, almost unbearably quiet—cut straight through her defenses.

She held his gaze, and something shifted. The silence between them wasn't empty anymore. It had weight. Shape. A pulse of its own.

"I probably need all night," she said.

The truth simply slipped out.

"Good thing I've got all night."

He nodded toward the lounge. "Come on. You're done here, whether you admit it or not."

She hesitated, the moment stretching taut and unreadable.

"Alright," she said at last. "But I might need a stiff drink before the night's over."

Gideon's lips curved slightly.

A flicker of amusement.

Then a glint of challenge.

"I can handle that."

The inner lounge was quieter than usual.

The muffled sounds of the main room vanished as the door closed behind them, replaced by low light and a hush that seemed to settle over everything.

Arden dropped into the leather chair, the cushions pulling her in as if they remembered the shape of her.

Worn comfort. Weighted silence.

Gideon moved to the bar cart, calm and unhurried. He poured two fingers of bourbon into both glasses, then handed one to her, the light catching in the amber just long enough to feel intentional.

Their fingers brushed.

Barely.

But the weight of the glass in her hand wasn't the only thing grounding her.

"Stiff enough for you?" His tone was light, almost effortless.

His eyes weren't.

She took a sip. The burn bloomed through her, warm and familiar and necessary.

"It'll do."

They sat in a quiet that wasn't awkward. It didn't demand to be filled. It simply settled around them.

Arden traced the rim of her glass with her thumb, her thoughts knotting in places she rarely let herself visit.

"You're different, you know."

Gideon's voice was steady, but something in it caught her attention. Something that sounded dangerously close to truth.

Her brow lifted, and a smirk slid into place like armor. "Careful, Blackwell. That almost sounded like a compliment."

"Almost?"

"Maybe if you said it like you meant it."

His gaze didn't flinch.

"I meant it."

THE QUIET BETWEEN them cracked open.

Not with tension this time, but invitation.

Arden hesitated, her heartbeat a steady thunder in her ears.

Fuck. What the hell am I doing?

But the way Gideon watched her—steady, patient, without judgment—made it possible to open her mouth. To try.

She took another slow drink, letting the bourbon brace her.

"I never talk about this."

He didn't answer. His silence simply made room for whatever came next.

"My father was the most dangerous kind of man," she said, her voice steady, though rough at the edges. "The kind who thought nothing could touch him. He dealt drugs—not just to survive, but because he was hooked on what he sold."

She stared down into her drink, watching the light catch in slow, smoky spirals.

"That place, whatever it was, never felt like home. It was a revolving door for hollow eyes and desperate hands. I learned early how to disappear, how to stay small and unnoticed, but..."

She lifted her gaze to his.

"It didn't always work."

Gideon didn't speak.

He didn't have to.

"One of them," she said, the words quieter now. "Someone I should've been able to trust. He confirmed every fear I had. He wasn't a stranger. He was close. Too close."

Her voice cracked but didn't break. "He waited until we were alone. Didn't leave bruises. No evidence. But he left a mark I couldn't scrub off."

Her fingers tightened around the glass.

"I froze. My mind just...went blank. And afterward, I hated myself for that. For not screaming. For not fighting. For letting him make me feel like I was nothing." She swallowed, forcing the rest through. "And it wasn't rape. Not technically. But it was a violation. Of trust. Of safety. Of everything."

The quiet wrapped around them, not with judgment, but with room to breathe.

"I never told anyone. What would I have said? That someone touched me wrong? That I was scared all the time? There was no proof. No clean way to explain how you start tensing every time someone moves too close, or how you live waiting for it to happen again."

A shaky breath left her, and she held the edges of her voice together by force.

"My grandparents were the only light in that house. My granddad's arm around my shoulders. My grandma's laugh echoing through the kitchen. They gave me something to hold onto." Her mouth tightened. "But when they died, that was taken from me too."

She set the glass down, her hands trembling.

"After that, I thought if I could just be perfect, it would keep me safe. Perfect grades. Perfect silence. Perfect obedience. But it never mattered. He always found something to punish. Some perceived wrongdoing. And the worst part wasn't even the punishment."

Her voice softened, thinning around the memory.

"It was the waiting. The silence before the next blow. The next storm."

Gideon remained still, but something had changed in him. Some deep, dangerous part of him had gone quiet in a way that did not feel calm at all.

"My mother..." Arden looked away, blinking hard. "She wasn't a mother. She was a shell. Every breath she took was for him. She waited on him like he was some god. Like keeping him happy was the only thing keeping us alive."

She swallowed.

"I used to think she'd wake up. Every time he went to jail, I thought maybe this would be it. Maybe she'd see the opening and leave." A bitter, fragile sound caught in her throat. "But she never did. She called it love. I called it survival. And eventually, I realized I had to choose one or the other."

When she looked up, the glassy sheen in her eyes didn't dull the fire behind them.

"So I walked away. I cut ties. I left it all behind. And people say that's selfish. That I abandoned my family." Her voice sharpened, not loud, but certain. "But it wasn't selfish. It was necessary. Because if I'd stayed, it wouldn't have been only my life I gave up. It would've been everything that made me."

Gideon leaned closer, his expression stripped of polish now, his words anchored in something deeper than comfort.

"You didn't deserve any of that," he said. "Not the fear. Not the silence. Not the betrayal."

She blinked, the words cutting straight through whatever armor she had left.

"Arden." His voice lowered around her name. "You've faced worse than most people ever will, and you're here. Still standing. Still burning."

She looked at him then—this man who did not seem to see someone broken beyond repair.

He saw fire.

Not fracture.

"Thank you," she whispered. "For listening. For not flinching."

He covered her hand with his own, solid and grounding.

"I'm right here."

ARDEN SPOKE INTO THE HUSH, her voice low.

"And you?" she murmured, her eyes fixed somewhere near his shoulder. "What are you carrying?"

His expression shifted. Shadows moved across his face like storm clouds gathering, but he didn't answer right away. Not out of reluctance, she thought. More with the care of someone who knew truth had weight, and once placed between two people, it could not be easily taken back.

"The weight of a family who sees worth as a transaction," he said finally, his voice low and rough at the edges. "People who only keep you close when there's something to gain."

Something sharp tugged in Arden's chest.

Not pity.

Recognition.

"That sounds lonely."

"It is," he admitted, barely above a whisper.

His thumb brushed hers as he released her hand, the contact lingering for one suspended second before it was gone.

"But it doesn't have to stay that way."

The moment held. Quiet. Honest.

And in it, Arden saw something familiar in him—not only pain, but persistence. The kind of resilience that didn't need to announce itself to be real.

She reached out slowly, her fingers brushing against his, more instinct than decision. The silence between them wasn't empty. It felt full, weighted with everything they had said and everything they still didn't know how to name.

With his hand in hers, doubt slid in beneath the warmth.

What if I'm wrong?

The question cracked something open, and others slipped through in its wake.

What if I'm not seeing everything?

What if hope is just another kind of lie?

She swallowed hard as the past pressed close, sharp as broken glass.

Then came another thought, softer this time. Fragile, but defiant.

What if I'm not wrong?

What if I jump and it feels like flying?

What if he's the one who catches me?

Gideon's touch moved across her hand, slow and sure, as if he could read every silent war she was fighting and chose to hold the line with her anyway.

When he spoke, his voice was a quiet anchor.

"I'm staying right here."

No doubt. No flinch.

And for once, Arden didn't question it. Didn't armor against it.

She let herself believe.

Outside, the city moved on, indifferent as ever. But in that quiet pocket of warmth and shadow, her hand stayed in his.

❧

The rest of the night blurred into something soft and unrushed.

141

They didn't talk much after that; not because there was nothing to say, but because the silence felt full enough without words. Gideon stayed close without crowding, his hand resting lightly against the back of her chair—a tether Arden didn't want to question.

She finished her bourbon slowly, letting the warmth settle in her chest, letting it fight the old chill that never seemed to leave completely.

When she finally stood, he rose too, easy and unthinking, as if gravity itself had pulled him toward her.

Neither of them spoke as they left the lounge, moving side by side through the sleeping hush of The Blackwell Room. The chandeliers were dim now, their reflections dulled and uneven across the marble. The air held the soft bite of whiskey and the faintest trace of lemon polish lingering in the corners.

At the door, Arden paused, one hand on the latch and her keys loose in the other.

Gideon didn't push.

He waited.

And that was the thing that undid her most of all.

She turned back, heart beating harder than she liked, and for one suspended second, she thought about reaching for him. About closing the last inch between them.

Instead, she offered a small smile—quiet, tired, real.

"Goodnight, Blackwell."

His lips curved slightly. "Goodnight, Rivers."

Their names held a different weight now. She heard it in the way he said hers, like something he wasn't ready to put down.

Neither was she.

The door clicked shut behind her with a hush of finality, but the night felt unfinished. Something had been set into motion, quiet and certain, too heavy to stop now.

And somewhere deep inside, beneath the fear and the old scars that still ached when she breathed too deeply, something else stirred.

Something that felt, terrifyingly, like hope.

CHAPTER 17

Brunch Among Friends

Sunlight crept through the apartment windows, soft and slanted, spilling across the scuffed wood floors and washing the living room in a sleepy kind of gold.

Arden stood at the counter with a mug still too hot to drink.

Across the room, Penny breezed past as if music lived somewhere in her bones. Her curls bounced with every step, and her pajama pants were purple chaos—loud enough to wake the dead, printed with cartoon cats mid-catastrophe. Tails tangled. Paws flailing. Somehow, it suited her.

Coffee filled the air, rich and warm, sweetened by the faint thread of vanilla from a candle Penny had stashed on a shelf as if it had always belonged there.

Arden breathed it in.

No rush. Only quiet.

The kind of serenity that lasted only until the world remembered you existed.

"I can't believe he called a staff meeting before nine," she muttered, lifting the mug. The first sip burned a little, but she didn't mind. "Gideon doesn't even pretend to like mornings."

Penny spun in a lazy circle, arms loose at her sides, her pajama cats caught mid-brawl. "Maybe he's had a revelation," she said, bright with mischief. "Woke up with the sunrise and decided to chase enlightenment."

Arden snorted into her coffee. "Or he's planning a deeply serious crash course in napkin origami."

"Oh yes, the thrilling world of upscale hospitality." Penny struck a dramatic pose, and her pants shifted so the cartoon cats looked as if they were mid-curtain call, tumbling over one another for applause.

The purple contrasted violently with the navy sofa.

Arden didn't comment.

She didn't have to.

"But seriously," Penny said, collapsing sideways onto the armrest with the tragic flair of a silent film star, "what's your gut telling you?"

Arden shrugged. "Not a damn thing. But I'm sure the answer's coming."

Penny groaned, letting her head loll back dramatically. "Well, if it's terrible news, at least bring me pastries. Two minimum. No forks. You know my policies."

Arden rolled her eyes, smiling despite herself. "I'll do my best."

With a final lazy spin, Penny blew a kiss over her shoulder, her pajama cats erupting into fresh chaos.

Arden shook her head, grabbed her bag off the counter, and made for the door, leaving behind the low hum of coffee, vanilla, and Penny's relentless, messy joy.

Whatever Gideon was planning, she would find out soon enough.

❦

The cold hit her face the moment she stepped out, crisp and biting. Arden pulled her coat snug and kept moving, her breath trailing in short puffs as the city blinked awake around her. A car grumbled to life somewhere nearby. A horn barked. Footsteps echoed behind her, quick and uneven, then faded.

She walked with purpose, her thoughts slipping elsewhere.

To Gideon.

Sharp. Unreadable. Tension stitched into his bones.

But something had shifted.

Subtle. Like he'd started loosening the reins enough to be seen.

And whatever was happening with Gideon? It was getting under her skin.

She hadn't named it yet.

But it was there. Unmistakable.

Like he was showing just enough of himself to make her wonder.

She reached the door before she was ready.

Tall. Black. Familiar.

The handle caught the light, bright against the darker frame. Arden hesitated long enough to draw a breath, then pushed it open.

Inside, the staff trickled in: quiet, yawning, half-dreaming. A few leaned near the bar, hands wrapped around coffee cups, eyes squinting toward the setup beyond them. The mood? Bleary. Suspicious. Definitely not normal.

Fatima spotted her first, brushing a stray curl from her forehead. "Didn't peg Mr. Tall-Dark-and-Broody for a sunrise kind of guy. What's with the early roll call?"

Arden shook her head. "No clue. Maybe we're getting certified in champagne saber techniques."

Fatima let out a low laugh. "Wouldn't put it past him."

Marco leaned on the bar, coffee in hand, eyes half-lidded. "If we're here this early, it's gotta be serious. Somebody must've butchered inventory."

"Doubt it," Arden muttered, her attention snagging on something further down the room.

She gave Fatima a nudge and tilted her head. "Does that really scream emergency staff meeting to you?"

Fatima followed her line of sight, then blinked.

Pastries lined a long table, warm and golden. Bright fruit spilled from polished bowls, the scent of cinnamon, butter, and coffee wrapping around her like a promise. Even a mimosa bar sparkled nearby, subtle jazz humming low in the background. The setup looked more like a brunch ad than anything corporate.

"What in the..." Fatima started, but her words trailed off as Gideon emerged from his office.

He moved through the room with his usual composed air, but...

Something was different.

Still authoritative. Still restrained.

But lighter.

He looked like a man just in from the cold; tense, but thawing at the edges.

His gaze skimmed the group, then lingered on Arden. Whatever passed between them... she couldn't name it, but it landed all the same.

"Good morning," he said, voice smooth but just a hair off, like the phrase didn't fit right in his mouth.

"I know this wasn't what you pictured when I asked you in early," he went on. "But I figured it was time to change things up."

Fatima leaned toward Arden, whispering, "Is he... smiling? Am I hallucinating?"

Arden elbowed her, fighting her own smile as Gideon went on.

"This isn't a meeting," he clarified. "It's a thank-you. You all work hard—harder than most. And it doesn't go unnoticed."

His fingers flexed at his sides, like he was unfamiliar, uncomfortable even, with this vulnerability.

"I've... realized lately that I don't say that enough." His gaze flicked, for the briefest moment, to Arden. "So, consider this brunch a small gesture of appreciation."

A murmur rippled through the group—surprised, amused, but mostly pleased.

Marco lifted his cup with a wide grin. "Look at that. The man bleeds after all."

Gideon gave him a dry look, but the corner of his mouth tipped up. "Try not to ruin the moment, Marco."

"This is new," Fatima whispered. Arden didn't disagree. Whatever it was, it stirred warmth beneath her ribs.

Arden shook her head, but warmth spread through her chest. "Not my idea. But he's full of surprises."

Gideon caught the exchange, lifting a brow.

Arden caught his eye, a crooked grin playing at her lips. "Trying to win us over, Blackwell?"

He didn't look away. Not right away. Something quiet flickered behind those eyes.

The question was light, almost teasing.

But something was underneath.

Something meant for her.

She held his gaze, smile tugging at the edge of her mouth. "Guess we'll see if your brunch game matches your brooding."

Laughter stirred the room. Mugs clinked against marble; chairs scraped back with sleepy groans; the usual tightness around Gideon loosened slightly. One by one, the staff drifted toward the spread, plates in hand, voices rising with something close to ease.

ARDEN HUNG BACK, letting the others claim their seats and dive into the spread. She watched from the edge of the room, arms crossed and coffee in hand, as her team laughed over syrup-drenched pancakes and piled their plates with buttery pastries and fruit so fresh it glistened.

A simple thing.

But from Gideon, it felt seismic.

He appeared at her side without a word, the soft tread of his shoes barely audible beneath the low murmur of conversation. His hands were tucked into his pockets, his gaze fixed on the table with a quiet, assessing focus, as if he were trying to determine whether this fragile ease would hold.

He didn't speak right away.

Neither did she.

Finally, he glanced her way. "Well?"

She looked over at him. "Well, what?"

His mouth twitched. "The food, Arden. The atmosphere. My...evolution into a halfway decent human being."

She arched a brow. "You want a Yelp review or a standing ovation?"

"I'll settle for the truth."

She studied him, coffee warming her hands, humor playing at the edge of her voice. "It's nice. Unexpected. But...really nice."

"They're not used to seeing this side of me," he said, almost to himself.

She tilted her head. "Neither are you."

That earned her a quick look, one part amusement and one part resignation. "Fair."

He shifted slightly, his stance loosening just enough to betray the weight beneath his words.

"I've been thinking," he said, quieter now. "About what you said. What this place could be. What I want it to be."

That stopped her.

Her amusement faded, something softer taking its place. She hadn't expected a follow-up, let alone reflection.

"I didn't think you were actually listening," she said, the words slipping out before she could pull them back.

His gaze moved to hers.

"I always listen," he said, quiet and certain.

The rawness in his tone made her stomach tighten. Not sharp. Not heavy. Just real. And for one rare second, she had nothing to offer in return. No joke. No sidestep. No polished little blade to slide between herself and the truth.

The silence stretched, but it didn't press down on them. It settled instead, still and open, something unfinished humming beneath it.

Then Gideon straightened, slipping the moment back into his pocket as if it hadn't happened at all. "Enjoy the brunch, Rivers. You've earned it."

And just like that, he turned and walked away.

Somewhere behind him, a glass clinked, or maybe a cork gave a soft pop, normal sounds returning as if nothing had shifted at all.

Arden let out a breath she hadn't realized she was holding.

She watched him from across the room: Marco's mug clinking against the bar as Gideon refilled it; Fatima's laugh lifting into the air like smoke; Gideon leaning in when someone spoke, not performing attention, but actually offering it.

It was subtle. Almost too subtle.

But Arden saw it.

Felt it.

Something had changed.

Maybe Penny was right. Maybe Gideon Blackwell really was turning over a new leaf. Or maybe he was finally letting them see the man he had always been beneath the steel and polish.

Either way, it suited him.

With a quiet huff that might have been a laugh, Arden grabbed a mimosa and slipped into an empty seat, letting the hum of easy conversation settle around her. Whatever had prompted this shift, she wasn't about to overthink it.

Not when it meant seeing her team like this: relaxed, happy, whole.

Not when the tension had loosened its grip on the room.

And not when, across the room, Gideon Blackwell finally looked like a man instead of a fortress.

The fact that he looked even better this way?

That alone was worth savoring.

And if it also meant catching glimpses of a different side of Gideon?

Well.

That was just a bonus.

An especially attractive bonus.

❦

As she walked, Arden couldn't shake the feeling that this hadn't been only a moment.

Not just Gideon letting his guard down.

Something had shifted.

Not in him, exactly.

In her understanding of him.

He wasn't only her boss. Wasn't merely the calculating man behind The Blackwell Room's empire, all strategy and restraint and polished control. He was a man trying to be better. Trying to become worthy of something beyond power or legacy.

And somehow, that made him more dangerous than ever.

Penny was going to have a field day.

Arden let out a breath, already bracing for the teasing, but as she climbed the stairs, her thoughts kept circling back to him.

His voice.

His restraint.

The way he looked at her as if she wasn't just anyone.

She was in trouble.

The kind of trouble that made her pulse kick before she was ready to admit why.

Because if Gideon Blackwell kept showing her the man beneath the mask, she might let him in.

And that was the real danger.

CHAPTER 18

Shadows in the Glow

Sunlight slashed through the floor-to-ceiling windows of Gideon's office, gilding the desk in unforgiving streaks. The brightness did nothing to soften the reality before him; it sharpened it, deepening the shadows around the scattered files until every page looked less like evidence and more like an indictment.

Every page was a crime scene. Aggressive acquisitions. Fabricated foreclosures. Generational wealth gutted under the guise of progress. The Blackwell empire had not been built on strategy. It had been built on predation, its foundation set in the bones of families who never saw it coming.

They hadn't simply exploited loopholes. They had created them, lobbied for them, funded campaigns to protect them. From courthouse clerks to state legislators, the Blackwell web ran wide, greased by favors and sealed beneath nondisclosure agreements. Time and silence had scrubbed the blood from the marble until brutality could call itself business.

Gideon exhaled and flipped the top folder closed. Leo Marcus hadn't uncovered anything Gideon hadn't known somewhere deep in the marrow. The former FBI agent had only confirmed what Gideon had spent a lifetime trying to deny: his family didn't just break laws; they rewrote them.

Their reach wasn't confined to West Virginia. Blackwell Enterprises had tentacles in every state where heirs' property laws lingered like ghosts—laws that turned promises into betrayals, that turned generations of belonging into sterile towers, manicured golf courses, and luxury developments that forgot the names buried beneath them.

Evelyn's urban revitalization projects were only a sterilized form of violence. A wrecking ball dressed in progress.

Erase the people. Keep the land.

That was the Blackwell method.

Always had been.

At the edge of his desk, one folder sat apart, its label stark against the chaos.

Leo Marcus—Federal Leads.

Gideon's fingers hovered over it for a moment before he flipped it open.

Not facts. Weapons.

At the top of the first page was a name: Special Agent Lauren Bishop, FBI, Public Corruption and Civil Rights Division. Her name had begun circulating in the right rooms, whispered with the inevitability of a storm edging closer to shore. She was known for taking down the untouchable, for scraping the polished veneer from men like his father and leaving nothing behind but raw, exposed rot.

Nathan Cole had been fighting these battles long before Gideon understood they existed. His grandfather's closest confidant, Nathan had spent decades cleaning up the Blackwell mess behind closed doors, and now he was helping Gideon drag it into the daylight.

It was happening. Piece by piece. Move by move.

Gideon leaned back, the weight of the mission lodged beneath his ribs, but the fire in his chest burned hotter than doubt. This club—his sanctuary, his clean slate— had been meant to remain untouched by his family's corruption. His name might be Blackwell, but The Blackwell Room had been built in defiance of everything that name stood for.

And still, Evelyn's shadow crept even here. A stain that refused to fade. A legacy that refused to die.

But even legacies weren't untouchable.

Not when you knew where to strike the match.

THE WEIGHT of the files clung to Gideon, the truth of his family's sins etched into every page.

Then she appeared.

Arden flickered onto the screen, her laughter breaking through the grainy security footage like sunlight through storm clouds. It disarmed him, that impossible warmth of hers, even rendered in black-and-white.

She leaned against the bar with easy confidence, her dark waves catching the light even in grayscale, her eyes bright with mischief as she teased Marco with a smirk sharp enough to draw blood. She looked entirely at ease in her own skin, and for reasons Gideon did not care to examine, that unsettled him more than her fear ever had.

Fatima stood beside her, bold and bright, the suggestion of pattern in her blouse lending energy to the otherwise monochrome feed. Marco gestured wildly as he spun another story, his hands cutting through the air with theatrical precision, and laughter rippled between the three of them—unrestrained, effortless, alive.

It was the only honest thing in a world built on careful facades.

Gideon exhaled, tension loosening beneath his ribs. Arden did not belong to this place, and yet she had done something no one else had managed. She had cracked the Blackwell family's polished illusion and made the ruins feel, for one dangerous moment, like something worth salvaging.

He leaned back, his fingers tapping once against the desk. He knew better than to hold on to moments like this. Better than to believe anything that made him feel human had been made to last.

Hope in the Blackwell family was dangerous, and Evelyn? She had noticed her. And that was a death sentence.

"MARCO, I swear—if I hear one more Paris story, I'm charging you fiction rates," Arden muttered, setting a crystal glass on the bar with the ease of muscle memory.

Fatima snorted and tucked a curl behind her ear. "She's not wrong. You can't go five minutes without name-dropping France."

Marco clutched his chest as if she'd shot him. "Wounded," he gasped. "Deeply."

Arden tilted her head, unimpressed. "Want me to fetch some smelling salts from the back?"

He straightened with exaggerated dignity. "For the record, I never said I played in those Parisian clubs. I simply...observed."

"Right." She wiped the counter with deliberate slowness. "Let me guess—Miles Davis begged for your input?"

Marco steepled his fingers, solemn as a priest. "Exactly. Told him trumpet was his thing. You're welcome, jazz."

Their laughter spilled through the room, loose and unrestrained, carving warmth into a place that had never been designed for anything so human. The club was polished, exclusive, a shrine to power and velvet restraint, but for once, it wasn't about roles or expectations. It was only the three of them, safe for the length of a joke, letting the room become something softer around them.

Marco leaned across the counter, grinning. "You know, Arden, for someone who claims to hate my stories, you sure remember all the details."

She rolled her eyes, but the way her fingers hovered guardingly over the next glass gave her away. "I have to," she said. "Otherwise, how would I know when you're full of it?"

Fatima bumped her shoulder. "Don't lie. You'd miss him if he stopped."

Arden opened her mouth to argue, but Marco was already pointing at her, triumphant.

"Aha. She likes my stories."

She sighed, long and dramatic. "This is what I get for growing soft."

"Too late now, Mountain Mama," Fatima said with a wide smile.

The words landed differently this time. Like a key sliding into a lock. Like something in Arden's bracing had finally loosened enough to let the shape of belonging press through.

She let out a quiet laugh and shook her head, but the knowing had already bloomed in her chest, quiet and sure. She had spent years surviving, keeping people at arm's length, choosing solitude over the risk of being left behind. This was different. It wasn't conditional or transactional. It didn't ask her to earn her place, or make herself smaller to keep it.

Marco would still talk too much. Fatima would still throw jabs with a grin. They would still make room for her at the bar as if her presence had become part of the rhythm here.

And maybe that was the dangerous thing.

Not the ache of wanting to belong, but the first soft terror of realizing she already did.

Arden pressed her palms to the bar, grounding herself in the moment. "Guess I'm doomed, then."

Fatima raised her coffee in a toast, tapping it gently against Arden's glass. "We all are."

And for once...Arden didn't mind the sound of that at all.

Miriam Harrington stepped into the office trailing winter in her wake—flawless, expected, and cold to the core. Her eyes swept the space with sharp, methodical precision before landing on the bar.

Arden stood there with Fatima and Marco, laughter moving between them. Light. Human. The antithesis of everything Miriam represented.

She saw it instantly.

Gideon didn't move. Didn't speak. Still, her judgment settled over the room like a veil of ash.

"Evelyn has concerns about...distractions," Miriam said, each word wrapped in velvet, all blade beneath.

Gideon's fingers tapped a steady rhythm against the desk. "My priorities are unchanged."

Miriam's smile barely moved. "Good. Because Evelyn has invested heavily in you, and she does not tolerate deviation." Her eyebrow quirked. "Or attachments that threaten to undermine what we've built."

Not a warning.

A verdict.

She started to turn, then stopped at the doorway. "Do remind Miss Rivers where she belongs," she said.

Her tone was calm. Polished. Sharp enough to draw blood.

"It would be unfortunate if she forgot."

Gideon's hand curled against the desk, tension threading up his arm. He said nothing.

The faint trace of Miriam's perfume lingered after her, heavy in the air, too sweet and too sharp—like something rotting beneath fresh-cut flowers. Then she disappeared, and the door clicked shut behind her with soft, surgical finality.

Gideon exhaled slowly, his fingers unfurling from the desk one by one.

Arden wasn't a weakness.

She was his line in the sand.

THE DOOR OPENED AGAIN—NO knock, no hesitation.

Alex.

"Baby brother," he drawled, smirking like the punchline was loaded. "Still brooding? Or are you finally plotting that family coup?"

Gideon didn't look up. "Do you need something, Alex?"

"I was just admiring your taste in bartenders," Alex said, sinking into the chair Miriam had vacated as if it had been reserved for him.

Gideon froze.

Alex's smile sharpened. "Arden, right? Rough edges. Strong presence. Very... compelling."

"Don't," Gideon said, the edge in his voice cutting sharper than any rise in volume.

"Don't what? Notice?"

Gideon set his pen down, calm but final. "Stay away from her."

"Careful," Alex said lightly. "You're starting to sound attached."

There it was. The pressure point. The invitation to crack.

Gideon said nothing.

Alex leaned back, arms spread, the picture of careless confidence. "Beautiful things don't last here, brother. Not in this family. They either break...or get carved into something unrecognizable. You've seen it happen."

A flicker moved through Gideon's jaw.

Seen it?

He'd survived it.

Alex smiled like he knew. Like he had put the blade there himself.

But Gideon didn't rise to it. He sat still, composed, every breath drawn through a sieve of willpower.

"You always were the fun one," Alex mused, standing. "Well, don't let me interrupt...whatever this is."

He lingered at the door, tossing the comment behind him.

"Always a pleasure."

The door clicked closed.

Only then did Gideon move, pushing back from the desk, his jaw tight, every muscle coiled like live wire. He turned toward the window and the city spread out below, all glass and distance and bright, indifferent ambition.

Not to find calm.

To remember what he was fighting for.

And who he was willing to burn it all down for.

Gideon turned from the window.

The city stretched below, his sanctuary of glass and steel, but tonight it felt less like something he owned and more like something bearing down on him. His world had always been built on careful control. Calculated moves. Silent wars. And the people in this family never stopped pushing.

Evelyn. Miriam. Alex.

Each of them, in their own way, tested the seams of his restraint.

He reached for his jacket and rolled his shoulders, but the movement did little to loosen the tension settled deep in his back. Somewhere below, The Blackwell Room pulsed with music and murmured deals, another elegant battlefield dressed in velvet and low light.

He wasn't looking for a fight tonight.

But then he saw Colton.

Colton leaning in, smirking. Arden squaring her shoulders, her expression steady.

Of course it was Colton.

Gideon drummed his fingers once against the desk.

Then he moved.

The club breathed around Arden in low music and whispered deals, though the sounds barely reached her. She was busy, focused, her attention narrowed to glassware and rhythm and the clean efficiency of work—until she wasn't.

The shift was subtle, like a cold draft slipping under a closed door.

A presence.

A pressure.

And then, a voice.

"You're a hard woman to get a moment with, Miss Rivers."

Arden turned, already knowing.

Colton Blake leaned against the bar, at ease in the way only men like him could be. The kind who didn't need to demand attention because the room had been trained to offer it.

She didn't react. Didn't tense. She only watched him, assessing.

Colton smiled. The slow kind. The practiced kind.

"Gideon keeps you all to himself." His gaze dipped to her hands, to the effortless efficiency of her movements. "I'd take it personally if I didn't admire the commitment."

Arden reached for a glass and wiped the rim with precise care. "Something I can get you?"

"I was hoping for a conversation."

She arched a brow. "That's unfortunate."

Disarmed.

Without even trying.

His amusement flickered, but he recovered quickly, tipping his head slightly. "Ah, but I'm a patient man."

"That makes one of us."

Another hit. Another shift.

Colton watched her for a beat, not merely looking now, but studying.

"You know," he mused, "most people show a little more interest when a Blackwell pays them attention."

Arden didn't pause. Didn't even blink. "Most people have lower standards."

Hook. Set. Twist.

Colton laughed, full and warm, but something tight hid beneath it. This wasn't how he had expected the conversation to go. She was supposed to play along, to flirt or flinch or give him some readable thread to pull.

Instead, she was playing him.

Worst of all, she wasn't even trying.

He dragged his fingers along the bar's edge, letting the silence sit long enough to be felt, then stepped back, smooth and unhurried.

"It's been a pleasure, Miss Rivers."

He paused and tilted his head, still trying to work her out.

"I'll see you around."

With that, he walked away. Not rushed. Not rattled. Only thoughtful, his footsteps fading into the low thrum of music until the club's velvet hush swallowed him whole.

Arden let the glass slip from her hand to the counter with a soft clink, small and grounding.

But she wasn't watching Colton anymore.

Because Gideon had entered the room.

She felt him before she saw him.

Not like Colton, not that cold shift in pressure or the sleek menace of something waiting to strike. Gideon's presence was different.

A weight.

A shadow.

A heat at her back.

She glanced up as he reached the bar, his gaze locked on Colton's retreating form.

"What did he want?"

Not a demand. Not a growl.

Low. Steady. Loaded.

Arden exhaled and tossed the bar towel over her shoulder. "Nothing."

She expected him to let it go.

He didn't.

His fingers curled around the bar's edge, his knuckles flexing once before he released his grip. "Arden."

She sighed and finally met his eyes.

Then, almost imperceptibly, she worried her lip. A small tug at the left corner of her mouth. A flicker of hesitation so slight she didn't seem to realize she had given it to him.

But Gideon did.

He had seen it before.

A habit. A tell. The quiet slip in her armor that meant there was something she wasn't willing to divulge.

One he hadn't yet decided how to play.

So he waited.

And Arden, unaware she had given herself away, shrugged. "Nothing important."

A beat of silence passed between them.

Gideon's jaw shifted, tension flickering beneath the surface as his gaze moved across her face, reading the shape of what she refused to say. Then, just as quickly, he stepped back and let it drop.

For now.

But that second of hesitation stayed with him.

———

FROM THE DIM glow of his study, he leaned over the screen—consuming every detail of Arden Rivers' life with ravenous precision.

The low whir of his hard drive was a mechanical heartbeat pulsing against the darkness as he leaned closer to the screen. She wasn't just a name anymore.

She was an obsession.

Pixel by pixel. Secret by secret.

He had stripped her bare.

Exposed her.

Silverbranch.

The word hit like a bruise. A tether she had tried to sever but could never quite escape.

Weeks of digging had peeled back her defenses, unearthing the fragile framework of her world.

A rundown bar.

A nursing career abandoned.
And Chad Dawson.
His fingers curled into a fist.
That nobody.
That pathetic excuse of a man who had once dared to call her his.
The thought of him touching her—breathing the same air—boiled in his blood.
She deserved so much more.
She deserved him.
Every choice she made, every scar etched into her skin, every silent battle fought in the dark,
They painted her in colors so raw, so vivid, he burned to look at her.
Little Fire.
She thought she had hidden the cracks in her armor.
But he saw them.
He had traced them.
Memorized them.
They weren't imperfections.
They were exquisite.
They were hers.
And that made them his.

A SLOW*, creeping smile curled at his lips.*
She had no idea.
How long he'd been watching.
How deep the hooks had sunk.
How far from safe she truly was.
His fingers drummed violently against the desk, his pulse thudding in his ears.
He scrolled through the files again, studying her past like scripture.
Her nursing days.
The way she'd clawed her way free.
And deeper still—the childhood nightmares she never spoke of.
A father whose rage and addiction left invisible scars.
A mother who had stood by, silent and complicit.
Arden had been forged in that fire.
She emerged strong. Unyielding.
But not untouched.
The fools circling her now? They didn't even recognize that kind of fire.
They were weak. Blind. Undeserving.
They didn't see her.
But he did.
His Little Fire.

Leaning back, he exhaled slow, controlled, his weight pressing into the leather chair.

Arden Rivers didn't belong in their shallow, plastic world of false smiles and hidden blades.

She needed something real.

Somewhere she could breathe.

Somewhere she could be seen.

Every crack. Every edge. Every wild, untamed piece of her.

She didn't need Gideon Blackwell. She needed him.

And when the dust settled—when the rest of them fell away—he'd make sure he was the only one left standing.

His plans were in motion.

And soon, his Little Fire would finally understand.

She had always belonged to him.

CHAPTER 19

Beneath the Glimmer

Evening light skimmed across the marble floors, catching on movement and muttering against the stone like a secret. The sconces glowed warm and low, but the corners stayed dark, where light didn't quite dare reach and secrets liked to settle.

Arden had spent weeks learning the unspoken rules of The Blackwell Room: how money amplified whispers into threats, how power moved across a room like smoke, how silence could be more deliberate than speech. Behind the bar, her hands worked on instinct, arranging bottles and aligning glasses with the precise efficiency of muscle memory. Usually, the motions were enough to settle her nerves.

Not tonight.

Something buzzed beneath her skin, a warning with no words yet.

"Arden." Marco's voice was low, more serious than usual. "You've been solid, but tonight? Be careful. The Blackwells are coming in."

The stemware creaked in her hand. She kept her voice neutral. "They're always here. What's different?"

"Evelyn's coming."

The name hit like a dropped stone in her chest.

Evelyn Hawthorne Blackwell.

The matriarch behind the curtain. Invisible but omnipresent.

Marco's eyes scanned the room with sharp focus. "And she'll be bringing the cavalry. They're staging a power play."

Arden hadn't met her, not officially. But she had felt her in every guarded glance, every subtle shift in atmosphere, every careful pause that entered the room before anyone dared speak. Evelyn was a force, and forces did not tolerate disruption.

"Should I curtsy?" Arden asked dryly.

Marco's laugh was flat, a crack across the surface of the room. "She doesn't need the curtsy. She cuts clean, no warning." He lowered his voice. "Watch yourself. Evelyn's ruthless. And she's already clocked the way Gideon looks at you."

A flush crept up Arden's neck. She turned, reaching for a bottle she didn't need. "Gideon doesn't—"

"Don't waste the breath," Marco said, cutting her off. "Everyone sees it."

Arden frowned, her voice quieter now. "Sees what, exactly?"

He gave her a look, equal parts knowing and exhausted. "The way he watches you. How you tense when he's near. It's not just you two anymore. The room's catching on."

Fatima passed with a tray of towels, catching the tail end of Marco's warning. Her expression was pure mischief. "If it's not a thing, it should be. The static between you two could take down the grid."

Arden shot her a flat look. "Really not the time."

Fatima gave her a side-eye. "Don't give me that face. I'm just stating the obvious."

Marco rubbed the back of his neck and exhaled loudly. "We're not giving you hell, Arden. Just be smart. The Blackwells don't lose. And if Evelyn's paying attention—and trust me, she is—you'd better tread carefully."

The doors opened with a hushed groan, and the air in The Blackwell Room shifted.

Something in the atmosphere tightened, like a wire pulled taut. An expectant silence moved through the room, the kind that warned of thunder before it broke.

Evelyn Hawthorne Blackwell entered first, her burgundy silk dress trailing behind her in a deliberate sweep of power and poise.

Evelyn did not arrive.

She claimed.

And the room adjusted accordingly.

Voices dimmed. Movements slowed. Some people leaned in, others instinctively pulled back, but no one looked away. Not when she was present.

Her gaze moved across the space with cold precision, and when it paused on Arden, it did so long enough to leave something behind.

Not interest. Not curiosity.

Judgment.

Already sealed.

Arden didn't flinch, but the weight of it lingered all the same, cold as frost against her skin.

Behind Evelyn came Alex Blackwell, arrogance worn like a second skin. He didn't so much walk as glide, sure of his place and his power, the smirk on his lips daring anyone to forget it. He did not need attention. He expected it.

Cate followed a step behind, pristine in pale pink, composed down to every eyelash. But her smile was stretched too thin, the shape of calm rather than the thing itself. Tension pulsed beneath it, taut and strained. Arden recognized it on sight.

Tori Langston swept in after them, silver and ambition shimmering with every step. She leaned toward the gravity of the table, aligning herself to it like a planet slipping into orbit.

Then, from the second floor, Gideon appeared.

He didn't descend like the rest of them. There was no pageantry to him, no performance. Only quiet command. Presence without demand.

He hadn't been summoned.

He knew.

The moment his family walked through the door, he had felt it.

His eyes swept the room, taking stock, measuring weight.

And then they found her.

Arden.

Their eyes met for only a flash, but the moment held like a struck chord.

Her pulse betrayed her, skipping before she could stop it. For weeks she had told herself it was nothing, some collision of circumstance and proximity, a trick of tension and timing.

But the flick of Evelyn's gaze between them. Tori's curling smirk. Alex's low-burn amusement.

Marco had been right.

Everyone could see it.

The Blackwells settled at the table like generals before a war. Evelyn took the head, regal and absolute, her expression immaculate in its indifference.

To her right sat Miriam Harrington, composed and sharp, an elegant extension of Evelyn's reach.

To her left, Grace Langston waited in olive-green Bottega, warm and deliberate.

Too warm.

The kind of warm that disarmed before it cut.

Tori leaned into Gideon, brushing his forearm, her voice spun sweet enough to rot the teeth. "Gideon," she purred. "It's been far too long since we've talked."

His fingers flexed, barely visible, a tell only the observant would catch.

"I've been busy."

Tori's smile wavered for a second, a hairline fracture in the polish. "I can't imagine what's been keeping you so occupied."

A pause followed.

Too pointed. Too deliberate.

Then, with the slow, syrupy precision of a woman convinced she had delivered checkmate, Tori turned her attention to the bar.

To Arden.

The glance was a thorn buried just beneath the skin.

Arden felt it: the weight of unspoken words, the assessment, the judgment.

Silly little girl.

She picked up the nearest bottle and poured a drink with calm, practiced ease. Tori could look. Could measure. Could stare. Could slice. Arden had seen her kind before—the girls who smiled like vipers in silk, who mistook breeding and a last name for power.

She didn't belong to their world.

She didn't need to.

And that meant she was the only one in the room not bound by its rules.

Arden placed the glass down with a quiet clink, a dismissal disguised as indifference.

Tori's smile stayed, but something in her eyes flickered.

Just for a second.

A miscalculation.

She could look. She could stare. She could size Arden up all she wanted.

It didn't change a damn thing.

ALEX MOVED FIRST.

He didn't just approach. He arrived, all polished confidence and predatory intent, the kind of presence that made space for itself whether it had been invited or not.

He claimed a spot at the bar like it had been waiting for him. His posture was relaxed, but every inch of him radiated control, ownership, the easy assumption that everything—and everyone—in the room existed within reach of his command.

Arden felt the weight of his gaze before she looked up. It crawled across her skin, measuring, possessing.

She didn't flinch.

She reached for the shaker and moved through the repetition of habit, refusing to let him dictate her rhythm. Men always looked. She wasn't built to be ignored; curves, confidence, presence—those were things she wore without apology.

But Alex didn't just look.

He assessed.

Sorted.

Filed away.

"Arden." Her name slipped off his tongue like a secret already claimed. "Gideon's latest...fascination."

He let the word linger, a smirk curving at the edge of his mouth.

A trap, gift-wrapped in velvet.

"What brought someone like you to a place like this?" he asked. "Luck? Wrong turn? Or are you playing the long game?"

Her response came as cool as the liquor she measured. "The job listing seemed straightforward enough."

Amusement flickered across his face, sharp and fleeting. "Clever. I like that."

He leaned in just far enough for it to register, his voice dropping. "But clever doesn't always keep you safe."

His eyes swept over her—slow, thorough. Not admiration. Not desire.

Calculation.

"Gideon has a thing for rare talent," he mused, his smirk curling wider. "You must be...exceptional."

Bait.

She didn't bite.

"Maybe not, Alex," she said, meeting his gaze head-on. "But it's gotten me this far."

Alex tilted his head, studying her like a predator watching something that had not yet realized it was cornered. He let the silence breathe, stretching the moment until it nearly snapped.

Then, voice low and rehearsed, "How does it feel...being the most interesting person in the room?"

A slow, thoughtful smile curved her lips. "I wouldn't know. You've been here the whole time."

His laugh came quick and tight, laced with something that didn't reach his eyes. Then those eyes darkened.

"You've got spirit." His tone sounded almost admiring.

Almost.

"But we'll see how long that lasts."

Before she could respond, another voice cut in.

Cool. Controlled. Precise.

"Alex."

Cate Blackwell didn't glide.

She cut.

All elegance. All angles. All steel wrapped in silk. Her pale pink sheath dress said perfection. Her voice said war.

She didn't look at Arden.

"Leave her alone."

Low. Unyielding. Command masked as courtesy.

Alex didn't flinch. Didn't blink. He turned slowly, indulging her.

"Only making conversation, darling," he said, the smirk never faltering. "You know how I enjoy meeting new people."

Cate's jaw ticked, barely enough to see, but enough to shift the air.

"And you know how I enjoy reminding you where to stop."

A pause followed. Neither cold nor warm.

Familiar.

Dangerous.

Whatever passed between them was old, well-worn, and sharp at the edges. Arden wasn't sure if it was resentment or resignation.

Or both.

Alex held Cate's gaze long enough to unsettle the space around them. Then something in him shifted. A retreat. A recalibration.

He chuckled softly and stepped away. "Don't be a stranger."

Light words.

Heavy weight.

He didn't look back.

Cate didn't watch him go. She looked at Arden instead, and for the first time, Arden saw beneath the surface. Not the flawless wife. Not the untouchable Blackwell. A woman who knew exactly who she was married to and what it cost to stay.

Something flickered across Cate's face.

A warning.

But if it had words, they stayed unspoken.

She turned and followed him, the crisp chill of her perfume cutting through the heavier warmth of the bar and leaving a sharper edge behind.

Only then did Arden exhale.

SEATED at the far end of the table beside Hawthorne cousin Julia Fenton, Colton Blake looked at ease—legs crossed, glass in hand, posture deceptively casual.

But anyone paying attention could see it.

He was a blade at rest.

Coiled, not careless. Idle, not inert.

He didn't speak often, but when he did, his words landed like a cocked gun in a quiet room.

Tonight was no different.

He caught Gideon's eye, his expression calm but sharpened at the edges. "Interesting choice," he said. "She seems competent enough. For now."

Gideon didn't blink. "She is."

Colton swirled his glass, the movement smooth and deliberate. "Competence is a fragile currency in this world. It's not just about keeping pace. It's knowing when to step back."

A test.

To anyone else, it might have sounded like advice.

To Gideon, it was a reminder: the family was watching.

And so was Colton.

Gideon's jaw ticked, but his voice stayed level. "She's not involved in anything that concerns the family."

Colton's smile barely formed, only a faint, knowing curve. "It needs to stay that way," he murmured.

His gaze drifted to the bar, where Arden worked with calm confidence. She looked like she belonged.

And still, she was being hunted.

"For her sake."

Gideon didn't respond. Not with words. But his posture shifted, shoulders squaring just enough to draw the line.

Colton didn't push.

He didn't have to.

His point had been made, and it lingered, quiet and barbed, in the space between them.

Sebastian moved through the room like gravity owed him something: unhurried, polished, and utterly sure of his place. His suit was flawless, his smile disarming, dangerous by design. His presence was intrusive in the way of men who never asked permission to take up space.

He stopped at the bar and rested a hand lightly on the edge as though he owned it. A smirk curled across his mouth, cool and entitled and practiced.

"So...Arden," he said, his voice low and easy. "Word is, you're hard to impress."

Arden lifted her head from the glass she was drying. She didn't smile. Didn't blink. She only met his eyes.

"Maybe don't believe everything you hear, Sebastian."

He gave a soft laugh, the kind meant to disarm. "I usually don't," he said, eyeing her with slow, curated confidence. "I prefer firsthand evaluations."

His gaze drifted, neither subtle nor rushed. He took her in the way some men window-shopped for things they planned to steal: the line of her waist, the curve of her hip, the way the fabric clung to her skin in all the wrong places for a conversation like this.

"Not every day someone walks into this world and holds their ground," he said, voice curling at the edges. "I can see why Gideon's...intrigued."

Arden's fingers went still against the rim of her glass.

That spark in her chest wasn't embarrassment. It was irritation held under restraint.

Her voice came cool and controlled. "I'm just here to work."

Sebastian tilted his head, studying her with careful, calculated quiet, testing for fractures.

"Is that all it is?" he asked, tone curious but edged with something sharper.

Something that wanted in.

Arden opened her mouth—

"That's enough."

Gideon's voice sliced through the room.

Cold. Commanding. Unmistakable.

Sebastian turned slowly, unbothered, a faint tick at the corner of his mouth as if the interruption amused him.

"Relax, Gideon," he said. "Just making conversation."

"Find someone else."

"Easy, brother." A few feet away, Alex let out a low, knowing laugh. "She's got a brain. You'll lose her to someone more entertaining soon enough."

Gideon didn't take the bait. He didn't even look Alex's way.

His focus stayed on Sebastian, gaze steady, jaw set.

"Stay in your lane."

The words didn't rise.

They dropped.

Sebastian held his gaze a half-second longer, then turned back to his drink.

"You might want to remind her," he said, dragging the words enough to twist them, "that being interesting in this family? That kind of attention can go sideways fast."

His fingertip traced the rim of his glass.

A warning disguised as small talk.

Gideon didn't flinch.

Sebastian stepped back with the same unbothered grace he'd entered, a storm in designer linen, leaving behind the echo of something that had not finished brewing.

Arden exhaled slowly, only then noticing the tightness in her chest. Beside her, Gideon said nothing, but the quiet between them had thickened into something that did not need volume to leave a mark.

The tension didn't let up.

It buried itself deeper.

The moment didn't end.

It simply waited.

EVELYN LIFTED HER WINEGLASS, the crystal catching the light with intentional brilliance—a quiet assertion of control, as effortless as it was absolute.

The moment stretched, tight with expectation, as Gideon felt her focus settle. Unforgiving.

The blade always came next.

"Tonight," she said, voice smooth as silk drawn taut, "is a reminder of what it means to carry this name. Success isn't a privilege. It's a requirement. And each of us has a role in ensuring it continues."

Her gaze moved slowly down the table, sharp and unhurried.

A sovereign taking inventory of her court.

Miriam nodded, untouched as ever.

Grace smiled, hands folded like a diplomat expecting applause.

Tori sat a touch straighter, her pale-blue eyes flicking toward Evelyn with quiet hunger.

It was all performance. Every gesture rehearsed.

And Evelyn, both audience and director, missed nothing.

She turned to Julia. Her voice warmed slightly.

"Julia, your work shaping the family's public image has been exemplary. That consistency doesn't go unnoticed."

"Thank you," Julia replied, poised. "We've worked hard."

Evelyn's lips curved, polite but bloodless. "Of course."

Her attention slid to Colton, who acknowledged her with a slight lift of his glass.

"And Colton, your discretion has proven... effective. It's men like you who ensure problems are handled before they become threats."

Colton inclined his head. Calm. Lethal.

Gideon stilled. Fingers curled beneath the table. Shoulders taut.

He knew the rhythm of her speeches.

Knew what came next.

The strike.

Evelyn's gaze turned to him like a tide pulling in. Certain. Unstoppable.

The glass in her hand balanced perfectly: weaponized elegance.

"Confidence is important, Gideon," she said, softening the edge of her tone with enough warmth to be mistaken for concern. "I trust you're prepared to defend your choices when the cracks begin to show. Because they will."

The pause wasn't silence.

It was suffocation.

Tori glanced toward him, lips twitching.

Alex, for once, said nothing.

Sebastian leaned back, watching her the way gamblers do when the dice are still in the air.

Gideon didn't flinch.

"I stand by my choices, Mother," he said. "All of them."

Evelyn's smile returned—slower. Purposeful.

She lifted her glass, sipped, then set it down with the finality of a closing ledger.

"Let's hope so," she murmured. "Because those choices won't cost only you."

It wasn't a threat.

It was a collar.

And Gideon felt the weight of it tighten, link by link.

Conversation resumed. Laughter. Posed smiles.

The illusion of normalcy stretched brittle as spun glass.

From behind the bar, Arden saw the shift in Gideon's posture. The way he looked at his drink a second too late.

Anyone else might've missed it.
But she felt it.
Like pressure before a storm.
A war fought in silence. Formality as armor.
No blood. But the wounds were fresh.
When the Blackwells finally departed, the room exhaled.
It wasn't relief.
Just release.
Their absence wasn't escape.
It was an echo.
Arden resumed her routine—wiping counters, replacing bottles—comfortable repetition.
But her thoughts spun.
Their eyes. Their words.
All sharp-edged.
All designed to draw blood without a blade.
It wasn't an emotion pressing against her chest. Not yet. Just weight, dense and unrelenting.
The quiet that followed wasn't peace. It felt suspended, the air itself waiting.

GIDEON APPROACHED the bar more slowly than usual, every step weighted. He stopped just short of her, one hand anchoring on the counter, the other curling restlessly at his hip.
His expression was shadowed. His control dimmed.
"You held your ground."
His voice was low. Even.
But something lived beneath it.
Pride, maybe.
Arden exhaled, and a half-smile ghosted across her lips. "They're...a lot."
But he didn't deflect. Didn't offer comfort dressed up as reassurance. Only truth, simple and stark.
"They're dangerous."
The warning was quiet but unmistakable.
He leaned in slightly, just enough for her to feel it: the heat of him, the gravity, the tension he carried like a second pulse. "Arden, they notice everything. And they don't forget."
The words landed, but fear wasn't what moved through her first. It was friction. Heat. Him.
His tension.
His restraint.
Her pulse jumped, but her voice held. "I can handle it."

Her hand hovered near his, fingertips almost brushing.

He didn't pull back.

He only watched her.

The silence stretched between them, delicate and exposed, neither of them looking away until something in his shoulders eased and his expression softened.

"I know you can."

He exhaled, quiet and heavy. "I need to head to Hawthorne."

His tone flattened again, control sliding back into place. "There's something I need to handle. Tonight."

Arden's brow furrowed. "It's late. Can't it wait?"

"It should." His lips curved faintly, but the smile never touched his eyes. "They don't wait, though. The moment they leave a room, the board changes. And if I don't move, someone else pays for it."

There was no anger in his voice. Only exhaustion, and the bitter clarity of a man who had been bearing too much for too long.

She studied him—the set of his jaw, the wear behind his eyes. "Do you ever get tired of it?"

"Every damn day."

No hesitation.

No facade.

"But if I walk away, there's no one left to stop them."

The truth cracked something open.

Then, slowly, tentatively, his fingers brushed her arm.

Just a touch. Barely there.

But it undid her all the same.

"Don't let them get in your head," he said, softer now. Not a warning this time. A reassurance. "They'll never see all you're made of. But I do."

Her throat tightened.

She nodded, small but certain. "Be careful."

"Always."

Then he stepped away.

Gone.

The space he left behind filled with cold. With silence. With everything he couldn't say.

Arden turned back to her work, and the faint clink of glass against wood became the only sound in the room. But the air hadn't cleared. It hung heavy, thick in her lungs and sharp at her spine.

A shadow that refused to leave.

❦

When she finally stepped outside, the cool air should have cleared her mind.

Instead, it seemed to press in tighter, carrying the city's silence with it—not soothing, not empty, but coiled.

A sound came from somewhere behind her.

Heels on pavement.

Arden kept walking and forced herself to breathe, each step measured, deliberate, too aware of the space at her back. She glanced over her shoulder once.

Nothing.

But nothing had never been the same as safety.

The city had too many shadows, and tonight they felt closer than usual.

———

He watched her move through a room that didn't deserve her.

She did not belong here.

Not among these polished ghosts with grasping hands and hollow smiles.

They thought they saw her.

Thought they could claim her fire.

Fools.

She wasn't meant to be held.

Not by them.

Not by him.

She was vivid. Untamed.

A wildfire given form, meant to be worshiped or burned by, not contained.

And her voice—God, her voice.

Not soft or sweet.

It struck like flint to stone.

Rough-edged. Intentional.

It stayed in the air long after she was gone.

And tonight, she had spoken to him.

Unwitting.

Unknowing.

But his name on her tongue.

The sound of it curled through him like smoke before the spark.

Slow. Intoxicating.

But she wasn't alone in her spotlight.

He saw them too.

The drunk at the bar,

Leaning too close.

The man in the corner with eyes too slick, too heavy.

Hunger disguised as interest.

AND GIDEON.
She softened for him.
And it twisted something dark inside.
Because that wasn't a glance. It was trust.
Misplaced. Foolish. Dangerous.

OH, Little Fire. Can't you see?

BENEATH THAT POLISHED CALM, Blackwell's a wolf.
And wolves smile when they bare their teeth.
They think they know you.
Think they can survive you.
They think they understand the burn. They don't.
Only he ever could.
His fists curled tighter as she smiled at Gideon.
Crescent moons carved into his skin.
She didn't need a man to tame her.
She needed one who would kneel in the fire and call it devotion.
Who wouldn't flinch when the heat rose.
Who would stoke it higher.
She didn't need saving.
She needed someone who'd burn for her.
They would never deserve her.
But he would.

CHAPTER 20

Blood & Leverage

The private lounge of the Blackwell estate glowed with low golden light. The air was steeped in old money and older rules, heavy with tradition, silence, and expectations no one said aloud.

Across from his mother, Alex Blackwell swirled his bourbon in slow, idle circles, the amber catching the light, performing under her gaze. The silence between them was denser than the cut crystal in his hand. Inescapable.

Evelyn sat upright, every inch composed. Not a single silver hair dared stray.

The teacup in front of her stayed untouched—just another part of the scene, more ornament than beverage.

This wasn't a conversation meant for warmth.

"You're distracted," she said evenly. Cool. Observant. "That's unlike you."

Alex took a slow sip, exhaled through his nose. "You wanted to talk business."

"I said I wanted to talk about family," she corrected, each word threaded with steel.

His smirk was faint. Bitter. Almost a sneer. "And you usually don't see a difference."

Her gaze narrowed enough to register displeasure.

"Family is business. And you, Alexander, are not holding up your end of the deal."

He set his glass down with a muted clink; his jaw tightened. "If this is about Cate—"

"Of course it's about Cate." Her voice didn't rise. "And the fact that she's failed at the only expectation that matters in this family."

His grip on the glass tightened. "That isn't something we can control."

Evelyn tapped her fingers against the armrest.

"Then perhaps you should take control of the situation." A pause. Calculated. "Cate may be incapable. But science has its... advantages."

A humorless huff escaped him. He leaned back in an attempt to stretch the tension from his neck. "You're pitching IVF like it's part of a quarterly strategy meeting."

"It is." Her words snapped like bone. "So is legacy."

"An investment in the future of this family. And currently, it's yielding no return."

He dragged a hand down his face. Irritation flared beneath the polished exterior.

"She's doing everything she can. We both are. But I suppose that's not good enough for you."

Her expression didn't shift.

"No. It isn't."

Silence settled. Thick. Choking.

Her tone cooled further. The air shifted with it.

"And while we're on the topic of your other... *deficiencies*—"

His jaw worked. "Here we go."

"I trust you haven't been foolish enough to try and remedy the situation elsewhere."

His posture stayed still, composed. But something in him tightened.

"You're reaching."

A quiet, dismissive laugh. "Please. Don't insult me." She leaned forward, voice dipping lower. Sharper.

"Let me make myself clear: I will not tolerate some bastard crawling out of the woodwork ten years from now, waving a blood claim."

Alex's smirk returned, but it had teeth now. "Worried about the family name being tarnished by some stray?"

"I'm worried about cleaning up another one of your messes."

He shook his head. "Relax. I know how to be discreet."

She arched a brow. "Do you?"

The question dangled, pointed and barbed.

"If you insist on your indulgences, fine. But if a Blackwell heir is to be born, it will be with our approval. On our terms."

Alex's mouth curved, all edge. "You always did make motherhood sound like a hostile takeover."

Her silence was answer enough.

"This family wasn't built on love, Alex. It was built on legacy. One you've yet to secure."

The words scraped something raw in him, but he buried it. He always did.

"Cate is trying," he said, voice tight. "We both are."

She gave him a long, unreadable look. Then leaned back, bored with the entire exchange.

"Try harder."

The silence that followed wasn't empty.

It pulsed with tension.

He finished his bourbon and set the glass down with finality. It rang like punctuation.

"You know," he murmured, not quite looking at her, "Gideon might not be the heir you wanted, but at least you don't have to remind him of his responsibilities every time he walks through the damn door."

Evelyn's lips curved. A phantom smile.

"That's because he understands the stakes."

Alex gave a short, humorless laugh, then he stood.

"Well, this has been enlightening."

She watched him rise. Composed. Unmoved. "It always is."

"Gideon may not want this family. But he understands it. And that's what makes him dangerous."

Alex stilled mid-step. *"Dangerous?"*

Evelyn swirled her tea with slow elegance, watching the spiral form.

"He thinks he can separate himself from us. That blood is something you can outrun with enough distance or disdain."

She finally looked up. Cold. Calculating. Like a knife behind fine china.

"But blood always leaves a trail."

He said nothing.

"And while you wrestle with your... domestic failure," she continued, "Gideon's been making decisions. Quiet ones. Strategic ones. And they concern me."

Alex lifted his brow, amused. "What decisions?"

She set her teacup down. The porcelain kissed the table with a soft, deliberate sound.

"Miss Rivers."

His expression flickered with amusement, mostly.

"The bartender?"

He took another sip of bourbon. No concern. No worry. Just mild interest.

"That's cute."

Evelyn said nothing. She didn't have to. She simply watched him, letting silence do the work.

He shook his head—dismissive, certain she was overreacting. "So what's the play?"

Her smile was serene. Her gaze? Surgical.

"One problem at a time, darling. For now, worry about yours."

He gave a shallow nod: not agreement, but acknowledgment. He didn't see the threat.

Not yet.

Arden Rivers was a passing novelty. A flicker of interest.

That was how Alex saw it.

But Evelyn? She saw more.

As Alex moved toward the door, she reached for her phone without hesitation. Dialed.

The door swung shut with a muted finality, but the warning stayed.

One ring.

"Colton," she said.

Calm. Controlled. Dangerous.

"We need to talk."

The late afternoon sun filtered through the heavy curtains, catching on the cup and saucer in Evelyn's hand. She sat perfectly still, as though posed for a portrait, every movement calculated down to the tilt of her teacup.

Colton lounged across from her with the ease of a man born into power and shaped by shadow. He didn't posture. He didn't need to. Presence radiated from him, quiet and dark and absolute.

"So," Evelyn murmured, setting her cup down with a gentle clink that carried more weight than porcelain should, "how is my wayward son?"

Colton's smirk was slow, indulgent. "Predictable. Still brimming with that signature moral superiority. And clinging to that bartender like she's the last hill he'll die on."

Evelyn's fingers drummed once, light and rhythmic, against the armrest. "Is that so?"

"He told me to keep my distance," Colton drawled, leaning forward just enough to show he was paying attention. "But I'm guessing you knew that."

Her smile was a flicker, polished and practiced and devoid of warmth.

"Gideon has always confused loyalty with weakness," she said smoothly. "It makes him easy to wound."

She studied Colton with a gaze sharpened for weak points. "And what do you make of her?"

He gave a low whistle. "Arden Rivers."

A pause followed as he considered the name.

"Not your typical distraction," he said. "She's got grit. Doesn't flinch. Doesn't fold. I'll give her that."

He tilted his head, almost admiring.

"She's not easy to shake."

Evelyn's expression sharpened. "Perhaps it's time someone did."

Colton's brows lifted, amused. "Is that an order?"

Her eyes didn't flicker. "A suggestion. A pressure test. You've been watching her. Let's not pretend otherwise."

He didn't bother denying it.

"But observation is passive," she continued. "What I want is impact. Nudge where it matters. Apply weight where it fractures."

She took a slow sip of tea.

"And if she proves...fragile—"

Her cup landed gently in its saucer.

Colton's grin stretched, edged with something feral. "She breaks. I'll make sure of it."

Evelyn reclined, the very image of satisfied calculation. "That's what I expected to hear."

Colton rose, straightening the cuffs of his shirt with bored elegance. "Gideon thinks she's untouchable. As if distance could protect her from bloodlines."

A pause.

A smirk.

"But we both know there's no such thing."

Evelyn's voice barely rose, but the words wrapped around the room like a noose. "Everyone becomes a Blackwell problem eventually."

Colton chuckled, darkly amused, and moved toward the door. Just before leaving, he turned back.

"I'll be watching."

The door shut with a decisive click.

And for one rare, private moment, Evelyn was alone with the thought she had refused to speak aloud.

Gideon wasn't merely rebelling anymore.

He was choosing.

And if Arden Rivers truly had his heart, then it was time to remind him.

Legacy would outlast love.

And in this family, legacy never lost.

CHAPTER 21

Danger at the Edges

The season's first warning rode the wind, threading cold air through Gideon's coat.

He stood beneath a streetlight that flickered overhead, casting jagged light across the bones of a building time had nearly buried. Cracked bricks. Boarded windows. A structure sagging beneath the weight of everything it had been forced to carry.

Across the broken pavement, a small group of tenants huddled close, drawn together by quiet fear, their silhouettes tight with unease. A boy's small hand tightened around his mother's, his fingers dark against her weathered palm, while his sneaker skimmed the broken curb with a soft scrape. Just behind them, a teenage girl tugged her backpack higher, her braids falling forward across her shoulder as she curled an arm around her sister. Their matching backpacks hung like shields across thin frames.

They looked as if they had just returned from school only to find the ground shifting beneath them.

Again.

Across the lot, Colton Blake leaned against a sleek black sedan, a monument to everything this place was not. His suit was sharp, his posture easy, his smirk as deliberate as the car's shine beneath the cold light. Indifference draped across him like a custom coat.

"You really think you can hold out?" he asked, his voice curling through the silence like a fuse waiting to catch. He gestured toward the building, contempt bleeding into every syllable. "This isn't a charity drive. Push too hard, and you'll find out how high the price gets."

The crunch of gravel under Gideon's oxfords cut through the night.

Slow steps.

Controlled.

Final.

"What the hell are you doing here, Colton?"

Colton turned leisurely, dragging out the moment as if it cost him nothing. The smirk stayed put.

"Cousin," he drawled, mock affection coating the word like cheap sugar. "Offering a little...guidance."

"Guidance?" Gideon's voice went flat. "This is intimidation."

Colton shrugged, tapping the hood as if his name had already been carved into the blueprints. Through the window, Gideon caught the edge of architectural renderings spread across the seat. He didn't need to see them clearly to know what they were.

Steel and glass. Towers of ego masquerading as progress.

Not homes.

Not for them.

"This neighborhood's had its time," Colton said, smoothing his sleeve. "The future doesn't wait for sentiment."

It hit like a slap. The same poison that had killed Richard II's dream, now dressed in finer clothes.

Two legacies warred inside Gideon.

Richard II: *A legacy built on broken backs will break under its own weight.*

Richard III: *Mercy is weakness. Control the board or be a pawn.*

"Back off," Gideon said, his voice sharp enough to draw blood. "You're not redeveloping. You're displacing."

Colton leaned in, voice dropping. "You think you're any different from the rest of us? Evelyn doesn't."

Press where it matters. See what cracks.

Gideon's jaw flexed.

But he held the line.

A new sound cut through the cold.

Low. Steady.

A cane against concrete.

An elderly woman stepped forward, her frame slight, her spine unbowed. Her hand trembled—not with fear, but with years. With survival. Her voice was quiet, but it carried.

"Your grandfather told us this place was ours. Not just buildings, but a future."

The words settled in Gideon's chest.

Not like sentiment.

Like anchors.

Richard II again: *Power protects. Or it destroys. You decide which.*

The mother beside her tightened her grip on her son's hand.

"Maybe you're different," she whispered to Gideon. "Maybe you haven't forgotten."

The older woman rested her hand gently on the mother's shoulder, generations of grit held in a single touch. Then her eyes found Gideon's, steady and unblinking.

"We've seen Blackwells come and go," she said. "But you—you've got your grandfather's eyes."

Colton scoffed, stepping away from the car.

"Aunt Evelyn won't let you wear that mask forever," he muttered. "We all play our parts. Time you figured out yours."

His engine kicked on with a low snarl. Tires spat gravel as he sped off, leaving only the reek of exhaust behind.

But it wasn't the sound of Colton's car that stayed with Gideon.

It was the shuffle of sneakers on pavement.

The tap of a cane.

The whisper of hope from a woman who should have had none left to give.

This was never only about him. It was about the promise Richard II had made, the one Gideon would keep if he had to carve the vow into his own bones.

He stood in the cold, breath ghosting in the air, fists still at his sides.

They would not lose their homes.

Not to Evelyn.

Not to Colton.

Not while he had blood left to spill.

❧

THE MARBLE BAR gleamed beneath the sconces' soft glow, all elegance and tension waiting for someone to name it.

Gideon stood behind it, his fingers trailing over the chilled surface, smudges vanishing almost as quickly as they appeared. A low jazz melody drifted through the room, its calm too smooth, too smug, against the chaos he carried.

Colton's smirk.

The old woman's trembling grip.

A pair of scuffed sneakers belonging to a boy who didn't yet know how quickly the world could shift beneath his feet.

Power should protect.

Not devour.

Footsteps interrupted the quiet.

Marco emerged from the back with a bucket of ice, rolling his shoulders as though trying to shake the night off. He saw Gideon and registered everything in a single look.

He set the bucket down and braced a hand on the counter, relaxed in posture and alert in every other way.

"What demon's got you tonight?" he asked, voice low. Ice clinked softly as he filled the wells with mechanical precision.

"Colton." The name landed like a blade against marble. "He was at one of my grandfather's buildings. Threatening tenants."

Marco's hands paused. The calm in his eyes evaporated on impact.

"Same playbook?"

Gideon nodded, reaching for the Blanton's out of habit more than want. "Bolder than usual. Evelyn's fingerprints are all over it."

Marco exhaled slowly and folded his arms. "Your grandfather wouldn't have stood for this."

The words hit hard.

Richard II had left something sturdy. Enduring. Legacy with roots, not wreckage.

Richard III had hollowed it from the inside and dressed the ruin in progress.

Now Gideon was left to hold the line in a war he hadn't declared but couldn't abandon.

Marco reached across the counter, plucked the bottle from Gideon's grip, and set it aside.

"You carry his name now," he said. "So tell me. What are you going to do with it?"

The question lingered like a match struck but not yet burning.

Something in Gideon locked into place. The weight in his chest solidified.

"I won't let it stand."

Marco studied him, then nodded, sharp and approving.

"Good." He returned to the wells. "Someone's gotta remind them what a real Blackwell looks like."

The air shifted. Less uncertain now. More like steel hammered flat and ready.

Gideon couldn't become his grandfather, but he could honor him. He could protect what mattered, even if it meant setting fire to every thread of inheritance binding him to the rest of them.

Some things were worth more than a name.

❦

Streetlights spilled fractured gold across Arden's midnight blue car, their glow catching on the paint in flickers of ember and shadow.

Her trunk was a study in precision: boxes labeled, supplies neatly stacked, every item in its place like a ritual against entropy. The kind of order born from a life that punished forgetfulness.

She straightened, box in hand.

"What are you doing out here?"

Through the city's noise, she heard him. Always calm. Always clear.

Arden turned, her lips curving into a dry smile as she swiped a loose strand of hair aside. Streetlight caught her eyes—keen, steady, aware.

"Stocking up," she said, hefting the box as if it were second nature. "Marco's list. I hate being unprepared."

Gideon drifted closer, his gaze skimming the trunk. Even the emergency kit was packed with intention: jumper cables looped tight, tools secured like they had been checked twice.

"Marco usually guards his supplies like a dragon hoarding gold."

Arden's smirk came quick, conspiratorial. "He was swamped." She shifted the box without thinking, her grip sure. "I like knowing what's in front of me. What to expect."

His brow lifted slightly, his eyes drifting to the car. "Still hanging on to this thing?"

For now.

"It's not made for city streets," she said, "but it's reliable. When I needed to leave, it never let me down."

The words lingered between them, like a memory she hadn't meant to unwrap.

In the distance, a siren wailed faintly. The pulse of the city filled the space they hadn't.

Gideon nodded, his voice lower now. "Manhattan's not big on mercy."

"Neither am I."

She slammed the trunk shut, the echo sharper than it should have been.

"And this thing's saved my ass more than once."

"You're full of surprises, Rivers."

"Says the billionaire playing bartender."

She adjusted the box on her hip, posture unshakable. For a moment, she looked untouchable—carved from the light instead of merely standing in it.

"Let me help you with that." He stepped in, reaching for the box, and the faint trace of her perfume moved with her: vanilla threaded with something rarer, something sharp. Barely there, but it landed in him like a memory.

She shifted the box just out of reach, her smirk deepening.

"I've got it."

Light. Resolute. No room for argument.

Gideon exhaled a dry breath. "Even legends need backup."

She glanced up, eyes glinting. "Who says I'm not vetting your secret identity?"

A low laugh broke from him, real and unarmored.

"Fine," he said. "But don't come whining when Marco doubles your workload for making it look too easy."

"Worth the risk."

Silence stretched between them.

Not empty.

Full.

The city's noise fell away, and for a moment, the quiet almost felt personal.

Gideon watched her move, measured and focused. Even the way she held the box said she was used to carrying more than people saw.

She didn't prepare for chaos.

She braced for it.

"I should get this inside before Marco starts barking." Her smirk flickered, her eyes locking with his. That look—half dare, half insight—always left him off balance. "You should rest. Saving the world's a full-time gig."

A chuckle slipped out of him. "I'll think about it."

She met his gaze for a moment too long. Something unreadable flickered behind it—curiosity, maybe. Or understanding. Then the guard slid back into place, though the corner of her mouth curved with defiance.

She moved past him, close enough to leave behind a trace of warmth. "Careful, Blackwell. You'll bruise that pretty head of yours."

He watched her disappear through the side door, light trailing after her.

Steady.

Unshaken.

Entirely her.

That strength, that rooted certainty, stayed with him like a melody he couldn't shake.

THEN, movement.

A shadow peeled itself from the alley wall, too fluid to be wind.

It was only a flicker at the edge of Gideon's vision. Subtle. Wrong. The kind of quiet that wasn't merely quiet at all, but loaded.

Alive.

Watching.

Every nerve in his body went taut, a pulse beneath his skin bracing to strike. His jaw tightened as his gaze swept the alley, the rooftops, the deep pockets of shadow gathered between buildings.

He wasn't looking.

He was hunting.

Something had shifted. He knew it in his bones, in the old, animal part of himself that understood danger before reason caught up. The city seemed to hold its breath around him.

He had seen how quickly the dark could take people. How easily it could swallow them whole.

And Arden?

She burned too bright to be lost to it.

Not while he stood breathing. Not while he could still put himself between her and the storm.

Even if it meant becoming the monster he was trying to fight.

———

From the shadows, he waited.

She moved like the world bent to her will. Even the streetlight existed just to catch her—the glint of her dark brown hair, the cut of her blue eyes through the dark.

Every detail, a gift.

Every motion, a scripture to be memorized.

Her scent lingered in the air. A whisper he could almost taste.

Her confidence wasn't armor. He knew better.

Every precise step, every deliberate gesture came from someone who'd forged strength from broken edges.

He'd traced those fractures. Memorized them.

The hesitation when someone moved too fast. The way she clocked exits before faces.

Beautiful. Telling.

But Gideon was one of those cracks.

The way she softened around him, how her guarded edges dulled into something intimate, something infuriating. It clawed at him, hot and visceral.

Her laugh, light and genuine in Gideon's presence, was a blade sliding between his ribs.

She was giving Gideon parts of herself that didn't belong to him.

Each smile, each lingering look—stolen moments. Not hers to give.

She didn't see it yet. Couldn't understand.

Every piece of her belonged to him.

He knew her rhythms better than she knew herself.

7:43 PM—almost always.

The way she packed her trunk. The way her fingers gripped her keys before she even closed the door behind her.

His breath quickened as she vanished into the club's gleaming façade.

For a moment, she was gone, absorbed into a world that didn't deserve her— polished perfection could never reflect her truth.

Arden wasn't made for their shallow kingdom of false smiles and hidden knives.

She needed something real.

Someone who saw straight to her soul and never looked away.

If she stayed, they'd smother her fire.
Piece by piece.
Men like Gideon always did.
Blind men, men who mistook a wildfire for something they could hold.

H*E* M*ELTED INTO THE NIGHT.*
The darkness folded around him.
Arden Rivers was already his.
He'd spent weeks learning her. Mapping every flicker of hesitation, every glance over her shoulder, feeling him there.
Could she?
The thought sent a shiver through him, electric and unsteady. A volatile mix of certainty and need.
Gideon Blackwell couldn't save her.
The club's gleaming walls couldn't contain her.
His footsteps fell silent into the pavement, merging with the city's pulse and the tight rhythm of his thoughts.

A*LL IT WOULD TAKE WAS* time.
Time for her to see.
Time for her to understand.
And when that moment came—when her defenses crumbled, when her eyes finally opened to the truth, his Little Fire would understand.
They weren't just drawn together.
They were fated.

❦

The cold slipped beneath Arden's jacket like a blade, clean and unapologetic.
Around her, the city lived and lingered: horns echoing down the block, laughter spilling from a window, an engine snarling at a stalled light. But something had shifted.
Subtle.
Wrong.
A disturbance too quiet to name.
She didn't see it at first. She felt it: a prickle at the base of her neck, that whisper of eyes waiting in the dark.
Then she saw it.
A single rose.
Blood red and flawless, resting against the deep midnight paint of her car.

Its petals curled open like a confession laid bare, waiting to be heard.

The night dimmed. Sounds dulled.

No.

The memory slammed into her, cold and unrelenting.

Morgantown.

A concrete garage.

A rose tucked beneath her wiper blade.

A whisper that had followed her for months.

Her stomach dropped as the voice that lived in her nightmares found her again.

You can't keep running.

Her hands twitched at her sides.

Keys or phone?

Move.

But she didn't.

Not this time.

She wasn't that girl.

One step. Another.

Her boots crunched over pavement until she stood in front of the rose, every muscle pulled tight, her chest drawn hard beneath the cold. It was too perfect. No thorns. No jagged edge.

She remembered the first one. Its stem had teeth.

A warning wrapped in beauty.

This wasn't that.

This was a message.

Clean. Intentional.

Her breath sharpened, heat coiling low in her gut as rage rose through the fear.

Try me.

She ripped the rose from the glass and crushed it in her palm.

Velvet petals gave beneath her grip. The bloom snapped with a sickening softness, and when she opened her hand, red fragments clung to her skin.

She let them fall.

The sidewalk didn't feel empty.

It felt watched.

A cab idled at the end of the block. A couple argued outside a bodega, their voices rising sharp against the cold. Three cars down, a black sedan sat tucked in shadow.

Too still.

Her jaw tensed.

She couldn't see inside.

But someone could see her.

She didn't flinch.

The door clicked open, then slammed shut. Locks engaged.

Her fingers curled around the steering wheel as she forced her breathing to even out.

Tomorrow, she would go back to the Krav Maga studio.

And the coward who left the rose?

They weren't going to break her.

Not again.

Not this time.

CHAPTER 22

A Fire in the Dark

The cold hit hard, sharp in her throat, but the heaviness in her chest didn't budge. She breathed out, the cold air catching it for a moment before it disappeared.

The city stirred: footsteps, steam, that sharp shriek underground she could never quite tune out.

She let out a slow breath and rolled her shoulders, but the tension stayed.

The rose lingered in her mind. That perfect, blood-red bloom: too pristine, too exact. Its smooth, thornless stem haunted her palm.

She hadn't slept much, but she'd woken up with one thought: *Not again.*

Upstairs in a converted warehouse, the Krav Maga studio pulsed with heat, windows misted over from the blur of bodies inside. That room was heat. Noise. Sweat. Control. Exactly what she needed.

The kind of place where fear had no footing.

Arden took the stairs in quick strides, hands flexing, bracing for impact, reflexes already primed.

The room was all grit and sweat—bare beams overhead, worn mats underfoot, the sharp bite of disinfectant mixing with leather and effort.

No distractions. Just motion.

"Morning, Arden!"

Kasha's voice rang out from behind the counter, all grin and caffeine-bright energy.

"Ready to knock someone on their ass today?"

Arden smirked, dropping her bag beside the cubbies. "More like get knocked on mine. But I'll take what I can get."

She wrapped her hands tight, pulled herself into the warm-up circle, and let the world shrink to nothing but breath and the thud of fists hitting pads.

The instructor didn't waste time: takedowns, defensive strikes, repetition until muscle overrode thought. Sweat poured down her back. Her arms ached. Her thighs burned.

And it helped.

The hour disappeared into grit and breath and bruises. When it was over, she sank against the wall, chest rising hard, muscles alive with a low, welcome burn.

"You've picked up speed," the instructor noted, giving her a short nod before moving on.

She gave a breathless, crooked smile. "That's the goal."

No fanfare. Just a glance, and he was gone.

Arden gathered her things and stepped back into the city's current. Her limbs throbbed, her pulse steady.

She wasn't that girl anymore.

Not the one from Morgantown.

Not the one who froze.

Not the one who let fear win.

❦

Just a few blocks down, tucked between a bookstore and a boutique, Arden's favorite café offered a hush the city hadn't touched. Ivy curled along the brick, and the old sign hung faded but familiar, as if it had been waiting for her.

Inside, warm light spilled over mismatched chairs and worn wood tables. The second she stepped in, the scent reached her—espresso and lavender, soft and grounding, settling into her chest like a name she hadn't heard in years.

"Lavender latte?" the barista called out, already halfway to pouring, a knowing grin tugging at her mouth.

"Make it a double," Arden said, pulling a bill from her pocket without looking.

The espresso machine kicked on with a soft whir, steady as breath.

She carried the cup to her usual corner, where sunlight slanted across the table just so, and wrapped both hands around the mug. The first sip moved through her slowly.

Bold espresso.

Just enough sweetness.

A floral finish that lingered.

For a few stolen minutes, she let herself breathe.

❦

The rest of the day passed uneventfully: errands, laundry, small tasks that served no real purpose beyond distraction.

Still, Arden couldn't stop replaying the moment outside her car.

The way the rose had waited.

The way it had made her feel.

Not afraid. Not anymore.

Watched.

By evening, she was back at The Blackwell Room, and she welcomed the rhythm of it—the structure, the simple and focused cadence of service. Polished counters. The clink of steel against glass. The reliable choreography of hands reaching, bottles lifting, liquor pouring clean.

She needed this. The ritual. The illusion of control.

Behind the bar, Marco was already halfway through setup. Fatima stacked glassware at the far end, bracelets catching the light each time she reached for another coupe.

"Busy night?" Arden asked.

"Manageable," Marco said, barely glancing up. "Steady, but not chaos."

She preferred those nights.

Enough to stay sharp.

Not enough to drown in.

So she slipped back into it: mixing, pouring, moving. Letting repetition wear down the restlessness curled at the base of her spine.

Near closing, the club had thinned to its regulars. Arden moved a rag across the bar, letting the quiet stretch a little longer than it needed to.

Then she heard it: Penny's voice, lilting and impossible to ignore.

"Hey."

Arden looked up, instantly suspicious. "Why do I feel like I'm about to regret this conversation?"

"Because you are. We're going out."

Arden groaned. "Nope."

"Oh, yes. Drinks. Dancing. Debauchery. The works."

"I'm tired."

"You're always tired."

"I've had a day."

"Exactly why you need a night."

Arden turned to Marco, desperate. "Marco, please."

"I'm with her."

"Traitor."

"You'll survive."

Penny arched a brow, smug. "Come on. You're already dressed like a sexy Bond villain. It'd be a shame to waste it."

Arden sighed and looked down at the bar, at the rag still folded beneath her hand. She thought about the rose. The unease. The quiet war she had fought all day to keep it from burrowing too deep. Maybe Penny had a point. Maybe one night of noise and bad decisions was better than going home to let fear sit beside her in the dark.

"Fine," Arden said. "One drink."

"Two," Penny corrected, looping her arm through Arden's. "And a few impulsive choices. They're good for the soul."

"This is probably a terrible idea, huh?"

"Obviously."

From across the room, Gideon watched.

He didn't speak. Didn't move.

He just stood there, glass in hand, eyes following every beat of her body language—the ease in her shoulders, the way Penny looped an arm through hers and pulled her toward the door like it was nothing. And maybe to her, it was.

But to him, it mattered.

He told himself it didn't. That she was free to go.

Free to laugh.

Free to leave without hesitation.

But when the door swung shut behind her, the sound of it echoed too loud.

Too final.

And something inside him went terrifyingly still.

———

He followed at a distance, never close enough to be seen. But always close enough to watch.

The crowd throbbed with light and sound, a living beast of bass and neon.

Music crawled through the floor, threading into bone like a second heartbeat.

Light fractured across the walls, casting flickering shadows that never stayed long enough to matter.

But none of it touched him.

Not the noise or the chaos.

Only her.

Arden moved like a clear note breaking through static—untouched, unshaken, effortless.

Penny, all wild limbs and clueless joy, tugged her toward the dance floor.

He watched the moment it shifted.

The hesitation in Arden's step.
The way her eyes swept the room's edges. Always scanning. Always attuned.
Then she let go.
And the music took her.
She didn't dance to be seen. Didn't perform for the crowd.
It wasn't rehearsed or polished. It was purer. A pulse from within.
Instinct.
A current all her own.
She was the flame in a sea of noise.
Light against a backdrop that never deserved her.
His Little Fire.
He didn't move. Didn't blink. Studied. Memorized. Possessed in silence.
Someone moved too close.
Heat flared beneath his skin. A fracture split through him.
The man leaned in, too familiar.
Arden shifted slightly, polite and practiced.
A faint smile. A measured step back. The space reclaimed.
She kept her composure.
But the stranger had been close enough to touch her.
Close enough to remind him how easily people forgot what she was worth.
His hands curled, fists buried deep in his coat.
Not yet.
Tonight wasn't for blood.
It was for learning.
She returned to the bar, breath short, cheeks flushed.
Penny that made her laugh, full and unguarded.
It gutted him.
That sound. That light.
She touched her hair again. Fingertips at her jaw, soft and unthinking. That tilt of her head—like she knew he was watching and wanted him to see. As if she were daring him to look.
She had no idea what she did to people.
No clue how the room shifted around her.
She didn't need the noise.
She didn't need the crowd.
She needed someone who saw her.
And he did.

*L*ATER, *she and Penny stepped into the cool air of the night.*
He stayed across the street.
Still. Watching.

Penny flagged down a car.

Horns cut through the wet air. Tires hissed across slick asphalt. Rain teased the edges of the sky.

But all he saw was Arden.

She laughed again, quieter now. Worn at the edges.

It hit him low, dull and certain.

She climbed into the car.

For one breathless second, she was framed in light—whole, ethereal, his.

And she was gone.

She hadn't seen him.

She never did.

But that was all right.

Because one day, she would.

And when that day came?

There'd be no more distance.

No more shadows.

Only them.

The heavy bag rocked violently, metal clinking overhead as though it might give way. Gideon's breath hitched, every muscle straining, sweat slick across his skin.

Still, he kept going.

He paused only long enough to catch his reflection in the mirror: jaw set, eyes dark, the face of a man who looked as though sleep had forgotten him weeks ago.

Colton's smirk.

The old woman's trembling hands.

The shuffle of a child's sneakers on cracked pavement.

His grandfather's voice rose through the chaos, steady and unyielding.

Power should shield, not consume.

Gideon slammed another punch into the bag, his knuckles burning in protest.

Not enough.

His vision narrowed until all he could feel was the need—raw and unrelenting—to hit, to break, to do something with the violence crawling beneath his skin.

And then he saw her.

Arden, standing at the bar, smirking at Penny. Her laugh drifting into the night. Her body turning toward the door.

Walking away without looking back.

The image hit harder than any punch.

A surge of adrenaline ripped through him, and he struck again, so hard the chain snapped taut and the bag swung wildly from its hook.

She was out there.

Dancing.

Laughing.

Drinking.

With strangers who didn't know her. Who hadn't earned that smile.

He had no right to feel this way.

He knew that.

It didn't stop the fury from coiling low in his gut. Didn't stop the ugly, helpless need to rip the bag from its hinges and reduce something—anything—to wreckage.

One final hit.

He stumbled back, bracing his hands on his knees, breath heaving, shirt soaked, every muscle burning.

But the ache in his chest remained.

Why did he care so much?

The answer hovered, dangerous and undeniable.

Because she wasn't just anyone.

Because she was flame and grit, sharp lines and soft silences. Untouchable.

And he wanted to touch.

Straightening, he grabbed a towel and scrubbed the sweat from his face. His reflection caught him again, jaw still set, eyes still hollowed by too much wanting and not enough sleep.

He barely recognized himself.

Holding back had always been second nature. Safer. Cleaner.

But tonight?

Tonight, he wasn't sure he wanted safe at all.

His phone buzzed.

He reached for it half-distracted, until he saw her name.

> Arden: Trivia tomorrow night. Bring Dan. Penny's making me go, so you're coming too. No excuses, Blackwell.

It wasn't an invitation.

It was a dare.

He stared at the message, something in his chest loosening against his will.

She wanted him there. Not for business. Not for appearances. Because she wanted him.

Maybe not the way he wanted her.

Not yet.

But it was something.

He thumbed out a reply.

> You'll regret letting Penny talk you into this. But fine. I'll see you there.

He hit send and tossed the phone onto the bench, but his hand hovered there, temptation tugging hard enough to feel like weakness.

Just one more message.

He shouldn't.

He knew that.

Still, his fingers moved.

> Are you home safe?

The pause stretched long enough to make his pulse kick.

> Arden: You checking on me, Blackwell?

He exhaled, his mouth twitching into a small smile.

> You shouldn't be walking around this late. Humor me.

Another pause.

He could almost picture her: head tilted, eyes narrowed, weighing how much softness she was willing to give him.

> Arden: Humoring you. I'm home.

Relief hit harder than he expected.

Gideon sank onto the bench, phone in hand. There were more things he could say. Things he wanted to say. Things better men might have known how to say without making them sound like possession, or confession, or a threat.

But he didn't send any of them.

Instead, he let the silence hold what he couldn't.

Tonight, she had let him in.

Tomorrow, he would get closer.

And for once, he didn't fight the full force of wanting her.

CHAPTER 23

The Art of Overthinking

Sunlight cut through the curtains in narrow streaks, pooling across the floor. Arden moved quietly through the apartment, leopard slippers soft against the wood, her black tank top clinging to sleep-warm skin and her lounge pants hanging low on her hips, as if the night hadn't quite let go.

She reached for her favorite mug. Coffee filled the air, comforting as breath, and for once, the morning felt still. Peaceful.

Across the room, Penny sprawled across the couch in flamingo-print pajamas—top and bottom just obnoxious enough to match. Her lavender-streaked hair was knotted into a chaotic bun, her laptop teetering on one knee, fingers frozen mid-keystroke.

"Morning," Arden said, raising her mug in lazy salute. "Love the birds. Subtle."

Penny didn't look up. "Don't start. I'm on the verge of throwing this thing through a window." She groaned and flopped the laptop down beside her. "Revision number eight, and he says it's 'close but not quite.' What does that even mean?"

Arden took a slow sip, the warmth settling behind her ribs. "It means he has no idea what he actually wants but enjoys watching you guess."

Penny gave her a dry look. "Wow. So helpful."

"Thank you for your insight, Dr. Sarcasm."

Arden crossed the room and eased onto the armrest of the couch. "Alright, genius. Walk me through it. Forget the revisions for a second. What was the original idea?"

Penny rubbed at her temples. "He said 'sleek and bold,' but every time I went modern, he shot it down. Tried minimalist. Still wrong."

"So maybe what he wants isn't what he said. What else did he tell you?"

Penny launched into a rant—half logic, half caffeine-fueled chaos—and Arden let her go, tossing in sarcastic quips and just enough nudging to keep the gears turning.

Then Penny stopped mid-word.

Her eyes widened. "Wait." She bolted upright and grabbed her sketchpad. "That's it. He doesn't want bold or edgy. He wants classic. Familiar, but sharp around the edges. I've been overthinking it. He's not after a statement. He wants something that feels like it belonged before you even noticed it."

She began sketching with new energy, the tension bleeding from her shoulders.

Arden sipped her coffee, smug and satisfied. "Told you. Sometimes you need someone annoying to poke holes in your thought process."

"You're insufferable," Penny muttered, but her smile gave her away. "Also—thanks. Talking it out actually helped."

"Anytime." Arden stretched and stood, rolling her shoulders. "But if he pushes for Revision Nine, I'm emailing him a PowerPoint titled 'This Is Final.™'"

"Deal." Penny's grin turned wicked. "Now, speaking of things that are 'close but not quite'—let's talk about Gideon."

Arden paused mid-sip, eyes narrowing. "What about him?"

"Oh, come on. The tension. The looks. The way you two circle each other like characters in a slow-burn romance with excellent lighting? Tells me something's happening."

Arden didn't answer at first. Her mug stayed near her mouth, but she wasn't drinking. Her teeth caught her lower lip, barely there; a nervous habit she hated because Penny never missed anything.

She sank into the cushions with a quiet breath. "I don't know, Pen." Her voice had gone softer. "There's something there. I haven't felt anything in a long time."

Penny's teasing vanished in an instant. "And that scares you?"

Arden nodded slowly, thumb running along the rim of her mug. "It's been years since I trusted anyone. Chad let me down. So did my parents. Letting someone close feels..." She trailed off, the words catching behind her teeth. "It feels dangerous."

Penny leaned in, her fingers pressing gently against Arden's arm—a silent promise, steady and sure. "But Gideon's different?"

Arden looked down. "He feels different. That's the part that terrifies me." Her voice barely rose above a whisper. "What if I let my guard down, and he ends up proving me right—just like everyone else?"

"I can't promise anything," Penny said. "But from where I'm sitting? He sees you. All of you. And he's still there. That's rare, Arden. It might be worth the risk."

Arden didn't reply right away. She only nodded once, slowly.

Maybe she believed it.

Maybe she wanted to.

Penny let the moment breathe, then grinned. "Okay—emotional vulnerability break is officially over. I need to wrap this sketch, and then we're pre-gaming for trivia night. I have a title to defend."

Arden chuckled, shaking her head. "If you start trash-talking too early, you're going solo."

"Please. You need me. I carry the team."

"Don't tempt me."

"I will throw you into traffic."

Penny didn't look back. "Love you too," she called, pencil already moving again.

The tightness in Arden's chest didn't vanish, but it loosened; just a little, just enough.

❧

Later, Arden tugged on her favorite leather jacket, the rasp of the zipper satisfying in a way she didn't care to examine. Grounding, maybe. Beneath it, the black lace top traced her skin, softness tucked under armor in a language her body understood too well.

Across the apartment, Penny twirled dramatically, her dress flaring like a celebration in motion. "Let's go win," she announced, every inch a queen entering battle.

Arden lifted a brow. "Trivia's not judged on dramatic flair."

"First of all, it should be. Second, if it were, we'd already have a trophy."

Arden rolled her eyes and tugged her sleeve straight, trying not to think about how aware she was of the lace beneath the leather, or what kind of reckless little truth that awareness had become.

"So..." Penny's grin sharpened. "Think Gideon's going to show up?"

A pause.

Long enough to register.

"Maybe."

Outside, the city stretched before them, cool air brushing against Arden's skin with the faint bite of oncoming winter. Penny spun once for effect, because apparently the sidewalk was also a stage.

"You ready?"

Arden smiled. Not only at Penny, but at the moment itself; at the dangerous, glittering promise of what the night might become.

"Let's go."

Maybe she'd look up and find him already watching. Those gray eyes never missed much, and tonight, she wasn't sure she wanted to be missed.

CHAPTER 24

A Night of Trivial Pursuits

The brewery was alive with sound—low music, bursts of laughter, chairs scraping over old wood. Outside, golden light spilled across the cobblestones, more invitation than ambience. Inside, string lights drooped from the rafters, their glow softening the sharp lines of brick and wood.

The air was thick with hops and fresh bread, edged by something sweeter Arden couldn't quite place—caramel, maybe, or toasted sugar. Rich. Comforting. Like a memory baked into the walls.

She kept pace behind Penny, who moved quickly through the crowd, lavender-streaked curls bouncing wildly and violet dress catching the light with every step. Penny didn't simply enter a room; she rearranged it. People moved for her without knowing why, their smiles lingering long after she passed.

They claimed a table near the back, just far enough to take the edge off the noise but still close to the heartbeat of the room. Penny tossed her jacket onto a chair and surveyed her domain as if she'd been crowned queen of the misfits and liked the weight of it.

"This," she declared, arms wide, "is the perfect launch point for our trivia world domination."

Arden slid into her seat, lifting a brow. "You've already decided we're winning?"

"Winning isn't something I decide. It's something I am." Penny's grin turned sly. "Let's be real, though. It's the beer I'm loyal to. Victory's just the glitter garnish."

Before Arden could fire back, two familiar figures stepped into view.

Gideon.

He moved like he owned the room but had no need to prove it; calm, assured, his presence quiet but absolute. Black button-down. Dark jeans. Broad shoulders relaxed, eyes sharp. When his gaze found hers, it held for a second too long, and whatever flickered behind it wasn't quite amusement. Wasn't quite warning.

Beside him, Dan was all easy swagger and unbothered charm. His eyes caught the light, brown with the amber gleam they got when he was amused, and he stood with his hands tucked into his pockets as though the room had already agreed to like him.

He reached for Penny's hand without fanfare, that crooked grin sliding into place with practiced ease. "You must be Penelope. The way Arden talks about you, I was expecting fireworks the minute you walked in."

Penny's grin widened as she shook his hand. "And you must be Daniel. The way she talks about you, I was expecting someone taller."

Dan laughed, unoffended. At well over six feet, the jab was pure sport. "Touché. But at least I bring the charm. And let's lose the formalities. Only my dentist calls me Daniel."

"And only my mother calls me Penelope," she countered.

Gideon slid into the seat beside Arden without a word, his presence settling with a quiet gravity that pulled her awareness tighter. She didn't have to look to know he was there. Warm. Steady. His cologne lingered in the space between them, subtle and expensive, and her pulse kicked before she could pretend it hadn't.

Dan leaned forward, mock-serious. "Alright. Ground rules. Arden and Gideon versus Penelope and me. Balance of power. Keeps it fair."

Penny scoffed, arms crossed. "Fair? Please. That's completely weighted in our favor." Her sharp eyes cut to Gideon, teasing. "No offense, but you don't exactly radiate trivia night energy."

Gideon's brow lifted. "And you don't exactly radiate humility."

Penny's grin widened. "Oh, he's got teeth. This just got interesting."

"The game hasn't even started," Dan said, flashing Arden a grin, "and I already know this is going to be good."

Arden rolled her eyes, but her smile slipped through anyway. "You two are out of control."

"And yet, here you are," Dan said, raising his glass. "To victory. And to Penelope terrorizing half the room."

Penny clinked her drink against his with wicked delight. "Equal-opportunity menace, thank you very much."

The clamor of the brewery pressed around them, but at their table, something shifted. The energy sharpened. The space between words stretched. And when Gideon leaned in—shoulder brushing hers, breath barely grazing the air between them—Arden didn't flinch.

She felt it.

And she knew he did too.

Arden leaned back in her seat, one long leg crossing over the other, the black leather of her pants molding to every curve as if it had been stitched on with intention and a grudge. Effortless, except nothing about Arden had ever been effortless; she had simply learned to make survival look like style.

She reached for her drink, fingers curling around the glass with the kind of casual poise that didn't demand attention.

It commanded it.

And Gideon was already watching.

Heat flickered behind his heavy gaze. One hand rested on his glass, thumb tracing the rim in a slow, exact arc, as if control could be kept one circle at a time.

Her eyes lifted to his.

The buzz of the room dulled around them—voices, glass, the steady thump of trivia night, all of it pushed to the edges as their gazes locked. It wasn't permission. It was gravity.

For one breath, they held there, tension winding taut between them; a question unspoken, a challenge issued.

Then she turned away.

Smooth as smoke. As if she hadn't just set the air between them on fire and left him to burn in it.

Arden tipped her head toward the table, the corner of her mouth curving as she reached for the pen. "Don't worry," she said, voice light but edged. "I'll carry us."

Gideon's smirk was slow, crooked, and full of the kind of intent that settled low and stayed there. He leaned in, his voice pitched for her alone.

"You're supposed to say I'll carry you."

Her smile was pure mischief, a slow curve of trouble. "Where's the fun in that?"

That voice hit him like it always did. Sexy. Dangerous. Impossible to shake.

He exhaled slowly, flexing his hand once around the glass.

He couldn't get enough of her.

This woman.

Trivia began, but neither of them seemed to hear it. The game became noise, a flimsy excuse for the current running under the table, through the air, along every careful inch of space they pretended not to notice.

"The Hanging Gardens," Gideon said smoothly, answering the first question as if it were reflex.

Arden frowned, tapping the pen against the table. "I thought it was—wait. No. You're right."

She sighed for effect, then smiled, already past the part where she'd been wrong. "Fine."

His smirk deepened. "Glad you trust me."

She scoffed, brow arching. "Trust? Let's not get ahead of ourselves."

Gideon laughed under his breath, a quiet sound with an edge of certainty, as if he knew exactly how dangerous the night had already become.

Oh, she was in trouble.

And maybe she wanted to be.

ACROSS THE TABLE, Penny and Dan were chaos in motion.

Penny whispered wrong answers just loud enough to draw amused glances from nearby tables, her grin unapologetic. Dan played along with exaggerated disapproval, shaking his head like a man who hadn't already surrendered to her particular brand of mayhem.

The host's voice cut through the chatter, booming with theatrical flair. "All right, everyone! The next category is... Science!"

A collective roar of "SCIENCE!" erupted across the brewery, part inside joke, part battle cry.

Penny sprang to her feet, fists raised. "Finally! All those hours of science podcasts are about to pay off."

Dan leaned back, arms crossed. "Sure. You probably think Schrödinger's cat is a meme."

Penny gasped, wounded. "Excuse me, Daniel—I'll have you know I was this close to becoming a mad scientist in another life."

Arden snorted. "You'd be more mad than scientist."

"Semantics," Penny said breezily, twirling a strand of lavender hair.

When the host asked, "What iconic structure was completed in 1889?" Arden didn't hesitate.

"Eiffel Tower," she said, scribbling the answer. "Took just over two years to build. Everyone hated it at first."

Gideon's voice came low beside her, thoughtful enough to turn the answer into something else. "Most great things are hated at first. People fear what they don't understand."

She glanced at him, catching the quiet weight beneath his words. "You're not wrong. Funny thing is, now they can't imagine the skyline without it."

He didn't look away. "Kind of like you here."

Her pen stilled; her pulse skipped.

"I don't think I'm exactly Eiffel Tower material," she said lightly. "Bit too blunt for that."

Gideon's smirk came slowly, but his eyes held steady. "Maybe. But you're hard to miss."

The air between them shifted again, charged and too aware.

Penny shouted, "See? Eiffel Tower! That's what I said!"

Dan groaned. "You said 'Big Ben.'"

"Close enough," she replied, unfazed.

HE NIGHT STRETCHED in a blur of laughter, drinks, and banter. Questions came and went. Arden and Gideon leaned closer with each round, their jabs turning quieter, sharper, skirting the edge of something neither of them seemed willing to name. Across from them, Penny and Dan escalated into full-blown performance art, drawing attention from half the room and pretending, badly, that they didn't love every second of it.

By the final round, anticipation pulsed through the crowd. The host stepped up to the mic and dragged out the reveal with shameless theatrical flair.

"And the winners are—"

Penny shot to her feet, arms raised like she'd snatched the trophy herself. "That's right! Bow to your trivia queen!"

Dan buried his face in his hands. "Beginner's luck is not a personality trait."

Penny leaned over the table, smug. "It is if you do it with style, Daniel."

Arden shook her head, a smirk curling at her lips as she turned to Gideon. "Told you I'd carry us."

His eyes met hers, something softer tugging at the edges of his smile. He lifted his glass.

"Maybe you did."

The buzz of the bar faded for a second, folding itself around the edges of the room until there was only him—his eyes, her breath, the quiet gravity of two people orbiting something neither of them dared name.

The pull between them wasn't new anymore. It had become constant now; invisible, inevitable, threaded through every glance they pretended not to hold too long.

Penny's laughter cracked the moment wide open.

Arden blinked, exhaled, and turned back to the table, but the heat stayed with her, low and insistent beneath her skin. Whatever had passed between them had not merely stirred something.

It had sparked.

And no matter how carefully she tried to ignore it, something in her had begun to catch.

The menu board blurred, chalk strokes swimming at the edge of Arden's vision. Pumpkin Patch Porter. Maple Moon Stout. Seasonal nonsense. She didn't register a single one—not when her senses sparked before her mind could catch up and name why.

Then he was there.

Gideon.

She didn't need to turn. The shift in the air gave him away, a sudden static that moved over her skin like a warning written there. She felt him drawing closer, heat and presence folding in until it pressed against her spine—weightless and suffocating all at once.

He saw her before she turned, and for one fractured heartbeat, forgot how to breathe.

She'd taken off the jacket. There was only the black lace now, sheer in places and deadly in all of them, clinging to her like a dare and catching the light in ways that made restraint feel thin. She was every contradiction that ever undid him—softness laid over sharpened steel. Her hips moved with that same dangerous grace he was already learning by heart, the kind born of survival rather than performance, and the scent of her—jasmine, vanilla, heat—drifted through the air with a sweetness that never once read as harmless.

She turned, slow as a trigger pull, and their eyes met.

Electricity.

It was the only word for it. Not lust alone. Not even longing.

Power—charged and volatile, a current neither of them could seem to break.

"Running away?" he asked, his voice low, velvet dragged over a blade.

She smiled, slow and dangerous. "Just thirsty."

The lie came easily, but her pulse told a different story, wild and uneven beneath her skin.

Her gaze held his. Her voice, when it came, was low and knowing. "What's your excuse?"

It wasn't only a question. It was a dare, dressed in casual ease.

He stepped in, too close and still not close enough, then lifted a hand to call the bartender as if it cost him nothing, though his pulse was beating hard enough to make that a lie.

"Two Autumn Ales," he said.

The authority in it made something wicked flicker low in her stomach.

She arched a brow. "Ordering for me now?"

"You looked undecided."

"And you looked cocky."

A smirk touched his mouth—small, but there.

The bartender slid the glasses forward. Gideon handed one to her, his fingers brushing hers in a touch so brief it should have passed for nothing.

It didn't.

The contact lit a fuse beneath her skin. Heat knotted low in her belly and climbed with every shallow breath. She took a sip—anything to anchor herself, anything to stop from leaning in.

Crisp. Spiced. Easy to like.

Unlike him.

"Bold move," she murmured.

His eyes caught hers over the rim of his glass, and for a second she could have sworn the air tilted.

"Says the woman questioning my taste."

"Maybe I'm testing it."

His gaze held hers, steady and dark. "Maybe I like that."

They hovered in the narrow space between maybe and more, the distance fragile, fleeting.

"You're awfully confident tonight," she said, her voice quieter than before, as if naming it too loudly might break the spell. No longer teasing.

"I just know what I want."

There it was—the quiet truth, dropped like a match in a room full of gasoline.

The words settled low and hot. He wasn't bluffing. This wasn't banter anymore. He meant it, and God help her, she felt it too.

She tilted her head, just slightly, testing the air between them. "Do you?"

He didn't blink. "You tell me."

He moved closer, each step an unspoken confession. Still no contact, but his restraint was a thread pulled tight, one breath from snapping.

She froze—not from fear, but from knowing. Because he wasn't playing. Not this time.

The crowd surged behind her. She swayed with it, and his hand was there, firm at her waist, spanning the curve as if he'd been there before and never forgot.

Not exactly possessive.

Protective.

Heat crawled up her throat.

His hand stayed.

Still, neither of them moved.

They stood locked in that too-small space, chests almost touching, lips inches apart. The bass from the speakers vibrated between them. She felt his breath against her cheek, saw the tight control in his jaw, the war in his eyes.

Her breath ghosted over his throat; his pulse stuttered beneath it. His hand flexed once at her side, grounding her and shattering her in the same motion.

She wanted to lean in.

Just a little.

Just enough.

Just a taste.

She didn't.

She held her ground, refusing to retreat.

"You're playing a dangerous game," he murmured, voice scraped raw.

The slow drag of his thumb at her hip left her skin tingling, the lace suddenly unbearable beneath her jacket, every inch of her too aware of him. Her eyes flicked to his mouth, and when he swallowed—hard—she felt it everywhere.

"I don't play games."

Her whisper curled between them, a blade sheathed in silk.

"And I don't back down."

His mouth was too close. His restraint was thinning by the second.

"Careful, Rivers," he said, voice rougher now, a crack forming beneath the surface. "You might not like what happens when I stop holding back."

Her pulse spiked.

She looked up, eyes locked on his, and saw the wreckage there. Felt something in herself break open in answer.

"Are you sure about that?" she asked, the words barely a breath.

The crowd jostled behind her, and for one exquisite second, her body pressed fully against his.

Chest to chest. Hip to hip.

She felt the restraint shudder through him, felt the war he waged to keep his mouth from hers. Her voice slipped out again, softer this time, reckless enough to ruin them both.

"Are you sure about that?"

He leaned in.

The world dimmed.

Their lips were so close it would have taken nothing. Less than nothing. A breath. A misstep.

She didn't kiss him.

But she didn't move away.

And he didn't dare blink.

Because this moment—this knife-edge of maybe—was the closest thing to surrender either of them had ever allowed.

Then the bartender dropped a beer stein, and the thud of stoneware sliced through the moment, a sharp reminder that they weren't alone.

She stepped back.

He let her.

Barely.

Her hand grazed his again, on purpose this time. A flicker of promise.

Then she turned, vanishing into the crowd with quiet finality.

He stood motionless, watching her disappear. The space she left behind still carried her heat, but somehow felt colder than before.

His chest ached in places he thought long since dead.

For the first time, he didn't wonder whether he could survive wanting her.

He wondered whether he could survive losing her.

THE BAR ROARED BACK to life, but none of it landed.

Gideon's world had narrowed to the echo of her touch, the scent she'd left behind, the magnetic pull refusing to fade. On his skin. In his blood. That lace top— God, he had never hated a fabric so much, or wanted to tear one away more.

And she was walking away.

Every step she took seemed to tug something vital from him, some connection drawn thin between them, taunting him, daring him to follow. He didn't. Not yet. But he wanted to with a violence that startled him; wanted to close the distance and say the thing that had been burning in his chest for weeks.

You're it.

You're the one I can't look away from. The one I can't stop wanting.

She moved through the crowd as if she hadn't just unraveled him. As if she hadn't left him standing there with the ghost of her laugh in his lungs, wondering whether he had imagined the way she'd leaned in. Whether that kiss had lived only in the breath between them.

And Arden?

She felt him behind her like momentum in reverse, pulling her back with every step; an ache at her spine, her ribs, her pulse.

Each step cost her. Her body still burned from the press of his, her skin tingling where his fingers had held her waist like he meant it. Not flirtation. Not a game.

A claim.

And it terrified her.

Because it would be so easy to turn around. To close that final inch and lose herself completely. To let him see what lived beneath all that sharpness and sass, how badly she wanted to be wanted by him.

But want was dangerous.

She'd wanted before, and it had nearly broken her.

So she kept walking.

She reached the edge of the crowd, chest tight, pulse hammering in her ears. Her fingers tightened around the glass, as if the weight of it might quiet everything else.

It couldn't.

Behind her, Gideon hadn't moved. He stood in the space they'd made, that fleeting pocket of charged silence, and stared.

He couldn't go after her.

Not yet.

Because if he touched her again, he wasn't sure he would stop. Not this time. And he wasn't sure he could survive what came after, when she inevitably remembered herself and walked away.

Then she turned, just slightly, glancing over her shoulder, her eyes finding his through the haze.

That look undid him.

Because she wasn't running.

She was waiting.

And the next time she looked at him like that—open, daring, almost his—he wouldn't hold back.

He wouldn't let her walk away.

THE BONUS ROUND hit like a drumroll, the entire room crackling with anticipation. Laughter echoed, pint glasses clinked, but at their table, the air tightened with focus.

Arden and Gideon were tied with Penny and Dan—still bantering, still circling, but beneath the laughter, both pairs were playing to win.

"What jazz standard is often called the greatest love song ever written?" the host boomed, drawing a low collective hum from the crowd.

Arden's pen hovered, her fingers still. She glanced at Gideon.

His eyes were steady on hers, unreadable but open, as if he already knew she had the answer. That silent confidence wrapped around her like a hand at her back; steadying, steadying, always steadying.

"Body and Soul," she said, her voice quiet but certain, tension threading tight around her ribs.

When the host confirmed the answer, a rare smile curved across Gideon's face—not the one meant to shield, but the devastating one. Raw. Pure. Unguarded.

It struck her breathless.

Arden looked away, but her smile felt far too triumphant for trivia.

"You carried us after all," he murmured, his voice low enough that only she could hear.

Feigning ease, she tilted her head, but her pulse betrayed her. The heat behind his gaze made her feel as if she'd stepped into sunlight without meaning to.

"Told you I could."

Across the table, Penny groaned and flopped backward in her seat with dramatic despair. "This is clearly rigged. Jazz standards? Who even likes jazz standards?"

Dan slid an arm around her shoulders, smug and shameless. "Face it, Penelope. Arden's brain crushed you."

"And Gideon's brooding," Penny countered, flicking her gaze toward him. "I'm sorry, is brooding now a trivia strategy?"

"It worked," Gideon replied, bone-dry, and Arden laughed before she could think better of it.

She dropped her pen and sighed with mock flair. "Don't inflate his ego, Penny. He'll be unbearable the rest of the night."

"Please." Penny sat up straight. "The only thing I care about now is snacks. Snacks are the real prize. Speaking of..." She turned to Dan. "Didn't you promise me nachos if I lost?"

Dan narrowed his eyes. "I promised nothing. You hallucinated that deal."

Penny gasped, clutching her heart like a spurned lover. "Wow. Treachery. Betrayal. This is how revolutions start."

Arden leaned back in her chair, laughter easing the tightness in her chest. Beside her, Gideon shifted closer, near enough that his arm brushed hers. The touch was subtle, barely more than contact, but her body answered anyway—a live wire drawn from his skin to hers.

"Good teamwork," he said softly.

"Surprised?" she asked, teasing, though her heart thudded as if he'd confessed something far more dangerous.

His voice stayed low, rough at the edges. "Not even a little."

The words sank into her, quiet but heavy, leaving ripples in their wake.

Before she could answer, Penny's voice barreled back in. "Okay, losers, we're not done until someone buys me dessert. Arden? Back me up here."

The moment fractured, sharp and sudden.

Arden blinked, startled by how quickly it vanished, and grabbed her bag with a little too much efficiency. "Always, Penny. Nachos and dessert. Let's make it happen."

Dan tossed his jacket over his shoulder, smirking. "Lead the way, Penelope. But don't think I'm paying just because you got smoked."

Penny sniffed, nose in the air. "I'm a woman of simple desires, Daniel. Just buy me one overpriced slice of cake, and I'll consider forgiving you."

As the chaos shifted toward the bar, Arden turned back.

Gideon sat unmoving, stone-carved and staring straight through her, that devastating smile still playing at the corner of his mouth.

"You coming?" she asked, aiming for breezy and failing miserably at casual.

His eyes locked on hers.

"Absolutely."

One word, but it hit like a promise.

She turned back, forcing her legs to carry her forward, but her heart pounded like it knew what was coming.

The night wasn't over.

And neither were they.

LAUGHTER FOLLOWED them into the night, sharp against the bite of cold air. Their boots clicked over rain-slick cobblestones while Penny linked her arm through Arden's, her hair flashing violet beneath the streetlights like a rebellious halo.

"Okay," Dan announced, slinging an arm around Penny's shoulders with exaggerated swagger. "Group tattoos. No backing out. Something bold. Possibly unhinged."

Penny gasped, clapping her hands as if he'd just proposed marriage. "Yes! Full chaos. Matching ink. And I'm documenting every moment. This is premium blackmail content."

Arden's smirk came easily, the kind that turned heads and made people wonder what she knew that they didn't. "Bold of you to assume I don't have one."

Dan stopped mid-stride, eyebrows leaping toward his hairline. "Wait. You're serious?"

Penny clutched at invisible pearls, gasping as if Arden had committed a felony. "Arden Rivers, you're holding out. What is it? A quote? A phoenix? A skull with roses and a tragic backstory?"

Arden tilted her head and let silence do the heavy lifting. They both stared, visibly aching to ask, and she let their curiosity stretch just long enough to become useful. A shield, if she needed one. A game, if she didn't.

Gideon stepped out of the shadow beside the lamppost, posture relaxed, though the look in his eyes was anything but.

The city light kissed the angles of his face, catching along the sharp edge of his jaw and the hollow at his throat. Controlled. Dangerous. Handsome in a way that didn't try to be.

His gaze found her—slow, precise, targeted.

"Now that's provocative," he said, his voice dark and smooth, like a secret poured neat over ice. "Where exactly is this mystery ink?"

His words draped over her skin like a touch she wasn't ready for. Heat threaded down her spine, pooling low, and for one breathless second, his fingers were there again, tracing the answer from memory.

But she didn't blink.

Didn't flinch.

Instead, she met his eyes, steady and unrepentant. "That's classified."

Gideon's mouth curved, half smirk, half mystery. Deeper than amusement. "Something that matters?" he asked, voice low and even, just enough to stir the butterflies loose in her stomach. "You don't exactly seem like the cutesy ink type."

"Wouldn't you like to know?" Her tone was light, but the edge in it was deliberate.

His eyes lingered, dropping to her mouth like a thought he hadn't decided against yet.

"I would."

Two words, low and razor-smooth, landed between them with the weight of inevitability.

The world tilted.

Their friends moved around them, laughing and talking, but the sound blurred beneath the hum rising in Arden's ears. His stare tethered her—unflinching, unapologetic—and the space between them seemed to shrink without either of them moving. No touch. No step. Only tension, thick enough to taste.

Arden's breath caught in her throat. He hadn't touched her, but her skin ached like he had.

Penny groaned, loud and theatrical, and the moment cracked like glass. "Okay, fine! Arden has secrets, probably etched in some very inconvenient location. But what about you, Blackwell?"

Dan grinned. "Yeah, come on. Family crest? Latin motto? Something moody and painfully elite?"

Gideon didn't move. Didn't break eye contact with Arden. But his smile turned sly. "I think I'll leave the ink to the rest of you."

Penny gasped as if it were a personal betrayal. "Unforgivable. Do you know how iconic you'd be with some dramatic ink across that chest?"

Arden didn't miss a beat, her voice turning syrupy-sweet and laced with steel. "He doesn't need ink. He's already brooding incarnate."

Gideon's laugh came low, worn at the edges, unfiltered. His gaze lingered on her. "Good to know I've earned your approval."

Their group's laughter rose around them again, but the heat between them hadn't dissipated. It lingered as they walked, a steady burn beneath Arden's skin, a hum she could feel every time Gideon's attention returned to her.

Penny and Dan bantered ahead, their silhouettes full of chaos and delight, but Arden felt Gideon behind her with impossible clarity.

Watching her.

Reading her.

Wanting her.

And when she glanced back, just once, he didn't look away.

Not even a little.

A promise flickered behind his expression, quiet, unspoken, and utterly certain; one she wasn't ready to name, though she felt it all the same.

And when it came, it was going to undo her.

———

From his corner of hell, he watched them play pretend.

A borrowed night. A borrowed table. Laughter that didn't belong to them, especially not to her.

Arden moved through the haze of clinking glasses and half-drunken banter like she'd forgotten.

Forgotten him.

He lingered in the shadows just beyond the reach of the lights, the warm pulse of the brewery brushing his skin like an insult.

Hidden, but not distant. Close enough to hear the shape of her laugh.

To see the way Gideon leaned in like he had staked his claim.

Every glance. Every unearned touch. Every look that lasted too long.

They didn't deserve to breathe the same air she did, let alone touch her.

That smug bastard sat there like he had a right to her, like expensive clothes and a family name were enough to protect her. To claim her.

As if watching her smile, hearing her voice, meant something.

But it didn't.

Because Arden wasn't theirs.

She was his.

Dan's theatrics were forgettable. Penny's glitter-coated charm was just noise.

But Gideon?

Gideon was the rot. Slick with confidence. All control and shadows and lingering looks, pretending that gave him power.

Pretending he could keep her safe.

He couldn't.

No one could.

When she laughed, he shattered inside.

Her laugh—his laugh—rising from her like smoke through stained glass, almost otherworldly.

God, how she glowed.

Even here, surrounded by dull-eyed people who didn't see her the way he did, she radiated that heat. That burn.

And still... she let them touch her. Let them fold her into their shallow world.

It made him sick.

Because they didn't know the truth of her. The damage she carried. The sharp, jagged edges she kept hidden beneath her calm. The fire beneath her skin didn't flicker. It waited.

He knew.

He had studied her like scripture.

The way she worried her lip when she wasn't sure how much to reveal.

The glance over her shoulder, automatic, every time she left a building.

The slight tension in her jaw when someone got too close.

Gideon didn't see those things. He wasn't paying attention.

But he always paid attention.

And now? He waited.

The trap was set.

They hadn't heard it snap yet.

They thought this was a game.

They were wrong.

She wasn't theirs to parade around in lace and leather and smug conversation. She wasn't some prize to be won in a bar game or some mystery to be solved by a man like Blackwell.

She was fire. His Little Fire.

And soon, she wouldn't just see it, she'd feel it.

Some fires don't go out. They come home.

And he'd be waiting.

CHAPTER 25

Cracks in the Foundation

A black car rolled through the mist, headlights brushing the cobblestones with a faint glow. It eased to a stop beneath the awning, engine barely audible, its restrained hum mirroring the tension tightening in Arden's chest.

She lingered under the canopy beside Penny while fine droplets caught in the streetlight overhead. Penny grumbled about wet shoes and frizzed hair, but Arden barely registered the sound.

Her attention had already found him.

Gideon stepped through the fog with quiet intent, every movement deliberate and grounded. The glow from the streetlight struck him mid-step, brushing over the cut of his jaw, the set of his shoulders, the weight in the way he moved. His coat stirred slightly in the breeze—no flourish, nothing theatrical. Just real.

Unreal all the same.

Mist clung to him as he passed, curling around his shoulders as though it hadn't quite finished with him yet. It wasn't magic, but it had the shape of it.

At the car, he opened the door with casual confidence. No show. No rush. Only that quiet certainty of his, the kind that never needed to prove itself.

"Ladies first," he said, voice low and steady.

It wasn't simply polite. It carried weight, like a quiet echo off stone; impossible to ignore.

Penny slipped past with a playful bow, smirking at Arden on her way to the car. "Try not to keep him waiting."

But the words barely landed.

Arden's focus stayed locked on him, on the way his eyes met hers and didn't flinch. The space between them held, stretched thin with everything they hadn't said. Overhead, the light flickered once, shadows shifting across the angles of his face. His features didn't soften beneath it.

They sharpened.

As if restraint itself had teeth.

The harsh line of his jaw. The unreadable set of his mouth. The clean, sharp cut of his cheekbones. He was striking in a way that stopped her breath, like lightning held still just long enough to admire before it struck.

But it was his eyes that undid her. Molten gray, threaded with silver, full of heat and history and something deadly serious.

They weren't only looking at her.

They were consuming her.

His stare felt like pressure. Gravity. A touch without contact. A promise without words.

Arden's skin prickled, her lungs tightening beneath the weight of his presence. It wasn't fair, the way he could look at her like that and still seem to want everything she tried so hard to hide.

Their gazes held, and in that single breathless stretch of silence, something broke open. Not loudly. Not with sound. With clarity.

This was the moment—the edge of the edge, the place where everything after would have to answer for everything before.

If she stepped forward, even an inch, nothing between them would stay the same.

The mist kissed her cheeks, cool and soft, a brutal contrast to the heat blooming low and rising with every heartbeat.

Penny's car door clicked shut behind her, muffled and distant.

And they were alone.

His eyes traced over Arden, slow and deliberate, lingering at her mouth, her throat, the place where damp hair clung to her collarbone. Not hurried. Not disguised.

Just taking her in.

His expression didn't change, but the air between them did.

It thrummed.

It dared.

Arden's lips parted, the breath she drew shallow and unsteady.

Still, she didn't move.

Neither did he.

They stood on the precipice, suspended in want and restraint, surrounded by city noise but locked inside a silence that screamed.

Gideon inhaled sharply, and the scent of her unraveled something deep and dangerously tethered.

It wrapped around him like silk and sin—intoxicating, inescapable. Every instinct in him demanded that he close the distance. Touch. Take. End the exquisite cruelty of restraint.

His hands fisted at his sides, tension threading through him like a live current. One wrong move, and control would no longer be a choice.

Then her breath caught.

Shallow.

Unsteady.

A crack in the composure she always wore like armor.

His fists tightened. His own breath faltered, brutal and unfinished, and he knew with a terrifying certainty that one more second might ruin him.

It leveled him.

When he spoke, his voice was unrecognizable, low, rough, a velvet rasp of restraint fraying at the edges.

"Are you getting in..."

A long pause.

"...or do I get to kiss you first?"

A question only in structure.

A promise in everything else.

The words hung there, thick and loaded, curling between them like smoke.

She smiled—slow, dangerous, deliberate.

It wasn't flirtation. It was surrender laced with fire.

"I'm not going to stop you, Gideon."

The storm in his eyes went still. Not calm, but focused.

Every thread of tension between them pulled taut, the moment stretching, daring either of them to make the first move.

And that was it.

His hands were on her before conscious thought caught up.

A hand gripped her jaw, tilting her face upward with a tenderness that stole her breath. The other slid into her hair, fingers threading through the waves until they found the nape of her neck and held: firm enough to make her gasp, soft enough to undo her.

The first brush of his mouth was gentle. Disarmingly slow and deliberate.

A tease.

A promise.

THEN... fire.

Arden felt it everywhere. It wasn't only the heat of his mouth or the way his hands gripped with such certainty. It was the way the world tipped sideways the moment his lips met hers—gravity had let go and left her weightless in his arms. Everything tilted, everything realigned.

She arched instinctively into him, electric, urgent, desperate.

And God, the feel of him.

Hard muscle. Heat. Tension wound dangerously tight, a storm seconds from breaking.

His hands roamed. One hand was tangled possessively in her hair, angling her exactly how he wanted her. The other slid boldly downward, spanning her waist, gripping the generous curve of her hip. His fingers dug in, pulling her closer, needing to feel, to anchor, to take.

She let him.

No—she matched him, met him, demanded as fiercely as he gave.

Because he might've been fire, but so was she.

The kiss was hungry and utterly unrestrained, then ignited and flared deeper.

He swept his tongue slowly, possessively against hers. Tasting. Claiming. Branding.

Her breaths quickened as she trembled with desperation and desire.

As she pressed her body flush against him, a sharp inhale betrayed how he was unraveling completely.

And God, she could feel him.

All of him.

Impossible to ignore. Undeniable.

Her heart stumbled, raced.

This was the opposite of careful and controlled.

It was wild, hungry, and primal.

His touch trailed down her body over the curve of her back to the dip of her waist, then settled possessively on the fullness of her ass.

He groaned into her mouth, his hands greedy on the soft give of her curves. Her body—lush, strong, sensual—molded against his, made for him alone.

Her fingers twisted fiercely into his hair. Her nails scraped gently against his scalp, holding tight. She was every bit as desperate to consume him as he was to drown in her.

A low sound vibrated in his chest, raw, primitive, a growl of surrender barely restrained.

He was dangerously close to losing control.

He should stop.

But fuck, she wasn't stopping either.

She was everywhere.

Her scent was midnight temptation, intoxicating and addictive.

Her breaths were quick and uneven, and she gasped sharply as he deepened the kiss. He teased her with tantalizingly delicious strokes of his tongue. When his teeth gently bit her bottom lip, a helpless, intoxicating whimper escaped her.

Her hips shifted against his with enough pressure to pull another broken sound from deep within his chest.

She knew exactly how affected he was. She felt every inch of his need, and he didn't try to hide it.

And she was right there with him.

The soft, breathless sounds slipping from her lips, tiny whimpers between each deep, consuming kiss, poured fuel onto the fire raging inside him.

His restraint was shattered, jagged and irreparable.

Her body fit against him flawlessly, curves melting into strength, soft yielding to hard in a connection so right it felt inevitable.

He wanted more.

Needed more.

When his hand slipped beneath her top and grazed the skin above her waistband, she shivered and sank into him too easily, too instinctively, like her body didn't get the memo to resist.

And that broke him.

She gasped softly against his lips—her body hot, responsive, and needy. Her hips shifted ever so slightly creating a tantalizing friction that stole his breath. He tightened his grip, pulled her even closer, and showed her exactly how utterly undone she'd made him.

Her low and involuntary moan tore him apart piece by piece.

His fingers flexed against her bare skin, memorizing every inch, every soft curve, and every enticing dip beneath his palms. There was only the heat and relentless ache of a desire between them.

His tongue traced her bottom lip before claiming her mouth again—slow, deep, torturous.

She whimpered softly, pressing herself against him until it blurred—them, the night, everything but heat and hunger. Her curves fit perfectly against the hard lines of his body. Her toned thighs brushed against his, pushing insistently when his grip tightened with desperate hunger.

Her breathing shattered into soft, ragged inhales.

She trembled.

So did he.

His control fractured entirely.

The kiss deepened, becoming more urgent, relentless. Slow. Demanding.

His hands continued roaming over her. Gripping. Claiming. Memorizing every inch of her, as though touch alone could bind her to him.

She didn't pull back.

She didn't hesitate.

Instead, she clung to him, matching his fierce abandon.

And that was his undoing.

"ARDEN! Get in the freaking car before the driver leaves!"

Penny's voice sliced through the charged moment, fracturing it sharply.

Arden jolted, but only barely. Her lips were still a breath from his, her heart pounding hard enough to drown out the street. Her fists remained tangled in his shirt, nails biting through fabric into the warmth beneath.

She stared up at him with dazed, wide eyes and swollen lips.

Gideon knew he should step back.

He didn't.

Instead, he rested his forehead against hers, brief and devastating, a fleeting acknowledgment of something irrevocable. Their breathing stayed ragged, uneven, almost in tandem.

His gaze dropped to her mouth, tempted past reason. He needed more; knew, with a certainty that unsettled him, that one kiss would never satisfy the fire she had set loose.

His thumb brushed her cheek, tender but deliberate. Possessive in the quietest, most ruinous way.

"We're not done."

Arden's pulse thundered, but her voice held steady, edged with defiance and surrender.

"Not even close."

The cool leather of the seat was jarring against Arden's still-buzzing skin.

Then he was there again, leaning in, invading her space, her breath, her senses. The car filled with the warmth of him—smoke, spice, something dark and smoldering—and her heart skipped before it stumbled into a frantic rhythm.

His fingers skimmed her arm as he reached across her, the barest brush against her skin, completely intentional.

A choice.

Not coincidence.

Gideon pulled the seatbelt slowly across her body, and his hand ghosted over the line of her chest, the sharp curve of her waist. Slow. Purposeful. His knuckles grazed close enough to make her breath catch, a touch so light it barely counted as contact, and yet every nerve beneath her skin sparked awake.

He didn't rush. Didn't fumble. Didn't waste a single, electrifying second.

The soft click of the buckle echoed between them.

But his touch lingered, fingers tracing over her ribs before he pulled back, and the restraint in it unraveled her more completely than force ever could.

Then his lips brushed hers.

Brief.

Tender.

A whisper-soft caress.

A promise rather than possession. A stolen moment he refused to surrender.

His breath warmed her cheek as he drew back slightly, lips grazing her ear.

"Stay safe," he whispered, voice roughened by everything he wasn't saying.

Her fingers curled into fists, and her breath caught sharply. She didn't dare move, because she knew if she did, she would pull him right back in.

The cool night air crept into the space where his body had been as he stepped away. The door closed firmly, final and hollow.

As the car eased from the curb, Arden leaned back into the seat. The low purr of the engine vibrated beneath her, steady and intimate, but the aftershock of him still thrummed through her skin.

Beside her, Penny mercifully stayed quiet, scrolling through her phone with a knowing smile.

Arden stubbornly ignored her.

Her pulse kept pounding. Her lips still tingled. Her body ached, traitorous and alive, craving the heat she had left behind.

Her phone buzzed against her leg, slicing through the thick remnants of want still coursing through her. When she checked the screen, his name lit up, and everything inside her answered.

Can I steal you away tomorrow evening?

A mischievous smile touched her mouth as she stared at the message. Arden typed back, letting wit do what it always did—stand guard over the flutter in her chest.

Stealing usually requires something valuable.

Gideon's response came almost immediately, as if he'd been waiting for exactly that.

Then you won't mind indulging me.

She hesitated, thumb poised above the screen, before sending another teasing retort.

What makes you so sure I don't mind?

This time, his silence stretched with intention. He made her wait, and when his reply finally appeared, it landed with enough precision to send her pulse racing.

Because I've learned to tell when you do.

Arden stared at the message, her heartbeat thudding beneath her skin. Beside her, Penny's fingers continued to tap quietly against her phone, mercifully absorbed in whatever digital chaos had spared Arden from immediate interrogation.

Swallowing the warmth creeping up her neck, Arden locked the screen and slipped her phone away, then turned her gaze toward the rain-streaked window.

But her reflection betrayed her.

That small, impossible curve of her mouth.

Some flames burned too fiercely to ignore, and Gideon Blackwell might be the one to leave her scorched.

————

FROM THE SHADOWS, he watched.

Gideon stood beneath the streetlight, hands in his pockets, the golden glow casting him in false divinity.

Serene. Sculpted. Untouchable.

Gideon Blackwell, the man who played god.

But tonight, the mask had slipped.

Tonight, the cracks bled through.

That kiss had broken him.

He'd seen it. How Gideon stiffened, spine gone taut like prey caught in the jaws of something stronger.

It was remarkable.

The unshakable, ice-veined heir brought low by her.

By Arden.

She had moved through the rain like lightning—raw, unrelenting, a storm made flesh.

She had kissed him, and Gideon had drunk her in.

Desperate. Starved.

Pathetic.

How dare he touch her?

Little Fire... how dare you let him?

Every flicker of that flame. Her defiant spark, her blade-edged grin, the chaos in her laugh—it all belonged to him.

Always had.

Not to this silver-spooned imposter with perfect posture and inherited power.

Not to this entitled prince with a crown he didn't earn.

Arden was his.

But she stood there, giving Gideon pieces of herself that were never his to take.

He had watched her for so long, studied her until she was carved into the inside of his skull.

He knew her better than she knew herself.

The tilt of her chin when challenged.

The wildfire in her eyes when cornered.

The way her laughter sliced through silence like a flare in the dark.

She was violence and velvet.
Steel in silk.
A woman made to bring men to their knees.
And Gideon couldn't see it.
Couldn't see her.
Not the way he ever had.
She didn't belong in Gideon's world of sterile glass towers and backroom betrayals.
She belonged in the shadows.
In truth.
In the blood and bone of real things.
She didn't belong to that world.
She belonged with him.
She hadn't realized it yet.
But he could wait.
He had waited.
Patient as breath.
He was meticulous. Careful. Like fate spinning its web, strand by strand.
And now?
The path had never been clearer.
That kiss had marked the beginning.
The slip.
The opening.
Soon, she would feel it.
The pull. The truth.
Soon, she'd open her eyes.
Soon, she'd see who truly knew her,
Who had always seen her fire, her fury, her worth.
Because she had always been his.
Had been since the first time he heard her name.
Would be until the last breath left their lungs.
And maybe—
Even after that.

CHAPTER 26

Blood in the Water

Rain turned savage by the time Arden and Penny reached their building. Wind sliced through the downpour, bending trees and splattering glass as if the sky had turned against them. The city blurred into smears of gold and gray while Penny wrestled her key into the front lock.

"Ruined," Penny muttered dramatically, flicking a soaked strand of lavender-streaked hair from her face. "My curls, my shoes, my faith in meteorologists—gone."

Arden barely heard her. Her pulse was rising, the night pressing too hard at the edges. Penny retreated toward her room, still grumbling, but Arden lingered in the living room, the low rumble of the storm vibrating through her chest.

She stood at the window, unmoving and silent, fingertips pressed to the cold glass as she watched the storm lash against the city like it was trying to wake something.

The kiss still burned through her.

Wild.

Electric.

She could still feel Gideon's hands, his mouth, the way he had looked at her as if he had never seen anything so real.

God.

It hadn't only rattled her. It had undone her completely.

It wasn't until her breathing began to steady that she moved toward her desk. The lamp's warm glow spilled across worn notebook pages, scraps of thought, pieces of herself; hope, hurt, and the mess between them.

She traced the curve of a half-finished sentence, her fingertip catching on the ridge of ink, then picked up the pen. The scent of ink and warm paper wrapped around her, comforting in its familiarity.

She sat.
Breathed.
Opened the notebook.
And then she wrote.
The words came slowly at first, hesitant, as though they had to wade through grief and fire to reach the page. But soon, the rhythm returned.
Steady.
Sure.
A reflection of everything stirring in her chest.

Starting over. It isn't about leaving.
It's about daring to believe that the past doesn't own you.
The cracks don't define you.
That trusting again isn't foolish.
It's brave.

Her hand hovered, pen tip catching slightly against the paper. She stared at the last line, and for one foolish, fragile moment, she let herself believe it was true.
But truth had sharp edges.
Her fingers drifted to the small, pale scar curved along her palm, a wound long healed but never forgotten. Trauma nursing had been her lifeline until it wasn't; until the relentless emergencies, the loss, the pressure, and Chad had all begun to blur into one long, unbearable stretch of survival. The manipulation. The slow, careful dismantling of her certainty. The way he had made her doubt herself until even instinct felt suspect.
And then the roses.
One after another, in places that shouldn't have made sense.
Her locker. Her windshield. Her porch. The back door of Dot's.
They hadn't stopped for weeks.
Silent. Chilling. Deliberate.
Each rose had arrived without warning, without explanation—perfect, crimson, and always alone.
A beautiful threat.
They haunted her. The scent. The precision. The silence that followed.
New York was supposed to be a reprieve. A reset. But Arden knew better than to believe safety came from distance.
You don't outrun this.
You survive it.
Moment to moment.
Breath to breath.

She didn't hear the knock at first.

Knock. Knock.

The pen slipped, a streak of ink cutting diagonally through her last line.

She froze.

Her eyes darted to the door, then to the clock.

After midnight.

Knock. Knock.

Too soft to be urgent.

Too precise to be innocent.

Her breath stilled in her throat. She rose slowly, fingers curling around the heavy brass candlestick she kept near the entry. A leftover habit from West Virginia.

One of many.

"Who is it?" Penny's voice came sleepy and muffled from her room.

"I don't know," Arden called back, her voice tighter than she meant it to be.

She approached slowly, staying in the shadows, pulse hammering behind her collarbone. At the door, she leaned in and pressed her eye to the peephole.

Empty hallway.

Wet footprints.

Leading away from the door.

Sharp. Deliberate. Too fresh to dismiss as accident.

She cracked the door open, inch by cautious inch.

There it was.

On the threshold.

A rose.

Single. Crimson. Rain-slicked.

Its petals curled in perfect, silent bloom against the welcome mat.

Not left carelessly. Not dropped in passing.

Placed.

Presented.

Offered.

The scent rolled in like a wave, sickly-sweet and artificial, a chemical sweetness that twisted the air wrong.

Then she saw them just beyond the lip of the doorway, trailing away from the threshold like breadcrumbs.

More roses.

Leading toward the stairwell.

Every nerve in her body ignited.

She slammed the door.

Bolted it.

Twice.

Her breath came shallow and fast, the air in the apartment suddenly too tight.

THE ROSE SAT on the kitchen counter now, its silent weight heavier than it had any right to be. Arden could still feel it in her hands. Could smell its perfume bleeding into her skin. The storm shifted—not outside this time, but in her.

Because this wasn't a rose.

It was a tether.

A warning.

A reminder.

Stalking wasn't one act. It was erosion; the slow, calculated unraveling of boundaries and breath, of peace and perspective. Fear delivered in inches. Terror dressed beautifully enough to make the world question whether it had ever been terror at all.

Each intrusion, each silence that followed, carved away at her bit by bit until her world no longer felt like it belonged to her.

She had thought if she ignored it, it would die.

But silence hadn't killed it.

Silence had fed it.

And now it had found her again.

She turned toward the hallway.

Checked every lock again.

Turned on every light.

Chased down every shadow.

But the weight in her chest stayed.

She wasn't imagining this.

She wasn't safe.

Not here.

Not anymore.

————

She didn't scream.

Not even when she saw it.

That was his Little Fire—composed.

Defiant even in fear.

He stood across the street beneath the edge of a rusted awning, shadowed from view, watching as the warm glow of her apartment flickered through the rain. The light bathed her in gold as she moved through the room, in slow, measured steps.

She was luminous tonight.

Still carrying the high of that kiss.

He had seen it.

Every second.

The way her body curved into Gideon's.

The way her lips parted.

The way she clung.
It had scorched him.
Because that kiss wasn't stolen.
It was offered. Given.
And Gideon had taken it like it belonged to him.
It didn't.
Gideon's hands had been on her.
Kissed her. Claimed her.
The memory scalded.
Gideon hadn't earned her. He couldn't.
Arden didn't belong to anyone.
Not unless she was choosing it.
And she hadn't chosen him yet.
But she would. She had to.
He could see her so clearly—the strength under her skin, the fire in her bones, the way the world bent around her without even realizing. They dulled her. Softened her.
But he knew better.
He knew what burned beneath the surface. He'd seen the spark in her long before Gideon even felt the heat.
That man was a storm chaser pretending he'd caught lightning.
But Arden wasn't meant to be captured.

WORSHIPPED. *Claimed. Eventually.*
He couldn't say how long he'd been watching, not in a way that would satisfy the timeline of law or logic, but long enough to know that Arden wasn't safe with Gideon.
She needed someone who understood her.
Someone who saw past the armor, straight into the war.
Someone who could survive the burn.
He watched the tension build in her posture as she bolted the door. Watched her press trembling fingers to her sternum, to quiet the riot inside.
And he admired her.
Even afraid, she didn't shatter.
She burned.
He stepped back into the shadows, the rain soaking his collar, crawling down his spine like ice.
The rose had done its job.
A red bloom to stir the embers.
A reminder that she wasn't alone.
That she never had been.
Let her pretend she was free.

But she wasn't.
Not yet.
But soon?
Soon.
She would see.
She'd burn for him.

CHAPTER 27

Electric Resolve

The storm had passed, but its ghost lingered; sky heavy with clouds, streets slick with memory. The world hadn't simply gone quiet. It held its breath, thick and suspended, as if both Arden and the air were waiting for something to shift.

She pushed through the doors of the Krav Maga studio, and the pulse of movement met her at once—the dull thud of fists against pads, the scrape of shoes over mats, the low rhythm of bodies choosing motion over fear.

Familiar.

Grounding.

Necessary.

Here, there were no roses. No whispers in the dark. No shadows that followed her home. Only sweat, breath, and strength.

"Morning, Arden!" Kasha's voice rang out from the front desk, chipper as always.

Arden offered a faint smirk and dropped her bag near the cubbies. The tang of disinfectant clung to the air as she wrapped her hands methodically, letting the repetition settle her frayed nerves. Each pull of the tape tightened her focus. Each turn brought her further back into herself.

"Partner up!"

The instructor's voice cut across the room, scattering the low murmur of chatter. Bodies shifted. Pairs formed.

"You're with Matt," Damon called, nodding toward a wiry guy bouncing on the balls of his feet with too much energy and not enough technique.

Matt grinned as he approached. "Go easy on me, okay? I'm new."

Arden tilted her head, unimpressed. "Keep your hands up and I won't have to."

They squared off. Within seconds, it was obvious Matt swung wide, stepped too soon, telegraphed every move before his body had committed to it.

She didn't exploit it at first.

Then Damon called across the room again. "Don't hold back, Arden."

So she didn't.

A pivot. A strike. A swift blow to the ribs that sent Matt stumbling back, breath catching.

"Damn." He lifted a hand, signaling a pause. "Okay. Got it."

Arden reset her stance. "You're chasing the hit. Watch your center."

He nodded, grin gone now, focus sharpening.

By the end of the session, her muscles ached in that honest, welcome way—earned through focus, not fear. She dropped against the wall near her bag and began unwrapping her hands as Matt approached again.

"Thanks for not totally obliterating me," he joked, still winded.

She shrugged, the corner of her mouth twitching. "You held your own. Slow down next time. Trust your body."

"Easier said than done," he muttered, then offered a grateful smile. "Thanks."

Damon passed, giving her a rare nod. "Good work today. That edge—that's what I want to see more of."

Arden slung her bag over her shoulder, but the words stayed with her.

That edge. That clarity.

It had nothing to do with the rose. Or fear.

It was hers.

Earned.

Reclaimed.

❦

By the time Arden stepped back onto the damp city streets, her resolve had solidified into something that felt, if not unshakable, then close enough to pass for it.

Still, a trace of last night clung to her skin—more than the rose, more than the shadows it had dragged back with it. She could still taste Gideon at the back of her throat, that kiss slow-burning beneath her skin as though it had never really ended.

Wanting Gideon wasn't the problem. It never had been.

The problem was trusting what it meant.

Trusting what he might mean.

That part made her chest tighten.

But Arden didn't want to come apart. Not again. So she walked faster, straighter, untouchable in posture even as her skin prickled with the memory of his hands.

❦

Arden stepped from the shower, steam curling behind her. The sting of hot water had washed away the last of the morning tension, but not the low hum of adrenaline still threading through her ribs.

She dressed in fitted jeans and a black tank, every motion deliberate. Measured. Her coffee mug warmed her palms as she crossed the kitchen, grounding her in something simple, something chosen.

The rose sat exactly where she'd left it. Its red bloom cut through the soft morning light, bold and intentional, beautiful in a way that made her want to hate it more. She picked it up, turned it once between her fingers, then set it back down.

Penny looked up from the couch, her mug resting on her knees. "So, are we burning it or pretending it's a decorative choice now?"

Arden leaned against the counter. "Neither."

"Right," Penny drawled, though her eyes didn't quite match the smirk. "Because it doesn't matter."

"It doesn't," Arden said, calm but unshakable this time. "I'm not letting it set the tone. Not today."

She took a slow sip of coffee, grounding herself in the heat, in the choice.

"And tonight?" Penny's tone softened, coaxing.

Arden met her gaze, chin lifting. "I'm going to Gideon's. And I plan on enjoying every damn second of it."

A slow grin spread across Penny's face. "Now that's my girl."

❦

The rain had stopped, but the hush outside felt unnatural, like the moment before a scream. Arden moved to close the blinds, gaze sweeping the windows.

Nothing.

She paused anyway.

The street below shimmered with post-storm quiet, reflections warped in puddles. It looked empty.

Too empty.

Unease curled beneath her ribs. Not fear exactly. Instinct.

She shook it off and tugged the blinds closed, but when she turned away, the feeling stayed; a prickle at the base of her neck, the inescapable sense that beyond the glass, someone was watching.

Later, Arden stepped into the hallway and found Penny waiting, arms crossed, devil's glint in her eyes.

"So..." Penny began, drawing the word out like silk. "You're seeing him tonight."

Arden groaned. "Please, not this."

"Oh, honey. Absolutely this." Penny marched toward her closet. "You kissed Gideon Blackwell. That's not a footnote. That's a headline."

"It was one kiss." Unconvincing, even to herself.

233

"And the electrical grid is still recovering." Penny yanked open the closet doors. "You're going over there. You need to wear an outfit that says, 'Yes, I might casually ruin your life with a single glance.'"

Arden flopped onto the bed. "It's not a date."

"It's an event. Stop talking." Penny tossed a sleek black top onto the bed. "This. With the dark jeans and those ankle boots you forget are hot."

Arden eyed the outfit. "I didn't even know I had that top."

"And yet the universe did. Now put it on."

Penny perched on the edge of the bed, curling iron in hand, examining Arden with the ruthless eye of a sculptor already seeing the finished form.

"You're thinking, 'He doesn't care what I look like,' right?" Penny said, eyes narrowed.

"Pretty much."

"Well, he does. And more importantly—you'll care. Confidence, my dear, is a weapon."

Arden let herself be handled—hair curled, mascara applied, lips tinted. They bantered lightly, the ease between them a balm against the strange pressure still lingering from the window.

"What exactly happened outside that car?" Penny asked, curling the last strand. "Because that kiss? I felt it in my spleen."

Arden paused, fingers curling in her lap. "It was... intense."

"Understatement of the century," Penny muttered. "Now stand up."

Arden obeyed, stepping in front of the mirror. The black top hugged her curves without trying too hard. Her jeans fit like armor. The boots gave her enough height to be dangerous.

She looked strong.

Poised.

Lit from the inside.

"Damn," Penny said with a slow nod. "He's not ready."

Arden grabbed her bag. "Thanks, Pen."

"Don't thank me yet. Thank me when you're walking funny tomorrow."

Arden laughed, flipping her hair over one shoulder. "Not happening."

"Call me if it does."

She stepped outside into the damp evening, the air charged in that post-storm way, as if the whole city were waiting to break open again.

But not her.

Not tonight.

⚘

Amber light carved Sebastian into something almost sacred in its wrongness.

Sharp lines. Precise angles. An engineered composure that barely disguised the hunger coiled beneath his skin.

Dylan sat across from him, taut and twitching, like a man forced to share a table with a loaded gun.

"You're sure about this?" he asked, eyes flicking toward the envelope on the table as if the paper might detonate if handled wrong.

Sebastian didn't answer.

He let the question rot in the air until the silence pressed on Dylan's chest, slow and suffocating. That was the beauty of silence—its invasive patience. Given enough of it, people always showed their cracks first.

At last, he spoke. Quiet. Precise.

"Red roses. One a week. Two, if I say so. No notes. No names. No mess."

Dylan shifted in his chair, a flicker of instinct tightening his muscles—flight, useless and already too late.

"You really think this is helping?"

A pause.

A smile.

Serene. Calculated. Terrifying.

"It's already working."

Sebastian leaned back, fingers steepled, his expression unreadable as Dylan's hand hesitated near the envelope; not over a piece of paper, but over the storm folded inside it.

"Fear makes people reach for something to hold onto." His smile fainted at the edges. "I'll be there when she falls. When she finally realizes she was never meant to stand alone."

Dylan's mouth opened, but the warning behind his lips never made it out. It collapsed beneath the weight of Sebastian's certainty.

"You think you're the anchor?" he asked instead, voice flat with disbelief.

Sebastian's smile returned, slow and deliberate—more omen than expression. "I'm not her anchor," he murmured, lifting his glass as the scotch caught the light like fire in a church. "I'm the answer."

His gaze sharpened.

Focused.

"I see what Gideon never will. Arden's not some delicate thing meant for safekeeping. She doesn't need a fucking pedestal. She needs permission to burn."

He leaned forward, voice lowering to something almost reverent.

"She's rage wrapped in silk. Built for fire. For destruction. For rebirth. And I'm the only one who sees that."

Dylan exhaled, sharp and uncertain. "You're playing with fire."

"I'm not playing," Sebastian whispered. "This isn't a game."

It was resurrection.

His thumb drifted along the rim of his glass, etching a halo into the condensation. The motion was idle, delicate—a lover's caress.

Then, softer still, "She needs to remember."

Dylan flinched. "This could destroy her."

Sebastian closed his eyes. He didn't flinch. Didn't waver.

Instead, he conjured her—Arden, wild and alive. Light caught in her hair. Fury parted her lips. Thunder moved beneath her skin.

Every spark in her blood, every flare of rebellion in her veins—he had mistaken all of it for a language meant for him. She hadn't learned that yet. Beautiful. Untouchable.

His.

"Aren't you just mimicking the other guy?" Dylan dared.

Sebastian's eyes opened, cold in a way devotion had no right to be. "I'm not mimicking him. He was careless. Clumsy. He thought fear alone could forge devotion. But I—" He breathed the word like scripture. "I understand her. I'm refining the narrative. Making it sharper. Making it worthy."

His gaze went glassy with something too polished to be madness and too intimate to be anything else.

"She was never his to break," Sebastian said. "But she'll be mine to rebuild. She doesn't know it yet. But she will."

LEFT ALONE WITH HIS SCOTCH, Sebastian traced the single red petal he'd placed on the table, his touch reverent and slow, as if even a fragment of beauty could bruise beneath the wrong pressure.

Everything was unfolding perfectly.

Dylan was playing his part. The messages were landing like depth charges in Arden's mind. Every reminder of her past had been crafted with precision, each one designed to press against the oldest wound until she moved exactly where Sebastian needed her to go.

Fear was never the end.

It was the doorway. The threshold. The first dark crossing into something inevitable; something waiting with his name already written into its bones.

Sebastian exhaled slowly, gaze fixed on the glass as amber light fractured through the scotch.

My Little Fire, he thought. She doesn't even know she's already burning for me.

Not yet.

But she would.

CHAPTER 28

A Garden Between Worlds

An hour later, Arden climbed the steps of Gideon's brownstone, the late chill slicing across her skin like a warning she did not need. The place wasn't grand. No sprawling estate, no gleaming monument to the Blackwell name; just brick and shadow and a kind of intentional quiet that felt more revealing than wealth ever could. It was him, she realized. Grounded. Controlled. Built to withstand weather without asking anyone to admire the architecture.

Before she could knock, the door opened.

And then he was there.

Dark jeans. A sweater that didn't try to make a statement. No designer flash, no sharp tailoring—only comfort, quiet ruggedness, restraint. He looked like the man from the club, but stripped of the armor; still unmistakably Gideon, and somehow more dangerous for being less protected.

It threw her for a second.

"I—" she began, but the word barely made it out.

Gideon didn't reply. One step closed the space between them, and his hand settled low on her back, the contact gentle but grounding. Even through the cotton of her shirt, the warmth of him sank deep, assured and impossible to mistake.

Then his mouth found hers.

Not tentative. Not careful.

Firm. Focused. Certain.

The kind of kiss that didn't ask for permission because it already knew the answer; the kind that moved through her low and deep, tightening her breath, scattering every thought before she could arrange them into something safe.

He pulled back slowly, but the look he gave her lingered, heavy and unreadable.

"Hi," he said, rough-edged, with that low, wreck-your-sanity voice of his.

She blinked, thrown by how quickly the air had shifted around them. "I thought we were keeping things uncomplicated," she said, her voice tighter than intended.

Gideon's mouth tugged at the corner. "Turns out I'm not great at uncomplicated."

Then he stepped back enough to give her space, letting the decision return to her without making a performance of it. Choice. Autonomy. Power. He offered all three by moving aside and saying nothing else.

Arden stood unmoving for a second, then crossed the threshold.

The warmth that met her wasn't only the radiator or the low, muted thrum of music somewhere deeper in the house. It lived in the atmosphere itself, in the subtle, lived-in quality of the space; clean soap, something herbal clinging to the air, the hush of a home designed for privacy rather than display. She felt it in her bones before she knew what to do with it.

Gideon didn't say much. He only motioned toward the staircase with a flick of his chin. "Upstairs."

No push. No pressure.

She followed anyway.

As they reached the second floor, everything shifted—closer, quieter. The scent of rosemary and cedar intensified, rich and familiar, settling in her chest like memory, though she couldn't place where or when.

Then the rooftop door opened, and Arden froze.

Overhead, string lights swayed in the breeze, casting the space in gentle gold. Ivy climbed the railing in loose, stubborn tendrils. Terra cotta pots flanked the walls, crowded with unruly herbs and clustered blooms, their edges softened by the damp evening air. It was a garden tucked into the bones of the city, wild and intimate, as if it had grown there in secret and been allowed, against all odds, to stay.

It wasn't some polished rooftop spread from a lifestyle magazine. It wasn't perfect.

But it was breathtaking.

A modest wooden table sat off-center, two places set with real plates and folded napkins. Beyond it, the skyline bled into a quiet, moving haze—light and motion and distance, softened by the mist until even the city seemed to be holding its voice down.

Her chest drew tight with something she didn't have a name for.

"This... isn't what I thought I'd find up here," she said softly, her gaze moving across the rooftop. "I expected... shinier."

Gideon stepped up beside her, hands in his pockets. "Something Blackwell?"

She glanced at him sideways. "Definitely not this." Her voice gentled despite herself. "It feels like you."

He didn't flinch. He didn't argue or deflect, didn't push her to explain what she meant. He simply let the silence stretch between them—quiet, unguarded, suspended like a held breath.

Arden looked past him, to the garden. To the city beyond it, veiled in a hush that felt almost sacred. The stillness settled inside her and twisted there too, soft enough to be comfort, sharp enough to be warning.

Her heart, loud and unruly, thudded against her ribs.

Something had changed. Not in what he said, but in what he allowed her to see. That was what scared her most—not the roses, not the watcher, not even the shadows she had spent years refusing to let catch her.

This.

The open door.

The chance she hadn't expected.

❦

Across the street, Colton leaned into the supple leather of the SUV's driver's seat, fingers tapping out a slow, aimless rhythm against the wheel. His eyes stayed fixed on the glowing windows of the brownstone.

He didn't bother hiding.

He didn't particularly care if anyone saw.

A billionaire with all the money in the damn world, and Gideon was playing house in a brownstone like some middle-class art dealer. *Jesus.*

Then he'd seen the kiss.

Seen Arden's body ease into it, seen the way she leaned toward Gideon like she wanted that kind of trouble. Amateur move. Want made people predictable; tenderness made them stupid.

Colton lifted his phone, snapped a photo, and sent it off without ceremony.

> She's here. They're comfortable. More than expected.

A pause. Then the reply came through.

> Aunt Evelyn: Keep tabs. I want everything.

Of course you do, Colton thought, slipping the phone back into his jacket.

The picture-perfect moment across the street wouldn't last. It never did. Whatever Gideon thought he was building in there—sanctuary, rebellion, some soft little life beyond the reach of the family name—he should have known better. Nothing survived this family untouched.

And Arden?

Sooner or later, she'd crack. They all did.

When she did, Colton would be there. Not to help. Not to catch her.

To report.

To watch her come apart, one piece at a time.

Dinner wasn't elaborate. It was beef stew, rich and hearty, ladled from a cast-iron Dutch oven Gideon pulled from a warming tray, the kind of meal that didn't announce itself so much as settle in and make a place feel lived in.

It felt... intimate.

The savory, earthy scent wrapped around them, mingling with the soft glow of string lights and the damp hush of the city beyond the railing. Like the world had stepped back. Like the night had exhaled. Like the warmth of him had found its way into everything.

Arden arched a brow as he lifted the lid.

"You're serving stew?" she teased, her voice half laugh, half curiosity. "Didn't see that coming."

Gideon laughed under his breath, warm and unbothered, and reached for the wine. "My grandfather used to make it when I was a kid," he said, pouring into two glasses. His voice carried a softer edge, shaped by memory. "Said simple food tells the best stories."

He handed her a glass, his lips tugging into a half-smirk. "Also, it's damn good."

The version of him she'd built in her mind—the polished, unreachable one—was crumbling. In its place stood something quieter. Truer. A man with herbs on his rooftop and stew in a cast-iron pot, offering memory as if it were something he had not meant to hand over but couldn't quite keep back.

She studied him. "He sounds like someone worth remembering."

"He was," Gideon said, the words quiet.

Then came the flicker of a dry smile. "Can't say the same for the rest."

The words hung between them, not bitter exactly, but unfinished. They settled into the space with all the things he did not say; old money, old damage, a family name polished smooth enough to hide the rot beneath.

They ate like they'd done it before. No performance. No careful arrangement of charm. Only presence, and the kind of rhythm that didn't need filling.

A little while later, Gideon set his fork down and leaned back. "This place... it's not what most people would expect." His thumb brushed the stem of his wineglass, the motion absent and telling. "But that's what I like about it."

Arden looked up. "Most people?"

He offered the faintest smile. "My family, mostly. They live for legacy and perception. I wanted it to feel like..."

He hesitated, not because he didn't know the word, but because saying it made the truth of it visible.

"Mine."

Arden lifted her wine. "And does it?"

His eyes moved across the rooftop—the imperfect brick, the tangled string lights, the mismatched pots, the small, stubborn life he had coaxed out of a city built to harden people. Something in him eased.

"It does now."

And somehow, so did she.

Conversation flowed after that, unrushed and unfiltered. Gideon talked about the brownstone like it was more than a home; a rebellion, maybe, or a refusal to keep playing the game on Blackwell terms. Brick by brick, room by room, he had built himself a life his family couldn't quite understand, which meant they couldn't fully control.

And Arden listened.

For once, she didn't armor up or pivot away. She let him be there in front of her without turning him into a problem to solve, a risk to assess, a threat to survive. She simply listened, and the quiet between them became something warmer than silence.

Her gaze drifted toward a small pot near the terrace edge, where roses bloomed defiantly against the chill. They should have looked delicate out there, fragile against the damp air and the hard lines of the city, but instead they seemed almost insolent with color. Arden reached out, her fingers brushing the soft edge of a petal.

"They're lovely," she murmured.

Gideon followed her gaze. "They're stubborn."

She glanced at him.

"The gardener said they wouldn't last," he said with a half-shrug. "I told him to plant them anyway."

Arden stilled. Not outwardly. Nothing so obvious. But something inside her held its breath.

"My grandmother grew roses," she said finally, her voice quiet. "She used to call me Rose—it's my middle name."

Her fingers hovered over the bloom. "I hated it when I was little. But now..." A shallow breath moved through her. "I miss how it sounded when she said it."

It was too much. She felt it the second the words left her mouth; the small, naked truth of it hanging there between the city and the string lights and this man who kept making quiet places feel dangerous.

But then—

"Arden Rose."

Her gaze snapped to his.

The way he said it was the problem. Not possessive. Not careless. Worse. Reverent in a way that made the name feel returned to her, polished free of grief and placed gently back in her hands.

The air didn't just shift. It thickened.

Her chest tightened. She hated how it sounded in his voice. She hated even more how much she didn't.

"Don't get used to it," she said, cool as ever.

Almost.

She threw him a smirk, quick and defensive, the shield raised before the wound could show. But Gideon didn't take the bait. He only watched her, quiet and unblinking, as if he could see every layer she had so carefully stacked between herself and the world.

Every deflection. Every discipline. Every lie she told herself about not needing anyone, about being fine on her own, about loneliness becoming safer if you learned to call it independence.

And for one terrifying, electric second, Arden wasn't sure she could look away.

As the night wore on, the noise of the world slipped farther away. Up here, the city felt held at a distance, all that glass and steel and restless motion softened beneath mist and string lights, as if the whole of New York had pressed pause and left them suspended in the hush.

For the first time in weeks, Arden felt it.

Peace.

No shadows gathering at the edges. No roses left in her wake. No phantom footsteps threading themselves through her memory. Only quiet, and the strange, fragile mercy of not having to brace for the next thing.

Gideon leaned back in his chair, the hard lines of him softened by wine and the kind of surrender he probably would have denied if she'd named it. When his voice came, it was low and thoughtful, raw in a way she wasn't used to hearing from him.

He spoke of his grandfather, Richard Blackwell II, the man whose legacy clung to the bones of everything they touched.

"He believed in creating a foundation that would last. Something good." Gideon's gaze drifted, his fingers brushing the rim of his glass, almost absently. "But that dream didn't survive him. It got swallowed by greed."

The shift in his tone sharpened the space between them.

"What happened?" Arden asked. No teasing now. No armor in the shape of wit. Only concern, quiet and direct.

"My father happened. And Evelyn." The names landed like dead weight. "They took what he built and twisted it—used it to control people. To erase them."

A bitter smirk flickered at the corner of his mouth and died there.

"The Blackwell name used to mean something," he said. "Now it's just... leverage."

His words settled over her, thick and unvarnished. But it wasn't self-pity. That would have been easier to dismiss, easier to file away as another rich man mourning the inconvenience of inheritance.

This was grief.

Arden leaned in, elbows braced against the table, her gaze steady on his. "You're doing more than surviving," she said, voice low but certain. "You're trying to rewrite it."

Not a question.

Gideon nodded once, a hard, quiet motion. "Trying." His voice roughened. "But Evelyn... she doesn't just want to shape the narrative. She wants to control it. Every word. Every page."

He looked at her then, really looked. "If she sees you as part of my story..."

He didn't finish.

He didn't have to.

Arden's chin lifted. "Let her."

No bravado. No reckless performance of courage. Just defiance, clean and steady, drawn from the same place that had kept her alive long before Gideon Blackwell ever looked at her like she mattered.

For a moment, Gideon didn't speak. He only watched her, as if she'd become something he hadn't dared let himself hope for.

"You don't make anything easy," he murmured.

"Would you really want me to?"

His smile came slow. Dangerous. "No. I'd hate it."

He didn't want easy.

He wanted her.

The moment stretched, pulling tighter with every breath. The air between them seemed to press closer, heavier, charged with all the things neither of them had been reckless enough to say.

He should have said something.

But for once in his life, Gideon Blackwell was speechless.

She was it. The most dangerous thing he had ever seen; not because she was fragile, not because she needed saving, but because she stood there with all that damage forged into discipline, all that ache sharpened into will, and looked at him as if she understood the parts of him no one else had bothered to name.

And fuck if he would ever let her go.

"You're chasing approval that doesn't matter," she murmured, almost conspiratorial.

His eyes lingered on her mouth, then lifted to hers, something unresolved passing between them.

Her breath snagged.

She hadn't seen that coming.

Arden's gaze fell to the table, searching for something safe to anchor herself to, but nothing felt steady. Not with him looking at her like that. Like he saw her.

All of her.

"I built walls," she admitted, her voice brittle. "Too high. Too thick. I built them so no one could get in."

Her fingers brushed his chest, catching in the fabric of his shirt, subtle and reflexive, as if some traitorous part of her had reached for him before the rest of her could stop it.

"It was survival," she said. "That's what it was. I got good at being alone."

Gideon didn't move, but his presence settled around her, anchored and certain.

She took a shaky breath. "Some people would call it selfish—cutting ties. Leaving them behind like they didn't matter."

She shook her head, her throat tightening around the rest.

"But that life... that wasn't living. It was barely breathing."

He said nothing. He only listened. Present. Anchored. One hand steady at her hip, his thumb tracing small, quiet circles there, not possessive, not demanding; only a reminder written against her skin.

You're not there anymore.

"I didn't have a choice," she said softly. "If I hadn't left... I don't think I'd have made it out whole."

When her eyes met his, there was no pity waiting for her. No soft, unbearable sympathy. Only steady resolve, the kind that did not flinch from ugly truths and did not insult her by trying to make them smaller.

"You're still standing," he said, voice low. "And not because someone saved you. You did that. You made a life out of what was left."

He lifted a hand to her face, cupping her cheek with slow, instinctive care. His thumb brushed her skin, and the touch sent a quiet ache through her ribs.

"In case no one ever said it out loud... you made the right call."

She stilled.

The words hit like truth always did—sharp, clean, undeniable.

Gideon leaned in, his breath warming her skin, and pressed a kiss to her forehead. Gentle. Unhurried. When he pulled back, he didn't say anything at first. He only looked at her, as if the pieces of her she had tried to make unlovable had never frightened him at all.

"And those walls you've built?" His voice was low but unyielding. "If I have to, I'll climb them. Scale them. Hell, I'll knock them down brick by brick if that's what it takes to get to you."

Her throat tightened.

For a moment, she could barely find her voice. "What if I never figured out how to let someone in?"

A beat.

Then, "You already have."

God help her.

He meant it.

The air between them charged in the silence that followed, every glance and breath somehow tethered to the other. Arden felt his steadiness, his restraint, the careful force of a man who knew exactly what he wanted and still refused to take what hadn't been offered.

"That's what makes this real, Arden." His hand found hers, threading their fingers together. "You're not hiding anymore."

She looked down at their joined hands, at the simple intimacy of his fingers between hers, and felt something inside her yield without breaking.

"Can we take it slow?" she asked. "See where it goes?"

His smile was quiet. Certain.

"We can take it as slow as you need," he said, voice firm, reverent. "But make no mistake…"

His fingers brushed hers, then entwined more fully.

His voice dropped.

"You're mine. I've known it since the night we met."

Her pulse skipped.

She didn't pull away. Didn't run. She stayed, and for once, the space between her and another person didn't feel like a battleground.

When Gideon rose and offered his hand, his voice was low and steady. "Come inside."

She didn't hesitate.

"Okay."

He didn't lead. He didn't pull. He waited.

And Arden took the step herself.

The room wasn't lavish or cold. It was lived in, softened by presence rather than décor, with a quiet kind of wear that made it feel less designed than inhabited. The scent of spice and temptation lingered in the air, unmistakably him, and it reached Arden before she had fully stepped inside.

She hovered in the doorway, fingers brushing the collar of her coat, because one more step felt significant. She wasn't sure why. She only knew she felt it in her chest like a warning.

She had faced down chaos. Stared down threats. Learned how to brace for danger long before anyone should have had to teach her.

But this was different entirely.

Gideon said nothing. He didn't crowd her or fill the silence with reassurance she hadn't asked for. He simply waited, quiet and steady, letting the choice remain hers.

Arden removed her coat and laid it across the armchair. A simple act, really; ordinary enough to mean nothing in any other room. Here, it felt seismic, as if she had crossed into a version of herself she wasn't used to being.

"I don't know how to do this," she said at last, her voice low. Not timid. Honest.

The admission landed between them with more weight than she expected.

Gideon crossed the space as if gravity had finally given him permission. No urgency. No resistance. His hands rose, rough palms brushing her jaw, thumbs tracing her cheekbones with aching precision. He didn't grasp. Didn't demand.

He simply touched.

Anchored.

"You don't need to," he murmured. "Just let me be here."

A quiet steadiness rose in her. Not all the way, but enough.

She nodded. A small motion, barely more than breath and consent, but for Arden, it was surrender wrapped in instinct. Not defeat. Something deeper, more dangerous. Permission.

She drifted toward the dresser, fingers gliding along the wood as if it held a current. No words. No glance back. Only a pause, a breath, and then she opened the drawer.

Her hand closed around the black tee—soft, broken-in, steeped in his scent—and a tightness curled low in her chest. She brushed her fingers over the cotton, then gathered it in her hand and walked toward the bathroom.

At the doorway, her eyes flicked back to him.

Not asking. Not explaining.

Only checking to see if he was still there.

He was.

Behind the bathroom door, each beat of her pulse sounded louder than the last. Her pulse wasn't warning her away this time; anticipation gathered low and molten, making every small movement feel charged.

Every movement felt like a choice: peeling off her layers, sliding into his shirt, adjusting the hem against her thighs. A line crossed. Not for him.

For her.

WHEN SHE STEPPED OUT, the air changed.

Gideon didn't speak. He went utterly still, jaw tight, every hard-won piece of his control suspended by the sight of her in his shirt.

The black cotton clung to her like a secret he had no business knowing. The hem grazed the tops of her thighs; the thin fabric skimmed the curve of her breasts, betraying the sharp evidence of her need. She stood there in bare skin and borrowed darkness, looking less like temptation than consequence.

His consequence.

As if she had no idea she had set him on fire.

Or worse—as if she did, and had decided to watch him burn.

When she walked toward him, slow and sure, it felt like a sentence being handed down.

He didn't reach for her.

She reached for him.

The second her hands found him, the room detonated.

The kiss wasn't patient or polished. It was filthy with want, wild and greedy, a collision of mouths and breath and months of restraint tearing loose at once. His hands found her hips and lifted her into him, dragging her against the hard line of his body with a desperation that shattered whatever discipline he had left. The heat of her through cotton, softness meeting steel, was goddamn lethal.

She wrapped her legs around him and moved against him with slow, dangerous rolls of her hips, dragging him along the ache between her thighs until the sound that tore from his chest barely sounded human. His hand slid higher, curling around the back of her thigh, dragging the shirt up until his palm found bare skin.

Hot. Smooth. Dangerous.

"Jesus, Arden," he rasped. "You're going to fucking destroy me."

She didn't answer. She kissed him again—deeper, darker, needier—with the kind of hunger that made the past feel like ash and her body the flame that had survived it.

Her fingers speared into his hair, tugging hard enough to drag another guttural sound from him, feral and helpless. Gideon kissed her like a man starving, like she was air and ruin and absolution all at once, like the next breath depended on the taste of her mouth.

When she pulled back, it wasn't distance. It was survival.

Their foreheads pressed together, breath tangled, pulses crashing in the hush between them. Her lips were kiss-bitten, parted and trembling. Her eyes were dark with promise, her chest rising with a need she made no attempt to hide.

And Gideon was already gone. Shattered. Worshipful. Held together by nothing but the thin, fraying thread of restraint.

Then she kissed him again, slower this time.

More lethal.

Gideon finally pulled back, just enough to see her. Really see her.

He circled her in a slow orbit, reverent and starved, like she was holy ground he had no right to touch. His gaze slid down her body, pausing at the swell of her breasts, the way his shirt clung and lifted, hinting at skin that begged to be touched. Her thighs were bare and breathtaking. Her nipples were hard, straining against cotton that couldn't hide a damn thing.

She was art.

Obscene.

Perfect.

His undoing.

Nothing had ever looked more right than Arden standing barefoot in his room, wearing his shirt, watching him like she had chosen this and wasn't going anywhere.

Gideon didn't speak. He reached for her hand, steady and quiet and sure, and the air between them shifted. He could have taken more; she would have let him. He felt that truth with a force that nearly wrecked him.

But instead, he stepped back just enough to meet her eyes.

What passed between them then went deeper than lust. It was recognition. Understanding. A line drawn carefully in the heat, because tonight was not about possession, no matter how badly his body wanted to forget the difference. It was about the quiet in between. The choice to stay. The ache beneath the armor.

So when he reached for her hand again—gently, open-palmed—it wasn't to pull her into more. It was to lead her toward something softer, into the hush between heartbeats, into a promise made without words.

The bed was warm, but Gideon's arm was what grounded her.

It rested against her like a vow. A tether. Steady. Solid. There, if she reached for it, and never asking for more than she was willing to give.

At first, her body resisted. Her muscles stayed tight, her spine stiff, old instincts whispering their warnings out of habit.

Don't relax. Don't trust. Don't let go.

Old reflexes didn't die easily.

But his touch never changed. It didn't coax or claim or try to persuade her body before her mind could catch up. It only offered.

His breath moved slow and even behind her, an anchor in a sea she didn't yet trust, and his hand—God, that hand—traced soft, aimless patterns along the small of her back. There was nothing calculated in it. Nothing performative. Only presence.

His thumb brushed her hip, featherlight and unhurried.

Take your time. I'm here.

Something opened in her chest, so tender it almost frightened her; the unfamiliar weight of being met gently, completely, without expectation.

She didn't know how to do this. How to be touched without consequence. How to rest in someone else's quiet without preparing for the silence to turn sharp. But maybe she didn't have to know everything yet. Maybe, for one breath, then another, she only had to stop fighting long enough to try.

So she breathed.

Hesitated.

And then she moved, curling into him by the smallest degree.

Barely.

But enough.

Gideon's breath hitched. Nothing loud or dramatic, but she felt it where his body rested against hers.

Then his arm tightened, just a little.

Enough to keep her close.

And she let him.

CHAPTER 29

The Dawn of Something More

The scent of him surrounded her now—warm, grounding, undeniably Gideon. It should have felt too soon.

Somehow, it didn't.

The worn cotton of his shirt clung to her skin, soft and oversized, brushing high along her bare thighs as she stretched beneath the covers. It drowned her in the best way; his scent, his warmth, his presence woven into every thread.

Oud Wood, that rich, smoky-spiced Tom Ford signature. Beneath it, something darker lingered. Earthier. Unmistakably him. A part of him she was beginning to crave.

His breath moved slow and steady beneath her cheek, the rise and fall of his chest lulling her into a dangerous calm, one that felt a little too much like peace. In the golden hush of morning, cocooned in scent and silence, Arden wondered if maybe—God help her—she could get used to this.

A shift stirred the sheets, the faintest pull of air, and her lashes fluttered open.

The covers had slipped down.

Her lungs seized around a breath she forgot how to take.

She blinked once, twice, her brain scrambling to reboot.

Oh.

Oh, hell.

Gideon lay beside her, half-covered and fully wrecking her. The man was obscene.

Black boxer briefs clung to him, criminally snug, and the fabric left nothing to the imagination. Least of all hers.

If he was devastating in a suit—untouchable, commanding, polished into something almost cruel—then like this, bare and sleep-warm and relaxed beside her, he was a different kind of ruin altogether.

God-tier.

Devastation in human form.

Not sculpted to be seen. Sculpted to unravel.

Her gaze wandered—no, devoured. Slowly. Shamelessly. The sculpted lines of his chest, the defined ridges of his abs, the impossible cut of his V—

And there.

Right there.

Her throat dried out.

The unmistakable shape beneath the cotton made her pulse stutter, and her body tightened with dangerous awareness.

Sweet merciful fuck.

She curled her fingers into the sheets, tethering herself there, because one more second of looking and she would crawl over him. Give in. Forget every fragile, careful thing they had built the night before beneath the weight of all that heat.

Except this wasn't only heat anymore.

It was gravity.

And God help her, she liked falling.

He shifted slowly, stretching with lazy, ruinous ease before dragging a hand through his messy hair, every muscle rippling with the motion. His head tilted slightly, as if he felt her gaze before he opened his eyes.

Nope.

Arden yanked the sheet over her head with a whispered curse.

Abort mission.

If she stayed hidden long enough, she could pretend she hadn't just spent two full minutes thirsting over him like a woman starved.

But then—

"Arden."

His voice broke through the silence, rough with sleep, deep enough to leave a mark.

One word, and she was wrecked.

His voice shouldn't have had the power to knock the breath from her lungs, but it did. She stilled beneath the sheet, trying to ignore the heat blooming under her skin, but the sound of him in the hush of morning unraveled her completely.

Slowly, cautiously, she peeled the sheet down enough to see him.

And there he was.

Gideon Blackwell, reclined against the pillows, bare chest kissed by morning light, sculpted lines made golden by the sun spilling through the window. His gray eyes were darker now, heavy with sleep, but trained only on her.

"Good morning."

His voice was gentler than she had ever heard it, as though he didn't want to break the fragile quiet stretching between them.

She blinked once, unsure how to navigate the truth of this. It wasn't banter, and it wasn't flirtation. It was quieter than that. Braver.

"Morning," she said, the word a soft echo.

His lips curved, slow and lazy, into the kind of smile that didn't belong to Gideon Blackwell, enigmatic businessman. It belonged to the man beneath the polish, the one who had held her like she wasn't delicate, but divine.

His thumb skimmed across her waist, casual and tender, sending a ripple through her that had less to do with lust than it should have and everything to do with care.

"You stayed."

No challenge. No smugness. Just wonder.

She swallowed hard, the weight of it catching in her throat. The way he said it made staying feel like something that mattered. Like she mattered.

"I did."

His gaze never left hers. "How do you feel?"

She hesitated, worrying her lip, unsure how much to reveal.

Like I should run.

Like I'm not built for this.

Like some part of me exhaled last night for the first time in years.

She tried for a smirk, but it fell a little short. "Okay," she said.

A pause, and then—quiet, raw, real: "Better than okay."

Relief softened his features, subtle but certain.

His hand came up to tuck a strand of hair behind her ear, and God, she leaned into it without thinking.

She should have pulled back. Should have found her shoes, her walls, her exit. Instead, she whispered, "You meant what you said last night."

Not a question.

A confession.

"I did." His voice was steady, grounded. "You don't have to rush, Arden. But you don't have to run, either."

The words pressed into her like a hand against her chest. Gentle, but there. A quiet truth she wasn't ready to hold and couldn't quite ignore.

Her gaze dropped to the blanket, where her fingers drew invisible patterns across the fabric.

"You didn't have to do that, you know."

He tilted his head. "Do what?"

She exhaled, the words catching somewhere between shame and gratitude.

"Hold me."

A breath.

"Make it feel like I wasn't too much."

His eyes darkened, not with heat this time, but with something that went bone-deep. He reached for her hand, slowly brushing over her knuckles before curling his fingers around hers.

"Arden," he said, voice roughened by conviction. "Last night wasn't about me. It was about you. What you needed."

Her throat tightened again, and she hated that it made her feel so exposed. So seen.

How did he do that?

How did he touch her without laying a single claim, yet make her feel like he'd reached every guarded place she had sworn no one would reach?

"I don't know how to let someone do that," she murmured, eyes fixed on their joined hands.

She didn't know how to stay. How to stop believing every battle had to be fought alone. How to rest inside tenderness without waiting for it to turn into debt.

His hand tightened enough to anchor her.

"You did," he said simply.

Then, after a moment that felt like a lifetime, "And you can."

The truth in his voice was gentle. Certain. Undeniable.

And she believed him.

Even if only for a moment.

Even if believing was the bravest thing she had done in years.

THE QUIET WASN'T UNCOMFORTABLE. It was expectant, the air between them thick with everything left unsaid.

Arden's pulse skipped, nerves flickering beneath the surface as a question rose in her throat, daring her to let it become real. She didn't overthink it.

"Gideon."

His name slipped out low and instinctive, a little too intimate to pretend she hadn't meant it.

It wasn't loud.

But it hit its mark.

He turned, gaze sharp and dialed in, as if she had cut clean through whatever quiet thoughts had been occupying him. One arm rested behind his head, the other sprawled across his abs like he had nowhere to be, every inch of him sleep-warm and unbothered.

He looked like a man who could stay like that forever.

Arden knew better.

His mouth tipped into a lazy half-smile, the slow-burn kind that always came with trouble.

"Hmm?"

She arched a brow, tipping her head with enough attitude to keep things balanced. "You have a spare toothbrush?"

He didn't answer right away. He only watched her for a beat, then let out a slow exhale, the kind that curled at the edges with smug satisfaction.

"A toothbrush?" he echoed, voice low, rough with sleep and unmistakable warmth. "So, you're planning to stick around?"

Arden rolled her eyes, but her smirk betrayed her. "Not forever, Blackwell. Just long enough to keep my teeth from falling out."

His laugh came low and unhurried, rough in that early-morning way that sent a ripple down her spine and heat straight to her center.

Then, like sin made casual, he swung his legs off the bed and rose in one smooth motion, stretching tall, muscles shifting like a slow, perfect problem.

"Top drawer in the bathroom," he said, nodding toward the ensuite. "I keep extras."

She raised a brow, arms crossing loosely. "Naturally."

He moved aside enough for her to slip past, flashing a grin that didn't even try to hide the spark in his eyes.

"I like to be prepared."

She stopped at the threshold, hand brushing lightly against the doorframe, and glanced back, one brow lifted, her expression threaded with playful challenge.

"Hopefully not prepared for just anyone."

She tossed it like a joke, a jab meant to keep the edge between them playful, but Gideon didn't let it stay there. His expression sharpened, the grin shifting into something subtler. More intent.

"You're not just anyone, Arden."

The way he said it landed in her chest like a punch wrapped in velvet.

Her heart kicked hard.

She opened her mouth, some smartass line already poised at the edge, but it caught halfway up her throat. Too dangerous. Too real. So she turned, calm as hell, and walked toward the bathroom like her legs weren't on fire.

Before the door clicked shut, she looked back once over her shoulder, only for a second.

That look wasn't teasing.

It was a warning.

Brace yourself.

ARDEN PEEKED out of the bathroom, feigning nonchalance while her pulse thrummed hard beneath her skin.

Dangerous. That was the only word for the way Gideon watched her—half-reclined, shirtless, breath-stealing, every inch of him looking too relaxed to be safe.

"I'm gonna grab a shower..."

A pause.

"Before I head home."

Gideon stilled.

For a moment, the only sound was the steady rush of water, steam curling past her like a slow-building storm.

Her words had been casual. Innocent, even.

Her eyes told a different story.

There was hunger there, dark and unmistakable, a dare wrapped in heat. She let him see it, let it hang between them with all the reckless confidence of a woman who had decided, at least for this morning, that running could wait.

Slowly, Gideon straightened, his eyes locked on hers, reading every unspoken challenge, every deliberate flicker of want. A muscle ticked in his jaw.

She knew exactly what she was doing.

God help her—so did he.

He repeated the words slowly, as if tasting the danger in them. "A shower."

Arden arched a brow, pretending not to notice the way his voice had dropped, rich and deep enough to slip beneath her skin.

"Yes, Gideon. A shower. Soap, water, the works."

His mouth curved into a slow smile, the kind that sent heat spiraling through her and threatened to make a ruin of every sensible thought she had ever had.

"You. In my shower." His gaze dragged over her, lazy, thorough, knowing. "You're making it very hard for me to leave this room."

Her cheeks warmed, but she didn't flinch. She didn't back down. Instead, she tilted her head and let the moment stretch, let him watch her standing there in his shirt, with steam at her back and trouble written all over her face.

Then, with a smirk—sharp, knowing, perfectly timed—she said, "Join me?"

His breath hitched.

For one charged second, Gideon Blackwell—the man who never hesitated, never faltered, never lost control—didn't move.

Then he snapped.

A growl, low and hungry, rumbled from his chest, and before she could take her next breath, he had her.

Arden squealed as he lifted her effortlessly into his arms, laughter bursting out of her, sharp and surprised and threaded with heat.

"Gideon!"

His grip was firm, his arms tightening around her as he carried her toward the bathroom like she weighed nothing.

His lips ghosted over her ear, his breath sending a delicious shiver down her spine.

"You can't say things like that and expect me to resist."

Gideon kicked the door shut behind them, sealing them inside the storm that had been building for months—inevitable, feral, consuming.

THE AIR THICKENED AROUND THEM, steam curling at the edges of Arden's vision as Gideon set her down. His hands lingered at her waist, his thumbs sweeping slow, teasing circles over her bare skin while the shower ran hot beside them.

Her lips parted, pulse hammering as she looked up at him.

A man unraveling.

A man barely holding back.

A man who wanted her completely.

"Well?" She took a single step back, the dare unspoken but unmistakable. "Are you just going to stand there?"

Gideon didn't answer.

The second her fingers brushed the hem of his shirt—the one she was wearing, the one he had imagined on her in a thousand filthy ways—his restraint fractured. He stepped forward and caught her wrist before she could pull the fabric over her head.

His voice, when it came, was slightly ragged.

"I want to undress you."

The words didn't ask. They promised.

And fuck, the way he said them.

Arden's breath stuttered, her body aching before he touched her again. Then his mouth was on hers, all need and heat and months of restraint tearing loose in a single, brutal rush. His hands slid beneath the shirt, palms dragging over her ribs before he lifted the cotton over her head in one smooth, ruthless motion and dropped it to the floor.

For one charged second, Gideon only looked at her.

Bare skin. Lace. Steam. The deliberate lift of her chin.

Then his fingers curled into her panties and dragged them down her thighs in one slow, devastating pull. His boxer briefs followed a moment later, and suddenly there was nothing left between them but heat, breath, and the raw, electric shock of him.

Arden wanted.

God help her, she wanted.

His hands found her again, gripping her thighs, her hips, the curve of her ass as if touch alone could tell him where the edges of her began and his restraint ended. The rush of water filled the silence around them, breath quickening beneath it, the promise between their mouths crackling like a live wire.

He needed more.

Gideon turned her effortlessly, pressing her back to the cold tile, his heat crashing into her in rough, unrelenting contrast. A shiver rippled through her. His mouth found her throat, tongue tracing fire over the flutter of her pulse before he dragged lower and nipped the skin above her collarbone.

Her knees buckled.

"Gideon—"

He caught her, pressing her back against the tile as his thigh slid between hers.

"No turning back now," he rasped, voice a low growl in her ear. "Not after that invitation. Not when I've imagined the sounds you make in my head."

His voice was rough. Ragged.

A confession, not a boast.

Her breath caught, sharp and unguarded, as his hands traced from her ribs to her hips—slow, certain, possessive enough to make her pulse riot, controlled enough to make her trust the fire. She arched into him, needy and fearless, offering the answer with her body before her mouth could catch up.

"Then stop imagining."

Her nails dug into his shoulders.

"Show me."

A low, broken sound tore from him.

And he did.

Gideon surged forward, hands gripping Arden's thighs as he lifted her against the cool tile. Her legs wrapped around his waist by instinct, locking him close, and the heat of her seared through every last shred of control he had left.

Water spilled over them, hot and relentless, but he barely felt it.

All he felt was her.

Her mouth parted on a gasp, and he caught it with his own. Brutal. Breathless. His tongue claimed hers, deep and hungry, and still it wasn't close enough. She was fire in his arms—arching, gasping, grinding against the thick press of him as if she wanted to burn the world down.

And fuck, he'd let her.

His mouth tore from hers and dragged down her throat, teeth grazing that sensitive spot beneath her ear, the one that made her shiver.

"You have no idea what you do to me," he ground out, voice shredded with restraint. His mouth trailed lower, nipping at her collarbone as his hips pressed into hers, deliberate and heavy.

She let out a breathy sigh, hot and unsteady, and lost it again when he rolled his hips, grinding her against the slick wall, making sure she felt every hard inch of what she was doing to him.

"Then stop talking," she whispered, voice trembling, daring. "Do something."

His answer was physical.

That was the crack that broke him open.

One hand gripped her ass, dragging her higher up his body, fitting her exactly where he wanted her. The other slid between them, fingers finding the heat between her thighs, moving through her with practiced confidence and devastating attention, as if he had studied every sound she hadn't made yet and meant to pull them from her one by one.

Her head fell back with a gasp, a moan tearing from her lips and echoing off the tile like a half-forgotten prayer.

"Fuck," he growled, watching her fall apart for him. "You're soaked—and it's not the water."

Her nails bit into his shoulders as his mouth found the swell of her breast, kissing and biting with a hunger that felt almost too reverent to survive. Desperation lived in the edges of it, in the way his breath dragged against her skin, in the way his hands held her as if she were the only thing anchoring him to the world.

Raw. Ferocious. His.

"You don't get it," he muttered against her skin. "This isn't a one-night thing. I'm not letting you walk away from this."

She met his eyes—wide, wild, and lethal—and dragged her fingers through his dripping hair.

"Then don't."

God, that voice.

Low and rough and pleading.

And he snapped. Again.

Because how the fuck was he supposed to survive her?

He slammed back into her mouth, the kiss raw and punishing, hips grinding, hands greedy. As she gasped into him—gone, shattered, burning bright enough to ruin him—he made her a silent vow. This wasn't the peak. This was the beginning.

And he'd make her feel it.

Every. Damn. Time.

Steam blurred the edges of everything, but not him.

Gideon pressed her harder into the tile, her back arching as water trailed rivulets down her skin. His mouth followed one over the swell of her breast, teeth catching on her nipple with enough bite to make her cry out—sharp, startled, desperate.

Her fingers clawed into his shoulders, holding on for dear life.

"Gideon—"

"I've got you," he growled, the words a promise, a threat, a vow.

His name had never sounded so ruined.

His hand slid down again, touching her with the same fierce certainty that had undone her all morning. He didn't rush. He didn't lose her in the heat. He found the rhythm of her body and followed it deeper, fingers thrusting, curling just right, hitting that spot that made her gasp like he'd stolen the air from her lungs.

And maybe he had.

He watched her come apart, completely consumed.

"Look at me."

She barely managed it—lashes wet, lips parted, every breath a moan—but she met his eyes, and he felt it.

The shift.

The surrender.

The trust.

A growl rumbled low in his throat, and he kissed her like he'd die if he didn't, like the taste of her was the only thing tethering him to the earth.

Her thighs trembled, her body clenching around his fingers, hips rolling with a rhythm that belonged to no one but them.

"Come for me," he ordered, dark and deadly. "Right here. Right now."

And she did.

Her cry shattered through the steam, her body breaking open in his arms, slick and trembling and so fucking his.

He held her through it, never letting go, never easing up, because she needed to know. This wasn't only sex. This was the line between before and after, crossed in heat and water and the kind of trust neither of them knew how to name yet.

When she collapsed against him, panting and ruined, Gideon pressed a kiss to her temple, his voice rough with reverence.

"We're not even close to done."

THE AIR BETWEEN THEM CRACKLED, heavy with want and the last fragile thread of restraint.

Gideon's gaze dropped, slow and reverent, then snapped back to hers as if looking too long might cost him the little control he had left. But the damage was done. His breath caught. His jaw flexed.

And when he moved, it was with purpose.

He backed her out of the shower and toward the counter, crowding into her space with the heat of a man unraveling by choice, not carelessness. His hands stayed on her, firm and sure, guiding without forcing, every touch another quiet answer to the question she had already asked.

"You're going to kill me," he murmured against her mouth.

"Then die knowing it was worth it," she whispered back, dragging her teeth across his bottom lip before pulling him down into a kiss that had nothing to do with patience and everything to do with possession.

Steam curled around them, the hiss of the shower fading behind the rush of breath and skin as he lifted her onto the cool marble counter. The contrast bit against her bare thighs while his hands burned along her body, sliding over wet skin with the kind of deliberate reverence that made her feel both ruined and held.

His mouth found her throat again, trailing fire along the delicate column of her neck and down to the curve of her shoulder. Arden arched, her legs tightening around his waist, hips rolling against the thick, aching evidence of how badly he wanted her.

"Arden," he rasped, his voice breaking.

She pulled him closer and managed, "Bed."

That single word shattered what remained of his restraint.

It was a gasp. A warning. A plea.

He wasn't stopping.

But he was still Gideon—feral at the edges, disciplined at the center, dangerous because even wrecked, he knew exactly how to hold her without taking more than she gave.

By the time he lifted her again, she was trembling—breathless, dizzy, wrecked. He carried her like a man who could ruin her and had already decided that wasn't enough. He wanted to keep her whole enough to feel every second of it.

The backs of her thighs hit the edge of the mattress, and he laid her down like she was the most breakable thing he had ever held.

The sheets were still warm beneath her, but the heat between them burned hotter.

Arden reached for him, pulling him down with her, legs parting as their bodies aligned with devastating ease—like this moment had always been waiting for them, patient and inevitable, beneath every glance they had refused to name.

He sank into her kiss with a groan that gutted them both, one hand braced above her head, the other trailing down her side until his fingers found the place where her skin was softest.

"Tell me what you want," he breathed, forehead pressed to hers, voice cracked open.

She looked at him then, really looked, and it was Gideon who came undone.

"This," she whispered. "You."

But what followed wasn't only hunger.

It was devotion.

He kissed her slow this time—deep and aching, his hands reverent as they slid down her sides, then up again to cup her face like he couldn't quite believe she was real.

Every kiss was a promise.

Every touch, a reckoning.

"I'm not rushing this," he breathed against her skin, lips ghosting over the swell of her breast, her ribs, her stomach. "Not when I've waited this long."

She could barely breathe, barely think, but she managed to whisper, "Then don't stop."

He didn't.

THE MATTRESS GAVE beneath Arden as she settled under the covers. Gideon followed, folding her into the hush of his body, his warmth easing into every breath.

They lay together for a while without words or rush.

Outside, the city carried on, dim and distant. But here, in the quiet between them, there was only the slow rhythm of his breath beneath her palm.

She drew aimless patterns over his side, committing the shape of him to memory. She had never been here before. Not like this. Not where it mattered.

Gideon broke the silence, his voice low. Careful. Certain.

"Arden."

She looked up, pulse skipping as his eyes found hers. Intent. Steady. All in.

"Yeah?"

His hand slid to the small of her back, warm and patient. A tether, not a hold; no urgency, no demand.

"I'm falling for you."

Her world shifted.

Her heart lurched, then leapt, fast and headlong, as if some reckless part of her had been waiting for this even while the rest of her prepared to run.

She should have made a joke. Deflected. Pulled away. But she didn't, because the words were real, and the worst part—the most terrifying part—was that they were not only his.

They clawed their way up past every wall she had built to survive.

"I think I'm falling for you too."

She didn't raise her voice. She didn't have to.

The confession hit like thunder.

Gideon went rigid beneath her. His hold tightened slightly, and his eyes searched hers—not for permission, but for doubt.

There was none.

Because it was true.

And it terrified her.

He exhaled, slow and steady.

Then he smiled.

Not a smirk. Not a tease. Something real, unguarded, almost boyish in its wonder, and it cracked her wide open.

"Can you do that?" he asked, voice rasping with vulnerability.

Her brows pulled together. "Do what?"

His fingers brushed her jaw, reverent, as if the answer mattered more than he knew how to say.

"Fall."

The word hit harder the second time, half invocation, half dare.

Her instinct screamed for retreat. For armor. For the old, familiar safety of distance. Instead, Arden stayed. She let herself be seen inside the silence, let the truth stand between them without trying to make it smaller.

When she finally spoke, it came quiet. Honest.

"I think I can... with you."

He released a breath like it cost him something.

Relief. Awe. Maybe both.

His arm tightened around her, sealing a vow neither of them knew how to name.

"There's no going back for me," he said, raw and unguarded. "I've tried to fight it. Tried to stay in control. But it's you, Arden. It's always been you."

The words hit hard—undeniable, and too much to hold all at once.

Something shifted in her chest, sharp and sudden, like a lock clicking open.

She pressed her hand over his heart, grounding herself there, as if the steady beat beneath her palm might slow the rush inside her.

"I don't know if I can give you enough," she whispered, the truth scraped raw at the edges. "Not what you deserve."

His hand covered hers, strong and certain.

"You don't have to know," he murmured. "You just have to try."

Her breath trembled.

But the words sank deep, into marrow and memory and the soft places she had once believed were gone for good.

Here she was.

Here he was.

Arden closed her eyes, exhaled, and let herself fall.

THE ROOM WAS BATHED in the muted glow of the city skyline, amber light stretching across tangled sheets and painting shadows over their skin.

The heat between them hadn't vanished. It had only changed shape, quieter now, threaded with something deeper than hunger.

Gideon lay beside her, his arm draped around her waist, fingertips gliding along her skin without urgency. There was no pattern to it, no destination; only a man learning her by touch, slow and reverent, as if he wasn't merely memorizing her body, but all the hidden places that had made her who she was.

His fingers found the curve of the lotus inked into her side.

Dark ink against pale skin.

Her breath caught, sharp and involuntary.

"A lotus," he murmured, voice low and unreadable.

His thumb brushed over the petals with deliberate delicacy, and Arden swallowed hard, the space between them somehow too close and not close enough.

"Got it after nursing school," she said softly. "New chapter. I needed something that felt like... survival."

He didn't respond right away. He only followed the lines of the bloom, every petal and shaded edge, as if the ink meant something sacred beneath his hand.

His eyes never left hers.

"Lotuses grow from the mud," he said finally, voice deeper now. "They bloom through the filth, the dark. That's the point."

Grief and gratitude twisted together in her chest, sharp and sudden and impossible to name.

He wasn't touching only a tattoo. He was touching what it meant, what it had cost, who she'd had to become in order to keep living after everything that tried to bury her.

And he touched it like she mattered.

Like all of it did.

"Fits you," he added quietly. "Even in the dark, you rise."

The words hit soft and unguarded, slipping beneath her defenses before she could decide whether to let them in. This was no longer only about surviving. It was about being seen all the way down to the root of it, and surviving that too.

Her throat closed around the ache forming there, and for once, she didn't try to speak around it.

She could have pulled away. Made a joke. Shifted the moment into safer territory before it asked too much of her.

Instead, she stayed still.

Let him learn her.

Let him trace the map of her past inked into skin.

When his lips slowly brushed over the tattoo, it didn't feel like possession.

It felt like recognition.

Arden didn't brace herself to be claimed.

She let herself be seen.

And God help her, she wanted to be.

❦

Across the city, Evelyn Blackwell sat alone in the hush of her private study, the skyline gleaming through the tall windows behind her and casting fractured shadows across the polished wood of her desk.

One perfectly manicured finger tapped the screen.

No surprise. No outrage. Only calculation.

Her eyes moved over the photos Colton had sent the night before.

They're getting close. She spent the night.

Evelyn exhaled once through her nose, the sound barely audible. At the corners of her mouth, the hint of a smile considered forming and thought better of it.

Foolish girl.

She set the phone down with surgical precision, then rose and crossed to the window, the hem of her silk robe whispering over the floor. Below, her gardens unfolded in orderly lines—every flowerbed symmetrical, every path exact, every bloom permitted to exist only where it had been placed.

Designed.

Controlled.

As she preferred.

Beyond them, the city stretched wide and glittering, an empire she had not merely inherited, but shaped.

The Blackwell legacy wasn't earned. It was enforced.

And Arden Rivers?

She was a weed. Tenacious, perhaps, but still a weed, and weeds had a tiresome habit of mistaking survival for significance.

Soon enough, Evelyn would remind the girl that wild things could be uprooted with the right blade.

Her fingers grazed the stem of an untouched wine glass, her nails clicking softly against the crystal.

Let them believe they mattered. Let Gideon pretend his decisions were his own. Let this girl think she was more than a phase, more than a temporary disruption, more than a brief, inconvenient softness in a man who should have known better.

Evelyn's mouth curved at last, cold and precise.

It'll make the fall that much sweeter.

Let them have their moment.

Let them play.

The game had only just begun.

And Evelyn Blackwell did not lose.

CHAPTER 30

Foundations

The sidewalks buzzed with Saturday grit—espresso machines steaming, bass lines leaking from open doors, sweet and savory scents colliding in the breeze. Arden zipped her jacket, the wind snatching loose strands of brown hair as a cab blared down the block.

She cast Gideon a sideways look as they fell into step. "Don't tell me you're anti-brunch."

Gideon huffed. "Brunch is just day-drinking with extra steps."

She laughed, nudging him lightly. "So, that's a no?"

"I never said no," he said, nudging his hands deeper into his pockets and giving her a look. "It's a half-assed excuse. The company makes or breaks it."

She bumped his arm with her elbow. "I see. So you do like seeing your favorite people in daylight."

His mouth twitched. "Favorite? That what we're calling it now?"

She gave a breathy laugh, brushing her hair back as he guided her gently past the crowd. "Penny and Dan beat us here somehow," she said, sliding the words out casually before he could get too close to whatever was twisting in her chest.

Gideon nodded, though a flicker of hesitation crossed his expression—quick, unreadable. "Figured we'd meet them. Felt like the right call."

Her head tilted. "You don't strike me as a group-brunch kind of guy, Blackwell."

"Maybe I'm here to watch Dan try to keep up with Penny for once."

She smirked. "Reasonable."

They ducked off the main strip, winding toward a narrow café wedged between two old brick buildings. A few locals lingered outside, half-drunk coffees on sun-warmed tables, their conversations rising and falling with the scrape of chairs and the clink of silverware.

At a table near the edge, Penny was mid-rant, her wild hair catching the light as she gestured with full-theatrical flair. Dan sat a chair apart, pointedly not engaging, stirring his drink like a man sentenced to watch interpretive jazz hands before caffeine.

When Penny spotted them, she pulled her sunglasses down. "Well, well, look who decided to show up after all."

Dan didn't even turn his head. "Honestly thought Gid would hold out for a place that served espresso dusted in gold leaf."

Arden dropped into the seat across from Penny and snatched up a menu like it owed her back pay for emotional labor. "No gold. Just caffeine and poor life choices."

Penny gasped in mock horror. "Who are you? First trivia night, now brunch? You're practically domesticated."

Arden gave her a look. "I can still ruin things."

Dan took a sip without glancing over. "She's out of practice."

"Daniel," Penny said sweetly, without missing a beat, "you're living proof that some people can ruin brunch just by showing up."

"Penelope," he replied dryly, "I live to serve."

Gideon took the seat beside Arden, setting his phone face-down on the table. "You two are unbearable."

Penny batted her lashes. "But you showed up."

Dan raised his mug. "For Arden. Obviously."

"Obviously," Penny echoed, sipping with mock elegance.

Arden hid her grin behind the menu. Their chaos was weirdly comforting, all sharp edges softened by familiarity. And being here, just the four of them, felt oddly easy—like she didn't have to brace for impact every second.

Penny pointed her straw at Gideon. "Alright, Mr. Grumble-and-Go. What's your order? Please say something absurd."

Gideon didn't blink. "Black coffee. Eggs. Bacon."

Dan groaned, throwing his head back. "Called it. Blackwell Special: sadness and cholesterol."

"No soufflé? No twelve-dollar truffle toast?" Penny mocked.

"You're all exhausting," Gideon muttered.

Dan leaned in, mock-concerned. "Come on, man. Do you even remember how to have fun, or did you have that surgically removed?"

Arden sipped her coffee, fighting a grin. "He knows. He just likes to suffer artistically."

Gideon cut her a sideways glance, something quiet and wicked flickering there. "So I'm that easy to read now?"

She smiled against the rim of her cup. "Only when you're trying not to smile."

He held her gaze for half a second too long, and the noise of the café seemed to dip around them. Arden rolled her eyes to save herself, but she couldn't stop the small smile creeping in. Maybe it was the banter. Maybe it was the rare ease of it all, the strange luxury of simply being here without armor or angle. Something tight stirred in her chest and loosened before she could stop it.

Dan raised his mug. "To suffering."

Penny clinked hers against it. "And the ones who weirdly enjoy it."

Gideon reached for his cup. Beneath the table, his fingers brushed Arden's—quick, intentional, and warm enough to send a pulse through her she hadn't expected.

She didn't pull away.

She let it stay.

And for one quiet, terrifying moment, Arden believed this could be real. Something steady. Something that didn't vanish in the morning light.

Something worth keeping.

"What's the matter?" Arden asked, one brow lifted in challenge. "Cat got your tongue?"

Gideon's smile came slow and unguarded, catching her off guard with its quiet realness. A laugh slipped from him, low and easy, as his gaze held hers.

"Something like that."

He leaned in, his hand settling lightly at the small of her back. Nothing showy. Only instinct. Familiar. He smelled like clean skin and the faint trace of cedar and warmth, whatever impossible thing had already worked its way into memory.

"Let me show you my New York," he said. "Not the version they put in guidebooks."

She studied him warily, then gave a small nod. "Okay, but this tour better be good."

He took her to Central Park first.

The trees filtered sunlight through amber leaves, casting long slants across the gravel path. Somewhere off to the side, a saxophone played—faint and wandering, weaving its mournful little thread between their steps.

Gideon reached for her hand. A simple, grounding gesture.

Arden slipped her fingers through his before she could overthink it, the motion so instinctive it startled her. Like she had done it a hundred times before. Like her body had decided on tenderness before the rest of her had finished negotiating terms.

They left the main trail, following worn paths softened by ivy and root. A weathered bench leaned behind a thicket of shrubs, half-lost to time, and a pale bridge curved over a lazy stream where the water barely seemed to move.

The city's edge fell away step by step, until only the trees, the saxophone, and the quiet beat of their footsteps remained.

"Is this your usual route?" she asked, nodding toward an artist hunched over a sketchpad beneath the wide shade of an elm.

"Often enough," Gideon said, his thumb skimming hers, barely a thought behind the motion. "It's one of the only spots in the city that doesn't feel like it's racing you."

She followed his gaze across the water, where sunlight shifted like breath over glass. "Yeah," she said. "It kind of makes sense."

They kept walking shoulder to shoulder, letting the quiet fill the space between them.

The rhythm came easily. Too easily, maybe. It didn't feel new so much as recovered, like a song she had known by heart and somehow forgotten until the first notes found her again.

And God, she didn't want it to stop playing.

Next was the Met: the towering steps, the cool hush of marble halls, the kind of silence that seemed to hold history in its mouth.

Arden hadn't expected Gideon to care about art, let alone have opinions. But then—

"That one," he said, nodding toward a canvas of a storm-torn sea. "Turner. He captured motion like no one else."

She tilted her head at the painting, at the waves wild and alive, crashing toward something unseen. "You're really interested in this stuff, huh?"

He glanced sideways, lips curving. "I like things with depth. The idea of control meeting chaos has always fascinated me."

The words landed deeper than she expected, slipping beneath the easy surface of the afternoon. He was talking about the painting. Of course he was.

Except he wasn't.

Arden looked at him, her heart tripping a little at how easily the idea fit between them.

Afterward, they ducked into a narrow bookstore tucked between a record shop and a florist. It was the kind of place a person could miss if they weren't looking, but Gideon had clearly been looking.

Tall wooden shelves climbed toward the ceiling, stacked with hardcovers and paperbacks and old editions with softened corners. The aisles were narrow, a little wild, a little magical; a shop that didn't merely sell books, but seemed to remember the hands that had loved them.

"You trying to seduce me in the poetry aisle?" she teased, eyeing him over the rim of a fiction display.

Gideon gave her that slow, private smile, the one that seemed reserved for her alone. "Would it work?"

Her heart kicked, and she smiled back. "Maybe."

She trailed her fingers over titles she didn't recognize and editions that looked older than she was. "This place is magic," she whispered.

He was already looking at her, making no effort to pretend otherwise. "I thought you'd like it."

They drifted separately, together—fingers tracing spines, pages fluttering open as if they had been waiting to be read. Gideon picked up a worn hardcover and handed it to her without a word, the gesture carrying the silent weight of I thought of you.

Somehow, that said more than any other man ever had.

He didn't reach for her, but she felt the pull anyway. Every aisle seemed to narrow until there was only the two of them, the hush of paper and dust and old glue, and the way Gideon looked at her like the rest of the world had become background noise.

She wasn't sure what made her look up. The sound of his breath, maybe. The stillness in his shoulders.

Either way, when their eyes met, it wasn't a bookstore anymore.

It was a moment.

Theirs.

They didn't stay long. Only long enough to forget the city outside, to feel the shift in the way they looked at each other.

Then they were walking again, through intermittent sunlight and low chatter, the late afternoon unfolding around them.

THEY SLIPPED into a small West Village bistro as the sun dipped low, golden hour casting lazy shadows across the candlelit table.

Over wine and quiet conversation, the space between them shifted. It didn't grow louder or more obvious; it only moved closer, subtle as breath, until the distance between what they said and what they meant began to thin.

Gideon told her about his grandfather. About architecture. About building things meant to last, not because they were grand, but because they were rooted. He spoke of stone and structure, of old buildings with good bones, of the quiet discipline it took to make something endure.

Arden offered pieces of herself, too. Not everything. She wasn't reckless enough for that. But enough to matter. She told him about Morgantown, about the strange loneliness of Silverbranch, about how exile could look peaceful from the outside if no one knew what had driven you there. She told him how sometimes surviving meant shrinking to fit inside whatever life still felt safe enough to keep.

Gideon listened with a kind of focus that rattled her.

Not polite interest.

Presence.

The kind of presence she didn't trust easily, because presence could become expectation if you weren't careful. It could become leverage. It could become a door closing behind you before you noticed the lock.

But with him... she was starting to believe it might simply be care.

His thumb found the edge of her hand, the smallest touch, steady and grounding.

He didn't speak.

He didn't need to.

BY THE TIME they reached the top of the Empire State Building, the sky had gone dark, and the city below burned with light—scattered, restless, alive.

Tourist spot or not, this was part of his New York. The one he wanted her to see.

Not for the view.

Not really.

For this.

The wind. The glow. Her.

Arden leaned against the railing, the wind tugging loose strands of hair across her face as her gaze held on the city sprawled before her.

"I've lived here for months," she said quietly, almost to herself. "But somehow... this feels new."

Gideon wasn't watching the view. He was watching her.

"Perspective's a hell of a thing."

She turned to him, her smile small but sure. "Yeah. It is."

He reached out, brushing a loose strand of hair behind her ear, his fingers slow and sure as they grazed her cheek. The touch lit a spark beneath her skin that didn't fade.

A breath caught between them. Hers, maybe. His. She wasn't sure.

The space narrowed, but neither of them moved quickly. There was no urgency to it, no rush toward the inevitable. Only gravity, steady and quiet, drawing them closer by degrees.

Then he pulled her in, his hands moving down her sides until they settled at her waist, strong and steady, as if letting go had become an option he no longer trusted himself to choose.

Arden turned into him without thinking.

Gideon leaned in.

The kiss started softly, like he was asking rather than assuming. But the second she met him there—answering with her breath, her mouth, her body—the space between them disappeared.

Nothing about it felt performative. There was no rush. No pretending. Only a deep pull, heat laced with reverence, leaving her dizzy in the cold night air.

He didn't kiss her like she was fragile. That mattered. Arden had spent too much of her life watching people mistake damage for weakness, softness for permission, fear for surrender. Gideon seemed to understand the difference. He held her like she was solid. Grounded. Lush and striking and completely real. He kissed her like he knew she could take the force of wanting and still choose what to do with it.

She gripped the front of his shirt, trying to slow the wild rhythm in her chest.

This wasn't only heat.

It was trust.

Timing.

When they finally parted, her breath came in uneven bursts, her skin humming with the imprint of him. Even then, Gideon didn't step away.

His forehead came to rest lightly against hers, breath to breath. The noise of the city fell away until it was only them, standing still in the middle of everything.

"Thank you," she said after a long moment.

He pulled back slightly to study her face. "For what?"

"For giving me a piece of myself I didn't know was gone," she said. "All of it."

His hands stayed at her waist, as if letting go simply wasn't on the table.

He had brought her here on purpose. Maybe to kiss her. Maybe to show her the city from a height that made it feel possible. Maybe just to stand beside her in the wind and remind her that the world could still hold beauty without demanding blood for it.

He watched her, eyes steady and unflinching.

"Whatever you want. However you want it," he murmured, voice low, deliberate. "It's yours."

The words hit lower than her chest, somewhere old and aching. Arden wasn't used to being given choices. She was used to consequences dressed up as inevitability, doors that locked after she walked through them, love that arrived with a ledger in its hand.

But maybe he meant it.

Maybe, terrifyingly, she believed he did.

They stood there, wrapped in the hush between them while the city carried on below, oblivious and electric and alive.

And the familiar pull to retreat—the instinct to step back, shut down, disappear —never came.

She didn't run. She didn't flinch.

She stayed.

With him.

CHAPTER 31

Ink & Intuition

The city rustled beyond the cracked window, distant and restless. Street sounds came and went, softened by walls that held the room in a hallowed hush.

The lamp beside Arden glowed against the shadows, casting warm light across the open notebook balanced on her knees. The page sat blank, patient as a held breath.

She curled deeper into the couch, pulling the throw blanket over her legs and tucking herself into its small, stubborn warmth. This was her spot. Her calm. The only space she had carved out that felt wholly hers, a shelter in a world that rarely offered one.

But tonight, even the familiar cushions couldn't hold her steady.

Not with his words still echoing in her head.

But make no mistake...

You're mine. I've known it since the night we met.

That sentence lingered in her chest like heat she couldn't shake. It should have made her bristle. Maybe a different man saying it would have. Maybe, from anyone else, those words would have felt like a hand closing too tight around her throat.

But from Gideon, they hadn't felt like a cage.

That was the dangerous part.

Arden blew out a breath and tapped her pen against the page, trying to drag her thoughts into order.

You're mine.

A statement.

A certainty.

Her fingers tightened around the pen as her pulse climbed. Images crashed behind her eyes—his hands on her, deliberate and reverent, learning her with a

273

patience that felt almost unbearable. His mouth against her skin. The steadiness in him when she trembled. The restraint, even when want had stripped his voice raw.

Gideon Blackwell had felt inevitable from the beginning. She had known it the first time she saw him at Dot's; the way he carried himself, the intensity in his gaze, the sharp-edged control that warned her he was a man accustomed to getting what he wanted.

But with her, he had never simply taken.

He had waited.

He hadn't tried to smash through the walls she had built with blood and discipline and years of necessary silence. He had stood outside them. Watched. Listened.

Let her decide.

And somehow, impossibly, she had let him in.

Her pen moved before she could second-guess it, scrawling words across the page in uneven lines.

> *What scares me more than the walls breaking down is that I want him to keep breaking them.*

She stared at the ink, jaw tight, the truth of it settling deep inside her. It sat there, too solid to ignore. Quiet, but enormous.

Because Gideon didn't only see the version of her she allowed the world to have. He saw the raw places too, the hidden ones, the parts she had buried beneath competence and dry humor and the particular discipline of surviving. And instead of recoiling, instead of trying to fix her, he held her like none of it made her harder to love.

When he whispered those words—You're mine—it hadn't felt like possession.

It had felt like a tether.

An anchor.

A promise that she was no longer standing alone in the dark.

Her chest tightened, fingers firm around the pen as her thoughts tumbled faster than she could catch them.

> *It is surrender and safety at once.*
> *Not the loss of control.*
> *The quiet relief of no longer carrying everything alone.*

Her pulse pounded against her ribs, insistent and undeniable. If she admitted this—if she wrote it down—it would become real. It would mean she wasn't merely letting him close because he had found some weakness in her defenses.

It would mean she was choosing him.

Arden held her breath as the final thought spilled onto the page, her scrawl uneven with urgency.

What scares me more than the words he said is that I want to believe them.

The ink dried slowly, sealing the truth she wasn't ready to say aloud.

She snapped the journal shut as the apartment door swung open.

"Babe!"

Arden blinked up as Penny strode into the room, holding a long-stemmed red rose like contraband.

"I swear to God, if I find one more of these outside the door, I'm filing a restraining order—or writing you into a trashy romance novel."

Arden turned, her stomach sinking. The warmth in her chest cooled fast, replaced by a slow, creeping dread.

"I mean, I love this for you, I do," Penny continued, wiggling the stem for emphasis. "Mysterious romance? Secret admirer? So on brand. But this was literally sitting outside our door. Again."

Arden's heart seemed to slow, then slammed into a sprint all in the same moment. She forced her voice to stay even.

"Again?"

Penny propped a hand on her hip, frowning at the rose like it might bite. "Yes, again. And I tried to get info from Mrs. Malone, too—you know, our resident 'private investigator.'" She let out a frustrated huff. "She sits by that lobby window with her cat, ready to dish out gossip the second anything happens. I asked if she saw whoever left this one."

Arden's breath caught. "And?"

"Nothing concrete," Penny said, rolling her eyes. "Mrs. Malone claims it was a nice guy with good posture. Didn't catch his face, though—had to save her muffins from burning."

Penny mimicked the old woman's voice, pitchy and distracted, then let out a sigh.

"She says it's romantic. Real helpful, right?"

"Basically, she saw someone stoop at our door, leave the rose, and then walk off. Midnight didn't even hiss, so now she's convinced it's all very 'meant to be.'"

She tossed the rose onto the coffee table. "Great help, right?"

Arden suppressed a shiver, imagining someone lingering beyond their threshold. "So basically, we're stuck with zero leads."

Penny's nod was grim. "Yeah. Mrs. Malone's already on 'high alert'—her words, not mine—so maybe next time, we'll get more than a partial glimpse of Mr. Polite Posture."

She flopped onto the couch with a grunt. "Uh, yeah. This isn't the first one I've brought in. And don't look at me like that—I figured it was, like, a sexy thing between you and you-know-who." She arched a knowing brow but kept going. "But I'm starting to think we should establish a 'no bouquets chilling in the hallway' rule. It's getting... weird."

Arden's breath caught.

She hadn't known Penny had been picking them up.

How many times?

Her gaze darted toward the door. One heavy beat struck against her ribs. Then another. Steady. Relentless. Each one louder than the last.

Penny followed her look and let out a sharp laugh. "If Prince Charming wants to send flowers, I'm not complaining, unless he's also building a shrine to you in his closet."

Arden didn't laugh.

She couldn't.

Because suddenly, the roses weren't an odd, unexplained mystery. They weren't only showing up at the bar or near her car.

They were here.

At their home.

Penny's teasing faltered as her expression shifted, catching the change in Arden's posture. She glanced toward the small collection near the door—some fresh, some wilted, petals scattered across the hardwood like careless drops of blood.

"For real though. Do we need to be concerned?" Her voice still carried humor, but unease had slipped beneath it now, a subtle note of worry under the sarcasm.

Arden forced her hands to stay loose, casual, instead of curling into fists. "No," she said too fast.

Then, trying again, she shook her head. "It's... weird, like you said."

Penny scoffed. "Weird is an understatement. This is, like, fairy-tale villain behavior. If a glass coffin shows up next, I'm moving out, and I'm not waiting for an explanation."

Arden should have laughed. Should have leaned into the banter, met Penny's wit with her own. But her stomach twisted.

Because if Penny had been finding them before Arden even got home, if the pile had been growing, then whoever was leaving them wasn't only watching her at work.

Worse, they weren't stopping.

Penny tilted her head, eyes narrowing. "Okay, whoa. Now, you just got seriously weird."

She straightened, setting the rose down on the coffee table with a soft thud. "What's up?"

Arden forced a smirk, though it felt wrong on her lips. "Nothing. I was only thinking. We need to invest in better locks."

Penny groaned. "Awesome. I already sleep with a bat next to my bed. Thank you, New York. But sure, let's add advanced paranoia to the list."

She flopped onto the couch with a grunt, tugging off her boots and letting them fall where they landed.

"Maybe I'll keep my meds by the door too. Ya know—keys, wallet, pepper spray, emotional stability."

Arden huffed out a laugh, sharp and shaky, but a laugh all the same.

Penny didn't miss it. She plowed right through, bright and shameless. "Or screw it, maybe I'll start hiding tasers in the couch cushions. 'Welcome home, have a snack, mind the electroshock therapy.'"

She pointed dramatically toward the hallway. "Fake trapdoor under the rug. Medieval spike pit in the foyer. One wrong step and—Bam! 'Home Alone' but make it violent."

Another startled laugh ripped out of Arden, jagged and halfway between amusement and adrenaline.

Penny softened at the edges but didn't push.

"Whatever it takes, babe. We survive. We laugh. And we're gonna keep doing both."

Arden nodded, the motion jerky, her throat tightening around a feeling she didn't have words for.

She pushed to her feet, grabbing her journal off the coffee table with hands steadier than she felt.

Penny didn't try to stop her. She offered a wink and another offhand comment about medieval booby traps as Arden slipped down the hall.

Inside her bedroom, Arden closed the door quietly and pressed her spine to the wood as if it could hold her upright.

Inhaled.

Exhaled.

Tried to find something solid in the dizzy rush of her chest.

A muffled voice called from the living room—Penny, trying for casual, though her words carried an edge now. "Grabbing my Xanax too, babe. Just in case Prince Creepy shows up with a carriage this time!"

Trust Penny to make survival feel like another thing you handled, no drama required.

Arden huffed a breath—half laugh, half exhale.

On the dresser, her small orange bottle sat tucked behind a row of worn paperbacks, forgotten but not gone. She crossed the room, unscrewed the cap with steady fingers, and slipped one pill beneath her tongue.

No shame. No collapse. Only breath.

She wasn't fighting the storm tonight. She was anchoring herself through it. The tightness in her chest didn't vanish, but it dulled enough to let her think through the fear instead of only feeling it.

She opened her notebook again. The pen felt heavy in her hand, but her grip didn't falter.

A question carved itself onto the page without permission, sharp and trembling and real.

Could it be him?

Her past had been creeping closer for weeks, pressing cold fingers against the life she was trying to build. She didn't want to believe it. Didn't want to believe he could have found her again.

But the roses were his signature.

If he had truly found her after all this time, then every fragile piece of this new life was now at risk.

And now it was inside her walls.

But Arden Rivers didn't shatter.

She braced.

She breathed.

She stayed.

Even when every instinct screamed to run.

She wasn't a girl who disappeared anymore. She wasn't a life waiting to be claimed or broken. She was here, choosing to stay, choosing to fight.

And tomorrow, she would show up. She would walk into that club with her head high, her heels sharp, her armor made of skin and grit and fucking fire.

Let him watch.

Let him think she was breakable.

Because she had learned a truth in the wreckage: you could plant a thousand roses at her feet, but that doesn't mean she had to bleed for them.

CHAPTER 32

Smoke & Embers

Arden didn't simply walk into the club; she claimed it as if it had always been hers, everyone else merely borrowing the space.

Confidence laced every move, unapologetic and sure. Low golden light flickered across her skin as she passed beneath the chandeliers, drawing glances in her wake. Conversation dipped for half a breath, long enough for people to track her path across the room, some staring longer than they should have.

Some looks held curiosity. Others, thinly veiled envy. A few women whispered behind manicured hands, eyes narrowing with cold appraisal.

And then there were the men—the ones who measured her with practiced interest, mistaking her presence for something they might be allowed to possess.

But one gaze burned hotter than the rest.

Gideon.

He stood near the bar, speaking with a patron, but the second Arden crossed the threshold, his attention snapped to her. He didn't move. Didn't smile. But she knew him now. She knew what that tightly held tension meant, the way his whole body stilled as if touch alone might tip him past pretending.

She saw it in the subtle shift of his grip around the glass in his hand. The careful roll of his shoulders as he adjusted his stance. The flicker in his eyes that gave him away before his expression ever changed.

Then his mouth curved at the corner.

Not a full smile.

Only hers.

Heat stirred low in her gut, slow and certain, but she didn't let it show. Her stride never faltered. She slipped behind the bar with ease, settling into the space like it had been waiting for her.

Marco caught the shift immediately, grinning like he'd spotted the lead in his favorite drama.

"Well, well, well," he said, draping his arms across the counter like the whole thing had been staged for his entertainment. His grin was lazy, but his eyes sparked with mischief. "Someone's strutting in like she owns the whole place." He tapped a knuckle against the bar. "Feelin' good, Mountain Mama?"

Arden tossed a bar towel over her shoulder with a smirk. "Why yes, Marco. I am. And no, I don't need anyone's permission to walk in like I own it."

Fatima breezed past a moment later, arching a brow as she gave Arden a once-over. "Oh, honey, you're lit from within. I don't know what you've been up to, but keep doing it."

She didn't have to say Gideon's name. The glance she shot toward him said plenty.

Arden rolled her eyes but didn't bother denying it. She reached for the bourbon, letting the silence do what words would have only made easier to mock.

Because the truth was simple.

She felt good.

She wasn't holding back, shrinking, or tucking pieces of herself away to make other people more comfortable. Tonight, she was all flame and steel, and the room bent to her heat.

Behind the bar, she became motion and precision—mixing drinks with practiced hands, flashing sharp smiles that made tips rain like confetti, charging the room with an energy that bordered on electric.

And Gideon?

She felt him watching.

Not in the overt way some men did, nothing crude or obvious in it. He was too controlled for that. Too measured. But she felt his attention in the air between them: in the pause of his breath when she stretched to reach the top shelf, in the way his gaze followed when she leaned over the bar just enough to tease, in the tension waiting there like a fuse begging for flame.

And she let him look.

Because when Gideon watched her, it didn't feel like possession. It felt like recognition. Like he saw every part of her she refused to dim and wanted the whole blazing truth of it.

After today—Central Park, the Met, the bookstore, the kiss that still lingered on her lips—this wasn't passing heat.

This was something that stayed.

Something that claimed space.

This was real.

By the time the last patrons trickled out, the room had quieted into a low, steady undertone, like the final crackle of embers after a long burn.

Arden moved through the space with practiced ease, wiping down the bar in slow, even strokes. Closing time always felt like an exhale, a small hour of order after the noise, hers to claim.

But tonight, she wasn't alone.

She didn't hear Gideon approach. She felt him first—that shift in the air, the prickle beneath her skin, the sudden awareness of warmth at her back.

He stood behind her, close enough that the heat of him raised goosebumps along her neck. He didn't touch her. Not yet. But his presence settled around her with the kind of weight that made her breath catch before she even turned to face him.

His expression was unreadable. His eyes held something slower. Deeper.

A gravity that didn't need to be named.

Her fingers stilled on the cloth in her hand. "What?" she asked, voice dry. "You sticking around to scare off the stragglers?"

He didn't smile, at least not all the way. Only a subtle lift at the corner of his mouth, a restrained pull that twisted low in her stomach.

"You're not a straggler."

She cocked her head. "No?"

"No." His gaze dropped for a moment, then lifted again, steady and intentional.

The air thickened between them, charged and impossible. Words hovered there, unspoken and undeniable.

Then Marco barked from the back.

"You two done smoldering over there, or should I dim the lights and set the mood?"

Arden laughed, shaking her head, but the moment didn't fully break. Not when she caught the way Gideon's jaw tightened, just slightly. The kind of tension that didn't announce itself; it simmered.

"Come on," he said, voice lower now. "I'll walk you."

She hesitated, not from doubt, but because she was still learning how to let care arrive without flinching from it. How to accept someone showing up in small, quiet ways without searching the gesture for its hidden cost.

Then she nodded, shrugged into her jacket, and followed him out into the dark.

❧

The city hadn't quite gone quiet, but it was close. As they walked, Manhattan's noise faded to a blur: snippets of conversation drifting from nearby patios, headlights casting fleeting shadows along the damp street, a lone car horn splitting the easy silence now and then.

The deeper they moved into the dark, the more the quiet thickened. Restless.

The kind of stillness that made a person listen harder before they knew what they were listening for.

They walked in step, their pace unhurried. Arden's car was parked several blocks away, typical for nights when luck didn't grant her a nearby spot. She had grown used to the inconvenience, the long walks, the small negotiations the city demanded from anyone trying to belong to it.

But tonight, the distance felt different.

Like space drawn tight.

Their steps slapped the concrete like punctuation marks. Rain still clung to the asphalt in a hush of petrichor and streetlight, as if the city itself were holding a warning between its teeth.

Then Arden stopped cold.

Her chest seized.

Gideon noticed the shift before she could speak. "Arden?"

She didn't answer.

She only stared.

Her car stood half a block ahead.

Or what was left of it.

The windows were gone. Every single one blown out, jagged glass clinging to the frames like teeth. The windshield was spiderwebbed with cracks, its surface dusted in red.

No rose this time.

Petals.

Torn. Ruined. Strewn across the shattered glass like confetti at a funeral. Some clung to the cracks. Others had drifted to the sidewalk, bright against the wet concrete.

And there, at the base of the front tire, lay the stem. Half-crushed. Split down the middle. The green gone pale where it had been torn apart.

This wasn't the same careful message left on her doorstep or tucked near her car before. This was anger. Escalation. The tantrum of someone whose fantasy had stopped obeying him.

Arden curled her hands into fists, the bite of her nails grounding her in the moment.

Months ago, this would have undone her. Left her gutted, hollow, shaking.

Now she was furious.

A hand touched the small of her back, steady and grounding.

Gideon.

He stepped forward without a word, surveying the damage with deadly composure. His breathing stayed measured. Too measured. Too even. The kind of calm that warned of violence held in check by a single, fraying thread.

Then he ground his heel into the stem.

The snap was soft.

Final.

A sound too sharp for the silence.

He stood there, unmoving, then turned to her.

"Tell me everything."

Not a suggestion.

A command.

Arden swallowed hard.

The wind stirred, sending petals tumbling across the sidewalk—red smudges against concrete, too vivid, too deliberate.

She didn't know who had left this message.

But she felt the intent in her bones.

Not yet.

Whatever this was, it wasn't only about her past anymore. She could feel the shape of it changing, widening, becoming something larger.

Darker.

And whoever had left this behind hadn't just made a mistake.

They had made an enemy.

———

FROM A DISTANCE, concealed in the layered dark of the city, Sebastian watched.

Not from hesitation.

From certainty.

Because he had left the rose—whole.

A gesture.

A vow.

Placed with reverence, meant to remind her of what she already knew.

She was never alone.

But someone had ruined it.

Shattered the glass.

Scattered the petals.

Crushed the stem.

Rage coiled through him—white-hot, unrelenting.

Amateurs.

They didn't understand her.

Didn't see her.

But he did.

Arden Rivers wasn't soft.

She wasn't meant to be coaxed or controlled.

Little Fire.

She wasn't some delicate thing to be warned away.

She wasn't just fire.

She was a goddess of ruin.

And these fools? These cowardly, scrambling hands that dared touch what was his?

All they'd done was make her burn hotter.
Let Gideon stand beside her.
Let him bask in her glow while it lasted.
He'd never earned the heat she gave so freely.
Soon, Gideon would know what it felt like to lose everything.
To watch the fire turn on him.
And Arden?
She'd see it.
She'd feel it.
The truth she kept running from.
The one written into her bones.
She was his.
Not Blackwell's.
Not anyone else's.
Only his.
And when she finally woke up to that truth?
She'd thank him.
She'd burn for him.
And she'd never even see it coming.

CHAPTER 33

Fractured Roses

The destroyed rose, the broken windows, and the shattered glass lay across the pavement like a warning shot.

Gideon had been in plenty of fights.

None of them had felt like this.

This wasn't an enemy he could see. He couldn't win it with fists or flawless strategy, couldn't step between Arden and a threat that had already learned how to move through shadows, thresholds, and memory.

This was worse.

Someone had made her feel small. Helpless. Unsafe, even with him standing right beside her.

And that was unforgivable.

His grip on Arden's wrist tightened, not enough to hurt, only enough to anchor her. Enough to keep her tethered to the street, to him, to the present moment, before she could retreat too far into that place inside her head where fear had once learned her name.

"Tell me everything," he said, his voice low.

Not a question.

A demand.

She inhaled sharply, fire flaring behind her eyes. For a moment, he wasn't sure she'd answer.

Then she exhaled.

And he saw the shift.

This wouldn't end until someone bled.

And it wouldn't be her.

The flashing red and blue lights had long faded, but the echo of them lingered, etched into the night and the space between them.

The city stretched wide and strange around them, its usual pulse dulled to a hush. The scent of damp pavement hung in the air, metallic and faintly electric. Arden's car was gone now, towed away, but the tension hadn't lifted.

Gideon stood beside her with his hands in his pockets, posture calm in a way that only meant trouble.

She could feel how tightly he held himself.

The storm inside him was building.

"I'll figure it out tomorrow," she muttered.

She meant the car.

Meant everything.

Gideon's jaw flexed. "You're not figuring this out alone."

And for once, she didn't argue.

He walked her to his car and unlocked the doors with a quiet click. Arden hesitated before sliding in, casting one last glance toward the empty stretch of street where her own car had been.

Her escape.

Her safety net.

Gone.

Untethered, she looked back at him.

He was already watching her.

"I don't need you to—"

"Let me take you home, Arden."

No demand. No plea. Just steady, grounding certainty.

She slid into the seat slowly, the chill of the night following her in. Before she could reach for the belt, Gideon was there, leaning in to buckle it for her with the same quiet care he had shown before. The click of it locking into place felt louder than it should have.

His hand lingered a second longer than necessary, fingers brushing her ribs, grounding her without a word. Then he stepped back, shut the door with muted finality, and circled to the driver's side.

For the first time since she'd seen the wreckage, Arden exhaled.

Shaky.

But real.

The apartment felt different.

Still hers, but too quiet. Too tight.

Penny sat on the couch in sweats, sipping tea, but the second Arden walked in, she straightened.

"What happened?"

Arden dropped her keys on the counter. The clatter cut sharp through the silence.

"My car got vandalized."

Penny's brows rose. "Vandalized as in..."

"As in shattered windows. Glass and rose petals everywhere."

The mug met the table with a muted thud. "Arden—"

"I'm fine." She toed off her boots and rolled her shoulders, as if she could shake the whole thing loose by force.

Penny wasn't buying it. "This isn't fine."

Arden didn't answer.

"And Gideon?" Penny asked, her voice softer now.

A muscle ticked in Arden's jaw. "He handled it."

Penny raised an eyebrow. "Handled it how?"

Arden shrugged, but her mind betrayed her, replaying the way Gideon had stepped forward. The way he'd crushed the stem beneath his boot like a declaration. The way his calm had felt more dangerous than anyone else's rage.

Penny exhaled, letting some of the tension roll off her shoulders. "Are you okay?"

Arden hesitated.

And that was all Penny needed.

She stepped closer and pressed a hand to Arden's arm. "No one gets to do this to you," she said, fierce now. "No one."

Arden nodded, jaw tight, but her fingers twitched at her side.

Penny saw it.

"You gonna sleep?"

"I—"

"Don't lie to me, Arden."

She tried to smile.

Failed.

"I'm gonna journal."

Penny gave her a look. "Good. Get it out."

Arden exhaled as Penny backed off, giving her the space without leaving her alone inside it.

She was safe here.

At least for tonight.

THE NOTEBOOK WAITED, open and blank.

Arden twirled the pen between her fingers as the silence pressed in around her.

She could still smell the crushed rose petals, still see the way the wind had scattered them across the pavement like ashes.

Finally, her thoughts bled onto the page.

> *Sometimes, ghosts don't stay buried.*
> *Sometimes, the past doesn't rot—it sharpens its teeth.*
> *And sometimes, you think you're free,*
> *only to realize the chains were simply waiting to tighten.*

She paused.

Swallowed hard.

This wasn't the same as before. She knew that. Felt it in the shape of the fear, in the violence of the message, in the way the threat had shifted from memory into something current and breathing.

But different didn't mean safer.

Her grip tightened around the pen.

She wasn't running.

Not this time.

She wasn't that girl anymore.

With a shaky breath, Arden flipped the journal shut.

Then she reached for her phone.

Gideon's name glowed on the screen.

She stared at it, thumb hovering above the keyboard.

Deciding.

❧

The gym was quiet except for the rhythmic pound of fists against leather.

Thud. Thud.

One more, and the bag shuddered.

Gideon didn't stop.

He didn't slow.

The bag swung violently with every strike, the chain creaking above him as sweat darkened the tape wrapped around his fists. But it wasn't enough. Nothing about this was enough.

All he could see was Arden standing in front of her ruined car, eyes wide and silent and scared.

Not because she was weak.

Because someone had dared to come for her.

Because someone had put her in their crosshairs and expected to walk away untouched.

His next punch was meant to break bone. The one after came faster.

The rage was there, simmering beneath his skin, cold and focused. Controlled, but barely.

A destroyed rose.

Petals like blood.

Windows shattered like bones.

And Evelyn?

She had been too quiet lately.

That wasn't like her.

He pictured Colton smirking from some polished corner, watching, reporting, carrying whatever scraps Evelyn asked for like a loyal blade waiting to be picked up.

Whoever it was—family or not—they had made a mistake.

His knuckles connected again, and the bag slammed back hard enough to strike the wall.

They thought they could scare her.

They thought they could shake him.

They had no idea what they had done.

His phone buzzed on the bench nearby. Gideon stopped mid-breath, grabbed it, and looked at the screen.

Arden: I'm okay.

Two words.

They made his pulse falter.

Made his hands still.

She didn't know what it meant. Didn't know those two words were the only thing keeping him from burning the world down and calling it justice.

Not yet.

But she would.

He hit the call button.

Christian picked up on the second ring. "Boss."

"Something happened." Gideon's voice was low, clipped. "Arden's car. Windows smashed in. Rose petals. It was a mess."

A pause crackled through the line, then concern. "Is she okay?"

"She wasn't there when it happened." He exhaled, jaw tight. "But I'm not taking any chances."

"I need two men on Arden. Twenty-four-seven. Quiet. She doesn't need to know."

Another beat. Then: "Consider it done."

"She doesn't leave her apartment alone. I want eyes on her every second. And if anyone even breathes wrong—"

"They won't get the chance."

Gideon ended the call, jaw locked, shoulders rigid.
At least now, he had a move to make.
Because this wasn't over.
Not even close.
And next time, he would be ready.

CHAPTER 34

A Lesson in Distraction

Penny adjusted her sunglasses as she sauntered into the glass-and-steel lobby of Hawthorne Holdings, her gaze sweeping the space like she was plotting a hostile takeover.

"Alright," she murmured under her breath as they neared the security desk, angling closer to Arden. "We're clear on the mission, right?"

Arden gave her a side-eye. "There's a mission now?"

"Yes," Penny said, too brightly. "Step one: deliver lunch. Step two: distract Dan. Step three: you do whatever it is you do when you're alone with Gideon."

Arden resisted the urge to rub her temples. "You're making it sound like we've launched a covert op."

"Please," Penny scoffed. "Everything about you two is covert. You think I don't notice when you come home looking all post-apocalypse wrecked?"

Arden shot her a sharp glare as heat crept up her neck. "I hate you."

"No, you don't." Penny grinned. "Now come on. Let's go feed your dangerously attractive billionaire before he starts snacking on underperforming executives."

Once the call upstairs cleared them, the guard waved them through. They stepped into the waiting elevator, polished brass gleaming from every surface, the faint scent of cologne and citrus lingering in the air. Penny let out a low whistle of appreciation as the doors closed.

"This place smells rich," she muttered, rocking back on her heels as if testing for red carpet. "Where do they keep the poor people? In the sub-basement?"

As they rose, Arden's pulse ticked faster.

She wasn't nervous, not exactly, but there was a gravity to entering his world. To seeing him in it.

Gideon.

She hadn't seen him since her car had been vandalized. Since the rose. Since the cold, surgical message carved into what used to be her safe escape.

She had spent half the night convincing herself it wasn't that serious. That she was overreacting. That fear didn't get to live here anymore. And now she was walking into Gideon's world with a bag of overpriced takeout and a half-formed plan to distract him. To keep him grounded.

Or, if she was being honest, to unground him completely.

Because one look from him, and the hunger in his eyes would have nothing to do with food.

The elevator chimed, opening onto the executive floor: sleek and gleaming, luxury muted beneath polished marble and glass walls.

Penny's jaw dropped slightly. "Tell me this place doesn't have a panic room and at least one button that opens a hidden weapons vault."

"Behave," Arden muttered.

"Define behave," Penny said under her breath, lips twitching as her gaze found a familiar face ahead.

But Arden had already tuned her out.

Because there he was.

Watching her like a decision he hadn't yet made.

Gideon stood at the end of the corridor, talking with Dan. He didn't have to move or speak to draw attention; he simply was. The air seemed to recalibrate around him, steady and self-possessed in that impeccably tailored suit, his posture perfect. Controlled. Powerful. Effortless.

When his eyes found hers across the space, everything shifted.

She saw it in the subtle change of his posture. The way his grip on the glass in his hand flexed slightly. The near-imperceptible curve at the corner of his mouth.

Her stomach tightened, heat sweeping low and deep, but she didn't break stride.

"Daniel," Penny called out, her voice syrupy sweet.

Dan turned toward her, a slow smirk tugging at his mouth. "Penelope... you bringing the chaos today?"

Penny tsked. "You know it. Didn't you feel the shift the second I walked through the lobby? Your productivity's tanking."

Dan chuckled, crossing his arms. "Explains the energy dip."

Arden sighed, already regretting this plan. "Penny..."

"What? He started it," Penny said innocently.

Dan's eyes flicked to Arden. "So, is this a visit to Gideon, or did you bring her for entertainment?"

"Both," Arden muttered, holding up the takeout bag like a peace treaty.

Dan smirked. "Well, if you're looking for a distraction, I could give Penelope a tour. We can sit in the executive lounge and pretend she belongs."

Penny gasped, clutching her chest. "You wound me, Daniel. I always belong."

"You belong in the world of chaos," Dan countered. "But come on. Let's see if you can sit for five minutes without launching a social experiment."

Penny didn't hesitate. She linked her arm through his as if they'd done it a hundred times. "Lead the way, Daniel. I promise not to turn the boardroom into a runway."

As they disappeared down the corridor, still bickering, Arden released a slow breath and turned toward Gideon.

The distraction crumbled, leaving only the magnetic pull of him, uncomplicated and undeniable.

This devastating man she had come to distract?

He was watching her like she was the only thing worth seeing.

Gideon's gaze didn't simply land.

It locked.

Not with surprise or amusement, but with a heat far more dangerous, something dark and unmistakable coiling beneath the polished line of his suit.

Possession.

The part of him that belonged to civility had stepped aside with unsettling ease.

Arden adjusted her grip on the takeout bag, as if overpriced lunch could anchor her against the pull in his stare.

"You brought me lunch?" he asked, voice deceptively smooth.

"You do need to eat, don't you?"

The smallest curve ghosted across his mouth, not quite a smile.

Hunger, barely contained.

His hand closed gently around her wrist, firm and unhurried, and the touch sent a clean line of heat through her before she could pretend otherwise.

She stepped in behind him, the quiet click of her boots muted by the plush carpet. The door eased shut behind them, soft but certain.

And the rest of the world fell away.

He had barely survived the morning—one relentless meeting after another, an endless churn of numbers, projections, and egos dressed up as strategy. His tie was loosened, his patience frayed.

And then she showed up.

Arden.

With a bag of overpriced takeout, a look that should have come with a warning label, and a smile that knocked every coherent strategy out of his head.

This space—his office, precise and controlled and arranged down to the last polished line—belonged to her now.

She set the bag on his desk with infuriating innocence, as if she hadn't knocked the air out of him by existing.

"Figured you wouldn't come up for air," she said. "Thought I'd be nice."

He studied her, jaw tense. "You're not being nice. You're baiting me."

"Would I do that?" She was grinning, and they both knew the answer.

Arden watched him watching her.

And Gideon was watching every inch of her.

"You're staring, Blackwell."

His voice dropped an octave. "And?"

She shifted slightly, and the motion nearly undid him. The curve of her hips. The unapologetic strength in her stance. The way her shirt clung to the sharp line of her waist. She knew exactly what she was doing.

And he loved her for it.

He stepped in, his hand curling around her waist with quiet claim. The desk was at her back, his mouth near her ear.

"You think my obscenely gorgeous girlfriend can walk in here looking like that and expect me to keep my distance?"

She quirked an eyebrow, but the word caught her. He saw it land before she recovered. "I thought you might be hungry."

"I am... but not for lunch."

Her breath slowed, but she didn't flinch.

She never did.

And that was what killed him.

Gideon lifted her onto the desk in one smooth motion. Papers scattered. Her legs parted to welcome him, and the last of his patience went with them.

The kiss landed hard, deep and unrelenting. His hands framed her face, pulling her in as her fingers tangled in his shirt and dragged him closer. Their mouths moved with intent, urgent and hungry, all that morning-after softness sharpened into something reckless beneath the glass walls and expensive silence of his office.

She gasped when his lips found her neck, his breath skating along skin that flushed beneath his touch. She clawed at his shoulders, trying not to melt and failing beautifully.

He barely heard his own voice when he rasped, "I should lock the door."

"You should."

Knock.

The sound cracked through the haze.

Dan.

Arden bit her lip, grinning. "You could ignore it."

Gideon groaned, resting his forehead against hers. "You have no idea how much I want to."

Knock.

"Gideon, you in there? The call with Paris is in five."

Then Penny's voice. "Ooooh, Paris. Fancy."

Dan muttered, exasperated, "I thought I asked you to stay in my office."

"Come on, Daniel. You knew that wasn't going to happen."

Arden laughed softly. "I swear, her timing is a weapon."

Gideon sighed, dragging one last kiss from her lips. "This is not over."

"I'd be disappointed if it was."

He stepped back, barely enough to let her slide off the desk.

She smoothed her clothes with the kind of composure that nearly ruined him all over again.

When the door opened, Dan looked mildly traumatized.

Penny looked smug.

Arden breezed past them like nothing had happened.

And Gideon?

He wanted to cancel every meeting for the rest of the year.

PENNY DIDN'T WAIT LONG to start in.

"So... how's Gideon?"

"Fine," Arden said tightly.

"Uh-huh. And how's your blood pressure?"

Arden leveled her with a look. "Penny."

"What? I didn't say anything," Penny said innocently.

They stepped into the elevator. Arden hit the lobby button and tried to ignore the way her body still buzzed from everywhere Gideon had touched her.

"You were going to."

Penny clasped a hand to her chest. "I would never."

The doors opened.

Arden walked fast.

Penny caught up faster, practically radiating glee. "Well, you do look a little... undone. Was that a lunch delivery or a hostile seduction?"

"Coffee," Arden muttered. "We're getting coffee. Not having an interrogation."

"I can multitask."

❦

By the time Penny had an oat milk latte and Arden had something... a bit stronger, the conversation had shifted to weekend plans.

"We should do karaoke again," Penny said, stirring her drink. "It's been too long since you belted out something tragic and sexy and had an entire room fall in love with you."

Arden snorted. "That is not what happens."

"It's literally what happens every time. Rachel has a conspiracy theory about it."

Arden shook her head, but the warmth settled in anyway.

While Penny waxed poetic about sequin dresses, Arden's mind drifted.

To Gideon. To his hands. To the way he had looked at her like she was the only thing he would ever need.

Penny waved a hand in front of her face. "Hello? Earth to Arden? Did you astral project back into your boyfriend's arms or—"

"Shut up."

Penny gasped. "You did."

Arden refused to confirm. "Tell me more about karaoke night."

Penny grinned, victorious. "You're on the list. No backing out."

Arden sighed. "Fine."

Penny clapped. "Perfect! Now let's go try on clothes we can't afford and pretend we're rich."

Arden laughed. "Lead the way."

And she let herself have it all: the caffeine, the chaos, the illusion of safety wrapped in laughter, and the fiery imprint of Gideon's mouth against her skin.

CHAPTER 35

The Family That Lies Together Stays Together

Evelyn Blackwell's dining room exuded a calculated elegance, every inch curated, commanding, and cold.

The gleaming mahogany table stretched beneath the chandelier's soft glow, polished to a mirror's edge until it shimmered with liquid light. The silverware and china had not been set for function. They were armor, silent messages arranged with surgical care: control was not given here. It was enforced.

Paintings lined the walls, gold-framed and deliberately muted, their brushstrokes too restrained to bleed emotion. They loomed like spectators.

Watchers.

At the head of the table, Evelyn sat with effortless authority, her charcoal Loro Piana dress tailored to perfection, cashmere worn as armor rather than comfort. The diamonds at her throat glinted under the light, understated but undeniable. A quiet warning: real power didn't raise its voice. It never had to.

"To the family," she said, lifting her crystal glass in a toast wrapped in steel. "And to preserving what is rightfully ours."

Glasses rose.

The chime was brittle as bone.

Gideon barely sipped. The deep red swirl in his glass looked like a stain, too much like everything the Blackwell name had cost.

Alex lounged with that signature smirk, entitlement dressed up as charm, all shine and no soul. He was enjoying himself. He had always thrived on illusion and cruelty.

Evelyn's gaze swept the table—sharp, assessing, lingering just long enough to remind them who held the knife.

"The media narrative," she said, her tone clean. Surgical.

Julia Fenton leaned forward, fingers delicate on her glass, her emerald blouse pristine enough to reflect the chandelier's light. "The Richardson property has generated some noise," she said with a practiced smile. "But I've secured local press highlighting our urban renewal campaign. By next week, we'll be praised for revitalizing the community."

"And the tenants?" Evelyn asked, already knowing the answer.

Alex answered for her. "Motivated," he said, lazy as ever. "Threats of no heat in January tend to move the needle."

Colton chuckled. "Well-timed outages," he said, amused. "Amazing what a little discomfort can accomplish."

BENEATH THE TABLE, Gideon's fist clenched hard enough for his nails to bite into his palm. He remembered the elderly woman who had thanked him for a simple repair last month, her hand trembling around the edge of her cane, gratitude offered for something that should never have been withheld in the first place.

The memory turned his stomach.

Evelyn's eyes darted to him, but his expression held. His rage had long since learned the rules of civility.

Then Sebastian spoke, his voice low and venomous. "Speaking of handling things, how is Miss Rivers? Quite unforgettable."

Gideon stilled.

Evelyn's gaze slid to him, curious. Alex's smirk widened, eager for blood, as always.

"Miss Rivers," Evelyn said smoothly, "appears competent. For now."

"Captivating, even," Alex added. "But girls like that? They always crack eventually."

At his side, Cate's grip tightened around her glass. Her composure faltered just enough to betray the truth: she knew exactly who they meant.

Harlan Atwood, family attorney, took a sip of scotch, his tone flat. "Let's hope she's worth the gamble. One wrong step and the private becomes public in an instant."

Sebastian's grin was all satisfaction. "Good question. Does she even realize what she's standing in?"

Gideon's voice cut clean through the rising tension. "The management of the club isn't up for discussion."

Sebastian leaned back, pleased. "Admirable. Your loyalty to your staff. She must be... special."

Evelyn's tone turned glacial. "Distractions," she said, eyes narrowing. "Are luxuries we cannot afford. Wouldn't you agree, son?"

The words fell heavy.

A challenge.

A test.

Gideon met her gaze without flinching. "Last I checked, I'm the sole owner of The Blackwell Room, thanks to both of my grandfathers." He let that land. "Richard Blackwell II and Henry Hawthorne."

A ripple passed through the room. Evelyn's eyes darkened, her lips pressing into a line thin enough to cut.

"My staff," he continued, voice ice cold, "is not yours to critique."

Colton's smirk turned mocking. "Until they are."

Evelyn leaned in, each word a blade. "The inheritance was an opportunity. We've all found ways to contribute. I trust you'll remember your place."

"Perhaps a little oversight would help," Alex said lightly, his tone laced with poison. "Keep things on brand."

Gideon didn't blink. "When have I ever needed, or wanted, your help with anything?"

Silence stretched.

Sebastian lifted his coffee cup in a slow, mocking toast. "Family dinners are always so... spirited."

Talk shifted to quarterly projections, but Gideon was no longer at the table in any way that mattered. His thoughts had gone to Arden, to the shattered glass and crushed petals, to the way she had stood in the wreckage with fear in her eyes and fire underneath it.

To how far he would go to keep her safe.

And what he was willing to burn to do it.

WHEN THE ROOM EMPTIED, Gideon stayed behind.

The silence wasn't peace. It was a void, echoing with everything left unsaid.

The air reeked of bourbon and ambition. The table gleamed beneath the chandelier's glow, but every reflection warped at the edges, fractured by crystal and shadow.

Gideon rested a hand on the back of his chair, fingers curling against the cool leather.

Power without principle isn't power; it's fear in disguise.

His grandfather's words echoed through him, as present as the fury threading through his blood.

Henry Hawthorne hadn't only left him wealth. He had left him a choice. A legacy Gideon had never asked for, but one he was determined to shape before the Blackwells could twist it into another instrument of control.

He remembered the day the will was read, every word slicing clean through the room. Evelyn's jaw locking. Alex pretending disinterest, even as his grip on the chair went white-knuckled. Colton watching too closely. Every one of them revealing, in the smallest betrayals of face and body, exactly what they valued when power shifted out of their hands.

Gideon had sat there knowing he was the outsider.

The threat.

The one who could dismantle the entire machine if he chose to.

And now the walls of that empire were closing in, and he was running out of time.

He looked to the window, the city glittering beyond the glass. His reflection hovered there—splintered, hollowed, restless.

What would walking away even mean?

Henry's voice returned, steel and warning.

Never leave your battles for someone else to finish.

Gideon's jaw set.

The empire could crumble.

Let it.

But they would not take her.

Not Arden.

He turned toward the door, spine straight, every step echoing a promise.

Let the empire fall.

She wouldn't.

And he was just getting started.

CHAPTER 36

Legacy of Shadows

Slants of sunlight carved gold through the room, catching on mahogany and cut crystal.

Evelyn Blackwell's dining room didn't merely showcase wealth; it broadcast control, every polished surface reflecting calculated legacy and restraint.

Gideon sat near the far end, posture composed, eyes sharp as he scanned the faces around the table. Evelyn, regal at the head, her diamond collar glinting like a threat. Alex, his smirk poorly disguising resentment. Cate, poised but tense, her fingers clenched too tightly around Alex's. Sebastian, lounging with predator's ease, his smile as cutting as the edge of his glass.

There were others—distant relatives, legal advisors, a handful of well-dressed vultures masquerading as mourners—but they blurred at the edges.

Only these few mattered.

This wasn't a reading of a will; it was a battlefield.

The lawyer cleared his throat, the scrape of sound cutting through the silence like a knife.

"To Evelyn Hawthorne Blackwell," he began. Each word was clipped. Careful. Cold. "I leave the Calloway Estate in Oregon, along with its vineyards."

Evelyn didn't flinch, but Gideon caught it anyway: the slight tension in her jaw, barely there and terribly telling. She had dismissed Calloway as insignificant more than once. Now it landed like a veiled insult, a thorn dressed as a rose.

"To Alexander Blackwell, Hawthorne Lodge in Wyoming, and its surrounding acreage. May its quiet offer space for reflection."

Alex's smirk slipped, his contempt barely masked. A remote lodge was not the crown he had expected. Evelyn's glance toward him carried decades of unspoken disappointment.

"To Catherine Blackwell," the lawyer continued, "the art collection housed at the estate, along with its archive. You've shown appreciation for its value, not as capital, but as legacy."

Cate dipped her head in acknowledgment, but her grip tightened around Alex's hand. Her polish cracked, if only for a second.

The room constricted with silence as the lawyer turned the page.

"To Sebastian Hawthorne, I leave Hawthorne House in Newport."

A ripple moved through the room. It wasn't only wealth. It was memory. A symbol of the friendship between Richard Blackwell II and Henry Hawthorne, long since frayed and buried beneath years of ambition.

Sebastian arched a brow. "A challenge from beyond the grave," he murmured, all charm and venom. "How fitting."

Evelyn's voice cut sharply. "It's a relic. A liability."

The lawyer didn't flinch. "To Henry, it represented loyalty. Community. A vision this family once aspired to, before it was lost."

Sebastian glanced toward Gideon. "Loyalty. Legacy. Lofty ideals for a room full of wolves."

Then came the pause.

The shift.

"To Gideon Blackwell," the lawyer announced, and the room seemed to hold its breath, the name itself disrupting the balance.

"I leave my shares in The Blackwell Room, an establishment co-founded with Richard Blackwell II. A space meant not for power, but for artistry, integrity, and sanctuary."

Gideon's fingers curled against the carved armrest.

He didn't blink.

The lawyer unfolded a letter. "And a personal note," he said, his voice quieter now. "'You are your grandfather's grandson. Richard and I dreamed of a legacy built on principle. That dream was lost, but I believe you can restore it. I entrust you with my share of The Blackwell Room.'"

Another pause.

"Additionally, I leave my controlling shares in Hawthorne Holdings to Gideon Blackwell. Combined with Richard Blackwell II's legacy, Gideon now holds full ownership of The Blackwell Room."

The silence cracked open.

Evelyn's composure fractured just enough for the fury beneath it to show. Alex looked stunned, his mouth hardening around everything he was too proud to say. Even Sebastian's smile faltered before it returned, colder than before.

Sebastian lifted his glass. "Well," he said, mock-toasting, "the golden child emerges."

Gideon rose, slow and certain, his gaze cutting across the room.

He didn't speak.

He didn't have to.

Each step toward the door echoed like a verdict.

Henry's final words followed him out like prophecy: Forge your own path. Don't let this family's darkness consume you.

Behind him, the empire seethed.

Ahead, there was only fire, and the ruins he was willing to leave behind.

Those words haunted him.

Forge your own path.

They weren't a mantra anymore. They were a test, and tonight, that test felt nearly impossible.

Gideon stepped into his office with tension pressing at his back. The city beyond the windows burned with light, but inside, the room waited quiet. Still. Heavy.

He reached for the photo in his wallet: his grandfathers standing outside The Blackwell Room, younger then, full of hope. Men who had believed they could build more than wealth, before ambition took root and turned so much of what they loved to rot.

He placed the photo on his desk, grounding himself in the proof of what had existed before the family learned how to corrupt it. This wasn't only about legacy. It was about truth. About honoring the club Henry had envisioned, and the man Richard Blackwell II had once tried to be.

But the family was closing in.

Evelyn's eyes at dinner. Sebastian's barbs. Alex's threats veiled as brotherly advice.

They were tightening the noose.

And then there was Arden.

Arden, who didn't fit in this world. Who didn't bend to it. Who scorched through every lie Gideon had been raised to live with.

She wasn't part of their war, but she had been pulled into it.

Because of him.

He reached for his phone.

Not her name.

Not yet.

Nathan Cole.

His grandfather's closest friend. The man who had never stopped warning Gideon that the real war would come from inside the family. His anchor in this fucked-up dynasty, and maybe the only person left who could help him navigate what came next without losing himself to it.

The moment Gideon hit send, it felt like crossing a line.

Gideon wasn't sure what he felt, not cleanly. Rage, fear, resolve, all of it moving through him with the same dangerous current. But he knew one thing.

Arden wasn't a secret to protect anymore.

She was the reason he had to fight.

The reason surrender was no longer an option.

She was the line in the sand.

Henry had warned him.

Don't let the darkness swallow you.

Gideon wasn't only protecting his grandfather's legacy. He was fighting for himself now. For her. For the future he was finally beginning to believe he deserved.

One built in trust, not shadows.

One worth burning everything else down for.

He stood at the window, the city reflecting back in fractured panes.

Let them come.

Let them try.

He knew who he was now.

And he knew exactly what—and who—he would burn for.

CHAPTER 37

Echoes of Loyalty

E ven in his club office, Gideon felt it: the inescapable reminder that nothing in his world was truly his, not while the Blackwell name remained stitched into every shadow.

Nathan Cole sat across from him, steadfast as ever, a presence anchoring the room against the tide Gideon felt rising beneath his skin.

The creak of leather cut through the silence as Nathan sat back, gaze deliberate. Years of shared history hung between them. Words weren't always required.

But tonight, they were.

"So," Nathan said, voice low and dry, edged with his signature calm. "Did family dinner live up to expectations?"

"Exceeded them." Gideon huffed a laugh, more exhale than sound, and rubbed roughly at the back of his neck. "Evelyn's watching. Alex is circling. And Sebastian?" He shook his head. "God knows what he wants this time."

He didn't finish the thought.

"This time, it's about her," Nathan said, cutting clean through the silence.

Gideon's eyes narrowed. Surprise flickered, then turned colder. "How the hell did you—"

"Because I know you." Nathan didn't need volume to make it land. His voice stayed low and even, but the conviction behind it hit hard. His eyes didn't waver from Gideon's.

"You've changed. You're a man who's finally found someone worth losing everything for. And tonight made it crystal clear who's got the family rattled."

The truth landed without buffer.

No room for denial.

"Arden," Gideon said quietly.

Her name sat between them, heavy as confession.

"She's..." He searched for a word that wouldn't collapse under the weight of what he meant. Nothing neat fit. Nothing simple. "Strong, but not performative. Rooted. She doesn't yield—to me, to them, to anyone. And it terrifies me, almost as much as it makes me want to watch her burn the whole damn map and make her own."

Nathan's mouth tugged, not quite a smile. More like recognition. Like he had seen enough men survive themselves to know when one was finally standing at the edge of something true.

"You don't fall for someone like her. You rise to meet her. And that changes everything."

Gideon dragged a hand through his hair, the burden of it all finally showing at the edges of his expression.

"She's on their radar," he muttered, more to himself than to Nathan. "Evelyn's playing chess. Alex is prowling. Cate's watching every damn move."

"And Sebastian?" Nathan asked, voice suddenly colder.

Gideon's answer came low and tight. "Sebastian doesn't give a shit about winning. He wants to break things, especially anything I care about."

Nathan didn't blink. "They think she's your weakness."

"They're wrong." Gideon's eyes were ice now. "She's not my weakness. She's a threat. And they know it."

The room quieted again, the weight of those words shifting the air.

Nathan studied him for a beat, then let out a low whistle.

"Well, damn," Nathan murmured, a crooked smirk forming as he leaned back. "She's under your skin. Doesn't happen often."

Gideon huffed a dry breath. "It's not just her. It's what she represents. She doesn't bend. She doesn't fit into the world they've built—and they can't stand that."

Nathan nodded slowly, eyes narrowing. "And it's exactly what scares Evelyn. She couldn't stomach Isabel either, and she was tame by comparison. You remember how fast she was gone."

Gideon's jaw clenched. "One conversation. One threat. One rumor. That's all it took."

"And you haven't let anyone close since." Nathan's voice dropped, not accusing, only honest. "Until now."

Gideon leaned forward, elbows braced against the desk.

"She's not like the others," he said, voice certain. "And I won't let them force her out."

Nathan's tone sharpened. "Then you know what's coming. She's not only a threat to your position, Gideon. She threatens the entire structure they've built."

Gideon exhaled heavily through his nose, his shoulders drawing tighter.

"So what the hell am I supposed to do?"

The frustration in his voice cut clean through the quiet. "She's already in it—there's no going back. If I push her away..." He stopped there, jaw locking around the rest.

"They'll see it as blood in the water," Nathan finished.

Gideon's silence told him enough.

Nathan's voice softened, but the truth in it did not. "She's not looking for someone to guard her, Gideon. She needs someone who won't break when things fall apart. Someone who doesn't protect her—someone who stands with her."

Gideon didn't answer right away. His thoughts had drifted to Arden, to the way she moved through a room without apology, to the way she saw him beneath the polish and power and all the inherited rot he had spent years trying to outpace.

She wasn't fragile.

She wasn't asking to be saved.

But she was stepping straight into chaos, and this time, he couldn't simply stand there and watch it unfold.

"She makes me want to believe," he admitted, voice low and raw. "But what if that's not enough?"

"Then you fight for it," Nathan said, without hesitation. "Because if she's worth it, and I think she is. You don't get to stand still."

Gideon let the words settle, his gaze drifting to the window. The city glittered beyond the glass, bright and distant.

But Arden was somewhere out there.

Not waiting.

Existing.

Defiant and brilliant.

The only real thing in a world full of illusion.

Silence fell again, broken only by the soft clink of Gideon's glass against the desk.

"You've always carried this family's legacy," Nathan said finally. "But carrying it doesn't mean you have to carry it alone."

Gideon didn't answer.

But in the quiet that followed, something shifted.

Not resignation.

Resolve.

THE DOOR swung open without a knock.

Dan.

He entered like a gust of sharp air, all energy and irreverence, cutting straight through the tension.

"Uncle Nathan, please tell me you're not trying to out-brood him," Dan said as he strolled in, casual as ever. "Because I hate to break it to you, but Gideon's had a head start since puberty. He's a professional."

Nathan's lips twitched, the faintest crack in his calm. "I'm trying to talk some sense into him," he said, nodding toward Gideon. "Feel free to join the intervention."

Dan flopped into the chair beside Nathan, sprawling like he owned the place. "What are we intervening about? Evelyn unleash her final form, or are we pretending this is about quarterly projections?"

Nathan gave him a dry look. "A little of column A, a little of 'the family's plotting against the woman Gideon actually cares about.'"

Dan's grin dimmed slightly. It didn't vanish, but concern tempered the edges. "So... we're talking about Arden."

Gideon didn't answer.

Dan nodded, his tone shifting with him. "I think your staff likes her more than they like you. She's got guts."

Gideon arched a brow, though a flicker of a smile ghosted across his mouth. "Careful, Dan."

"I'm just saying," Dan continued, his grin widening again, though it didn't quite reach the earlier ease. "Anyone who can face off with Sebastian without flinching? She's got more backbone than half the board. Including me."

Gideon's smirk faded. "That's what I'm afraid of," he muttered.

The air shifted, playfulness draining into something heavier. More honest.

Nathan leaned forward slightly, reading the undercurrent. He and Dan exchanged a glance, silent and instinctive.

They had both heard it.

The unsaid thing beneath Gideon's words.

NATHAN STOOD, the leather creaking beneath him as he placed a firm hand on Gideon's shoulder.

"You've always carried this family's weight," he said. "But this? This is different. And some things—some people—are worth carrying it for."

Dan leaned in too, the sharp edges of his humor softened by rare clarity. "If Arden can walk into your world and not just survive, but make you want something more? Then she's already fighting for you. The question is whether you're ready to fight back."

Gideon exhaled slowly, the pressure in his chest shifting into something that no longer felt only like weight.

Purpose.

Arden.

She wasn't fragile. She wasn't a phase. She was wildfire in a world built on ice, and she didn't flinch.

She made him believe there could be more.

Even if believing terrified him.

"You two are relentless," Gideon muttered, but his tone held more than recognition now.

It held conviction.

Nathan didn't remove his hand. "Someone has to be. You've spent so long guarding yourself, you don't even see what's right in front of you."

Dan smirked, sharp again. "Besides, I'm not about to let you sabotage this. Arden isn't just some woman, Gideon. She's changing you."

Gideon looked between them. The silence thickened again, but it was no longer oppressive.

Only real.

Clear.

He let out a breath. "I won't let them get to her."

Dan leaned back like he'd won a bet. "Now that sounds like the Gideon Blackwell I know and tolerate."

Nathan shook his head, but his approval showed in the smallest shift of his mouth.

"Don't wait too long," he said, voice lower now. Measured. "Time has a way of running out when you least expect it."

Gideon didn't answer right away.

Because Nathan was right.

And he knew it.

What the hell was he waiting for?

Not Arden. She wasn't the one hesitating.

Not clarity. He had already chosen.

He was waiting for the moment to move. To act. To finally do what needed to be done before the people circling them decided to strike first.

Because Evelyn was circling.

Colton was watching from the shadows.

Alex was weighing his next move, calculating loyalty the way a predator measures distance.

Sebastian didn't need a reason. Only an opening.

And Arden had been targeted.

Her car. The shattered windows. Glass everywhere. Rose petals torn and scattered across the dash—a warning dressed in beauty. It hadn't been random. It hadn't been noise.

It was a message.

But from whom?

Family?

Someone else?

She hadn't told him everything. He had seen it—the flicker in her eyes, the hesitation before she said she was fine. Maybe she knew more than she was saying. Maybe she carried it alone because she didn't believe anyone could lift it with her.

That cut deeper than the glass.

Because if she didn't trust him with this, how the hell was he supposed to stand beside her when the next blow came?

His jaw tightened.

No more waiting. No more silence.

Whatever storm was coming, Gideon would meet it head-on.

Because Arden wasn't a liability.

She was the line in the sand.

And he would burn every name on the Blackwell ledger before he let anyone cross it.

THE LOUNGE HUSHED the moment Gideon stepped inside.

Not because he demanded attention, but because he didn't have to.

Real power didn't announce itself. It walked in and made the room forget what it had been saying.

He didn't scan the crowd. Didn't hesitate.

He knew who he was looking for.

His gaze found Alex first, seated near the bar like he owned it, arrogance coiled around him in the loose sprawl of his body and the lazy tilt of his glass. Gideon didn't stop for him.

Not yet.

His eyes found Arden next, and the world narrowed to her.

She noticed him instantly. No flinch, no double take. Only a shift in her posture, a spark in her gaze—relief, recognition, and something deeper.

Connection.

It settled between them like a current.

Then Alex turned too, tracking Gideon's line of sight.

His posture shifted, not much, but enough. The smirk faltered, barely and briefly, before returning smooth and deliberate, as if it had never left.

Gideon moved forward, every step measured. Controlled. But his intent pulsed through the room, unmistakable as a warning beneath the music and low conversation.

He didn't look at anyone else. Didn't break stride. He only closed the distance with surgical precision.

"Alex." His voice was calm. Even. But it held weight. "I wasn't aware you were still in the building."

Alex turned fully, lifting his glass with lazy arrogance. "Just catching up with your staff," he said, his smile easy. "Miss Rivers is quite the conversationalist. Smart. Interesting. Very... compelling."

His eyes dragged toward Arden again, blatant and assessing.

Gideon stepped between them, silent and absolute.

It wasn't dramatic. It wasn't showy.

It was final.

His presence became a wall of silent fury, impenetrable and cold enough to cut.

"She is," Gideon said, his voice perfectly level. "And she has work to do."

He didn't look at Arden, but the message was clear.

Not a command.

A lifeline.

She caught it instantly.

"Always," she replied, cool as glass, her voice level despite the discomfort tightening the air around her.

When her gaze flicked toward Gideon, it said everything she couldn't risk saying out loud.

She turned and walked away without looking back, each step deliberate and composed. She didn't rush. She didn't stumble.

She didn't spare Alex another glance.

And that was what made Gideon's blood run colder than anything else.

Because Alex had seen it too.

The way she looked at Gideon. The connection between them, clean and wordless and impossible to disguise.

As soon as she was gone, Gideon leaned in, just slightly.

Just enough.

"Stay away from her." His voice was calm, but violence lived beneath it.

Alex chuckled low in his throat, swirling his drink. "Awfully protective of a bartender, little brother."

Gideon didn't blink. "You know damn well she's not just a bartender."

A pause stretched between them.

Alex's smile didn't fade, but it turned colder. Sharper.

"No," he said. "She's not."

And that was the problem.

The flicker of awareness. The calculation behind his eyes.

Alex wasn't merely intrigued now. He saw Arden. Saw her as useful. Dangerous. Valuable.

Gideon stepped closer, voice dropping lower, cutting sharper. "She's not yours to watch. Not yours to provoke. Not yours. Period."

Alex held his gaze, a glint of calculation behind the smirk.

A warning, returned in kind.

"Relax, Gideon," he drawled, lifting his hands in mock surrender. "I'm not making a move. I'm... observing."

Gideon didn't answer.

He didn't have to.

The silence that followed said it all.

Don't.

Not her.

Alex finally pushed off from the bar, adjusting the cuff of his sleeve like he had all the time in the world.

"Good chat," he said over his shoulder. "Let's do this again sometime."

Then he was gone—casual, composed, calculated.

THE LOUNGE slowly eased back to life around him, the spell breaking by degrees. Laughter resumed. Glasses clinked. Conversations lifted and folded over one another until the room remembered itself.

The world moved on.

Gideon didn't.

Not yet.

He stood rooted to the floor, jaw tight, hands fisted at his sides.

Because Alex wasn't merely sniffing around.

Gideon had seen Arden's car. The smashed windows. The petals scattered across the dashboard like a message someone had meant him to find.

A threat, yes.

But more than that.

A declaration.

And Arden hadn't told him everything. He knew it. There had been a look in her eye that night, a flash of knowledge she had swallowed before it could become words.

Whether it was family or someone else, someone had made her a target.

And now Gideon wasn't only protecting her from the people outside the circle.

He was protecting her from the ones within it.

❦

The loud buzz of his phone cut through the silence.

Gideon didn't check the screen. He knew who it was.

"Talk to me," he answered, voice flat.

Leo didn't waste time. "It's escalating. Alex isn't even trying to be subtle. My team's trailing one of his guys. He's been shadowing Arden. No direct contact yet, but it's deliberate. He's testing boundaries. Watching her. Watching you."

Gideon's grip tightened around the phone. His pulse thudded slow and dangerous. "And Sebastian?"

"Digging," Leo said. "He's been reaching out to people from her past. Nursing school contacts, old employers, even neighbors from Morgantown. He's hunting for leverage, anything that'll give him a crack to pry open."

Gideon stood, tension rolling through his frame as he crossed to the security monitor. The feed showed Arden behind the bar, sharp and composed, untouched by the storm she didn't yet realize was closing in.

"What about Evelyn?" he asked, lower now, but no less dangerous.

Leo's voice darkened. "Same tactics. She's casting lines. Seeing what bites. Corporate records, off-the-books firms. Requests for old HR files, employment history, sealed background checks. Someone at her old law firm tipped us off."

Gideon's jaw locked. "She's fishing. Quietly."

"She's good at it," Leo admitted. "Knows how to keep her fingerprints off the file."

"Then don't just watch her," Gideon said, pacing slowly behind his desk. "Watch Colton."

Leo's voice sharpened. "You think he's the one on point?"

"I don't think—I know. Evelyn doesn't make moves herself. She keeps people like Julia whispering and people like Colton enforcing. If there's pressure to apply—if it gets physical—it'll come from him."

Leo didn't argue. "Then I'll have a second team follow him directly. He's not in any of the usual surveillance networks, but I've got a guy who can get inside that orbit."

"Do it quietly. If Colton suspects he's being followed, he'll vanish."

Leo's voice came back crisp. "Understood. We'll keep eyes close."

Gideon let the information settle. The fury had chilled into something worse now—measured, merciless, ice that only burned once it was too deep to stop.

"And the car?"

Leo hesitated. "No movement from the precinct yet. No leads on the vandalism. Whoever did it—no prints, no cameras. Too clean. But you know the rose petals... that wasn't random."

"I do," Gideon muttered. "Christian's had her covered since the report came in. Soft shadow. She doesn't know."

Leo's tone shifted. "You trust him to keep her close?"

"He's not just good," Gideon said. "He's mine. Former military. Loyal. The second anything looks off, he'll move."

"Good," Leo replied. "Because this isn't about surveillance anymore. It's a warning."

"No," Gideon said coldly, watching the screen where Arden moved behind the bar, oblivious to the storm circling her. "It was a mistake. And they're going to learn the hard way."

"I want Alex and Sebastian tracked. Every move. Every call. If they so much as breathe in her direction, I want to know."

"Already done. But Gideon..." Leo's voice lowered. "You can't protect her from all of it. Not without her knowing the full picture."

"I'm not..." Gideon stopped himself, his gaze fixed on Arden's image. "I'm buying time."

A pause.

"Time for what?"

Gideon looked at the screen again. Arden's silhouette was framed by the soft overhead light.

Glowing.

Beautiful.

Defiant.

He didn't look away. "To burn it all down."

Leo didn't respond immediately. When he did, there was no doubt in his voice. "Then we'll be ready."

Gideon ended the call and dropped the phone on the desk with hushed finality. His hand moved to the rotation schedule Christian had updated earlier. Without hesitation, he crossed out two names and scribbled in replacements—his best, sharpest detail.

Unseen.

Unrelenting.

Let them come. Let them believe Arden was unprotected. Let them underestimate the one thing he would kill to defend.

The rules had changed.

So had the battlefield.

❦

Christian Sampson didn't move, not until Arden disappeared down the subway steps.

Her gait was steady. Her chin lifted. But the set of her shoulders told him the pressure had returned, the same weight she had carried that night with the shattered glass, red petals, and no clear answers.

She didn't have her car anymore. No repair orders had crossed his desk. No update had been passed to management. No mention of it at all.

Which meant one thing.

She didn't feel safe enough to ask.

Christian exhaled through his nose, the cold biting against his skin. At this point, Arden didn't know she was being followed, for protection or otherwise.

And that was a problem.

Because she was.

Gideon had given the order the minute the car was hit. Christian and his team shadowed her now, not always visible or near, but constant.

He wasn't alone.

Another agent waited near her apartment, ready to pick her up from the subway entrance and track the walk home. They rotated through posts and methods, always close enough to intervene, never close enough to be seen.

A parked car.

A bench.

A camera feed from the corner bodega.

Quiet. Efficient. Unrelenting.

Christian tapped his earpiece, checking in with the night detail. Routine coverage. No activity.

Yet.

Even so, he didn't like the vulnerability in this new pattern. The subway created gaps, and gaps bred risk. Arden Rivers needed a fortress right now, not blind spots dressed up as transit.

His gaze lingered on the dark mouth of the station, his instincts gnawing at him. He made a mental note to tighten the coverage. Add another post near her apartment. Adjust the subway handoff. Close the spaces where a careful threat might breathe.

Because whatever was coming for her would not arrive with a bang.

It would slip in like smoke.

CHAPTER 38

Into the Fire

The streets pressed in—eerily quiet, strangely still—as if the city itself had paused to listen.

Arden kept a brisk pace, shoulders hunched, her breath curling in fast white ribbons as the cold bit deeper. The scarf at her throat felt too thin. Her boots struck the pavement in sharp, uneven warnings she couldn't ignore, and every flicker at the edge of her vision made her spine straighten, her jaw clench.

You're tired, she told herself. Overthinking.

Then she heard it.

A footstep.

Too deliberate to be coincidence.

Her breath faltered, her heart kicking hard beneath her ribs. Logic warred with instinct. Coincidence, she reasoned. Just someone else heading home. Just another body moving through the same cold stretch of city.

Then she heard it again.

The exact same rhythm.

Right behind her.

Shit.

Panic snapped through her, fast and bright. Her pulse spiked, and every sound sharpened at once. She picked up her pace, forcing her breathing to slow even as her body screamed for speed.

Don't run.

If she ran, she was prey.

And prey didn't win.

Her fingers fumbled in her pocket, brushing the edge of her phone. Call

Gideon. Call Penny. Call someone. Her thumb hovered, frozen by one second too much fear.

One second too slow.

She glanced over her shoulder.

A shadow trailed her.

Too tall. Too close. Face obscured beneath a hood. Their gait matched hers, barely a step behind.

A cold jolt shot through her, and she turned sharply down a side street, her boots slipping slightly on the slick pavement.

The alley stretched ahead, narrow and dark. The city noise faded, swallowed by the kind of quiet that lived between buildings.

Arden darted behind a dumpster and crouched low, the chill of the metal bleeding through her coat. Her breaths came fast and shallow, but her mind snapped into place.

Control the space.

Control the outcome.

She listened.

Waited.

Footsteps approached.

Even. Measured.

One scrape of rubber on concrete.

Then another.

A tall figure stepped to the mouth of the alley and stopped, head tilted, listening.

Arden didn't move.

She could strike if she had to. Run, if she timed it right. She measured distance, angle, weight, the slickness of the pavement beneath her boots. Every lesson came back as instinct, cold and precise.

But the figure only lingered, shifting slightly.

A beat passed.

Then another.

And then they turned and disappeared, as if they had never been there at all.

She waited five seconds.

Then ten.

Slow. Calculated. Every nerve firing.

Arden slipped from her hiding place and moved back toward the main street, breathing ragged, muscles trembling with held tension.

They were gone.

But the dread clung to her skin like smoke.

And now she knew for certain.

She wasn't imagining it anymore.

———

SEBASTIAN LINGERED IN THE SHADOWS, *alive in the city's pulse.*

Invisible.

Intent.

Each flicker of movement, each distant sound, sharpened his focus.

Arden walked ahead of him, head high, steps clipped, carving through the night as if she didn't have a care in the world. But he could see it—the strain in her shoulders, the too-quick glances, the tension simmering beneath all that practiced control.

She moved like a woman who belonged entirely to herself.

But he knew better.

She had no idea.

No idea how magnetic she was. No idea that each step, every stubborn breath, only pulled him in deeper.

That was the thing about Arden.

She didn't merely stand out.

She burned.

Too bright.

Too bold.

Too dangerous.

Little Fire.

A flare he would follow into oblivion if he had to.

She thought independence was armor. She thought strength could protect her. But strength only made her visible to the wrong people, and visibility was a dangerous kind of beauty.

For men like him.

For worse.

Especially worse.

Men like Gideon Blackwell didn't see the real her. Not the way she tried so hard to outrun her past, to stay ahead of the world closing in around her. Gideon would strip her down piece by piece until she no longer recognized herself, not out of cruelty, perhaps, but through the slow, elegant violence of misunderstanding.

Men like him always meant well.

They always destroyed.

Arden didn't belong in Gideon's world of glass towers and silent threats, in his empire of lies dressed up as legacy. She belonged with someone who saw through it. Someone who could handle the heat without trying to tame it.

Someone who wouldn't put her on a pedestal.

Sebastian would worship the fire and guard it with his life.

She didn't understand that yet.

But he did.

That was why he was here. Why he would always be here.

Not just to watch.
To keep her safe.
To keep her his.

*

Arden turned to leave the alley.
Then—impact.
Solid.
Immediate.
She collided with a wall of muscle instead of brick, and instinct took over. Her hands flew up, ready to shove, to strike, to survive.
A lifeline, not panic.
A sharp inhale clawed through her. She looked up, wide-eyed, and met his gaze. Gideon.
"It's me," he said, calm but urgent, his hands slightly raised in reassurance. His stance didn't demand her trust. It made room for it.
Relief slammed into adrenaline, stealing the strength from her legs. For one dizzy second, the only real thing in the alley was him.
And Gideon was already assessing.
His eyes swept over her face, then the alley, then the dark mouth behind her, each shift in his posture tighter than the last. No wasted movement. No unnecessary words. He didn't need details to know the threat had already reached her.
"What happened?" The question was clipped, restraint drawn taut over rage.
"I..." The syllable snagged in her throat, too breathless to carry anything more.
She swallowed, trying to steady the rush in her chest while facts, training, and instinct scrambled for dominance. "I heard footsteps. Deliberate. Too close. I tried to shake them—cut down an alley to gain some distance. To get a better angle."
She watched the shift in him as she spoke: his stance widening, his hand settling at the small of her back, protective but careful.
"Did you see him?" he asked, voice clipped.
"Not clearly," she said. "He paused at the alley's mouth. Then walked away."
A beat of silence passed, tension crackling between them like a storm waiting to break.
"Next time," he said quietly, "you call me. The second you feel off. You don't walk alone."
She opened her mouth to argue, but one look at him—at the steel behind his eyes, the fear he wasn't saying out loud—stopped her cold.
"You think I'd rather find you in an alley than answer my phone?" His voice was low and sharp, anger laced with worry so exposed it hurt.
"I didn't want to sound paranoid," she murmured, her voice small.

"Arden, paranoia keeps you alive," he said, eyes hard on the shadows behind her.

His hand pressed more firmly at her back, a subtle pull drawing her closer. "And you're not crazy. You were right to run."

The words lodged deep, warming something she hadn't realized had gone cold.

Her fingers knotted in the front of his coat, grounding herself in the only steady thing left. When he inhaled like he felt it too, it nearly undid her.

"I'm fine," she whispered, too soft to sound convincing.

"No," he said simply. "But you will be. Because I'm not letting anything happen to you."

His hand shifted, sliding from her back to the dip of her waist, the gesture steadying her even as it sent a flicker of heat crawling up her spine. She didn't pull away. Couldn't. The warmth of his touch was the only thing keeping the cold from getting in.

When they started walking again, her body drifted closer, his hand firm at her waist.

It wasn't a choice.

It was instinct.

And for the first time in blocks, Arden could finally exhale.

THEY WALKED IN SILENCE, but it wasn't the kind that offered peace. Each step dragged, slow and heavy, while the city seemed to hold its breath alongside her.

Gideon's hand stayed at her waist, steady and sure. More than comfort. More than guidance. It reminded her where she was in the dark, tethered her to the present before fear could drag her back into old rooms and older shadows.

Arden barely felt the cold anymore. Each shadow along the sidewalk tugged at her focus, setting her nerves on edge. Maybe it was nothing, another trick of adrenaline and exhaustion.

But she couldn't shake the feeling they weren't alone.

"Let me walk you up," he said, his voice low but resolute.

The way he said it made the offer feel less optional than she wanted it to be.

She turned at the door, already shaking her head. "I'm fine," she said too quickly, the words brittle, a defense dressed as strength.

His jaw flexed. Not anger. Restraint.

"I know you are," he said. "But humor me."

The words wrapped around her like a truth she wasn't ready for. They were dangerous because they didn't threaten her; because they sounded too much like care, like trust, like someone willing to stand close without turning her fear into proof that she couldn't stand on her own.

And that was what scared her most.

She didn't argue. Couldn't, not with him this close, not with his presence slipping through cracks she had been trying too hard to ignore.

THEY CLIMBED THE STAIRS, the creak of old wood the only sound between them. The silence stretched tight, thick with everything neither of them could say.

At her door, Arden reached for her keys, but her fingers fumbled. They slipped from her grasp and clattered against the floor.

She muttered a curse under her breath.

Gideon was already there.

He closed the last inches between them, his hand brushing hers as he steadied her. The touch hit like a spark, short-circuiting every instinct she had spent years sharpening into discipline.

For a second, she couldn't move.

Only feel.

"Let me," he murmured.

Her fingers loosened, surrendering the keys. Not because she couldn't manage. Because she didn't want to keep pretending she had to.

He unlocked the door but didn't move away. His hand settled back at her waist, slow and deliberate this time. His thumb slid beneath the edge of her sweater, barely a touch, and still it lit her from the inside.

Immediate.

Unmistakable.

Her heart pounded, the heat of him cutting through the cold. He was close, grounding in a way that made her feel a little less unmoored, a little less alone in the dark hallway with her pulse still trying to outrun the footsteps behind her.

"I've got it from here," she said, but her voice cracked under the weight of it, too soft and uneven to pass for strength.

His reply came lower, rougher. "I know."

His fingers tightened.

Just enough to anchor her.

But he didn't let go.

CHAPTER 39

Dangerous Territory

Where his fingers touched, heat flared—sharp and immediate. It slipped beneath her coat like purposeful fire, a visceral current she couldn't outrun.

Her heart slammed against her ribs, not from fear, but desire; dark, reckless, and dangerous enough to unravel everything she had spent years holding together.

Her lips parted on a shaky breath. "We should—"

The words dissolved as Gideon turned fully and pressed her back against the door, gentle enough to give her room, firm enough to make every nerve in her body pay attention. His hand stayed at her waist, unwavering, control wrapped around restraint. His scent curled around her—warm, dark, utterly intoxicating—and she hated how much she needed it.

He leaned closer, the charged air between them crackling.

Fierce.

Untamed.

"Should what?" His voice dripped with sin, velvet against her skin. "Pretend I can't feel the way your pulse betrays you?"

She inhaled sharply, chin tilting upward in stubborn defiance. "I'm not—"

But the hesitation fractured the lie.

His smile came slow and deliberate, less seduction now than predator recognizing the first drop of blood in the water. His fingers tightened at her hip, testing the edge of her resistance without crossing it.

"No? Prove it," he shot back, but the way his voice hit her when he repeated it, low and dangerous, left her breathless.

"Prove it?" Her voice sharpened, a tremor of defiance in it. "That's dangerous territory, Blackwell."

His eyes darkened, intense and unyielding. "I live in dangerous territory."

He moved even closer, his breath ghosting across her skin, cedar and danger tangling in her senses. "And sweetheart? You're already deep in my woods."

Her palms landed on his chest, drawn there by instinct. Beneath her touch, his heartbeat beat steady and controlled, but there was violence in the restraint of it, a promise held taut beneath bone and muscle.

His hold on her waist cinched, unmistakable now. Not a warning, not quite a claim, but something perilously close to both.

His free hand lifted, fingers grazing her throat with maddening calm. Gentle, but laced with power. His thumb traced the race of her pulse, precise and relentless, as if her body had already confessed what her mouth still refused to say.

"Still not shaking?" he murmured, lips grazing her jaw, each word dark with knowing.

"Shut up," she said, hands gripping his jacket. She dragged him closer because restraint had become a language neither of them was willing to speak.

His low laugh vibrated through her, a dark challenge. "Make me."

He pushed. She pulled.

They collided.

Their mouths crashed together, restraint giving way to something wilder; want and war, tongue and teeth, breath tangling until patience became impossible and reason turned useless at the door.

Gideon pressed her hard against the wood, every muscle carved with tension, his grip tight at her waist. His other hand slid into her hair, angling her mouth to his, pulling her closer, deeper, until the world narrowed to heat and pressure and the impossible certainty of him.

He broke away just enough to breathe, his voice brushing her lips, rough and raw. "Still think you're fine?"

She bit his bottom lip in response, deliberate and sharp. "Still think you're in control?"

The flare in his eyes could have set fire to the world. Not anger. Intensity. A dangerous heat that dared her to challenge him again. His grip tightened, and the kiss deepened with a hunger that made her knees threaten betrayal.

"Control?" he rasped at her throat, teeth grazing skin. "Sweetheart, I lost that the second you walked into my storm."

Her head fell back, fingers curling into his hair, pulling him closer. His answering groan wasn't only sound; it was surrender, devotion, and defiance caught in the same ruined breath.

"Someone could see," she whispered, her voice no longer steady. No longer certain.

"Let them." His kisses scorched a path down her collarbone, each word a brand. "Let them see who you run to when the dark gets too loud."

His intensity should have sent her retreating. Instead, she clung harder, anchored by him and by the dangerous weight of his certainty.

"This is insane," she murmured against his lips.

"No." His voice dropped, soft but lethal. "This is inevitable."

A broken laugh slipped out, ragged and breathless. "Inevitable? That's bold. Even for you."

He pulled back to meet her eyes, his gaze sharpened to a blade. "It's not bold. It's truth. You're the match, Arden. I've waited my whole damn life to burn."

Her fingers traced his jaw, feeling the strain there, the fracture line between control and surrender. "We'll burn it all down."

His forehead rested against hers, their breath tangled, slow and searing. "Then it all deserves to burn. Maybe I've been holding the match for too long."

The quiet truth slipped out of her before she could bury it. "Your mother will destroy me."

"She'll try." His tone turned to steel, his arms iron around her. "But she forgets. I'm a Blackwell too. And I protect what's mine."

The word detonated between them.

Mine.

A promise. A warning. A vow.

"Yours?" she echoed, voice stripped raw, somewhere between challenge and surrender.

His eyes darkened, a dare burning in their depths. "Prove me wrong. Walk away. Go inside."

She didn't move.

Couldn't.

"Can't," she whispered.

His voice was a blade wrapped in silk. "Or won't?"

Her lips brushed his, the space between them evaporating.

"Both."

He kissed her again, slower this time, but no less consuming. The urgency shifted into something deeper, more dangerous for its restraint. Reverent. Possessive. A claim laid not against her body, but across the space between them—unchallenged, undeniable.

Before Arden could catch her breath, Gideon gathered her into his arms, effortless and commanding, as if she weighed nothing and meant everything. Her legs wrapped around him on instinct, her arms locking around his shoulders as though the ground beneath her had vanished.

He backed her into the wall, the chill biting through fabric enough to make the heat pouring off him feel combustible. His chest rose against hers in uneven rhythm, every breath laced with tension and want, a firestorm held together by the last fraying thread of control.

His mouth found hers again, scorching through what little thought she had left. He kissed her like she was the only thing tethering him to the earth, like stopping would fracture something vital inside him. His grip on her thighs didn't waver. He held her as if every impossible truth between them had finally taken shape in flesh and fire.

His mouth trailed down the edge of her jaw, lingering low, lower, until he found the sensitive place below her ear. When his teeth grazed that spot, her gasp broke loose—guttural, needy, dangerously soft.

Her head tipped back, body arching into him, hips aligning to his. Her fingers tangled in his hair. She trembled, but fear had no place in it.

He tasted her like he meant to leave a memory on her skin. Something indelible. Something she would feel long after the night had ended.

"Gideon," she breathed, her voice breaking.

His teeth skimmed her neck again, his hips pressing hard into hers, and every last ounce of resistance shattered.

When he finally stilled, their foreheads met, breath tangled between them like smoke.

"You're mine," he said again, voice hoarse with certainty. The words seemed to tether him to the ground.

She gripped the lapels of his coat, her body trembling from the sheer weight of how right it felt.

He lowered her with deliberate care, palms sliding along her thighs in slow descent until the soles of her boots kissed the floor. But the current between them stayed live-wire. Ruinous.

Neither moved.

Neither spoke.

His hands settled at her hips, wide and unapologetic, holding the kind of curves a man didn't merely touch; he studied them like scripture. He stood there grounded in the weight of her, the heat of her, as if she were something holy he had no intention of pretending he didn't worship.

Then he dipped his head and kissed her again, slow and reverent.

One final burn.

"I'm yours," she whispered into his mouth, steadier this time. Undeniable.

"Damn right you are." The grin that broke across his face was dark and shameless, but behind it flickered something unguarded.

He leaned into her ear, lips grazing skin that still burned. "Go inside," he murmured. "Like a good girl."

She blinked up at him, sharp and defiant. "I'm not a good girl."

His smile curved, molten.

"I know." His voice dropped lower. "I prefer it that way."

Gideon stepped back deliberately, dragging the moment out so she would feel it long after he left.

"Goodnight, Arden."

Then he turned, his stride unhurried and confident, a man who knew he had just razed the ground and left her standing in the ash.

Arden stood frozen, breath jagged, the echo of him painted across her skin.

"Bastard," she whispered, dazed and far too fond.

The door clicked shut behind her.

She didn't move. She only leaned into the wood, chest rising and falling as if she had barely survived a cataclysm. Her fingers brushed her lips, swollen and burning.

His voice looped in her memory.

I prefer it that way.

The words coiled low in her belly, molten and wild.

For one reckless, unraveling second, she let them consume her.

The click of her door echoed louder than it should have.

Final.

Unbearable.

Gideon didn't move at first. Every muscle remained drawn taut, his body locked in the space Arden had left behind. His pulse hammered against his ribs, never steady where she was concerned, never obedient enough to remember who he was supposed to be.

Her scent still hung in the air—warm, defiant, delicate only in the way fire was before it spread. It wrapped around him, unshakable and inescapable.

He should have walked away. Should have turned on his heel and put distance between them before his restraint cracked clean down the center.

His body hadn't gotten the memo.

His palms still remembered her: soft where she scorched him, strong where it mattered more. That little gasp she'd made when he found her pulse point had lodged somewhere deep and ruinous, the kind of sound a man heard later in dreams.

Or nightmares.

Either way, he was a dead man.

Gideon dragged a hand through his hair, jaw clenched hard enough to ache. Every part of him thrummed with the aftermath of her—wanting her, needing her, and worse, needing to protect her with a force that felt almost primal.

Not because she was weak.

Because the world would try to break her, and he would burn it down before he let that happen.

She had no idea what she'd done. What she was still doing.

That wasn't only lust.

That was collapse.

Her breathless "I'm yours" had detonated the last thread of his control and blown straight through every disciplined part of him, leaving nothing behind but ash. He wasn't built to hear those words and stay sane. Not from her. Not with the world closing in.

Gideon exhaled hard. He flexed his knuckles and forced himself to take a step back, then another.

The space between them was physical now, but it didn't matter.

She was in his blood.

There was no more pretending.

Arden Rivers was his.

And heaven help anyone who tried to take her from him.

Arden had paused in the doorway, still on edge from the alley and Gideon's last words at her door.

Go inside like a good girl.

She had almost flared up at the command. Almost. But spellbound had gotten there first, heat and defiance tangling too tightly to separate. Her sass had kicked in on instinct—I'm not a good girl—half rebellion, half truth.

Then his voice at her ear, low and sinful.

I prefer it that way.

That whisper had sent a shiver winding down her spine, reigniting every spark they had set off against the door. Her heart still throbbed from all of it: the fear, the relief, the heat, the unbearable intimacy of being seen too clearly and still wanting him closer.

By the time she crossed the threshold, the door clicked shut with a soft snick, and the silence sealed itself around her.

She stood there, back against the wood, trying to get her breathing under control.

Part of her still rattled, the memory of being followed scraped raw and too recent. Another part felt nothing but fierce, aching gratitude that Gideon had appeared in the alley right when the dark began to close its hand around her. And a third couldn't stop replaying every single word he had murmured against her skin.

Kicking off her boots, Arden drifted into the living room. She turned on a lamp, tossed her keys onto the table, and caught sight of herself in the hallway mirror.

Wild hair. Flushed lips. Ravaged. Radiant.

The worst part?

She wanted more.

But beneath the heat still pulsing through her skin, a chill crept in.

How did he find me in that alley?

Gideon had been intense ever since the rose. Since the car. Since the glass. But that timing hadn't been coincidence. It couldn't have been.

She grabbed her phone and hesitated only once before her fingers flew.

> You left me at my door all heated. But I'm curious... how'd you know I was in that alley?

She tossed the phone onto the couch and started pacing.
The light buzzed.

> Gideon: I'm guessing "Hey, are you okay?" is out of the question first?

She huffed. Typical. Deflective.

> I'm fine. Answer me

> Gideon: Arden...

> Don't "Arden" me. Spill it: how'd you know I was there?

A beat.

> Gideon: After the rose petals, the broken windows... I couldn't shake the feeling someone was targeting you. I asked Christian's team to keep tabs. For your safety.

She stared at the words.
So he'd had her followed.
Her stomach knotted. Her mouth went dry.
No.
No, no, no.
She wasn't doing this again. Not with him. Not with someone she was beginning to let in.

Her phone trembled in her hand as she paced the room, her heart beating out a warning she hadn't wanted to hear. The heat from the alley hadn't even cooled before this new fury rose up, blistering and raw.
She hadn't been paranoid.
She hadn't imagined it.
She had been watched.

And the worst part was that he hadn't said a word.
Her fingers flew across the screen, messy and fast, edits abandoned halfway through.

> Are you fucking kidding me?

> You had people watching me and didn't think I deserved to know?

She started another message, deleted it, then retyped with shaking hands.

> If I feel like I'm being watched, and I am being watched because you decided to keep me in the dark, then it's not paranoia. I deserve to know the difference.

The three dots appeared on his side.
She sent another message before he could answer.

> You had me followed. And you didn't think to TELL me?

> Gideon: I'm sorry. But after seeing you spooked, after your car got hit, I couldn't just let it go. If anything happened to you…

She exhaled, heartbeat climbing. The alley came back in sharp flashes: the silence, the shadow, then Gideon breathing hard, his arm sliding around her like armor.

> So Christian's people texted you? And you rushed over?

> Gideon: Exactly. They sent me a pin the second they spotted trouble.

A reluctant warmth spread through her chest.
He'd dropped everything.
He'd come like a storm.

> You should have told me sooner. Damn it.

> Gideon: I know. I didn't want you looking over your shoulder constantly. I wanted you safe. Not scared. That wasn't my intention.

The knot in her chest loosened, but not all the way.
Controlling? Yes.
Infuriating? Absolutely.

And still… undeniably his kind of care, reckless and overreaching and terrified beneath the polish.

God, he meant it.

She sank onto the couch.

Says the guy who told me "Go inside like a good girl."

His reply came fast.

Gideon: So, you do listen sometimes.

She barked a laugh, scrubbing a hand over her face.

In your dreams, Blackwell.

This time, the pause felt longer. When the message finally arrived, it was stripped down. Bare.

Gideon: Arden, I am sorry I kept it from you. But I can't handle letting you face this alone.

She sat with that one. Let it fill the quiet.

I get it. Doesn't mean I like it. But yeah… you helped.

Thank you.

Another buzz.

Gideon: If you need me. Anytime. Call or text. Especially if you feel followed again. No hesitation.

She bit her lip. Her fingers hovered, then tapped.

Arden: So you really think I'm a good girl?

She didn't know why she sent it. Maybe to feel the heat again. Maybe to make him squirm. Maybe because fear had left her nerves raw, and flirting with Gideon Blackwell was apparently how her body had decided to prove it was still alive.

His answer was immediate.

Gideon: Not for a second. I prefer it that way, remember?

She closed her eyes as a reckless smile tugged at her lips.

Oh, she remembered.

Arden: Thanks for having my back, Blackwell. I'd say don't pull that secret spy stuff again, but... I suspect you're not good at following orders.

> Gideon: I follow them when they make sense.

> Gideon: Lock your door, Rivers.

She rolled her eyes.

And she locked it.

But that other door, the one inside her—the one she had kept sealed shut for years—had cracked open now.

And God help her, she wasn't sure she wanted it closed again.

CHAPTER 40

Unseen Gestures

The Blackwell Room wasn't merely a club. It was a stage for glances and low murmurs, for wealth dressed as leisure, for Gideon's maddeningly timed smirk arriving exactly when it could do the most damage.

Tonight, though, something had shifted.

No circling. No defense.

Gideon's presence clung to Arden like a vow, woven through every glance cast across the bar, every footstep in those familiar halls, every silence that carried more than words ever could. It followed her from her apartment to the club, from the rasp of his voice still seared into her skin to the memory of his hands, a heat she could feel beneath her clothes long after he'd left.

You're mine, he had told her. I've known it since the night we met.

And the terrifying part—the part that unsettled her most—was how much she had wanted to believe him.

The chandeliers threw warm amber light across the room, catching on crystal and splintering into soft prisms that skimmed polished wood and velvet trim. The lounge thrummed with quiet wealth: ice striking crystal, silk brushing against tailored suits, the kind of laughter reserved for people who knew they were being observed.

Arden moved behind the bar with practiced ease, every motion second nature, but the rhythm of the night felt unsettled. Unease threaded through her thoughts, too faint to name and too persistent to dismiss.

Across the lounge, Alex and Harlan leaned in close, their laughter low and intimate, coated in charm and edged with a chill that didn't match the room's warmth. Their grins were easy, practiced—old money and older games.

She didn't trust the camaraderie.

333

Not from them.

Not here.

Sebastian sat tucked into his usual corner, flanked by a brunette Arden didn't recognize—elegant, sharp-eyed, clearly bored. He murmured something Arden couldn't catch, coaxing a faint smile from the woman as she reached for her drink, but his attention never quite stayed where it belonged. One arm draped loosely along the back of the booth, the other curled around his glass, his posture too calculated to be casual.

Arden didn't flinch when she felt his gaze sweep toward her. She met it evenly, letting the moment stretch longer than politeness allowed.

Then she turned away.

No rush. No rattle. Only resolve.

Beside her, Fatima moved in sync, their rhythm built over long nights, shared shifts, and wordless trust.

"I'm thinking of a twist on a classic," Arden murmured, reaching for the lavender syrup. The scent bloomed gently, floral and calming. "Gin, lavender, chamomile. Hit it with citrus. Clean, unexpected. Smooth."

Fatima's brows lifted. "Goddess-tier. If that's your vibe, you've gotta try Delancey's. Lavender-chamomile tea, loose leaf. It's like a spa in a cup. Tiny place, overpriced as hell, but you'll want to frame the box."

Arden chuckled, and some of the tension eased from her spine. "I've walked past it. Always figured it was too bougie for me."

Fatima grinned. "You're bougie now, babe. Own it. After dealing with..." She swept a hand around them. "...this? You deserve all the overpriced nonsense your heart desires."

Arden felt the shift before she saw him.

Gideon.

He appeared at the far end of the bar, silent and intentional, as though summoned by the change in her pulse. An untouched espresso and a precisely stacked folder of documents marked his place. His collar was open, sleeves rolled to reveal forearms corded with quiet strength.

No performance.

Only presence.

Her breath stuttered before she forced it steady again.

GIDEON'S GAZE swept the lounge like a scalpel—precise, methodical. It passed over Alex and Harlan, paused briefly at Sebastian's table, and moved on. It was a silent inventory, enough to register every player without revealing his hand.

Then his eyes found hers.

Heat curled low in Arden's stomach. He claimed her with a glance, but it was different now. This wasn't the simmering pull of stolen looks or backstage flirtation.

It was control threaded through devotion—a quiet declaration forged in shadowed moments, in the heat of his sheets, in the way he had held her afterward, and in the way she hadn't pulled away.

He leaned forward, elbows braced on the bar. To the room, it was a relaxed pose —intentional, nonchalant. To Arden, it was a shield. Without a single word, he had placed himself between her and everything else.

Sebastian might posture with smirks and curated charm, but Gideon didn't need to perform. He was power in its quietest form: watchful, restrained, and impossible to mistake. And for the first time in a room full of eyes, Arden didn't feel exposed. She felt protected. Chosen.

This was different, because this time she wasn't navigating the storm alone.

This time, she was his.

And every person in that room knew it.

SHE SENSED Sebastian before he came into view; an itch beneath her skin, as if the air changed simply because he had entered it.

He drifted through the lounge with calculated grace, his gait too smooth to be casual, each step placed with careful precision. The crowd shifted around him without realizing it, unconsciously parting in his path.

Arden's chest tightened.

"Busy night?" Sebastian asked as he approached, his tone light, conversational. "Looks like you're holding court."

Then his voice dropped, smooth as silk pulled tight over broken glass.

"You've got a sharp mind, Arden," he murmured, eyes never quite leaving hers. "It's rare in a place so obsessed with polish. Most people only know how to reflect. But you? You cut through it."

She tilted her head, the compliment landing with the wrong kind of weight. "Thanks. Though I wouldn't underestimate the depth around here. It tends to surprise you."

A soft chuckle. Controlled. Calculated.

"Touché." His gaze lingered too long. "But you stand out here, in ways I doubt even you realize."

His glance drifted toward Gideon, a flick of amusement buried inside it. A subtle dare.

Gideon didn't move, but his jaw flexed.

A silent acknowledgment.

A warning.

Sebastian caught it, and his smirk widened.

"Still," he mused, "working under Gideon must come with its own... complexities. He's always had a reputation for playing too rough. Doesn't always leave the pieces intact."

The jab slid between the words like a blade, veiled enough to feign innocence.

Arden straightened, tension bristling through her limbs before she could stop it. "Sebastian."

Gideon's voice cut clean through the din, quiet and razor-sharp, violent in its restraint.

He hadn't raised it.

He never needed to.

Sebastian pivoted with disconcerting calm, the smile on his lips unchanged. His eyes, though, had gone sharp. Darker.

"No need to be territorial," he said mildly. "I was being polite."

"Don't."

One word.

A command.

Sebastian's grin held, then flickered. He backed away a single step, retreat masquerading as grace.

"Of course," he murmured. "I'd never stir the pot."

Arden focused on the glass in her hand, unwilling to meet either gaze. She refused to give Sebastian the satisfaction of reaction.

But as he walked away, every step landed with intention, echoing like punctuation. His eyes dragged over her one last time, no longer curious or admiring.

Appraising.

Ice needled down her spine.

But the heat beside her—Gideon's silent, unmoving presence—rooted her. A shield in the storm. One she hadn't asked for, but wasn't about to refuse.

Fatima nudged her, smirking like she had discovered a secret. "You know, I've said it before, but there's definitely something going on between you and our brooding boss."

Arden raised a brow, slicing clean through a wedge of lime. "You've said it more than a few times."

"And I'll keep saying it," Fatima said breezily, though her voice carried more insight than humor. "But it's different now. He's... less 'storm cloud about to explode' and more 'cloud that might let the sun peek through.'"

She laughed at her own metaphor, setting the citrus aside. "Still intense, obviously. But when you're around, he looks... human."

Arden huffed a soft laugh, the corners of her mouth betraying her before she could stop them. "That's dramatic."

Fatima grinned. "Maybe. But I see the way he watches you. That's not managerial concern. That's a man who'd burn the world down without a second glance."

Arden didn't reply immediately.

The heat blooming beneath her skin had nothing to do with the gin. She reached for the chamomile syrup and measured it with steady hands.

"He's... Gideon," she said finally.

No scoff. No dismissal. Only his name, heavy with meaning she hadn't figured out how to hold.

Fatima's expression softened. She didn't press, only tilted her head toward the drink Arden was building. "Well, finish your spellwork, witch. I need five minutes of peace, and your cocktails are the closest thing I've got to a religious experience."

Arden smiled and focused on the delicate pour.

Lavender. Citrus. Light stirred into shadows.

Her rhythm returned, practiced and precise, even if her body still hummed with memory, even if her mind refused to stop whispering what she already knew.

Everything had shifted.

She slid the glass across the bar, and Fatima took one sip before groaning like she'd seen salvation.

"Arden, this is dangerous. Give me three and I'll forget I work here."

A real laugh slipped out this time, but it faltered the moment her gaze drifted toward the far end of the bar.

Gideon was there.

Still.

Unwavering.

And this time, he didn't pretend to look away.

THE CLUB HUMMED with wealth and power, every polished surface reflecting some piece of the carefully curated world Gideon had built.

His world.

A world shaped by legacy and lineage, one Sebastian had been groomed to inherit until it slipped through his fingers like sand.

He lingered at the edge of the room, a shadow rendered in flesh and tailored wool, his smirk coiled with irony as Gideon moved through the space with the entitled ease of someone who had never had to earn it.

Because he hadn't, had he?

The perfect heir.

The one Henry Hawthorne had chosen.

Sebastian's grip tightened around his glass, the polished weight of it a small anchor against the rising tide of betrayal—familiar, corrosive, and sharp-edged with everything he had once believed was his.

For years, their family had whispered his name first.

Sebastian, the eldest grandchild.

Sebastian, the natural successor.

Sebastian, the one who should have carried the Hawthorne name forward.

But when Henry died, the will told a different story. A story where Sebastian was cast aside. A story where Gideon took everything.

And why?

Because Henry had believed in potential. Because Gideon, at twenty-three, had been the perfect blend of Blackwell ruthlessness and Hawthorne control.

Sebastian had spent his life preparing for the crown, only to watch it fall uncontested into the hands of a boy who hadn't even reached for it.

That had always been Gideon's trick, hadn't it?

To be chosen without trying.

To want nothing and still walk away with everything.

He took what Sebastian wanted most without even trying.

And now?

Now he was doing it again.

Sebastian's eyes flicked to Arden.

She didn't even realize she was stepping into a war.

Because this wasn't only about her. It was about him and Gideon. About history repeating itself. About Gideon taking something that should have belonged to Sebastian before the thought had even finished forming.

This time, Sebastian wasn't going to let it happen.

He watched as Gideon's gaze locked onto Arden, a territorial edge in his eyes, the kind that made the truth painfully clear.

Arden wasn't merely someone Gideon wanted.

She was someone he thought he owned.

Sebastian's fingers tightened around his glass until the pressure threatened to crack it.

Mine.

He had heard it before, or something close enough to leave the same scar.

Spoken in a different lifetime.

From a different Gideon.

He had heard it the summer Gideon was twelve, the year Henry started choosing him over Sebastian.

THE YEAR EVERYTHING CHANGED

August hung heavy in the air, the scent of sun-warmed grass and sweat clinging to their skin as they stood at the edge of the estate. The football lay between them, scuffed and dirt-streaked from hours of adolescent war.

Sebastian, seventeen and still burning with the clean violence of victory, had just finished running circles around the younger boys. His muscles hummed with adrenaline, his grin sharp with satisfaction.

He had turned to grab the ball, only to find Gideon standing there, holding it.

"Give it back," Sebastian had said, voice even.

Gideon had only smiled.

Not a taunt. Not quite a challenge. Something worse—calm, unwavering certainty.

"Make me."

The words had cut deep because there had been no hesitation in Gideon's eyes. No doubt. No awareness, even, of what he had taken by standing there with the ball in his hands and that effortless little smile on his face.

As if he had already won.

As if he knew something Sebastian didn't.

That was the first moment Sebastian had truly hated him.

The moment he understood that Gideon had no idea what want felt like, because he had never had to want. Things simply fell into his hands, as if the universe had been designed around the shape of his palm.

Lucky.

Chosen.

Henry's heir before anyone had dared say it aloud.

And now, twenty-one years later, Gideon wore that same fucking look.

Standing at the bar, staring at Arden like she belonged to him.

Make me.

Sebastian exhaled slowly, dragging himself back to the present, and set his glass down before it shattered in his grip.

This time, Gideon wasn't going to win.

He had taken Sebastian's birthright. He had taken the future that had been promised to him, the crown Sebastian had been trained to carry, the legacy that should have bent toward him by blood and order and right.

But he wasn't going to take Arden.

Because unlike before, Sebastian wasn't going to wait for Gideon to hand over what he had stolen.

He was going to make Arden see the truth.

Gideon wasn't her salvation.

He was her cage.

And when she finally realized that, she would come to Sebastian instead.

Where she belonged.

Where she had always belonged.

This time, he wasn't going to let her slip away.

Not now.

Not ever.

CHAPTER 41

The Weight of Gifts

A sleek, meticulously wrapped box lay exactly where Arden kept her things behind the bar.

Not casually placed.

Not forgotten.

Deliberate.

The wrapping paper was dark and velvety, its surface seeming to drink in the room's amber light. A satin ribbon—smooth as water, black as ink—coiled around the package with quiet opulence.

This wasn't a gift.

It was a statement.

Arden froze.

A sharp current snapped through her nerves. Years of bartending and trauma nursing had honed her instincts into something precise, a sixth sense for the subtle shifts most people missed.

And this? This didn't whisper danger. It howled.

The air thinned around her, charged with the awful intimacy of being observed. Her pulse drummed in her ears while her mind sliced through possibilities with surgical focus.

Tell Gideon and risk accelerating a problem she didn't yet understand. Loop in Marco or Fatima and risk pulling them into it. Ignore it and let the thing fester in the dark.

Every option came with a cost, and Arden wasn't ready to surrender control before she knew what she was holding.

First, she would watch. Assess. Let the room settle before she moved.

Her fingers hovered above the ribbon, a breath from unraveling whatever waited beneath. One tug, and the curtain would lift. One tug, and she would be pulled deeper into whatever this was.

The act of giving could be soft. Sincere. Human.

But this wasn't tender. It was curated. A performance dressed in luxury, sharpened to a point. A message disguised as generosity.

"Holy shit."

Fatima's voice snapped the spell, sliding in beside her like a jolt of current.

Arden didn't flinch, but her fingers trembled above the ribbon.

Fatima's eyes locked on the box, her easy expression gone. Concern flickered across her face, raw and unguarded.

"What the hell is that?" she asked, voice pitched somewhere between disbelief and dread. "Looks like a gift a rich psychopath sends before the third act."

"If only I knew." Arden's voice came clipped and dry.

She tugged the ribbon. It unfurled without resistance, silk whispering over itself, and the paper opened as if it had been waiting.

Lavender.

The scent rose first, familiar and disarming. It didn't merely linger; it carried memory in its wake, spilling from the box like a ghost in velvet, soft on the surface and laced with static underneath.

Inside sat a sleek tin of Delancey's lavender-chamomile tea, centered with unsettling precision. Beside it, a glass bottle of lavender syrup. Delicate. Pristine. Expensive.

Atop them rested a single ivory card.

The handwriting was clean. Practiced. Stripped of personality.

For your creations and relaxation.
—Your Secret Admirer

Her stomach dropped.

This wasn't flirtation.

This was intrusion.

Fatima exhaled slowly. "Okay, that's... not—"

"It's not random," Arden murmured.

Her teeth caught the edge of her bottom lip, her eyes fixed on the box as though acknowledging it too directly might shift the entire room.

Her thumb skimmed the syrup's label.

The memory landed like a punch.

The night they had talked about that blend. Fatima had mentioned Delancey's. A throwaway conversation, spoken right here over citrus and glass and the ordinary rhythm of service.

Someone had been listening.

Closely.

Fatima's eyes narrowed. The warmth in her face vanished, replaced by quiet steel. Protective. Unflinching.

"You think it's a customer?"

"I don't think it matters," Arden said.

Her gaze lifted, quiet but unyielding. "The question is how long they've been watching and listening."

Then Arden swept the lounge, not idly, but like a scanner on alert.

EVERY CORNER, every flicker of motion fed the churn in Arden's gut.

Alex sat stiffer than usual, his smug ease stripped thin. When their eyes met, his smirk faltered—not fear, exactly, but something close enough to leave a shadow.

Harlan was worse. Jittery. Eyes darting. Hands unsure where to land.

Sebastian sprawled as if the room had been built to accommodate him, legs stretched, one arm thrown over the back of the chair, a glass turning slowly in his hand. But the stillness was camouflage. That faint smile never reached his eyes.

"Still clinging to the edges of the family business, Harlan?" Sebastian asked, voice cool and casual, venom tucked neatly beneath the surface.

Harlan bristled. "I'm not the one on the edge."

The air tensed, one word away from sparking.

Alex's laugh came next. Low. Measured. The kind that reminded everyone who held the leash.

"Careful, boys. No need to make a scene."

Not camaraderie.

Control.

Conflict didn't belong in the open. Not here. At The Blackwell Room, everything whispered, and anything that couldn't be hidden had to be spun.

Arty Barrett dropped into a lounge chair as though ownership were a posture, his whiskey catching the light as he lifted it. His fingers wrapped a touch too tightly around the glass. When he looked at Arden, he held her gaze long enough to unsettle, then dipped his head.

Gentlemanly.

Respectful.

Underneath, expectation waited.

A couple near the fireplace caught her eye. The man was mid-performance, all flourish and charm, but the woman beside him hardly moved. Her gaze wandered, then landed—not on Arden, but on the box.

Recognition flickered in her eyes.

Sharp. Quick. Gone.

She turned back to her date, her smile too polished, too empty.

Arden slid the note into her pocket and pushed the gift beneath the bar, out of sight.

But not out of mind.

The weight of it pressed beneath her ribs. This wasn't a gift. It was a declaration.

And maybe an accusation.

She kept moving—mixing, pouring, calculating orders with mechanical precision—but beneath the rhythm of service, her thoughts spun.

Tell Gideon? Pull Marco in? Fatima already knew too much.

But keeping it to herself felt dangerous.

The scent of lavender lingered, sticky now instead of soothing.

Someone had been listening.

Watching.

Waiting.

She didn't know who.

Or why.

But something had shifted.

And Arden felt it in her bones.

LATER THAT EVENING, Gideon approached the bar with too much deliberation.

From a distance, he looked calm. Controlled. But real control had a scent, and this wasn't it.

The moment he crossed into her space, Arden felt the shift—a hum beneath her skin that had less to do with proximity than awareness.

His eyes dropped briefly to the counter.

To the package she had thought she'd hidden.

His jaw tensed.

This time, visibly.

When his gaze met hers, the air thickened. "What's this?"

His voice was smooth, but wrong. Too even. Too quiet in the way a blade was quiet before it touched skin.

"It was waiting for me," she said. "No note at first. Just... placed there."

"And now?"

She reached beneath the bar and slid the message to him. Their fingers touched, brief and electric.

Gideon picked it up carefully. Not because it was delicate, but because he was already recalculating.

For your creations and relaxation.

—Your Secret Admirer

A muscle in his jaw ticked. He ran his thumb along the edge of the note once, then again.

When he set it down, his whole face had changed.

Gone was the polished restraint.

What replaced it was quieter.

Deadlier.

"This isn't casual."

"No." Her voice dropped to match his.

"You don't know who?"

"If I did," she murmured, "we wouldn't be having this conversation."

He leaned in, one hand braced on the bar, the other hovering near the note as if touching it again might give him something to punish.

His presence wasn't suffocating. It was protective, but barely leashed.

"I need you to tell me if anything else happens." Not a request.

"I can handle—"

"Don't." His eyes cut to hers. "Don't give me the practiced line. Not tonight."

Her breath caught.

He wasn't asking for control. He was offering protection, and that made the ground beneath her feel more dangerous than it should have.

Gideon leaned in a breath more, his voice barely audible. "Not everyone's attention is harmless, Arden."

THE LOUNGE BUZZED AROUND THEM, laughter threading through candlelight, but none of it touched them.

This moment lived outside time.

Gideon's eyes never left hers, and Arden—who had spent years refusing to be protected because protection too often came with a price—felt the weight of knowing she wasn't alone in this anymore.

He wasn't angry because he wanted control.

He was angry because he cared.

And he wasn't merely warning her.

He was planning for war.

GIDEON MOVED DOWN the private hallway like a weapon sheathed in quiet.

The note burned in his pocket.

Not everyone's attention is harmless.

No shit.

He flicked open his phone and called Christian.

"I need eyes on every camera at the club. Someone left a package behind the bar. Wrapped. No name. Between eight and eleven."

"Think it was delivered in person?"

"If it was, I want a face."

He hung up and texted Leo.

> Heads up. Cross-check all entries and deliveries from 8 to 11. Targeting Arden. Someone's getting bold.

> Leo: Done.

Someone had gotten close.

Too close.

Which meant they were inside the perimeter.

Gideon exhaled slowly, forcing himself back to center. Control. Focus. Precision.

They had made a move.

Now it was his turn.

THE REST of the night crawled forward, taut and stretched thin. Glances lingered too long. Smiles felt rehearsed. Somewhere beneath the polished murmur of the room, something was testing Arden, watching for the place her armor might give.

The usual soundtrack of clinking glass and soft flirtation warped at the edges.

When the last patron left, Marco stepped from the back hallway.

Even he looked different.

He nodded toward the box beneath the bar. "Quite the admirer you've got." His tone was light. Too light. But the warning beneath it wasn't. "In this place, even gifts come with price tags."

Arden scrubbed the counter with unnecessary precision. "Tell me about it."

Marco leaned in, his voice dropping beneath the last hum of the room. "Seriously. If the vibe turns, if the air shifts, trust it." His gaze dropped to the gift again, jaw tight. "This crowd doesn't deal in accidents. Everything is intentional. Games are their native tongue, and they don't play to lose."

She nodded once. "Thanks. I'll keep that in mind."

The lights buzzed out one by one.

Marco disappeared to finish closing, but Arden didn't move.

The box remained beneath the bar. Elegant. Unsettling. A velvet-wrapped dare.

It wasn't the tea. It wasn't the syrup. It wasn't even the note.

It was the intimacy of the gesture. The precision. The power wrapped in civility and laced with control. A message disguised as affection, laid exactly where she would find it by someone who wanted her to understand she had been seen.

Her fingers twitched with the urge to throw it out. But that was the trick, wasn't it? Someone had made a move, not to win her over, but to claim space inside her head.

To claim her.

Arden exhaled slowly, the towel in her grip biting into her palms.

She didn't know who had left it. Didn't know what they wanted. But she knew one thing with a clarity that settled cold and clean beneath her ribs.

This wasn't a gift.

It was a test.

A leash dressed in luxury.

And whoever thought she would flinch had made the wrong calculation.

She wasn't that girl anymore.

If they tried to control her, she would burn the whole game down.

MARCO'S WORDS echoed as Arden stepped into the night air.

If the air shifts, trust it.

Something was off.

The city had a rhythm she knew by heart, but tonight, it stuttered. Fell out of sync. Never quite found the beat again.

Cold kissed her skin, but that wasn't what made her shoulders rise. Every step felt observed. Not overtly. Nothing she could prove. Only a hum beneath her skin that refused to quiet.

She glanced back once, casual enough to pass for nothing. Shadows moved the way they always did, slipping beneath streetlight and pooling behind parked cars.

Then her building came into view, a familiar silhouette that should have soothed her.

It didn't.

Her pulse tripped, chasing a thread of dread she hadn't earned but couldn't shake.

Inside, the hallway lights flickered in stuttering bursts. Color bled in and out, stabbing, then retreating. Arden reached for her keys with cold fingers, metal fumbling against metal before they slipped from her grasp.

Clink.

The sound landed louder than it should have, sharp and invasive.

"Shit."

She crouched to grab them, ears tracking the echo as it stretched too far down the corridor, as if the building itself had stopped breathing.

She looked again.

Nothing.

The key slid into the lock.

It stuck.

Only for a second, but long enough to feel like hesitation.

Then—click.

She exhaled.

Froze.

At her feet lay a single rose.

Blood-red and drenched, it gleamed like a warning whispered in her sleep, soft enough to haunt and impossible to forget. Its petals shimmered beneath the flickering light like stained glass.

She hadn't seen it when she walked up. Maybe the lighting had hidden it.

Maybe it hadn't been there.

But it was there now.

Too perfect.

Too placed.

Her pulse thundered.

This wasn't a gift.

It was a lie.

IN THE KITCHEN's soft glow, Arden laid the rose beside the tin of tea.

Side by side, they looked almost graceful.

But not to her.

To her, they painted an entirely different picture: menace cloaked in elegance, beauty sharpened into threat.

Her gut knotted. She drew a shallow breath that didn't quite reach her chest. Her fingers drifted to the scar on her palm, finding the rough skin there, the familiar anchor. It steadied her, but barely.

From Penny's room, laughter rose—muffled, warm, alive.

It startled her.

Because Penny was alive in the next room, wrapped in ordinary noise, and Arden stood frozen in the kitchen with a rose and a tin of tea that felt like evidence from a crime no one had named yet.

Penny didn't know. Not about the package. Not about the rose. Not about the storm that had been winding tighter inside Arden since she unwrapped that first box.

Telling her would change everything.

It would pull her in.

Not tonight.

Instead, Arden crossed the room and sank onto the couch, arms folding tight around her ribs. It wasn't the cold. Her eyes found the rose again, sitting there as if it belonged, crimson petals catching the low light, too vivid to be natural.

It whispered.

Watched.

The apartment buzzed with familiar sounds—the fridge, Penny's TV, the soft shift and murmur of life continuing on the other side of the wall.

Normal.

But not safe.

Camouflage.

Arden exhaled, slow and shallow.

The anonymous messages. The gifts. The way ordinary things had been turned against her. Tea. Flowers. Doorways. Conversations. Every harmless object made suspect by the hands that had chosen it.

Her arms tightened, but the knot in her chest stayed.

Her eyes darted to the rose.

It wasn't a gesture.

It was a move.

A warning.

A promise.

Someone was ahead of her.

This wasn't affection.

This was control, wrapped in satin and thorns.

And whoever thought she would fold had made the wrong mistake.

They didn't know her.

Not anymore.

She wasn't easy.

She wasn't breakable.

And she wasn't going down without a fight.

————

FROM HIS SEAT at the table, the world sharpened.

Sebastian swirled the amber liquid in his glass, slow and deliberate.

His eyes never left her.

Arden.

Steel beneath silk.

Others noticed her. Admired her fire. Feared it. But they didn't see her. Not like he did. They didn't speak her language. They didn't know how her smile changed only when she forgot the room, how her head tilted when she was pensive, how her laugh carried its own rhythm beneath the noise.

But he did.

Every flick of her wrist behind the bar was gospel.

She didn't belong here. Not among these shallow men in pressed suits, these polished pretenders who wanted only her surface.

Sebastian wanted the truth.

The girl beneath the grit. The fire beneath the calm.

And she did have fire. She didn't know how to wield it yet, but he did.

The tea. The syrup. The roses.

Not gifts.

Touchpoints.

A language made for two.

He remembered the way her fingers had lingered on the label, the softness in her voice when she said the word lavender. The details others missed, he worshipped.

And the rose, stripped of thorns but no less sharp, wasn't merely a gesture. It was a promise. A thread between them, tied in red.

She hadn't thrown them away.

Hadn't hidden them.

She had kept them.

All of them.

That was enough.

She didn't flinch.

Not yet.

Curiosity was the first crack.

Still, there was Gideon.

Always in the way.

Watching. Hovering. Caging.

He didn't see Arden's fire. He saw a belonging to keep, to possess, to lock behind glass.

But Sebastian?

Sebastian would let her burn.

He would be the one to set her free.

Across the room, she paused. A hand too slow. A breath caught in her chest.

She felt it.

The shift.

She didn't look for him.

She didn't have to.

Soon, he thought, finishing his drink.

When she left, he followed.

Not close.

Not careless.

Just enough.

The night wrapped around him. The hallway outside her apartment buzzed with flickering, sickly light, the air alive and expectant.

And there, at her door, waited the rose.

Crimson.

Rain-kissed.

Perfect.

Placed not as a gift, but as a sign.

Little Fire.

Perfect.

Fierce.

Chosen.

He pictured the way her fingers would reach. The breath she would catch. How the knowledge would settle inside her, slow and undeniable.

This wasn't coincidence.

This was craft.

A thread pulling tighter with every beat.

She hadn't unraveled it yet.

But she would.

Sebastian lingered too long, just to imagine the moment she would understand. The moment she would know she had been seen.

Claimed.

And once she felt that knowing, there would be no undoing it.

No escape.

Once she saw the thread for what it was, there would be no going back.

CHAPTER 42

Strength in Small Things

Arden took a slow sip of coffee, letting the bitterness settle over the unrest coiled in her chest.

Penny swept into the room the way she always did—half windstorm, half caffeine buzz, coffee in one hand and laptop in the other. "Morning, sunshine!"

She slowed the moment her gaze landed on Arden. "Whoa. You look like someone hit pause mid-apocalypse." Her mug hit the counter with a thunk. "Spill it. Blackwell drama again?"

Arden settled into the couch. The cushions gave beneath her, but the tension in her body didn't. She circled the rim of her mug with one finger, her mind still caught somewhere between the rose, the tea, and the sickly flicker of hallway light.

"It feels like someone's always watching," she said quietly, her voice rougher than she meant it to be. "Breathing wrong feels like giving someone front-row seats to the worst version of yourself."

Penny wrinkled her nose. "Ugh. That's a nightmare."

Then her gaze shifted.

She spotted it.

On the counter, the rose and the tin of tea sat intact, side by side.

Untouched.

Wrong.

Penny zeroed in. "Wait. Is that... Delancey's?"

Arden followed her line of sight, and a fresh ripple of tension coiled low in her chest.

Penny crossed the room in three brisk strides, scooping up the tin like it might vanish. "The Delancey's tea? Arden, this stuff costs more than rent."

She turned, holding it up like damning evidence. "Okay, who's sending you gifts fit for royalty?"

The question hit harder than Arden expected. She groped for an easy answer. A glib excuse. Anything that would make the whole thing smaller.

Nothing came.

She shrugged instead. "It was... left for me at work."

Penny's brows shot up. "Left? Like, anonymously?"

Her stare sharpened, one hand landing on her hip. "You really weren't going to bring that up?"

"It's tea, Pen." Arden forced a half-laugh. "Maybe it's a thank-you from a client. People get sentimental over cocktails."

But Penny's expression dimmed, suspicion gathering fast.

Then she saw the rose.

Unmoved.

Watching.

Her face sharpened. "Okay, but what about that?"

She pointed like it might bite.

"You're not seriously calling that a coincidence."

A flicker passed across Arden's face.

Subtle.

Unmistakable.

Her jaw tightened, fingers wrapping more firmly around the mug.

"It was at the door last night."

Her voice came steady. Detached. As if facts alone could strip meaning from them.

"They're probably not even connected."

She knew better.

Penny narrowed her eyes, seeing straight through it. "You're not worried?"

Arden took another sip. "No."

Lie.

Another sip.

Longer this time.

"It's the timing. That's all."

Penny didn't buy it. She crossed her arms, her stance sharpening.

"'Weird timing' is how every Dateline episode starts. If someone's playing secret admirer, they need to read the room and back off."

Arden shook her head. "It's nothing. Let's not make it a big deal."

A pause.

Then, "Fine."

But the word dripped with doubt.

Penny pointed a finger at her like it was a vow. "But if anything else shows up? You tell me. No more pretending this isn't real."

Arden managed a small smile. "Deal."

Penny set the tin down harder than necessary, bristling.

Then, without warning, Penny said, "I have a great idea."

Arden narrowed her eyes. Penny's great ideas were usually code for chaotic joyrides with no exits.

"You're coming home with me this afternoon. No arguments."

Arden blinked. "What?"

"You heard me. It's our usual Sunday chaos—glitter, bread, and someone getting irrationally competitive over charades. It's basically emotional CPR."

"Penny—"

"My mom's been dying to meet you. And I promise: no roses, no mysterious tea, no tailored-suit weirdos. Just a lot of carbs and too many siblings. I mean, it's just me and Mia, but you get it."

Arden's lips twitched.

The thought of Penny's family, warm and messy and uncomplicated, felt like stepping into sunlight after weeks of storm.

And the alternative?

Sitting alone in the apartment with that crimson monstrosity?

Unbearable.

She sighed. "Okay."

"I knew you'd come around." Penny beamed. "But don't show up with gym injuries. My family's nosy. They'll assume you're a spy or something."

Arden rolled her eyes and grabbed her gym bag. "I'll be fine. Want me to grab a pastry or something on the way back?"

"Do you even have to ask?" Penny pressed a hand to her chest, mock-serious. "Oat milk latte, extra foam. And if you find a chocolate croissant? I'll put you in my will."

"You already love me," Arden muttered, heading for the door.

She paused, glancing back.

A smile.

Small.

Real.

"See you soon."

Penny waved her off. "Don't forget the croissant!"

———

THE RHYTHMIC THUD of fists striking pads. The low murmur of breath and instruction. The sharp crack of controlled hits reverberating off concrete walls.

It all wrapped around Arden like armor.

No whispers.

No watching eyes.

No games.

Only discipline. Movement. Precision.

She moved through each drill with purpose, tension burning off her limbs as her focus narrowed into heat and instinct, channeled through every breath, every strike.

Fierce. Powerful. Controlled.

Damon Hale circled like a sentinel, his gaze slicing through the motion.

Sharp. Observant. No nonsense.

"Rivers," he called. "You're with Drake. Try not to kill him."

Evan Drake stepped forward, already smirking. He rolled his shoulders like he had something to prove.

"Don't worry about me," he said, light and cocky. "I can hold my own."

Arden gave him a once-over, lifting a brow. The corner of her mouth twitched.

"Famous last words."

Damon snorted. "Good luck, Drake. You're gonna need it."

The first drill was straightforward: measured strikes and counter blocks. No ego. No improvisation. Just fundamentals.

Evan blew it in the first ten seconds.

He overreached, telegraphing the hit before he committed to it. Arden's counter came fast, clean, and direct, a strike to the ribs that landed with a dull thud. Not enough to hurt. Just enough to educate.

He exhaled with a grunt, his grin slipping for half a breath.

"Okay. Message received."

Arden reset without a word, rolling her shoulders and settling back into her stance.

"Guard's still wide," she said, calm and clipped. "Don't give away space you'll have to earn back."

By the third round, sweat carved a line down his temple. He was improving, tighter and quicker now, but still a beat behind.

She saw the flaw in his footing a second before he did.

A pivot. A hook. A clean takedown.

He hit the mat with a grunt and a curse.

"Damn, Rivers," he groaned, half-laughing. "Remind me never to cross you outside this building."

She offered a faint smirk as she peeled the wraps from her hands. Adrenaline coursed through her, fast and hot, but cleaner now. Useful.

Damon passed by, nodding once as he clapped her shoulder.

"Good work today. Stay sharp."

She nodded back.

Focus.

Discipline.

Control.

Everything she needed, everything she felt slipping, was here—tucked between the strike and the silence that followed it.

And Arden wasn't letting go.

On her way back, Arden slipped into the corner café Penny swore by, a cozy little place with antique brass fixtures and the steady hiss of espresso warming the air.

The baristas didn't even bother asking for names. They gave a knowing nod and got to work.

Arden ordered Penny's usual: an oat milk latte with extra foam and a chocolate croissant so golden it looked freshly pulled from a dream. The pastry flaked at the edges, light catching on the sugar-crusted top.

As she waited, she fired off a quick text.

> Latte and croissant acquired. Don't say I never do anything for you.

Penny's reply came before she could lock her screen.

> Penny: You're my favorite person alive. Except maybe whoever invented extra foam.

Arden laughed under her breath, shaking her head as the barista handed her the warm cup and bag.

When she stepped inside the apartment, Penny was mid-spin, practically vibrating with energy, her laptop abandoned on the counter.

"You're a lifesaver," she declared, clutching the latte and croissant with reverence.

She took a long sip, eyes closing as if she had found inner peace.

"Okay. Now we move."

She pointed at Arden with croissant-crumb conviction.

"Mom's already prepping a bread tasting, and if we don't leave in five, we risk missing the cinnamon rolls. And Arden?"

Her voice dropped to a dramatic whisper.

"They. Are. Legendary."

Arden laughed, pulling on her coat. "You weren't kidding about the chaos, huh?"

Penny's grin widened, all brightness and mischief. "Please. Haverford chaos is a lifestyle. Consider yourself formally initiated."

She slung her bag over one shoulder. "Come on. If we're late, my mom will serve a pre-appetizer. Don't ask."

Arden followed her out, grateful for the first genuine smile of the day.

❧

As they stepped into the brisk afternoon, Arden glanced back at the apartment.

The stark image of the rose against the threshold clung to her like a whisper that refused to fade. The unease hadn't left. It hovered, quiet and watchful, threaded through the ordinary sounds of the hallway and the city beyond it.

Then Penny linked their arms, warm and grounding, and pulled Arden forward with the effortless certainty only she could manage.

Away from unanswered questions.

Away from the shadows gathering at the edges of her life.

Toward laughter and light.

Toward something unfiltered and fiercely alive.

Toward a kind of safety that didn't demand silence.

———

THE TRAIN ROCKED GENTLY beneath them, carrying them farther from the city's steel and precision into a softer sprawl of trees and hills. The skyline receded behind them, glass and ambition fading into memory.

Arden leaned against the window, her breath fogging the glass.

The motion should have calmed her—the rattle of the tracks, the warmth of coffee lingering in her hands—but her thoughts refused to settle.

The rose.

The tea.

That tight, unmistakable sense that someone had been watching.

Still watching.

And layered beneath that, quieter but no less relentless, was a pull she didn't understand and couldn't ignore.

Gideon's voice echoed in her chest, low and sure and unshakable.

You've been mine since the night we met.

It hadn't been flirtation. It hadn't been a line tossed out in the heat of a moment he didn't mean to keep. There had been weight in his voice, the kind that didn't come without consequence.

She remembered the look in his eyes, storm-dark and unwavering.

He hadn't been trying to seduce her.

He had been claiming her.

The thought made her heart tighten in her ribs. Her fingers curled around the paper cup in her lap.

Part of her wanted to bristle. Push back.

She didn't do ownership. Didn't do surrender. Didn't hand anyone the keys to the parts of herself she had spent years learning how to guard.

But another part, quieter and harder to ignore, wanted to believe him. To lean into the gravity of him. To trust the unspoken promise in his presence.

Claimed.

Seen.

Safe.

The last word snagged.

Safety wasn't a truth she believed in easily. Not after everything. Not when a rose on the floor could shake her. Not when lavender came laced with unease. Nothing in her life had ever arrived without strings, without cost, without some hidden clause waiting to collect.

And yet...

Gideon hadn't offered her comfort in any gentle, polished way. He wasn't warmth wrapped in illusion.

He was storm.

Fire.

Unapologetically sharp-edged.

Maybe that was the only reason she believed him. Because nothing about Gideon Blackwell had ever been easy, and somehow, that made him harder to doubt.

Beside her, Penny had one earbud in, singing along to a song only she could hear while her fingers scrolled aimlessly across her phone.

Earlier, she had launched into a full-color monologue about her dad baking through a new bread cookbook, her mother's excitement bordering on party-planning mode, and a younger sister named Mia who, according to Penny, might actually be louder and more unfiltered than she was.

Arden wanted to focus on that.

On the comfort wrapped inside Penny's stories.

A family messy in the best ways—loud, affectionate, alive. The kind of chaos that didn't require armor.

She wanted to believe she could step into it.

If only for a day.

Even as an outsider.

But could she?

Would she ever fit in a space built on ease and belonging?

Penny pulled out her earbud and nudged her gently. "Oh, and heads-up—my family doesn't ease into things. You're basically being adopted the second we walk through the door."

Arden exhaled, somewhere between disbelief and a laugh. "That intense?"

"But in the best way." Penny slung her bag over her shoulder, already gathering momentum.

Arden shook her head, a low chuckle slipping out.

"You'll feel right at home," Penny said, no hesitation.

She wasn't trying to convince her. It wasn't a pitch. Just truth, plain and simple.

"You're going to leave wondering how you survived this long without cinnamon rolls, unsolicited opinions, and way too many group hugs."

The laugh caught in Arden's throat, almost staying there.

Because Penny made it sound easy. Effortless. As if a place had already been set at the table with her name on it, no performance required, no careful audition for belonging. Just welcome, waiting warm and loud on the other side of the door.

Arden turned toward the window, her voice barely audible. "You said your family collects people?"

Penny's tone softened. "It's kind of our thing. Why?"

Arden paused, fingers dragging a slow line across her jeans.

Then came a quiet, tentative smile.

"I think... I might need that today."

CHAPTER 43

The Warmth of Family

The door opened before they could knock.

"There you are!"

Lillian Haverford's voice spilled out like a welcome mat, her presence filling the doorway before Arden and Penny had even crossed the threshold. Her arms were already open, silver strands slipping free from the knot at the back of her head as if the day had tugged loose every last pin.

She smelled faintly of cinnamon and something pleasantly floral, warm and comforting but impossible to place. Arden breathed it in, caught off guard by how much it reminded her of a memory she couldn't quite reach. A warmth she might have missed without ever knowing its name.

This must be what love looks like.

Before Arden could speak, Lillian wrapped her in a hug, solid and certain, as though she had already decided Arden belonged. It wasn't formal. It wasn't cautious.

It was natural.

Unfiltered.

Arden stiffened at first. Instinct flared, the old reflex to brace, pull back, scan for the catch.

But there was no transaction here. No performance. No hidden cost pressed between her ribs.

After a breath she hadn't realized she'd been holding, she leaned in, tentative at first, then fully, as if her body understood something her heart hadn't yet learned how to trust.

Her walls wavered.

Her eyes stung before she could stop it, tears rising too quickly to deny. She blinked them back, but the moment had already found its place inside her.

Too warm.

Too real.

"Inside, inside," Lillian urged, her voice as easy as sunlight through an open window.

THE HAVERFORD HOUSE unfolded like a living thing—soft, cozy, inviting. Books lined every surface, some shelved, most not. They leaned in corners, spilled off end tables, nestled under windows. A well-worn quilt draped across the back of the couch, the kind of fabric that had soaked up years of Sunday naps and late-night movies. A candle burned low on the mantel, its scent—vanilla and clove—softening the air with quiet persistence. Wax had pooled and hardened around the base as if it had nowhere better to be.

The walls were covered in photographs, none of them staged, none of them neat. Pure moments. Overlapping prints and curling corners, full of smiling chaos: beach trips, flour-dusted kids on kitchen stools, Robert, Penny, and Mia in matching Christmas pajamas, laughing until they couldn't breathe. Lillian and Robert dancing barefoot on a porch, a summer sunset glowing behind them.

This wasn't perfection.

This was joy.

Arden's chest tightened. For so long, home had meant silence. Measured tones. Unspoken rules. Control. But here, home was noise. Mess. Laughter that spilled without apology. A place where people took up space without asking.

It was a language she didn't speak, but God, she wanted to learn it.

"Here they are!" Robert's voice rang out from the kitchen, full of welcome. He rounded the corner in a Yankees apron dusted with flour, a tray of cookies balanced in his hands like second nature. His smile stretched wide, warm, and uncomplicated —the kind that made a person feel expected, even when they had only just arrived.

"Arden," he said, as if her name were reason enough to celebrate. "House rule— nobody leaves hungry."

She hesitated for a second. Then, carefully, she took a cookie. The scent hit her first: rich chocolate, butter a shade past golden, warmth rising soft against her face.

"Thank you. This smells incredible."

Robert beamed, visibly pleased. Penny had already snatched two, taking a dramatic bite like she hadn't eaten in days.

"Therapy in chocolate chip form," she said around a mouthful.

Robert nodded solemnly. "Better than half the prescriptions out there."

Lillian laughed, brushing flour from her sleeve. "Don't let him fool you, Arden. He bakes to avoid my honey-do list."

Robert's grin widened, eyes bright. "Family tradition."

Lillian gave him a look that could only be described as long-suffering affection, the kind built over decades, the kind that made space and kept it warm.

They moved around each other so easily, so naturally, as if affection were second nature.

Arden let herself lean into it.

Only for a moment.

But she did.

HAVERFORD-STYLE CHARADES WAS unlike anything Arden had ever seen. Rules were optional. Cheating was encouraged. Chaos was required.

The living room had become a war zone of flailing limbs, wild guesses, and exaggerated performances. Robert, ever the showman, threw himself dramatically to the floor. His clue? "A whale trying to escape."

What followed defied logic. He rolled. Flopped. Twisted and thrashed like a tragic sea creature mid-rescue attempt, his apron flaring out with every committed, deeply unnecessary movement.

"A beached seal!" Mia shrieked, nearly doubled over.

"A breakdancing caterpillar!" Penny gasped between wheezes.

Arden pressed her lips together, trying—and failing—to stay composed.

Then Robert flopped onto one side, gasping like a dying fish, and her laughter broke free.

Pure.

Uncontrolled.

Real.

"A whale trying to escape?" she guessed, hesitant but hopeful.

Robert popped up, triumphant. "Exactly! See? She gets me!"

Penny slung an arm around her shoulders.

"Told you," she said, her voice quieter now. "You're already one of us."

The words hit somewhere deep, somewhere Arden hadn't let anyone touch in years.

The game carried on, each round more ridiculous than the last. Lillian's "pirate searching for love in a library" left them breathless. Robert's "tap-dancing giraffe" made Penny cry-laugh, her head tipped back, tears streaking down her cheeks.

And when Penny pantomimed "a dog auditioning for a reality show," Arden lost it.

She laughed—really laughed. The kind that knocked the air out of her and left her shoulders shaking, one hand pressed to her side. She couldn't remember the last time it had come that easily.

Or hit that deep.

The room didn't quiet around her. It held her.

Not like a blanket or some tidy metaphor, but in the real way a room could hold a person: familiar voices, warm light, bodies shifting comfortably through shared space, someone tossing a cookie across the couch and missing by an impressive margin.

It didn't ask anything of her.

For once, Arden stopped asking so much of herself.

Here, laughter wasn't curated. Joy didn't come with strings. Love moved loudly and badly across the living room in socks, flung cookies, terrible guesses, and people who didn't care how ridiculous they looked as long as someone else was laughing.

She had never known a family like this.

No masks. No rules worth keeping. Only love, messy and loud and relentless.

She didn't feel like an outsider.

She belonged.

At least for now.

Arden sank into the couch, her heart lighter than it had felt in months, and breathed it in.

Let herself believe.

Let herself feel safe.

HER PHONE BUZZED.

Sharp.

Jarring.

Arden reached for it, expecting nothing.

Unknown number.

One line.

> Do you feel safe with them?

The words cleaved through her.

Cold.

Calculated.

Unmistakable.

Her grip tightened around the phone, her pulse kicking fast and loud in her ears.

"Everything okay?" Penny's voice was soft now, her concern immediate.

"Spam," Arden said quickly.

The lie scratched at her throat.

The warmth in the room hadn't vanished. Lillian laughed from the kitchen. Penny argued over the score. Robert offered "victory cookies" to anyone willing to take his side. Mia somersaulted into the next round like a woman possessed.

The light held.

But the dark was there.

Patient.
Watching.
Waiting.
Untouched by the laughter filling the room.

The train cut through the dark, its lights slicing the night into flickers of motion and memory. Outside the window, the city blurred past in jagged shapes, too fast to hold, too familiar to surprise.

The steady rhythm of the tracks should have been calming. A lull. Almost peaceful.

Beside her, Penny had drifted off, curled into her seat with one arm slung across her stomach, her breath quiet and even. Arden watched the rise and fall of it—soft, steady, untouchable—and felt something inside her twist.

Penny had given her sunlight for an afternoon. Noise. Bread. Ridiculous games. A family that collected people like spare warmth and made room before anyone thought to ask.

And somehow, even there, the message had found her.

Do you feel safe with them?

Her thumb hovered over the screen, but she didn't open the thread again. She didn't need to. The words had already burned themselves into her memory, elegant in their cruelty, intimate in a way that made her skin crawl.

Not a threat shouted from the dark.

A question.

That was worse.

A question meant to make her doubt the room she had been standing in. To turn laughter suspicious. To make warmth feel watched. To remind her that wherever she went, whatever comfort she tried to accept, someone believed they had the right to follow.

Arden swallowed hard and looked back out the window.

The glass reflected her face in fragments: pale skin, tired eyes, mouth set too firmly for someone who had spent the afternoon laughing.

She should tell Penny.

She should tell Gideon.

She should hand the phone over, let someone else hold the weight for once.

Instead, her fingers curled around the device until the edges bit into her palm.

Not yet.

The thought came too fast, too familiar. A reflex dressed as control.

But the train kept moving, carrying them back toward the city, toward the apartment, toward the rose and the tea and whatever came next.

Penny shifted in her sleep, murmuring something unintelligible before settling again.

Arden looked at her, at the friend who had dragged her into warmth without asking for a confession first, and guilt pressed sharp beneath her ribs.

The message hadn't only followed Arden.

It had followed her there.

Into Penny's family.

Into the place that had made her feel safe for one reckless, impossible afternoon.

Her jaw tightened.

No.

Whoever this was didn't get to take that too.

She turned the phone face down on her thigh, breathing through the cold bloom of fear until something steadier rose beneath it.

Anger.

Quiet.

Clean.

Awake.

The city lights flashed across the window like warnings, but Arden didn't look away.

HER PHONE VIBRATED, muffled and distant.

Arden dug for it blindly, her mind still miles away.

A notification blinked on-screen.

Her stomach knotted briefly, automatically.

Then she saw his name.

Gideon.

The weight in her chest shifted. It didn't vanish, but it lightened enough for her to breathe around it.

> Gideon: Hey, beautiful. Hope your day went well. Can I see you tomorrow evening?

She read it twice.

Blushed.

Smiled.

She realized her expression had changed only when Penny stirred beside her, cracking one eye open.

"That from your secret admirer?" she murmured, voice raspy and soft from sleep. Then, with a lazy smirk, "Or someone... less annoying?"

Arden rolled her eyes, but the corner of her mouth tugged upward. "It's Gideon."

Penny grinned, satisfied. "Ah, yes. Brooding boss with hidden depths. Solid choice."

Arden ignored her and tapped out a reply.

> The day was good... Penny's family is a force of nature. Tomorrow sounds good. What time?

The answer came almost immediately.

> Gideon: I'll pick you up at 7.

She stared at the screen a moment longer, her thumb resting against the edge as if she wasn't ready to put him away yet.

Gideon and the Haverfords were nothing alike. One was heat held tight beneath restraint. The other, unfiltered warmth spilling everywhere. Both had found their way to her.

Both steadied her, but in different ways.

Penny's voice slipped through the quiet, half-mumbled and half-anchored in dream.

"You've got people now."

Arden turned slightly, catching Penny's gaze in the reflection of the window.

Penny didn't smile this time. She said it again, softer now. Clearer. "Whether you want them or not."

Arden didn't answer.

Couldn't.

The words landed in the space between them and stayed there.

Outside, the city stretched toward them, sharp and bright. Manhattan's skyline blinked into view—familiar, fast, unyielding. The train rattled forward, pulling them back into its grip.

Back into reality.

Back into the shadows.

The warmth of the Haverfords' kitchen already felt too far behind, too soft and safe to trust for long.

And deep in Arden's chest, where instinct lived, a cold certainty unfurled— quiet, primitive, impossible to shake.

Whoever had sent the note...

Whoever had left the rose...

They weren't gone.

They were only getting started.

CHAPTER 44

The Legacy of Chains

The Blackwell Enterprises building rose sleek and unyielding, all mirrored glass and sharp lines. Its windows didn't mirror the skyline in awe; they thrust it back like a warning.

Inside, everything shone. Marble stretched wall to wall beneath gold trim and steel's gleam. Light scattered from chandeliers above, glass prisms catching enough sparkle to say: you don't belong here unless we decide you do.

Gideon walked the corridors unhurried. The place knew him—his footsteps, his authority, the silence he carried like a weapon. His coat shifted with each stride, black wool cutting clean lines through the building's golden sheen.

Ahead, the doors to Evelyn's office stood open.

She was already seated, posture straight, every movement intentional. The skyline stretched behind her in glass and steel, casting a cool glow across the room. Evelyn Blackwell didn't need to rise or speak to assert control; her presence did the work. The sleek twist of her silver hair. The gleam of polished wood. The way she folded her hands with quiet precision.

"Gideon," she said with a cool smile, "always punctual. Have a seat."

He didn't sit.

"You asked for this meeting. What is it?"

She gestured to the chair across from her. Gideon stayed standing.

If she noticed, or cared, it didn't show.

"I want to revisit your place in this family," she said. "The expectations that come with it. Responsibilities."

"My responsibilities," he said evenly, "are to Hawthorne Holdings. And the people depending on it."

Her mouth curved, a gesture shaped like a smile and void of softness.

"Hawthorne Holdings may carry your grandfather's name, but don't kid yourself. Everything you do reflects back on us."

"No," Gideon said. "It reflects on you."

She exhaled, quiet and dismissive, like she was entertaining the complaint of a child.

"You are my son, Gideon. That means you don't get to pretend. Independence isn't permanent."

His hands curled at his sides, but his voice stayed level. "Do you say the same to Alex?"

For a breath, something flickered through Evelyn's expression—irritation, maybe disdain. Gone before he could name it.

"Alex and Cate haven't given this family an heir," she said. "Which means the future rests on you, whether you want it or not."

His breath caught, then left him slow and quiet. "Funny. I thought you already cut your losses."

She shifted slightly, eyes narrowing with a knowing edge that stripped away any trace of amusement. "Not completely. There's time to course-correct. But that window is closing."

She laced her fingers. "You should be choosing the right people. Building something that lasts—not chasing distractions."

His jaw flexed. "You mean Arden."

She didn't deny it. Her expression stayed neutral, but cold triumph flickered behind her eyes. Less surprise than satisfaction.

"Yes. If we're naming names, then yes."

Gideon stepped closer, the shift in his stance quiet but unmistakable.

"She's not your business."

Evelyn raised a brow, smooth and practiced. "She's very much my business. Because she's a distraction. And she's not Blackwell material."

A chill settled low in his chest. "Say that again."

She gave a sigh, all theatrical patience.

"Gideon. Let's not play pretend. You're the heir. Not because it flatters you— but because it's required. Alex failed. That burden falls to you now. And a Blackwell doesn't throw away a legacy for a... passing indulgence."

His hands hovered near the edge of her pristine desk, tension flickering through his fingertips. But he didn't let them shake.

"Say what you really mean."

She leaned in slightly, her voice cold and flat.

"She is no one. No name. No standing. Just complication. You want her? Fine. But you don't build a future on a charity case."

The words didn't rise.

They didn't need to.

Evelyn had spent a lifetime perfecting the art of damage, cutting clean without raising a blade. And this was a direct hit, the kind of precision that left bruises where no one could see. No theatrics. No venom.

For a moment, the room held its breath.

The silence wasn't peace. It was pressure.

Thick.

Measured.

Intentional.

Beyond the glass, the city pulsed on—bright, indifferent, and unaware of the war being waged in its highest tower.

Then Gideon laughed.

Low. Dark. Sharp enough to draw blood.

Evelyn's eyes narrowed, a hairline crack in her otherwise impenetrable veneer.

"Let me make one thing clear," he said, voice like glass under pressure. "You don't decide my future. And you don't get to dictate who I let into my life."

Her mouth curved, but it wasn't a smile. It was contempt dressed in pearls.

"That woman will cost you more than you're prepared to lose."

He stepped closer. His presence filled the room, casting its own kind of shadow.

"And you think you have the power to make that happen?"

Evelyn didn't blink. "I don't think, Gideon. I know."

The silence between them wasn't empty. It was loaded, smoke-thick and crackling with every unspoken threat.

"Consider this your warning," she said, tone pristine. "Arden Rivers is nothing more than a distraction. If you insist on keeping her, so be it. But don't fool yourself into thinking she belongs in your future."

His words came cold and surgical. "You ran one woman out of my life. You won't lay a hand on Arden."

Evelyn's composure didn't waver. If anything, her calm deepened.

"You're fighting a war that's already been won."

"Stay out of my business." His voice dropped, low and vicious. "This is your warning."

She laughed—soft, elegant, dismissive. "Warnings are for people without power, darling. And in this family, we both know which of us holds it."

Gideon turned, every muscle coiled, breath tight as he stalked toward the door.

"Oh, and Gideon?" she called as his hand touched the frame.

He paused.

Didn't turn.

"Colton dropped by earlier," she said lightly. "Something about tenants causing trouble again. Perhaps you should remind him where your loyalties truly lie."

His grip tightened on the doorframe.

"Colton knows exactly where I stand."

"Do you?"

Gideon didn't answer. Didn't flinch.

He simply turned away.

THE DOOR WHISPERED shut behind him, but Evelyn's voice lingered, sharp and precise.

Gideon slowed in the hallway, jaw set, rolling his shoulders back as he dragged in a breath he didn't quite trust.

"You look tense."

Colton Blake leaned against the wall, posture relaxed as if he had been there all along, waiting to catch the fallout. Sleeves rolled. Collar undone just enough to suggest ease.

Gideon knew better.

Colton never moved without motive.

A snake in a suit.

Gideon's fists curled before he could stop them.

"Rough meeting with the queen?" Colton pushed off the wall and fell into step beside him. "She give you the legacy talk again? Or was this one about your woman problem?"

"Stay out of my way, Colton."

Gideon didn't look at him.

Colton chuckled under his breath. "You used to be a lot more fun. Back before you went soft."

Gideon stopped short.

Turned.

Their height was close, but power had never been about inches.

"You think I'm blind. That I don't know what you're doing?" His voice dropped low. Deliberate. "The intimidation. The strong-arming. You're Evelyn's leash. Nothing more."

Colton's smile widened, slow and slick. "Funny. I thought I was her blade."

Gideon didn't blink. "You're a shadow. Feeding off what's left after she's done bleeding people dry."

Colton's gaze sharpened. "You forget who you are."

"No," Gideon said. "I remember too well. That's why I'm not like you."

"But I hear you've been busy," Colton said. "Putting down roots. Getting sentimental. Risky move."

"If you even breathe in Arden's direction—"

Colton raised both hands in mock surrender. "Relax. I've got better things to do than play watchdog over your bartender."

Gideon stepped in, the space between them razor-thin.

His voice was low. Precise. "You go near her, and you'll regret it."

Colton didn't flinch, but the smirk dimmed for half a second.

He turned, took a few steps, then looked back.

"Funny thing," he said. "You've never gone this far for anyone."

He let the words sit, poisonous and precise.

Then came the final cut.

"So what does that make her?"

Gideon didn't move.

But the air shifted, volatile and charged.

Colton saw it.

Registered the hit.

"That's what I thought," he said, turning his back as if the conversation were over.

But Gideon wasn't finished.

Not even close.

His fists stayed curled, his mind already on Arden.

Because if Evelyn had set her sights, Colton would be circling.

And Gideon would burn the entire legacy to the ground before he let either of them touch her.

She hadn't left his thoughts in days.

Maybe longer.

It wasn't only her sharp tongue or the way she stood her ground. It was everything in between: the pause before a smile, the stillness before trust, the rare softness that surfaced when she thought no one was looking.

Arden moved through the world like someone waiting for it to shift beneath her feet.

And even in that tension, there was grace.

Quiet bravery he couldn't stop seeing.

Every piece of trust she gave him felt earned. Real. A weight he had no intention of taking lightly.

Gideon exhaled slowly, pulled out his phone, and typed.

Have dinner with me tonight?

He stared at the screen.

Just a question.

Her reply came faster than he expected.

Arden: I'd like that. What time?

His jaw softened.

He could almost hear her voice in the words, measured and a little reserved, but not closed off.

Trust.
Uneven and new, but unmistakable.
A thread of openness where there used to be armor.

Pick you up at 7:30.

Arden: I'll be ready.

He set the phone down, exhaling slowly.
She was stitching herself into spaces he hadn't known were empty.
And for the first time in years, he didn't feel the need to retreat.

CHAPTER 45

Full Throttle

The low growl of an engine outside cut through their banter.

Penny's head snapped toward the window, her green eyes going wide. "Oh my God." She spun around, practically vibrating. "Your chariot awaits..." Her grin widened. "And it's even sexier than I expected."

Arden frowned, amused. "What are you talking about?"

She tugged on her coat, glancing at Penny, whose expression had turned downright gleeful.

"I knew he was pulling out all the stops tonight," Penny said. "He's always thoughtful, but this?" She gestured toward the window like she was unveiling a masterpiece. "This is on another level."

Arden shook her head, brushing off the comment even as her pulse began to quicken. "It's dinner, Pen."

Penny's arched brow said otherwise. Her grin only deepened.

"Sure, it is. Just dinner with the gorgeous billionaire who clearly worships the ground you walk on."

Arden rolled her eyes, but the corner of her mouth betrayed her. "You're way too invested in this."

"Of course I am." Penny threw up her hands. "If you're not going to appreciate the sexy-AF boss situation, someone has to pick up the slack."

Then, turning mock-serious, she added, "Oh, and if he actually brings you back, I want details." She paused, tilting her head. "Actually, scratch that—I want dessert. Something fancy."

Arden smirked, shaking her head as she opened the door.

Outside, the engine purred again, smooth as velvet and deep as a promise. The evening air curled around her, cool against her skin, threaded with a tension that had nothing to do with the weather.

Her breath caught.

The car gleamed beneath the streetlights, a midnight-black Roadster SV with curves that promised speed and sin. Every inch of it whispered power and indulgence.

But even that came second to the man beside it.

Gideon leaned against the driver's side as if he owned the night itself. The navy jacket stretched clean across his shoulders, tailored to distraction. His collar stood open just enough to tempt, offering the smallest glimpse of skin and the suggestion that beneath all that control, something wilder waited, coiled and watchful.

There was nothing careless about him.

Everything about him looked chosen.

ARDEN STEPPED OUTSIDE, her heels meeting the pavement in a slow, percussive rhythm that seemed to wind the tension tighter with every step. She took her time, her gaze drifting from the gleam of the car to the man who made it look like an accessory.

She stopped at the curb, folding her arms as her mouth curved. "Hmm... I'm not sure which is sexier," she said, her voice low and sensual. "You... or the car."

Gideon pushed off the door, that crooked smile already in place. He moved toward her with unhurried confidence, every step a dare.

"Tough call," he murmured, low and rough. "But I think I can tip the scales."

Before she could answer, his hands were at her waist—firm, certain. He lifted her onto the hood like she weighed nothing, and her breath caught at the chill of metal beneath her, followed a second later by the heat of him settling between her thighs.

"Gideon—"

"I'm making my case," he said, his mouth brushing hers once, then again, teasing and tasting.

Then he kissed her.

There was no hesitation in it, no space left for second thoughts—only heat, certainty, and that dangerous control of his that always felt one breath away from fracture. His hands slipped beneath her coat and glided up her sides, anchoring her as if even this small distance was too much. Possessive, yes, but measured.

She gasped, sharp and soft all at once, gripping the lapels of his jacket like she needed the leverage to stay upright. But upright was a lie. He had her, and they both knew it.

The scent of him wrapped around her, that familiar mix of heat and restraint, the whisper of smoke beneath skin. He kissed her deeper then, hungrier, his mouth opening over hers with slow, dangerous purpose. His tongue brushed hers, and the rest of the world fell away.

Her thighs tightened around his hips. Her heels pressed against the curve of the Roadster, reaching for some anchor in the steel while the rest of her came undone. Her hands slid beneath his coat, finding heat and muscle and tension drawn tight to the edge. She opened to him on a sound she couldn't contain, and he answered with a low growl that curled straight down her spine.

"Arden," he said against her mouth—rough, reverent, barely controlled.

Her name landed like a vow.

His thumbs traced the barest edge of skin at her waist, and she arched into him, chasing the contact, wanting more, needing it.

But not yet.

Not here.

This moment, against the gleaming hood of his very expensive car with the city only steps away, wasn't about taking. It was about promise. About everything her body could say before her mouth was ready to.

He kissed her once more, slower this time—a drag, a vow—and when he pulled back, he didn't step away.

He just looked at her.

The look said everything.

And Gideon looked like a man who knew exactly how far she would let him go.

And exactly how far he planned to take her.

"For the record," he said, voice low and rough with satisfaction, "you never answered the question."

Arden blinked, still caught in the aftershocks. "What question?"

Gideon didn't rush. He only let his gaze wander, slow and unapologetic, before it settled on hers with enough weight to make swallowing difficult.

"Which one of us you decided was sexier."

Her lips parted, then curved.

She didn't hurry.

With her chin tilted slightly, she murmured, "Still deliberating."

His chuckle was velvet and smoke. "Take your time."

She almost did, if only to spite him. But before she could fire back, his hands were at her waist again, gentler now but no less sure. When he lifted her from the car, her whole body remembered what it had felt like to have him settled between her thighs.

Her boots hit pavement.

Her balance didn't.

Then, with that maddening confidence she couldn't stand and kept craving anyway, he opened the passenger door and gave a half-bow, mock formality thick in the air.

"After you."

She rolled her eyes, but her mouth betrayed her, forming a smile she tried and failed to kill.

"So chivalrous."

His brow lifted. "Only when it gets me what I want."

She gave him a look, sharp-edged and amused, but her legs carried her into the car anyway. She sank into the seat, his scent wrapping around her like a trap she had stopped trying to escape.

Leather. Spice. Him.

The door shut behind her with a soft click.

A second later, he was there. Close. Composed. Every inch of him unreadable and infuriating and unfairly attractive.

He reached for the ignition, then stilled.

"You forgot something," he said.

She blinked. "What?"

He didn't answer.

He only leaned in.

Not fast. Not showy. Just there, with the kind of quiet confidence that made her stomach flip and her pulse stumble.

His arm brushed hers as he reached across her chest. The seatbelt slid over her collarbone, warm from his touch. The buckle clicked into place, but it wasn't the sound that made her breath hitch.

It was the way he didn't move.

The way he hovered.

Close enough for his breath to whisper along her jaw.

Close enough for her body to remember every inch he hadn't touched yet.

Her pulse climbed.

The heat of him soaked through her skin as if he belonged there.

His mouth brushed the shell of her ear, his voice low enough to leave marks.

"Safety first."

She didn't breathe.

Didn't dare.

For one suspended second, neither did he.

He didn't pull back. Didn't look away. His lips hovered just shy of her neck, his gaze locked on hers, watching closely—not for surrender, but for the moment she chose it.

Her voice was gone.

Her composure, a lost cause.

Still, she didn't move.

Couldn't.

Then finally, Gideon eased back. Not far. Only enough to shift gears as if nothing had happened.

THE ENGINE PURRED TO LIFE, low and smooth, a perfect echo of the tension still running through her blood. As the car rolled forward, city lights sliced through the windshield, gold and silver streaking across the dark.

But Arden wasn't watching the road.

She was stuck on the way a seatbelt had ruined her composure. On the way Gideon had used silence like a weapon. On the ache coiling low in her belly, and the truth she wasn't ready to admit.

He knew exactly what he was doing.

"So," she said, her voice casual despite the riot beneath her skin, "where are we going? Or is that classified?"

His mouth twitched. "You'll see."

She narrowed her eyes. "Let me guess—somewhere expensive and full of people who never blink?"

"Maybe." He glanced at her, that insufferable smirk back in full force. "Maybe not."

"You're infuriating."

"I've been told."

His fingers brushed hers on the gearshift, subtle but not accidental.

"You'll forgive me."

She leaned back slowly, pretending her skin wasn't still tingling from that touch.

They both knew she already had.

As they pulled in, floodlights blinked on overhead, cutting sharp paths through the dark. The track unfolded in front of them—smooth and shadowless, its curves catching the light like something alive and waiting.

Somewhere on the far side, an engine tore through the silence, deep and rough, the kind of sound that made her pulse jump before her thoughts could catch up.

Adrenaline stirred before she could stop it.

Arden blinked. "Is this...?"

Gideon cut the engine. The glint in his eyes said everything.

"You said you liked excitement."

"I thought you meant something like sushi."

He didn't smile, not quite.

"This felt more fitting."

She stared at him for a moment, caught between disbelief and the kind of thrill that licked at the edges of fear. Then her mouth tugged into a grin, slow and sly, a flicker of fire behind it.

"You really don't hold back, do you?" she said, bone-dry.

But her eyes gave her away.

His gaze held hers. "Not when it counts."

He stepped out and came around to her side. When the door opened, a rush of air swept in—cool against her skin, tinged with the raw bite of fuel and track rubber. The low throb of engines carried across the lot, steady as a heartbeat.

She folded her arms, cocking her head as her eyes tracked the nearest curve. "Okay," she said slowly. "What exactly are we doing here?"

He didn't answer right away. He only slipped a hand into his pocket and held out the keys.

"You drive."

She looked from the keys to him. "You're seriously letting me drive this?"

"Just don't crash it."

Arden took the keys. Their fingers brushed—heat, intent, a quiet exchange of control.

"Oh, I won't."

She slid behind the wheel. The Roadster came alive beneath her, its growl deep and steady, like it had been waiting to be unleashed.

She gripped the wheel.

Breathed.

Hit the gas.

The car launched forward, tires gripping the track as if it knew the way. Laughter broke from her chest, sharp and unexpected, as speed wrapped around her, reckless and clean.

The Roadster devoured the asphalt, cornering with effortless precision. Each curve pulled tighter, and Arden moved with it, fluid and reactive, her pulse rising to meet the rhythm of the machine.

Beside her, Gideon said nothing, but she felt his eyes.

Watching.

Measuring.

Tracking her with quiet precision.

"Enjoying the show?" she asked, breathless, glancing at him.

"You've got good instincts," he said, voice calm but edged with something else.

A smirk tugged at her lips as she eased into another turn, seamless and sharp. "You sound surprised."

"Not even a little." His voice stayed even, his jaw tight. "I've watched you work."

The words hit like impact aimed straight at center.

Not flirtation.

Conviction.

She pushed the car harder. "Careful, Blackwell," she said, eyes forward. "Keep talking like that and I'll think you're impressed."

"I am."

Low.

Steady.

Undeniable.

"But I figured you already knew that."

Her breath caught behind a laugh that never quite made it out.

Another turn.

Another rush of speed.

For a moment, there was nothing else. Only the Roadster beneath her, the track unraveling ahead, and Gideon's gaze beside her—steady, unrelenting, lit with something that felt too much like pride.

Control.

Velocity.

Heat.

She didn't need permission to take the wheel.

And she wasn't giving it back.

As SHE GUIDED the car into the pit lane, the rush clung to her, pulse still thrumming.

She turned toward him.

Gideon was already watching.

There was a flicker in his eyes—pride, maybe. Or something darker. Hungrier.

Her breath came fast. "You're far too calm for a man who just handed over the keys to his outrageously priced car."

Gideon leaned back, lips curving, more dangerous now. More intent.

"I like you like this."

She angled her head, still catching her breath. "Like what?"

His answer didn't waver.

"Lit up. Unapologetic. Alive."

No performance. No distance. Just truth, bare and searing.

It landed between them like an open flame—unexpected, electric, undeniable.

This wasn't about the car.

It was about her.

With the car idling in the soft glow of the diner's lights, Arden eased back into the seat, claiming the space like it was hers.

The cabin carried the echo of motion, saturated with heat, leather, and the trace of him. Gideon dropped into the seat beside her with quiet ease, all coiled composure.

But his eyes didn't lie.

They moved over her slowly. Not lewd. Not polite, either.

Her legs crossed, high-waisted denim tightening across her hips, the shimmer of her blouse catching enough light to draw the eye. She didn't rush the movement.

He noticed.

She smiled, slow and unhurried.

"I've made my decision."

His brow lifted, interest flickering like a match. "About?"

"Which of you wins."

Gideon leaned back, one arm settling on the wheel like he had all night to wait her out. "And?"

She let the silence stretch, curling between them, until anticipation sparked behind his eyes.

"I've decided…" She leaned in slightly, voice low. "The car is definitely sexier."

He didn't flinch.

Not at first.

But something shifted.

His gaze dropped to her mouth, then lower, a slow, predatory sweep that made the air inside the car feel suddenly too thin.

"Is that so?"

"Mmm." She bit back a grin, her hand resting lightly on the center console.

His smirk reappeared—cocky, dangerous, impossible. "Then let's raise the stakes."

"Oh?" Her voice was pure challenge now. "You want a rematch?"

"I want a bet." His tone dropped as he turned toward her fully, crowding the space without touching her.

"I bet I can change your mind before the night's over."

"And if you lose?"

His smile turned wicked.

"I don't."

She laughed, breathless, shaking her head as she leaned back. "You're impossible."

"And yet…" His eyes dipped again—mouth, neck, legs. "You're here."

Her grin came slow. Satisfied. "Or maybe I like a challenge."

He leaned in, his breath brushing past her cheek, close enough to feel but not quite touch.

"Then buckle up."

CHAPTER 46

Reckless Devotion

The drive back into the city passed in a quiet blur, but the silence wasn't empty. It hummed between them, alive and electric with everything neither of them had said.

Arden rested her temple against the window, the glass cool against her skin. Outside, the city unfurled in golden blurs; each flash of light slipped over her reflection and disappeared. She let herself look at him in the fractured glow—his rigid profile, the hard line of his jaw, his hands steady on the wheel.

He didn't look at her once.

Didn't dare.

When they finally pulled into the garage beneath his brownstone, the Roadster settled with a low purr, its last rumble fading like a held breath. Gideon cut the engine, but neither of them moved.

Then, slowly, he turned to her.

The storm in his eyes had gone quiet; steady now, but no less dangerous for it.

"Still think the car is sexier?" His voice was low, edged with something darker.

She tried to smirk, bold and flippant, but it cracked under the heat of his stare. The space between them had tightened to a breath.

"I don't know…" She lifted one shoulder, casual by sheer force of will. "It's close."

His jaw flexed.

Just once.

A warning.

Then he was out of the car.

She barely had time to track him before he was there, rounding the hood with that quiet, coiled stride she'd learned to recognize. He opened her door without a word and offered his hand like a man who knew she'd take it.

"I still think I can tilt things in my favor," he said, voice rough and threaded with the control he was barely keeping.

Inside, the brownstone welcomed them with a hush, familiar and expectant. Arden slipped out of her coat, the fabric whispering down her arms before she draped it over the armrest in a soft, deliberate fall.

When she turned, he was there.

No rush. No hesitation. Just Gideon, closing the space between them as if gravity had made its choice.

"You know," he said, voice low and teasing, but anchored, "I've been patient."

The word landed like a spark.

Heat stirred low in her belly. She didn't bother pretending otherwise.

"Patient?" she asked, brow lifting.

He traced her wrist, only a brush of contact, but her breath caught anyway.

"Letting you take the wheel. Sitting through dinner. Watching you move in that brutally intoxicating outfit..." His hands slid to her waist, thumbs slipping just beneath the hem of her blouse. "You've been testing me."

She laughed quietly, but the sound thinned as he leaned in, his mouth grazing just shy of her throat.

"You're wrong, by the way," he murmured.

She swallowed. "About what?"

"That the car is sexier."

His hands moved lower, slow and certain, anchoring her. Then his mouth met hers, and the last careful inch between them burned away.

Arden melted into him. Her fingers gripped his shirt, dragging him closer until nothing remained but friction and heat and the ruthless honesty of want. His hands tightened on her hips, fitting her to him with a precision that felt less like impulse than inevitability.

He kissed her like he had imagined it a hundred times and still hadn't come close.

When they parted, their foreheads stayed pressed together, breath mingling in the narrow space between them. Gideon brushed his thumb over her lower lip; the touch was slow, reverent, edged with possession, like a vow written without words.

Her smile curved, slow and certain. "I might need more proof."

His gaze sharpened—dark, intent, unraveling. "Come on," he said, voice rasped and wrecked. "Let me prove it."

He kissed her again, an invitation and a promise, his mouth lingering long enough to make her knees remember they had options.

"I've got all night," he said. "And I'm done holding back."

Arden let the weight of that land. Then she met his eyes, sharp as ever, her voice steadier than her pulse.

"You're awfully confident for a man who might be losing."

"Losing?" His smirk curled, molten and sure. "You're still here."

The truth in it struck deeper than she wanted to admit. She pressed her hand to his chest, firm and grounding, feeling the steady force of him beneath her palm.

Because she wasn't unsure anymore. Not about him. Not about this.

"Lead the way, Blackwell," she said.

And she let go.

The door clicked shut behind them, sealing the room around them—and everything they were becoming.

Gideon didn't wait. He didn't ask. He crossed the space like the decision had already been made somewhere deep in him, somewhere older than restraint. His eyes weren't teasing now. They were focused, hungry, intent.

"This isn't a game to me."

"I know," she said.

His hand came up slowly, open and unhurried. His fingers brushed the side of her neck, then followed the line of her collarbone before gliding down her arm. From there, he found her waist, and lingered there—mapping. Learning. Holding himself back by fractions.

"You can still walk away."

She didn't.

Instead, Arden stepped closer and set her palms against his chest, feeling the restraint beneath the expensive fabric, the storm locked under skin and bone.

"I'm not going anywhere."

His breath caught.

So did hers.

The moment shifted; not rushed, not careless, but irreversible in the way some choices became true the instant they were spoken. His hands tightened at her waist, anchoring her, and the last of his restraint looked almost painful.

"Then let me have you," he said, voice hoarse, reverent.

She kissed him first. Not shy. Not soft.

"I'm already yours."

His next kiss wasn't a continuation. It was a reckoning.

Unhurried but hungry, his mouth moved against hers as if spelling out every vow he couldn't yet say. Intentional. Focused. This wasn't only seduction, and it wasn't only want. It was Gideon looking at her with that devastating, disciplined attention and making her feel seen in places she had taught herself not to name.

He moved with that infuriating, beautiful certainty, and the rest of the world seemed to go quiet for this...for her. Gideon didn't just touch her; he memorized her, as though this wasn't indulgence but survival. His weight anchored her, firm and steady, while his hands found the places she hadn't known were aching until he reached them.

A shiver raced down her spine as his palm slid along her ribs, each brush sending sparks beneath her skin. He wasn't taking. He was asking, and somehow that undid her more completely. Every pass of his fingers, every breath against her, carried the same quiet question.

He was still learning her, reading her body like a prayer whispered in the dark. Every gasp, every arch, every tremor became part of the answer.

His lips moved from her mouth to the tender place beneath her ear, and there he paused. Kissed. Tasted her like a man savoring something he wasn't sure he deserved. Slow. Open-mouthed. Addicted. She felt it in the way his breath caught, the way his jaw flexed, the way his whole body responded to the smallest sound she failed to hold back.

When his mouth grazed her collarbone, she moaned softly, almost helplessly. Almost.

His name barely formed on her tongue.

And Gideon breathed her in like her scent alone could anchor him.

THEN HE MOVED LOWER, inch by agonizing inch, his mouth tracing the curve of her breast, the hollow between, the tender edge of her ribcage. Each press of his lips left heat behind—reverent, ruthless, wrecking.

Arden's hands threaded through his hair, nails grazing the line of his jaw, and when she moaned—really moaned—his whole body jerked. He trembled beneath her touch, as though the sound had struck something vital and left him unsure he could survive the echo.

Then his mouth closed over her nipple.

The pleasure was sharp enough to steal the air from her lungs. His tongue moved slowly, insistently, sending heat spiraling through her until her back arched and another broken sound slipped free. When he dragged his teeth over her, gentle and precise, just once, her gasp nearly undid him.

"Fuck," he rasped.

The word wasn't thrown at her. It was dragged out of him—for her, for himself, for the disbelief of having her beneath his mouth and still needing more.

He wasn't only touching her; he was coming apart with every inch he claimed. Her hands found his shoulders, then his back, tracing the strength that bracketed her, and she felt the strain in him—the restraint stretching, fraying, threatening to snap. Still, he let her guide the rhythm until the careful control inside him fractured.

He lifted his head and met her eyes.

The look he gave her carried lust, yes, but lust sharpened by everything beneath it: need, awe, hunger, something fierce enough to frighten a more sensible woman.

"You're a fucking masterpiece."

His voice shook with something almost sacred, not because of what he saw, but because of what he felt. For her.

Her breath caught.

Then he was kissing lower.

Slower.

Her ribs. The soft slope of her stomach. Her hips, where his hands found her again, fingers flexing, thumbs grazing bone like he could keep her there by touch alone. When he glanced up, the look in his eyes knocked the breath from her lungs.

"You're unreal," he rasped, voice uneven. "I don't know what to do with you."

His hands settled at her hips, fingers splayed wide, anchoring her as he kissed his way down her body in a slow, deliberate descent. His mouth dragged over her skin with a hunger that made knowing her feel insufficient. He wanted to learn her again—inch by inch, breath by breath—until she had no choice but to understand exactly what she did to him.

And then, lower.

His mouth found her with devastating certainty. No hesitation. No apology. Just heat and hunger and a rhythm so deliberate it made her toes curl. He kissed her like she was a promise he meant to keep with his hands, his mouth, his body, every ruined piece of restraint he had left.

She felt the shape of his grin before she saw it, the wicked curve of his mouth against her thigh.

"Gideon," she breathed, voice already frayed. "Please..."

Her fingers slid into his hair, desperate for something to hold as the world narrowed to heat, anticipation, and the unbearable patience of his mouth.

His laugh was low and dark, a promise delivered straight to her skin.

"Since you asked so nicely..."

Then he gave her everything.

His mouth closed over her, tongue circling with unrelenting precision, controlled and consuming. He didn't rush her. He didn't waste her. He learned every sound she made and answered it, lips coaxing, tongue tormenting, his mouth working her with the same disciplined focus he brought to everything—except now that discipline had teeth.

Arden cried out, hips jerking, thighs trembling, but he held her steady. Let her come undone. Made her feel every second of it; every flick, every pull, every relentless wave of pleasure until her body locked and shattered in his hands.

Still, he didn't stop.

Not right away.

He softened only when she gasped his name again, broken and blissed-out, her breath coming apart beneath the weight of him. His kisses gentled then, featherlight along her thighs and hips, reverent again, his murmured words lost beneath the pulse roaring in her ears.

Only when she sagged back into the mattress, boneless and trembling, did he rise.

Slowly. Deliberately.

Over her.

Body to body. Heat to heat. His skin slick against hers, his mouth found hers in a kiss that said he was nowhere near finished.

Because he wasn't.

And neither was she.

His mouth crushed hers, no preamble, no apology. His tongue slid deep, claiming the taste of her, the broken sound she made when he pressed closer. His hips surged forward, grinding against her with dizzying pressure, and Arden opened for him on instinct—shameless now, greedy for every inch of heat and weight and want.

She moaned into his mouth, fingers clawing at his back as she dragged him closer, until there was no distance left to collapse. His body was hard and hot between her thighs, the thick length of him pressing against her, slick from the wet heat of her. She arched up, seeking friction, and the low, ruined sound he made against her throat nearly undid her.

"Fuck, Arden…" His voice was guttural and reverent, her name dragged from him like a curse and a prayer. His hand slid between them, fingers parting her with a kind of desperate precision, as if he could not bear the thought of missing a single response.

"So wet for me." One thick finger pushed inside her, then another, curling deep until her body clenched around him. His breath fractured. "Look at you."

Her thighs trembled. "Gideon…"

"I've got you." His voice was rough, steady, hungry. "I've got every single part of you."

Arden gripped the nape of his neck and dragged his mouth back to hers, tasting the last thread of his restraint before it finally burned away. He pulled his fingers free, then moved the head of his cock through her slick heat, teasing her entrance with a patience that made her ache. His hips shook from the effort of holding back.

"Please," she whispered, and the word carried more than want. It carried need, surrender, and the sharp little fury of a woman done being patient. "I need you inside me."

That was all it took.

He pushed into her in one slow, overwhelming stroke, filling her to the hilt. Arden arched beneath him, the thick, delicious pressure tearing a gasp from her throat as her body stretched around him, took him, knew him. Gideon didn't move at first. He stayed buried inside her, chest rising in sharp bursts, his forehead pressed to hers while he tried to breathe through the wreckage.

"You fit me," he ground out. "So...fucking well. So perfect." His jaw tightened, and his hands flexed against her hips. "Like you were made for me."

Then he began to move.

Long, deep thrusts rolled through her, each one sending shockwaves through her core. His rhythm was controlled at first, almost punishing in its restraint, but need kept breaking through—the snap of his hips, the rough drag of his breath, the way he watched her as if every sound she made cost him another piece of himself. Arden clung to him, legs locked around his waist, nails scoring down his back as he drove into her with the force of everything they had held back too long.

She wasn't passive beneath him. She was not delicate. She met him stroke for stroke, fierce and hungry, taking him as much as he took her.

"Harder," she gasped. "I can take it."

His growl moved through his chest and into hers. "You'll get everything."

And she did.

Gideon's control snapped into something darker, harder, devastatingly precise. One hand gripped her thigh. The other tangled in her hair. He drove her closer and closer to the edge, his body relentless over hers, every thrust pushing pleasure deeper until heat built low and vicious, coiling tight enough to steal her breath.

Her climax hovered just out of reach, maddening and bright, threatening to tear through her if only he would—

His hand slipped between them again, thumb finding her clit and circling in time with each thrust, fast and unrelenting.

"Gideon—" Her voice broke.

The pressure snapped.

The orgasm ripped through her like fire and light, and she cried out his name as her body locked around him, pulsing in hard, helpless waves. Pleasure took her apart from the inside out. Gideon followed with a guttural sound torn from somewhere deep in his chest, spilling into her with a final, shuddering thrust.

His release moved through him like a quake, all clenched fists and shaking muscle, his body bowed over hers as his forehead dropped to her shoulder. He groaned through the wreckage and kept grinding into her, riding the aftershocks, refusing to let the connection slip too soon.

They stayed tangled like that, hot and breathless, his cock still inside her, her body still fluttering around him. Sweat cooled slowly on their skin. Her thighs were slick. Their hearts hammered against each other in the heavy, ruined quiet.

When Gideon finally lifted his head, his eyes locked on hers—dark, blown, still reeling. His voice cracked, raw and wrecked, as though he had not quite survived her.

"You ruin me."

She touched his face, brushing the damp hair from his temple. "Good."

He was still inside her, not only in the way that mattered, but in all the ways that did. His breath at her throat. His hands at her waist. The heat of him still pulsing through her like an aftershock that refused to fade.

And then, because it wasn't over—not yet—he started to move again.

Slow.

Deep.

Because once was never going to be enough.

Not for him.

Not for her.

Not when they were finally laid bare, with no distance left between them, and every inch of her body had already learned to answer his like a prayer.

THEN SOMETHING SHIFTED.

A flicker. A twitch of muscle beneath her palms. The tension that had unraveled moments before began to gather again, low and sharp, like a storm regrouping in the calm.

His fingers skimmed up her thigh and dragged through the sweat-slicked heat between them as though he couldn't bear the thought of letting her go. Then his mouth followed, lower now, slower, pressing kisses to the center of her chest with a hunger that had lost its polish. Teeth. Tongue. The last ragged edge of his control. There was no caution left in him, only Gideon and the wreckage of what she had given him, and the greedy, aching need to take more.

"You're shaking," he murmured, voice gravel-soft and reverent all at once, his mouth grazing the underside of her breast as his hand slid up her ribs.

"Not cold," she whispered.

That was all it took.

He surged up, mouth crashing into hers, and this time there was nothing gentle in it. The kiss was possession and surrender, fire unleashed beneath fragile skin. His fingers fisted in her hair, tugging her head back to bare her throat, and his mouth was there a second later, biting, tasting, dragging a groan from his chest as her hips lifted to meet him on instinct.

Her legs wrapped around him; her ankles locked at the base of his spine as if she could keep him there forever. His name spilled from her lips again, but this time her voice was hoarse, low, entirely unguarded.

He didn't make her wait.

He was already hard again, and the moment she shifted beneath him, inviting and aching, he found her. No warning. No pause. Just the desperate sound they both made when he sank back into her, hot and deep and too much, too soon, and still not enough.

Not nearly enough.

Her back arched, body bowing off the mattress, hands scrambling for purchase—

his arms, his shoulders, the slick curve of his neck. She needed something to hold onto, and he gave her everything.

They moved together like instinct, like war and worship tangled in the same breath. There were no slow thrusts now, no easing in, only rhythm and friction and the raw, brutal beauty of two people who knew exactly how they fit and were too far gone to pretend they didn't need it.

He pressed his forehead to hers, breath ragged, one hand fisted in the sheets beside her head.

"Look at me."

She did.

And what she saw broke something open. Gideon wasn't in control anymore. Not fully. Not beautifully. He was undone above her, stripped of strategy and restraint, and he wanted her to witness it.

His hips snapped harder, dragging a gasp from her throat as she clung to him. Her fingers dug into his back. Her lips brushed his jaw, whispering nothing and everything, and she met him thrust for thrust, nails leaving red marks down his spine as she tried to ground herself in him. Her moans caught on every breath.

"Gideon," she gasped, again and again, as though the shape of his name might keep her from unraveling too fast.

But unravel she did.

He felt it.

"Let go for me," he said, voice low and thick, barely more than a growl.

And she did.

She shattered again—violently, exquisitely—body arching, breath breaking, hips rising to meet every relentless inch of him until she cried out and clutched him like she might never stop. Gideon followed her over the edge with a rough curse and a final, deep thrust that left him trembling above her, spilling into her with a sound that was part prayer, part surrender.

They collapsed together, chests heaving, skin slick and burning, their mouths brushing between heartbeats.

He didn't say her name this time.

He kissed it into her mouth.

Neither of them moved for a long time.

The room held its hush, not from distance but from weight—the kind that followed something intimate, something real. Gideon exhaled against her temple, his body still warm and heavy over hers, grounding her beneath the steady rise and fall of his chest.

When he lifted his head, his voice moved across her skin like another touch.

"Arden..."

It wasn't a question.

It was a vow.

They stayed tangled in the aftermath, breathless and spent, both of them undone in ways that had very little to do with the body anymore. The world outside had faded—the city's hum, the stretch of traffic, the slow creep of night. None of it touched them here.

Gideon didn't retreat. He held her, anchored her, one hand still at her waist as if letting go required more courage than he had yet gathered.

Her fingers traced his spine, lazy and soft.

"You're incredible," he whispered, brushing a kiss to her temple.

"I almost think you mean that."

His mouth curved against her jaw. "I don't say things I don't mean."

The way he said it caught something inside her.

She believed him.

His hand slid down her back, gentle now, as though he still wasn't done committing every inch of her to memory. Arden kissed the center of his chest, right where his heart thundered beneath her lips, and he flinched—not from pain, but from something quieter. More fragile.

THEY STAYED WRAPPED around each other in the kind of stillness that wasn't silence. Her leg hooked around his hip. His hand rested at her waist, warm and possessive in the softened aftermath, as though some part of him still needed proof she was there.

Then her phone buzzed.

A soft vibration against the nightstand.

Arden hesitated.

"Leave it," he murmured, eyes closed.

She almost did.

Almost.

But something twisted low in her gut, cold and instinctive. She reached for the phone before she could talk herself out of it.

One glance at the screen drained the heat from her skin.

Unknown: You looked beautiful last night. Did he tell you?

The words landed like a blade.

The illusion cracked. The safety she had dared to believe in—the quiet room, his body beside hers, the fragile mercy of being held—shattered all at once.

Her grip tightened around the phone.

Gideon stirred, his voice low and rough with concern. "Arden?"

She locked the screen and forced her voice steady.

"It's nothing."

Too fast.

He scanned her face and said nothing, but she felt the warning in his silence.

Don't lie to me.

He didn't push. Instead, he drew her close again, his arm coming around her with careful strength.

"Whatever it is..." His mouth brushed her hair. "We'll handle it. Together."

She wanted to believe that.

God, she wanted to.

But the message burned in her hand.

You looked beautiful last night. Did he tell you?

Her eyes drifted to the window.

Outside, the night felt heavier now, pressed close to the glass, watching.

Because someone had been there.

Someone had seen.

And Arden didn't know how much longer she could pretend she didn't feel it.

CHAPTER 47

Where You Are

Arden stirred against sheets that no longer held his weight. The warmth of him had faded, but his presence hadn't. His scent lingered—clean, masculine, a little dangerous—clinging to the linen, clinging to her skin. Something dark, threaded with heat. Sex. Him. The kind of scent that didn't let go.

She didn't panic.

Morning light pushed through the curtains in soft gold stripes, brushing over the rumpled space beside her. Gideon had left something behind: a cup of coffee on the nightstand, still warm; the echo of a kiss at her temple, tender and lingering; and on her phone, the soft buzz of a message.

> Gideon: Didn't want to wake you. You looked like peace I didn't deserve to disturb. Coffee's hot. Lock the door. Text me when you're up. Please.

She read it twice, the corners of her mouth twitching despite herself.
Then another message came through.

> Gideon: You wrecked me, Rivers. And I'd let you do it again.

The heat that coiled low in her stomach had nothing to do with caffeine.

Arden sank deeper into the pillow, her body deliciously sore from the night before, every inch of her tingling with the memory of his touch. The ache between her thighs wasn't a complaint. It was a memory. A promise.

Proof.

But even as warmth curled through her like smoke, something colder edged in.

395

Not fear.

Awareness.

That feeling again.

She shifted toward the window, and there it was: the same silver car from the week before. Parked. Unassuming. Unmoving. Too still.

Not paranoia. Not anymore.

She knew Christian's team was watching. Gideon had told her—after the destroyed rose, after the shattered glass, after the gift of lavender tea with the note from a secret admirer. He had wanted her protected, and part of her had believed him. Wanted to believe him.

But this didn't feel like protection.

It felt like surveillance. Pointed. Precise. Like someone wasn't keeping her safe so much as keeping her.

She made it through her morning routine: Krav Maga, a long shower, extra concealer under her eyes. Still, the feeling clung to her like sweat before a storm, heavy and unshakable. Even the burn of training hadn't bled it out. The adrenaline helped, but only temporarily.

When she slowed down, it crept back in, coiling tight beneath her skin.

❧

By the time Arden stepped through the employee entrance, the tension had settled squarely between her shoulder blades.

The air shifted.

And she knew.

Something was off.

She felt them before she saw them.

Evelyn Blackwell entered like a woman sealing a fate. Every movement carried the precision of a final chess move. Her midnight-blue Chanel suit was tailored to perfection, severe in cut and colder in tone—the kind of fabric that dared anyone to wrinkle it, the kind of look that warned you not to try.

Beside her, draped in tailored black, Miriam followed with quiet threat and tightly coiled judgment. If Evelyn was the ice, Miriam was the air before it shattered.

They weren't women in power. They were predators who had mistaken polish for mercy.

And tonight, they had come to hunt.

Arden didn't need to look up to know they'd arrived. The room had changed around them, the air tightening, the walls seeming to brace. When she finally lifted her head, her gaze met Evelyn's without flinching.

Steel met steel.

"Welcome to The Blackwell Room, Mrs. Blackwell. Mrs. Harrington."

Her voice didn't waver. Didn't bend. Cool, direct, equal parts courtesy and warning.

Evelyn's smile was more blade than warmth.

"Arden Rivers." She let the name roll slowly from her tongue, each syllable laced with distaste. "We need a word. In private."

The leather groaned faintly as Evelyn slid into the booth like a woman used to being waited on. Miriam followed, mirroring her posture—hands folded, gaze unreadable.

Arden didn't sit.

She wouldn't lower herself beneath them.

Evelyn tilted her wrist. A diamond bracelet caught the light, scattering it in sharp little shards across the table. The gesture was practiced. Controlled. A weapon disguised as elegance.

"I understand you've managed to capture my son's attention."

There it was.

The first cut, wrapped in silk.

Arden's heart ticked once, then steadied. "Gideon and I are together. Yes."

Evelyn's expression didn't shift, but something beneath it turned colder.

"Together." She repeated the word as if it offended her.

Miriam reached for her drink, took a measured sip, and set it down with a gentle clink.

"The Blackwell name carries weight, Miss Rivers. History. Responsibility. It was never meant to be shared lightly."

A pause.

Then, smoothly, "Especially not with someone of your...background."

The unspoken part of the sentence filled the silence like smoke.

Your kind.

Arden didn't flinch. Not anymore. Her hand curled once at her side, only once, and then stilled.

"What exactly do you think I am, Mrs. Harrington?"

Miriam's smile was small. Icy.

"A distraction. A phase. Something he'll move on from."

Arden leaned in slightly, her voice calm and razor-clean.

"Let me guess—you'd prefer someone more...suitable?"

Evelyn tapped her fingers once against the table. Sharp. Deliberate.

"Let me be clear, Miss Rivers. Gideon is expected to marry well. To carry on the Blackwell name with someone who understands legacy. That woman—" she tilted her head, gaze sliding over Arden like a dissection, "—is not you."

She paused, and then came the twist of the blade, spoken so casually it almost passed as observation.

"Not exactly the elegant, willowy type, are you?"

The insult landed exactly where Evelyn meant it to.

Miriam's smirk confirmed it.

But Arden didn't break.

She had never wanted to be one of them. The words cut clean, but they found no wound deep enough to open.

Instead, she smiled, slow and cutting.

"Not exactly your type, either, is it?" Her voice was silk-wrapped steel. "Funny —I was thinking the same about you."

She didn't blink. Didn't back down.

"You've got the diamonds. The breeding. The bloodline." Her gaze flicked once over Evelyn's flawless suit, Miriam's folded hands, the practiced stillness between them. "But none of that means a thing if you can't stand to be alone in your own skin."

Her chin lifted, casual. Controlled.

"And I can. I am."

She didn't raise her voice.

"Gideon didn't choose me because I'm willowy or elegant or bred to play a role. He chose me because I don't pretend. And I don't need to."

Her gaze slid briefly to Miriam, then landed back on Evelyn with quiet finality.

"I know exactly who I am."

The game changed.

The air tightened.

Evelyn's lips thinned. Miriam shifted, fingers curling once against the leather.

Arden tilted her head, cool and collected.

"It must be exhausting, living a life someone else scripted for you. Chasing approval you never asked for. But Gideon?" Her smile sharpened by a fraction. "He's not chasing. Not anymore."

The silence that followed wasn't heavy.

It was hollowed out. Gutted.

Evelyn's voice went cold as steel. "Doors close quickly in this world, Miss Rivers. You'd do well to remember that."

Arden's exhale was smooth. Confident.

"And yet, here I am. Still standing."

She turned without waiting for dismissal, leaving them both in the booth—two women who had spent their lives controlling the board, realizing too late they had threatened a queen they had never bothered to see coming.

And that kind of power couldn't be bought.

Only earned.

THE CONVERSATION ENDED, but the tension didn't.

It followed Arden out of the club like smoke clinging to her skin, invisible and impossible to shake. The night air cut cool across her cheeks. Manhattan buzzed around them—horns in the distance, music bleeding from open windows, the occasional burst of laughter from late-night wanderers. The city didn't care what had happened. It kept moving.

Arden didn't.

Not really.

She stayed close, her heels tapping out a quiet challenge with every step. Her arms were crossed, shoulders stiff, jaw clenched around everything she hadn't said inside. Every clipped stride tried to shake off the frost Evelyn Blackwell had left behind.

It didn't work.

She exhaled through her nose, then finally broke the silence.

"Do you always let her treat people like pawns?"

The words snapped harder than she meant them to. She knew that. But bitterness had teeth, and hers were showing.

Gideon stopped walking.

Abrupt. Still.

The streetlight caught the angles of his face, carving sharper lines into his expression than had been there a moment before. He stood there in silence, as though the wrong words would do more damage than none at all.

He didn't rush to defend Evelyn. He didn't rush to defend himself.

He only looked at Arden, jaw tight, eyes unreadable, a storm held back by discipline and very little else. Then his hand dragged through his hair, frustration flashing across his features.

"No." His voice cut clean through the night, controlled but edged. "And I don't let her intimidate the people I care about."

Her heart stuttered.

The people I care about.

The words weren't loud, but they echoed.

Arden looked away and scoffed, soft and sharp. "That's funny. She just spent the last twenty minutes making sure I know I don't belong anywhere near you."

Gideon stepped closer.

Measured. Steady.

Not to dominate. To be seen.

"She doesn't get a say," he said, the edge in his voice all steel and certainty. "You're in this with me because I chose you."

Her breath caught.

He made it sound so simple.

Too simple.

"And what if that choice stops being enough?" she asked, quiet but unflinching.

Something shifted in his eyes—sharpened, storm-bound. His control coiled tighter, but he didn't look away.

"Then I burn it all down."

It wasn't said like a threat.

It was a promise.

Something cold and electric slid down her spine. Not fear. Something deeper. Because he meant it. She should have pushed back, should have told him he didn't have to burn anything for her, but the truth was uglier and far more honest.

If someone came for him, she would light the match herself.

She swallowed hard, gaze dropping to the sidewalk as the city blurred around the edges of her thoughts. Then she saw it: a sliver of soft light across the street, small and tucked between glass towers and late-night taxis. A café, still open. Still warm.

She nodded toward it.

"I need coffee."

Gideon didn't flinch. Didn't press. He only nodded once.

"Come on," he said quietly.

His hand grazed the small of her back—not steering, not leading. Just there.

They crossed together in silence, slipping through the thin stream of traffic. The café's neon sign buzzed overhead, and inside, the scent of espresso drifted out into the cold, curling around her like comfort.

Arden breathed in deeply, letting it settle somewhere beneath her ribs.

She didn't know what came next. She didn't know how to silence the voice whispering that none of this could last.

But tonight, Gideon stood beside her.

And for now, that was enough.

The café was warm and quiet, the kind of place where people whispered truths over chipped porcelain mugs and left pieces of themselves behind in the grain of old wood.

Gideon sat across from Arden, fingers loose around a coffee cup gone cold. Steam curled between them, a fragile barrier neither of them fully wanted to break. The overhead light caught her cheekbones, softening her edges in gold.

But he knew better.

She wasn't made of gold.

She was fire.

Always had been.

And tonight, he had watched Evelyn try to smother it.

He had watched Arden stand her ground while his mother sliced at her with words polished to a sheen. The only reason he hadn't stepped in—the only reason he hadn't dragged Evelyn from the room by sheer force of will—was because he knew Arden wouldn't have wanted him to.

She hadn't needed saving.

But God, it had gutted him.

Because she shouldn't have had to fight at all. Not against Evelyn. Not against anyone.

Not alone.

Across the table, Arden exhaled, quiet but weighted. Her fingers tapped the rim of her cup in an uneven rhythm he recognized now, restless and guarded, carrying Evelyn's poison beneath the skin: the old ache of never being enough, the ghost of a world that never invited her in.

It made him want to set something on fire.

She glanced up, catching him mid-thought, and her expression softened just enough to see through.

"You're quiet."

He didn't answer.

He only looked at her—the sharp blue of her eyes, the stubborn tilt of her jaw, the tension in her shoulders she probably didn't know she carried.

Maybe that was what cracked something open in him.

When his voice came, it was low. Certain. A promise wrapped in iron.

"You don't have to fight them alone."

A flicker passed across her face. Surprise, maybe. Doubt.

Gone before he could name it.

Her hand curled tighter around the mug. "I know."

But she didn't.

Not really.

He could hear it in the way the words landed, too brittle to be belief, too careful to be truth. Gideon didn't push. Not yet. Instead, he reached across the table, his fingers brushing the back of hers.

She didn't pull away.

His thumb traced a slow arc across her knuckles, and he felt her breath catch.

Only for a second.

But it was enough.

"Evelyn's never going to accept this," she said, voice low.

Still, she didn't move her hand. Didn't pull back.

He kept his hold light but sure. "I don't need her to. But you..."

He paused.

"You do."

That made her look at him.

Sharp. Direct. Wary.

And God help him, he wanted to kiss her so badly it hurt. But this wasn't about taking. This was about proving something she had every reason to doubt: that Evelyn didn't get to define her, that no one did. Not in his world. Not anymore.

His fingers tightened around hers slightly before he let go, before he did something she wasn't ready for.

Her throat moved as she swallowed. He could see the war happening behind her eyes.

But then—

She turned her hand over, palm up, fingers open, and laced them through his.

Gideon Blackwell, a man who had built empires on control, nearly came undone.

Arden didn't say a word. She only exhaled, a soft, fragile sound.

But he felt it.

The walls cracking.

Her fingers tightened around his, a whisper of pressure. Then she let go.

Not rejection.

Space.

Breath.

A promise.

He ran a hand through his hair and exhaled slowly, his heartbeat a steady riot.

"Okay," she said, quiet but steady. "Let's go."

He didn't ask where.

He didn't need to.

Wherever she was, that was where he would be.

CHAPTER 48

The Cost of Control

Each blow traveled through her frame, fists landing sharp and deliberate, cutting through the quiet of the cavernous space.

Sweat dripped into Arden's eyes and carved slow trails down her back. Beneath it, bruises throbbed—earned and blooming in a slow rise beneath the surface.

Again.

Harder.

Once more.

Her breath hit in steady beats, tight and controlled, keeping time with the chaos flashing behind her eyes.

Damon absorbed the impact with practiced ease and snapped, "Rivers, focus. You're not fighting a ghost."

She exhaled through her nose and rolled her shoulders.

If only it were a ghost.

Ghosts didn't wear midnight-blue Chanel or speak in blade-edged pleasantries. Ghosts didn't wield legacy like a weapon, didn't smile as if they were sealing your fate, didn't make you feel like you had only been allowed in the room as a favor.

She reset her stance, fists clenching tighter.

Control it.

Channel it.

Her knee drove into the mitt—fast, precise, punishing. The force snapped through her body and grounded her in something tangible. Something real. The rest of her life felt too much like smoke and mirrors lately, too much like polished rooms and hidden eyes and people deciding what she was worth before she ever opened her mouth.

But this wasn't enough.

Not today.

Damon grunted and shifted his stance. Block. Strike. Pivot.

Arden moved on instinct. Efficient. Dangerous.

Only this time, it wasn't discipline.

It was purge.

The violence wasn't clean. It was therapy.

Adrenaline spiked hot through her veins, burning through the hollow space where sleep should have been. She hadn't rested, not after Evelyn's voice had wrapped around her like a noose. Not after standing her ground with steel in her spine and a storm behind her eyes. Not after Gideon had watched her, silent and furious, restraining the kind of rage that might have destroyed the whole room if she had let him loose.

And afterward, he hadn't tried to save her.

He had simply held her.

Like an anchor.

Like a vow.

Her fists slammed into the mitts—one, two, three—too hard, too fast.

Damon stumbled half a step. His brow lifted, and then he gave a low, amused grunt.

"Well. Someone's pissed."

Arden swiped her forearm across her forehead, catching her breath. "Something like that."

His gaze lingered. He saw it, the fire she hadn't extinguished, the fury still smoldering under sweat and skin.

"You good?"

She reached for her towel and offered a crooked smirk. "Ask the next guy who crosses me."

A bark of laughter. "Noted."

She turned away, chest still tight with leftover adrenaline. The sweat helped. The burn helped. But it hadn't burned everything away. The ache in her shoulders was a comfort, something blunt and honest, but unease still curled beneath her sternum like a warning.

Her phone buzzed.

Gideon: Did you sleep? Or are you working out your frustration by beating the shit out of something?

She smiled.

Define "something."

Gideon: That's my girl. I'll see you this evening.

She stared at the screen, thumb hovering above the glass. Her smile faltered, softer now.

And for the first time all morning, her breath came easy.

The heat hadn't faded, but it had direction now.

Arden tucked the phone away, slung the towel over her shoulder, and headed out into the cold morning air, still wound tighter than she would admit.

The water was scalding. Steam hung heavy in the air, curling along the glass in restless, shifting patterns.

Gideon barely felt it.

He stood motionless beneath the spray, hands braced against cool tile, every muscle drawn tight beneath his skin. Water poured down his back, carving along the ridges of his spine, pooling at his feet before spiraling into the drain.

It should have burned. Should have snapped him back into his body.

It didn't.

Not against the fire inside him.

Evelyn. Arden. The storm gathering behind his ribs.

Every carefully constructed part of his life was shifting now, colliding, forcing pressure against the walls he had spent years reinforcing. Those walls were starting to crack, and at the center of it all was her.

Arden Rivers.

He should have been thinking about Leo. About Christian. About the file waiting on his desk, the one that could reduce Blackwell Enterprises to ash.

Instead, all he could think about was her.

The night before.

Her hand in his.

That brief, real flicker of trust when she let him hold on.

She hadn't pulled away.

The moment hadn't felt small. It had felt fragile and borrowed, like something he had no right to keep and every intention of protecting anyway.

Deep down, he knew she was already waiting for him to fuck it up. Not because she was cruel, but because she had seen this story before. She knew what men like him chose in the end.

Power. Control. Legacy.

And if Gideon didn't move carefully, she would be gone before he ever got the chance to prove her wrong.

A low breath scraped from his chest. He dragged a hand through his wet hair, eyes closing for half a second.

Control.

That was what mattered.

Not Evelyn. Not the simmering rage locked behind his teeth. Not the echo of Arden's voice in his head, quiet and uncertain, as though some part of her had already accepted how this would end.

That was what gutted him.

He shut off the water with a sharp twist, steam thick around him as he stepped onto the heated tile. He dried himself quickly, jaw set, movements crisp, every muscle wound tight.

Control meant nothing if you didn't know who your enemies were.

And right now, he had too many.

By the time he rolled his sleeves, adjusted his cuffs, and stepped into the backseat of the waiting car, the storm inside him wasn't only heat anymore.

It was direction.

Focus.

Purpose.

And maybe...

Retribution.

The expansive office of Hawthorne Holdings reflected Gideon Blackwell's deliberate separation from the legacy that had shaped, and stained, so much of his life. Sleek, modern, purposeful—the space held quiet strength rather than ostentation, all clean lines and muted tones, the kind of focused minimalism that stood in stark contrast to the gilded decadence of Blackwell Enterprises, where Evelyn still ruled with an iron fist.

Sunlight slashed through the floor-to-ceiling windows, casting long, angular shadows across the polished wood of his desk. Beyond the glass, Manhattan stretched in a hard glitter of ambition and power.

But inside these walls, Gideon had built something different.

Something stripped of illusion.

Here, precision reigned.

Papers lay in careful disorder across the desk, the faint scent of ink mingling with the hum of the city far below. Gideon leaned forward, scanning the latest report from Leo Marcus, each line deepening the knot coiling in his chest.

A knock came at the door.

Sharp. Steady.

"Come in."

Leo entered first, methodical and unshaken, carrying a thick, worn folder Gideon recognized as both necessary and damning. Christian Sampson followed, his gaze sweeping the room with quiet, coiled vigilance.

Where Leo was calculation, Christian was instinct.

Leo placed the folder on the desk. "We've got more." He paused, expression grim. "Bishop's team is circling tighter. Financials, emails, property deals—your family hasn't just bent the law. They've pulverized it."

He crossed his arms and settled against the edge of the desk. "Skeletons in every closet. Not enough doors to hide them."

Gideon flipped the folder open. The contents stared back at him, line after line of corruption laid bare: shell companies, coerced land acquisitions, money rerouted through redevelopment projects that had produced little beyond displaced families and padded pockets.

"And Alex?" His voice stayed low.

Leo nodded. "Up to his neck. He's the front man, but it all funnels back to Evelyn. Every dollar. Every contract. Clean on paper, but scratch the surface and it's rot all the way through."

His jaw tightened. "The tenants who tried to speak out were...handled."

Threats. Legal pressure. Bribes.

Gideon's stomach turned.

"Colton?" he asked, already knowing the answer.

Leo nodded. "He's the messenger. Your cousin is the one delivering the threats."

The memory hit hard: Colton's smug face, leaning across the bar like a man too accustomed to getting what he wanted.

"It doesn't bother him," Gideon muttered, voice tight.

A beat passed, and another memory rose, unwelcome and precise.

"It used to not bother you either."

Colton's voice, weeks earlier. Disdain curling off every word.

"People grow up," Gideon had shot back. "And they grow a conscience."

He pushed the memory aside.

Focused.

"And Sebastian?"

Christian straightened, barely, but enough.

"He's not on the books," he said. "Not tied to the business officially. But something's off."

Leo stepped forward. "He's been watching Arden. Digging into her past—old jobs, addresses, contacts. Even following trails in Morgantown."

Heat uncoiled in Gideon's chest.

Not panic. Not fear.

Something heavier. Tighter.

A warning before the wire snapped.

His jaw ticked. "And?"

Leo didn't answer right away. His silence stretched.

"It's not just Arden."

The words landed like a punch to the ribs.

"He's accessed old Blackwell trial records," Leo continued. "Cases tied to those medical facilities your grandfather shut down decades ago."

Westchester.

The name alone sent something cold sliding through Gideon's bloodstream.

"Sebastian's been visiting the site," Leo said. "Deliveries. Security personnel. Refrigeration units." His eyes met Gideon's. "Something's happening there."

Gideon's jaw tightened. He remembered those facilities, remembered his grandfather halting Evelyn's so-called research when the lawsuits poured in. Injuries. Deaths. Human experimentation parading as innovation. Even the Blackwell name hadn't been able to scrub that stain clean.

"Bishop needs to see this," Gideon said, voice low but sure. "But not yet. If the feds move too soon—"

"Evelyn will bury it," Leo finished. "Understood. I'll keep Bishop cautious, but out of the loop on timing until we have enough to make it stick."

Gideon turned to Christian. "I want surveillance on the Westchester facilities. Eyes on Sebastian. And check Arden's coverage—if there are weak points, I want them closed."

Christian nodded once, sharp and silent. "Already on it."

As Leo and Christian exited, the silence that fell over the room was suffocating.

The storm wasn't coming anymore.

It was here.

In the walls.

In the blood.

Gideon's gaze dropped back to the open folder, but the words blurred at the edges. He couldn't stop thinking about Arden.

He reached for his phone and sent the message before he could turn it into strategy.

> Meetings all day, but can I stop by later?

Her reply came a moment later.

> Arden: I'd like that. Not for long though. I have plans tonight.

Plans.

Karaoke night with Penny and the others. A rare pocket of lightness in a life too often shadowed by threat and memory.

A flicker of a smile tugged at his mouth.

Then faded.

His attention returned to the folder. Pages of corruption. Evidence. Collateral damage. Names and numbers arranged in careful lines, as if ruin became more civilized when printed in black ink.

And through it all, his thoughts circled one place.

One person.

Arden.

The idea of her being dragged into this web, of her name existing anywhere near Evelyn's schemes, left a bitter taste in his mouth. Arden had nothing to do with any of this, and still she stood in the middle of it.

Because of him.

Because he let her in.

Because she stayed.

Gideon leaned back in his chair as the sun spilled molten gold across his desk, painting everything in the quiet glow of a promise he hadn't made yet, but would. Whatever was coming, Arden wouldn't face it alone.

The line between business and personal had blurred long ago.

But tonight, it felt like a fuse.

Lit.

CHAPTER 49

A Rose and a Warning

Her muscles ached with the deep, satisfying burn of exertion. Every strike, every pivot, every ruthless takedown from the Krav Maga session she'd thrown herself into hours earlier still lived in her frame. The sweat had long since dried, but adrenaline lingered in her blood, her pulse ticking slightly faster than normal.

Not restless.

Ready.

Still tuned for combat.

Arden stretched her fingers, rolled one shoulder, then stepped up to the counter. The scent of espresso curled around her—warm, rich, anchoring—but her mind was miles away.

Evelyn's voice still coiled around her ribs like a vise, a poisonous echo that refused to fade. Beneath it, though, moved something quieter. Stronger. More dangerous.

Gideon.

The way he had looked at her. The promise in his voice.

Then I burn it all down.

Her fingers flexed.

She hadn't come here for indulgence. Only a moment to breathe.

A slow inhale.

A long exhale.

The simple act of staying in her own body.

Wrapped in the low clatter of mugs and whispered conversation, in the comfort of baked vanilla and dark roast, Arden allowed herself the smallest reprieve. Her shoulders eased as she placed her order, the warmth of the café sinking into her skin like filtered sunlight on a cold day.

The barista slid a cup and saucer toward her.

And beside it, a rose.

She stilled.

A single stem. Deep red. Impossibly perfect.

Out of place.

It wasn't the rose itself that made her pulse lurch. It was the contrast. Here, in this café with its soft lighting and cozy charm, the rose didn't feel romantic.

It felt wrong.

It didn't belong.

Arden's fingers hovered above the stem, her expression sharpening as she looked up. "What's this?"

The barista barely glanced at her before pivoting to the next order. "Guy came in. Said to make sure it got to a woman named Arden." His tone was bored. Unconcerned. "That's you, right?"

A slow ripple of unease moved beneath her skin.

"Did he leave a name?" she asked, voice quieter now. More precise. "Did he say anything else?"

The guy shrugged, wiping down the counter with practiced detachment. "Nope. Just said you'd know what it meant."

Her stomach turned.

You'd know what it meant.

But she didn't.

And that was the problem.

She carried the rose and her coffee to a table near the window, her gaze scanning the café once, then again. No one lingered. No one watched. Still, the prickling under her skin didn't ease.

She sat, fingers curling tight around the warm ceramic. Steam spiraled upward in soft coils, catching the light—so ordinary, so familiar.

Nothing about this felt ordinary.

The rose lay between her and the window, flawless and unblemished.

A message.

But from whom?

Her jaw tightened, and for the first time in days, she couldn't decide which possibility was worse: that it might be a warning from Evelyn, or that it wasn't.

She was still staring at the rose when something shifted behind her.

Not a sound. Not movement.

A presence.

Barely there. Unmistakable.

Like a static charge in the air before a storm breaks. It moved too close, lingered too long, deliberate in a way that didn't belong inside the comfort of a café.

A shadow where there shouldn't have been one.

"Fancy running into you here."

The voice cut through the low hum of conversation, threading through her thoughts like a needle—precise, practiced.

Sebastian.

Arden didn't turn right away. Didn't flinch. But her focus narrowed instantly, her pulse ticking upward.

THE SHIFT in the atmosphere wasn't imagined.

Arden felt it.

The invisible compression of space, as though gravity had tilted toward him the moment he stepped in.

Sebastian moved through the room with a confidence too casual to be genuine. Every step looked designed, not instinctive, as if he had been waiting just out of frame, watching the scene unfold until it was his cue to enter. His suit was immaculate, tie knotted with perfect tension, posture deceptively relaxed.

A performance, down to the breath.

He slid into the seat across from her without so much as a glance for permission.

A quiet invasion.

The kind that didn't require force, only presence.

His eyes drifted to the rose, and a slow smirk lifted the corner of his mouth. "Secret admirer?"

Arden didn't answer right away. Her fingers curled more tightly around her coffee cup, the heat a welcome contrast to the cold uncoiling beneath her ribs.

"Apparently." Her voice stayed calm. Unshaken. "Some guy left it with the barista. Said I'd know what it meant."

Sebastian studied the flower like it was a riddle only he could solve.

"No note? No signature?"

"Just the rose."

Her smile was small, unreadable, measured.

She wasn't going to give him anything more.

He leaned back, tilting his head. "Curious."

There was something too focused in his stare, as if he were collecting her responses and filing them away for later. He was good at that—quietly gathering, silently circling, watching for the smallest weakness he could turn into leverage.

Then, as though on cue, his gaze returned to the flower.

"Here I thought lavender lattes were your thing."

Her throat tightened before she could stop it. Barely a breath, but he caught it.

His smile deepened, just enough to show teeth.

"Thought so."

He shouldn't have known that.

She had never told him. Never told anyone except, maybe, Gideon in passing. But Sebastian wasn't guessing. He was letting her know he had been watching.

Lavender. Roses. Warnings dressed as gifts.

She lifted her cup and took a slow sip, letting the ceramic shield her face.

"Not today."

That was all she gave him.

No confirmation. No denial. Just a wall.

He didn't press.

He was already in the room.

That was the point.

His hand drifted toward the flower again, not touching, but close enough to cast another shadow.

"It's bold," he said, voice low and even. "That kind of attention tends to come with a cost."

Arden set the cup down with deliberate care, the soft clink of porcelain against saucer grounding her. She met his eyes with a gaze as even as his tone.

"Or perhaps a rose is just a rose. Not everything is a warning."

Sebastian's smile didn't budge, but something in his expression cooled.

"You, of all people, should know better than that."

Her jaw tightened, fingers finding the edge of the table.

"I'll let you know if I get the bill."

He laughed then, softly. Almost indulgently. As though her sharpness amused him more than it threatened him.

Sebastian stood, brushed invisible lint from his sleeve, then adjusted his cuffs with meticulous precision.

"Enjoy your coffee," he murmured. "And the rose."

He didn't wait for a reply. He only turned and walked out, his retreat as staged as his entrance.

Arden didn't move.

Not right away.

The babble of the café returned slowly, like someone had turned the volume back up on the world.

But the rose stayed.

Unbothered.

Still perfect.

Still out of place.

She reached for her cup again, fingers tracing the rim. The warmth hadn't faded, not entirely. But underneath the coffee and cinnamon and faint sweetness from the counter, something else lingered.

Not unease.

Not memory.

A warning.

And this time, she didn't doubt it.

————

SEBASTIAN HADN'T NEEDED to stay.

Not after the look in her eyes.

Not after the hesitation.

She had felt it—the shift, the thread pulling taut.

He watched from the corner, unnoticed, as the moment sealed itself inside her. A whisper she couldn't shake. A question she wouldn't answer.

She hadn't run.

Not yet.

And she wouldn't.

Because deep down, Arden Rivers already knew some warnings weren't meant to be avoided.

They were meant to be followed.

❦

Arden's phone buzzed.

The sound cut through her thoughts like a sudden knock at a closed door. Her shoulders jumped before her eyes found his name.

Gideon.

Something unspooled in her chest. Not completely, but enough.

She exhaled, the smallest breath of relief.

> Gideon: Meetings all day, but can I stop by later?

A line. Simple. Uncomplicated.

It shouldn't have steadied her, but it did.

Her thumbs hovered, then moved.

> I'd like that. Not for long though. I have plans tonight.

His reply landed fast, no hesitation.

> Gideon: I'll see you soon.

A smile touched the edge of her mouth, small and real. He always did that—found her center without trying.

Sebastian's words still clung to the edges of her thoughts, low and needling, like a song stuck in the wrong key. But the sight of Gideon's name on her screen had quieted something.

Not all of it.

Enough.

She slid the phone back into her jacket and leaned into the chair, the motion subtle, automatic. Even that small shift stirred something tight in her chest, something she hadn't realized was still wound so hard.

The unease hadn't left.

It had buried itself deeper.

One word lingered.

Lavender.

She rolled it over and over in her mind. Had it been careless? Coincidence? Or had Sebastian known exactly what he was doing?

Her arms folded over her chest, more muscle memory than defense, but the tension stayed there—coiled, low, unsettled.

Across the café, the barista made a joke to someone in line. A laugh followed, loud and easy. Behind the counter, steam hissed. Cups clinked. Espresso poured. The usual rhythm of a weekday afternoon kept moving around her.

The world didn't feel any different.

But Arden did.

Something in the air had shifted, tilted slightly off balance, just enough to make everything feel misaligned.

❧

The apartment looked like it had lost a fight with a fashion tornado. Fabric had been flung across chairs, tossed over lamps, and scattered over the floor in a bright, reckless patchwork of chaos. Sequins, satin, leather—every shade of rebellion laid bare.

Penny's closet had clearly waged war, and the battlefield was her living room.

In the eye of it all spun Penny, a one-woman storm, limbs flailing with uncontainable energy. Her laughter was bright and loud, incapable of leaving room for shadows.

"Tonight," she announced, stepping out of her room like she had just been awarded a Tony, "we forget all of it. Mysterious flowers. Brooding men. Creepy run-ins. We remind this city what we're made of."

Arden lounged on the couch, holding up the burgundy top Penny had launched at her like a challenge. Soft fabric. Sheer sleeves. A neckline that dared to go lower than her comfort zone. It caught the light with a quiet shimmer, bolder than her usual choices, but not wrong.

She raised an eyebrow. "And how are we doing that, exactly?"

Penny struck a pose and nearly toppled off her silver heels. "First, we make you look dangerously gorgeous. Then, drinks. Karaoke. And if necessary, emotional exorcism."

She vanished into the closet and emerged seconds later, holding up a pair of high-waisted leather leggings with the triumph of someone who had discovered buried treasure.

"These could double as a weapon. Perfect for shattering hearts and ghosting billionaires."

Arden took them with mock suspicion. "You're lucky I trust your chaos."

"Trust," Penny said solemnly, hand over heart, "is the foundation of our sacred friendship."

With a dramatic flourish, she spun around and revealed her own outfit: a sequined mini dress so reflective it could probably redirect traffic. Cutout back. Hemline legally questionable. Pure Penny.

Arden stepped into the leggings and adjusted them over her hips. They clung to her body, daring in all the right ways. She paused, looked in the mirror, and nodded once.

Screw it.

"Shoes?" she asked.

Penny gasped like she had been mortally wounded. "Shoes are everything, Arden. They set the emotional tone."

She produced a pair of stiletto ankle boots—shiny, black, and unapologetically sharp.

Arden zipped them up and struck a mock pose. "Dangerous enough yet?"

Penny's eyes lit up. "Lethal. You're a storm in heels. A goddess with grievances. The city won't survive."

Arden laughed, lighter now. Looser.

"You're something else."

"I prefer iconic," Penny said, looping an arm around her, sequins catching the light like stardust. "And tonight? So are you. Let's go be legendary."

CHAPTER 50

The Weight of a Promise

The knock came as Penny vanished in a whirlwind of sequins and heels, muttering about a "wardrobe emergency of epic proportions."

Arden opened the door, and there he was.

Gideon Blackwell, all sharp lines and quiet intensity, standing at the edge of her world.

"You made it," she said, voice even despite the way her heart thundered.

"I did," he said, tone low and deliberate.

His eyes swept over her slowly. Taking her in. Arden caught the shift in his expression—the smallest flicker of something raw, the pause of his gaze, the slight clench in his jaw, the twitch of his fingers at his sides. He was trying not to reach for her.

She wore the burgundy top Penny had chosen, tailored elegance teetering on indecency. The sheer sleeves shimmered in the light, whispering secrets, while the leather pants gripped her hips like they had no intention of letting go. Her stiletto boots gave her just enough height to level the playing field.

Gideon exhaled, slow and controlled.

Not unaffected.

That tension in his hands was still there.

"You did that on purpose," he said, voice rougher now, edged.

Arden lifted a brow. "What—got dressed?"

She played it off, but the gleam in her eyes gave her away.

The look on his face said the rest. Dark. Dangerous. Knowing.

"Dressed like that."

She fought her own smile. "If I say yes, what does that get me?"

His eyes dipped—not only to her mouth, but lower, down the length of her body. Taking his time. Making her feel it.

"Trouble," he said finally. Quiet. Certain. "A whole lot of trouble."

The few inches between them felt combustible. Arden felt every glance like a touch dragged slowly over her skin, and her stomach dropped, dizzy and delicious.

She stepped aside, letting him in, pretending not to feel the heat that radiated from him as he passed. Gideon moved into her apartment with the ease of a man who knew how to belong anywhere he decided to stand. In the low kitchen light, he looked even more dangerous—shoulders broad, presence coiled, every inch of him shifting the gravity in the room.

His cologne trailed behind him.

Warm spice. Late-night temptation.

Unmistakably him.

Arden breathed him in before she could stop herself.

He didn't say anything. Only let that smirk deepen.

"See?" he murmured. "Trouble."

She brushed past him with a roll of her eyes, but the heat he left in his wake settled low in her spine, stubborn and slow to fade.

Gideon leaned against the counter, his eyes locked on her like she was the only thing in the room worth studying. Arden turned to grab two glasses from the cabinet. She needed something to do, something to keep her hands occupied, because he was watching her like a predator watches a flicker of movement—calm, alert, focused.

Thread by thread, her composure began to unravel.

He broke the silence first. "Nice place."

She glanced back. "You sound surprised."

"I'm not," he said. "Just wasn't expecting..."

She narrowed her eyes. "Expecting what?"

He didn't answer right away.

He read the apartment the way he read her—slow, sharp, thorough. His fingers tapped once, twice against the counter, then stopped.

His gaze had landed on the rose.

The shift was subtle enough that Arden almost missed it, but when she turned back to face him, his expression had changed. Hardened. Something cold slipped beneath the surface, and the tension in the room tilted.

At first, it was the single bloom on the counter, its petals pristine, waiting for admiration. Then his gaze tracked the rest: roses by the door, stems stacked carelessly, petals bruised and wilting.

Some fresh.

Some not.

Something clicked.

His breath stayed even, but the quiet tension in his body told her he had seen it for what it was. This wasn't one gesture. It wasn't a strange coincidence or some passing inconvenience she could tuck into a drawer and ignore.

It was a pattern.

Deliberate.

Gideon's expression hardened further. Not anger—not only anger—but concern sharpened into something furious and controlled.

"You've been getting these."

It wasn't a question.

Arden's fingers drifted toward the counter but didn't touch the petals. She hovered near them, as if distance alone could make them less real.

"It's nothing," she said. "Some weirdo with a flower budget and too much time to kill."

The words rang false, even to her.

Gideon closed the distance between them.

"One rose might be nothing," he said, gaze cutting to the door. "But that? That's not nothing."

His eyes met hers. Steady. Burning.

"How long?" he asked.

Quiet. Controlled. The restrained edge in his tone should have soothed her. It didn't.

"It's—" She faltered, gaze dropping. "A while."

Gideon went rigid.

THE SILENCE that followed was worse than shouting. Her admission hung between them, shameful and fragile.

Gideon's jaw clenched.

She didn't elaborate, and he didn't pressure. Not yet. But the silence thickened anyway, gathering weight in the small space between them.

He stepped closer, slow and deliberate, and the movement made Arden lift her eyes to his. Whatever she saw there made her blink once, then brace.

"And you didn't tell me."

She shrugged, a poor imitation of indifference. "It's harmless. Just dumb gifts from someone with too much money and not enough sanity."

He didn't move. His fingers flexed once at his sides.

And then he saw it.

Her tell.

A tiny tug at her bottom lip, left side first. A flicker of hesitation so small she probably didn't even know she was doing it. She always did that when she was holding something back.

She wasn't brushing this off.

She was hiding it.

A slow breath left him. Measured. Controlled.

"You weren't supposed to care," she added quietly, then hated herself the second it slipped out.

The fire in his gaze dimmed, replaced by something raw.

He leaned in, voice dropping. "Wrong."

She flinched.

Gideon backed off a fraction. Not far. Enough to make room for the anger to cool before it became something she would mistake for threat. He exhaled slowly, reining himself in.

"Tell me everything," he said. "Please."

Her throat tightened. She wanted to. God, she wanted to. But saying it aloud would give the fear shape, and once it had shape, she would have to admit it had been standing beside her for weeks.

"It's not your problem," she whispered.

Gideon didn't move.

Then he said softly, "It became my problem the second I met you."

Something in his voice broke through her.

Arden dropped her gaze, blinking hard. She wouldn't cry. Not over roses or fear. Not over him. But the pressure had been building for days. Weeks.

"Look at me," he said.

She did.

His face was too close. His eyes relentless. There was nothing cold in them now; only heat, only care, only the kind of fury that had nowhere safe to go.

"Arden." His voice came low, a warning wrapped in restraint.

Her lips parted as if she might answer, but instead her teeth caught her bottom lip again. The first rose on her windshield. The notes at the bar. The anonymous texts. The silent weight of being watched.

It all rose up like smoke.

A pause.

"It's not a big deal."

His patience snapped.

He moved fast, one hand at her waist, the other at the back of her neck, and suddenly she was pressed full against him, flush from shoulders to knees.

"You don't get to decide that. Not when someone is trying to scare you. Not when—"

He broke off, jaw clenched.

Not when I care about you.

He didn't say it.

She felt it anyway.

Her eyes burned.

She didn't answer. Didn't argue.

Because she knew.

Gideon exhaled through his nose, slow and sharp. He wouldn't press. Not now. Not when she was already bracing for a fight. But this wasn't over.

"You're not facing this—or anything else—alone."

She swallowed, gaze flicking up to meet his. Something moved behind her eyes, vulnerable and raw.

Gone before he could name it.

Her hands had fisted in his shirt. At some point, she had started holding on. She didn't know when.

It wasn't calculated.

It was instinct.

And he let her.

Let her hold on.

His hands settled at her waist, firm and grounding, his fingers flexing once as though anchoring them both.

She wasn't delicate. She wasn't small. But he felt her there—the tension in every breath, every ache she refused to name, every quiet thing she hadn't said.

And God, he revered her for it.

"Promise me," he said, low and reverent, one hand skimming the side of her neck before trailing to her jaw. "If anything feels off. If you see something. Hear something. If your gut so much as twitches—you call me. Day or night."

She blew out a long, heavy breath.

She could argue. Push back. Remind him that care and control wore the same face often enough to make a woman cautious.

But this wasn't that.

This was care. This was the way he anchored her without demanding she stay.

"I promise," she whispered.

Then the air shifted again.

The promise hung between them.

Unshaken.

Unbreakable.

GIDEON'S JAW RELAXED. Not because the fury was gone. It wasn't. Not because he wasn't already building a plan in his head.

But because, right now, she was in his arms.

And that mattered more than anything else.

His fingers brushed her wrist, lingering long enough for his thumb to trace the inside of it. A small, grounding touch. Not demanding. Just there.

"Good." His voice dropped lower, quieter. "That's all I need."

A lie.

He needed more than that.

But he wouldn't ask.

Not yet.

Arden swallowed, and for the first time that night, something inside her eased. Barely, but enough. Her breath slowed. Her shoulders lowered.

And then, before she even realized it, she reached for him.

Her fingers fisted the front of his shirt, unthinking and instinctive.

He was solid.

And she needed solid.

Gideon let her hold on.

His hands found her waist—steady, unmoving. Where she was soft, he was stone, but it wasn't fragility he felt beneath his palms. It was strength. Tension. Will.

She met him there, in the storm.

And she never flinched.

God, he adored her for that.

His fingers dipped beneath the hem of her shirt, skimming warm skin with the barest touch. An anchor. A truth.

The tension between them didn't break.

It deepened.

Something curled in the silence, thick with meaning.

His hand slid to her hip, slow and sure, fingers pressing into her as though he needed proof that she was real. That she was here. That she had chosen to stay within reach.

When she didn't pull away, his grip tightened.

A quiet claim.

His lips brushed her temple—soft, hesitant. Testing.

Arden's breath caught.

Gideon nuzzled closer, the bridge of his nose skimming down her cheek. His stubble scraped lightly over her skin, and her breath hitched again.

"You drive me insane."

A soft smile touched her lips. "Feeling's mutual."

Her fingers stayed curled in his shirt. She could feel every inch of him, even through the fabric.

His hand skimmed higher, not in haste, but in reverence. She was warmth and power, soft skin and sharp edges, and he wanted to know every part of her.

Arden smoothed her palms down the front of his shirt, slow and deliberate. Not pulling away. Not pushing, either. Committing the moment to memory as if she understood exactly how rare it was.

Gideon's breath deepened, deliberate, as though he could rein it in.

He couldn't.

She felt the shift before he made it: the firmer press of his hands, the tension in his jaw, the parting of his lips like he meant to speak.

He didn't.

She licked her lips.

His eyes tracked the movement like a man who had already lost the battle. "Arden."

Her name was a rasp. A confession. A warning.

The space between them frayed, held together by a thread. Her breath caught, her chest rising and falling against his as his pupils darkened with hunger, restraint bleeding out of him with every second.

She tightened her grip on his shirt.

Don't pull away.

Don't stop.

His hands curved around her hips, steady and claiming.

One motion.

That was all it took.

WITH PRECISION AND INTENT, Gideon lifted her onto the counter.

The marble was cold against her thighs through the leather, but Arden barely noticed. His mouth moved over hers with aching precision—hungry, yes, but restrained, savoring every taste as if he were afraid of going too far and more afraid of stopping.

The rose slid from the counter, crimson petals scattering across the tile like silent witnesses.

Arden exhaled sharply. Her legs parted enough for him to step between them, and then he was close.

So damn close.

"Gideon—"

Her voice barely made it past her lips before he silenced it.

Not with a word.

With his mouth.

The kiss wasn't soft. It wasn't careful. It was collision. Breaking point. Her hands pulled him closer as if she needed him to burn everything else away—every thought, every fear, every hesitation—and Gideon let her.

Let her take. Let her lead. Let her have him.

His fingers slid into her hair, tilting her head back, deepening the kiss, taking control only when she met him with equal force. She tasted like slow heat and quiet defiance, and he was too far gone now—wrapped in her, ruled by her, undone in ways he hadn't seen coming.

His breath came hard against her chest, uneven and rough, each exhale betraying the war burning inside him. He was strength, stone and steel, but in that moment, he held her like something precious.

That contrast struck her hard.

Beautiful.

A little feral.

Her thighs drew tighter around his hips, instinct answering instinct. His groan rumbled low in his chest, swallowed by her mouth, and she felt it everywhere.

She was heat and danger beneath his hands—soft where it mattered, sharp where the world had taught her to be—and he wanted every inch of her.

Wanted more.

His lips trailed from her mouth to the line of her jaw, then down her neck, fire over her pulse, and Arden let him. Let him savor. Let him breathe her in like she was something rare. Something he didn't deserve, but had no intention of letting go.

She thought about speaking, saying something sharp, something to remind herself this was dangerous, but she couldn't. Not with Gideon between her legs, not with every inch of him pressing close enough to make thought feel unnecessary.

Instead, she tilted her head, giving him more.

A surrender.

A dare.

And Gideon took it.

His hands slid higher, slow and deliberate, as if this wasn't only a kiss.

As if it were something holy.

A reckoning.

Neither of them moved to stop it. The air between them crackled—charged, molten, alive—and her body curved into his like it belonged there.

Maybe it did.

Her fingers slid into his hair, not to pull him away, but to anchor herself. She arched into him on instinct, breath hitching, pulse racing like it couldn't catch up.

He kissed her like breathing had become negotiable. Like she was the only thing holding him steady. Deep. Devouring. A wild surrender.

His hands gripped her hips as if he needed the proof of her, of this, imprinted in his palms.

And when he finally tore himself away, it wasn't distance.

It was breath.

A pause.

A moment to steady the storm.

Forehead to forehead. Heart to heart.

Their breaths tangled.

"Come to the Blackwell Charity Gala with me," he said, voice low, a vow wrapped in a question.

Arden's eyes searched his. "Your family's gala?"

He dragged his thumb along her cheek, reverent, unexpectedly gentle for a man still coiled with heat.

"Early spring," he said. "Come with me. As my date."

It wasn't only an invitation.

It was a line in the sand.

Her throat thickened. "You're sure?" she asked. "I'm not exactly high-society material."

His mouth curved, slow and sure. Not quite a smile. Something sharper. Something deeper.

He cupped her face in both hands, grounding her. "It doesn't matter if you're society material."

His gaze held hers, unflinching.

"You weren't made for them."

His grip tightened, and his next words came like a truth he had carried too long. "You were made for me."

Her heart slammed into her ribs.

Arden didn't believe in being swept away. Not by promises. Not by pretty lines. But this wasn't a line. This felt like him.

Like truth.

His hands slipped lower, tracing her waist, his palms memorizing every curve like a man cataloging what he could no longer afford to lose.

She should have pushed back.

She didn't.

Her thumb brushed his jaw, rough with stubble, anchoring her.

"Okay," she whispered. "I'll be there."

Something wavered in his eyes.

Relief. Possession. Maybe even permanence.

His mouth found hers again, slower this time, his lips moving with a reverence that made her dizzy.

This wasn't hunger now.

It wasn't urgency.

It was devotion.

Silent.

Unrelenting.

Penny's music created a muffled backdrop to the moment. Laughter echoed from the other room, bright and careless, a reminder that the world still turned.

But here, there was only him.

Only her.

Arden pulled back slightly, her lips still tingling from the heat of him. Their foreheads bumped gently, and she exhaled a laugh that still carried the edge of a smirk.

"You really don't know what you're in for," she said, though the sharpness in her voice had softened into something warmer.

His thumb traced a slow line down her back, steady and unhurried. The way he looked at her—like she was rare, ruinous, already under his skin—left her breath caught in her throat.

"With you?" His voice was steady, utterly certain. "Absolutely everything."

The weight of his words settled deep in her chest, heavy with promise. With inevitability. Her fingers drifted along his collarbone, mapping the moment, memorizing it, while the quiet intimacy between them became its own kind of gravity.

For a long moment, they remained locked in each other's orbit, tethered by everything they hadn't said. The outside world loomed at the edges, no more than a shadow, while what they were building here—raw, electric, undeniable—felt impossible to dismiss, even in its newness.

Penny's laughter cut through the quiet again, distant but insistent, pulling at the moment like an inevitable tide.

Reality beckoning.

Arden shifted slightly, lips curving into a small, private smile as she caught Gideon's gaze.

But she didn't move away.

And Gideon wasn't ready to let go.

His hands moved over her waist, fingers brushing the curve of her hips as if trying to hold on a little longer. His thumbs caught beneath her shirt, right where her waist narrowed, and she felt the slight flex of his grip. Reverent. Possessive. Careful enough to be a question and dangerous enough to feel like an answer.

His gaze roamed over her, unapologetic and deliberate. The way her top hugged every curve, the way those sheer sleeves softened the sharp edge of black leather at her hips, nearly did him in. She was heat and tension beneath his hands, impossible not to touch, impossible to let walk away without feeling the loss of it first.

His thumb skimmed along her jaw, an anchor and a spark.

"I meant what I said." His voice was rough, deliberate. A vow. "You're mine. And you're not alone. Not now. Not ever."

Something shifted inside her.

The words landed. She felt them settle, felt them burrow deep, threading through places she had kept guarded for so long she'd almost forgotten they could open. For years, she had carried everything alone. Had been alone.

But now...

His lips brushed hers again, soft and fleeting, no less disarming for its restraint.

And she let herself believe him.

His smirk was pure sin, but it didn't disguise the dark flicker in his eyes, the one that said he was barely holding himself back.

"Letting you go doesn't mean I'm done with you."

His lips ghosted over hers, too soft, too reverent, too dangerous because of what it did to her. The world fell away for one breath more, the silence between them thick with understanding, with inevitability.

His hand stayed at her waist.

Branding her.

Staking his claim.

Strength and tenderness, both at once.

The contrast of him stole her breath, and Arden let herself feel it all without walls, without hesitation.

From the other room, Penny's cheerful voice usurped the moment. "Arden! Subway leaves in fifteen!"

Arden laughed under her breath, forehead resting against his. "Guess that's my cue."

His jaw tightened. A shadow passed through his eyes—quiet, reluctant, raw. Gideon didn't answer at first. He only gave a low, frustrated sound and held her tighter before easing her off the counter with a care that made letting her go feel like its own confession.

Once her boots hit the floor, he adjusted her top and smoothed her hair.

Intimate. Domestic. Maddeningly tender.

"You're not taking the subway," he said, voice low and final.

Arden's chin lifted, a familiar spark in her eyes. "It's only a few stops. We'll be fine."

His hand held hers a little tighter. "Car's already en route."

She blinked, clearly not expecting the gentle steel in his tone. "You didn't have to."

"I know," he said, steady as stone. "I wanted to."

A subtle shiver moved through her, not from fear, but from the quiet care beneath his certainty.

Her lips curved. "Thank you. For everything."

"Anytime." His gaze lingered, unreadable and full.

PENNY SWANNED into the room like a Broadway finale. "We're on a schedule, people! And schedules don't wait—not even for smoldering billionaire makeouts!"

She paused, green eyes darting between them before a slow, delighted grin overtook her face.

"Oh. Did I interrupt foreplay?"

Gideon's smirk was effortless, but his eyes told a different story. "Nothing that won't pick back up later."

Arden snorted and stepped toward Penny, but the heat of Gideon's hands still clung to her skin, the taste of his kiss lingering on her lips.

"You've got a car downstairs," he said, addressing Penny with quiet authority. "No subway tonight."

"Ooh, we've officially entered my rich-girl era," Penny crowed. "I'm choosing not to question it."

She bumped Arden's shoulder, and for once, Arden didn't roll her eyes. Instead, she turned back to Gideon, something softer slipping through her expression.

"Thanks," she said, quiet but unflinching.

He nodded once, gaze locking with hers. "Have fun tonight."

The way he said it shouldn't have landed the way it did.

But it did.

Like he was already feeling her absence before she had even walked out the door.

Arden hesitated, then smiled. Not coy. Not careless. Warmth sparked in her chest as her fingers found the doorknob, but she paused and turned back again.

"Oh, don't look so tragic," she teased, the edge in her voice softened. "I'm not exactly running off with someone new."

"No." His eyes moved over her, slow and unapologetic. "But I'm not thrilled about you stepping out looking like that."

"Like what?" She arched a brow.

He let the silence stretch. Then, quietly, "Like trouble I don't want to share."

She smirked, sharp and knowing. "Perfect. That's the look I was going for."

He stepped in, too close now. Close enough for her to feel the hum between them.

"Menace," he murmured.

She tilted closer, her mouth barely skimming his jaw. "You say that like I should apologize."

His hand found her waist again, holding her there as though the act of letting go required more restraint than touching her ever had. He didn't kiss her. He only rested his forehead against hers, keeping her close for one last breath.

"Don't make me wish I'd stopped you," he said, low and gravel-laced.

Her heart kicked, but she didn't back down.

"You won't," she said softly. "But you'll be thinking about me all night."

They stood there for one last suspended moment. Then she slipped away, and the door clicked shut behind her.

Gideon didn't move.

In the hallway, Arden let her spine touch the wall, breath catching sharp in her throat. She wasn't fragile. Never had been. But letting him in hadn't felt like surrender. It felt like armor. Like choosing softness and keeping her edge. Like handing someone the weight of your world and knowing they would carry it if they had to.

Downstairs, Penny's voice echoed by the curb.

But all Arden felt was the imprint of Gideon's touch.

THE DOOR SHUT behind her with a soft click.

Gideon didn't move. Not immediately.

Arden's scent lingered in the air—wild floral, soft and sharp at once. Unexpected. Unruly. Untamed. The apartment smelled like her.

But beneath it, something else waited.

Rot.

He scanned the space. Penny's shoes sat near the door, kicked off in a swirl of color. A sweater draped carelessly over the couch. Her presence was loud, unmistakable, impossible to miss. But beneath the chaos, the apartment still felt like Arden too—clean, minimal, intentional.

His gaze drifted left.

The roses.

Dozens of them, wilting in silence. Petals dried and curling like old wounds. Crimson blooms scattered across the floor.

It wasn't one or two.

It wasn't love.

It was a graveyard.

The mood of moments ago—the heat, the laughter, the bright reckless edge of her smile—bled out of the air.

Gideon stepped forward, jaw tight, the stillness in his body coiled and dangerous. He crouched and picked up one of the roses from the floor. The thorns had been clipped like warnings removed from the evidence. The stem was clean. Too clean. The petals still perfect.

A warning.

Not a gift.

He rose without a word and crossed to the kitchen. Under the sink, he found the trash bags and gathered every single rose: fresh, fading, fallen.

One by one.

Methodical.

Final.

He tied the bag tight, his knuckles pale.

She was out there laughing. Singing. Finally letting herself breathe. And here, in the quiet, he was calculating the breach.

His hand brushed along the counter's edge, the same place her body had pressed against his minutes before.

Then he reached for his phone.

He didn't call immediately. Not until the anger had settled low in his chest, dense and deliberate.

His gaze dropped to the bag by the door.

Heavier than it should have been.

How the hell had no one seen this?

Christian's team was supposed to be watching the building. After the shattered window, there had been protocols. Surveillance. Coverage. Oversight. Someone had trespassed over and over—unseen, unchallenged—and left pieces of himself inside her life like offerings.

Gideon's jaw flexed.

She hadn't told him. He understood that now. Her silence wasn't forgetfulness.

It was fear.

He tapped Christian's name and waited. When the line picked up, Gideon didn't pace. He didn't shout.

"She didn't say anything," he said. "But I'm looking at more than a dozen. Some fresh. Some rotting."

A pause.

"Find out how the hell they got there."

Another pause.

"And if your team missed this," he said, voice low and cold, "I want to know why."

He ended the call and set the phone down, the quiet click like a final nail.

His gaze stayed fixed on the door.

She hadn't been gone long, but already the air felt wrong without her.

———

SEBASTIAN HADN'T EXPECTED him to cross the line so soon.

Gideon was in her space.

Not orbiting.

Inside.

Among her things. Breathing her air. Touching the edges of a life he had not earned the right to enter.

The boundaries were dissolving.

To walk in like it meant nothing.

Like she already belonged to him.

The cameras didn't catch everything.

Not yet.

But they caught enough.

The way she moved toward him. The pause. The look.

That look.

He hated it.

Too soft. Too trusting. As if she had forgotten everything that came before.

She was stunning tonight.

Not dressed up.

Set on fire.

Hair down. Eyes bright with something dangerously close to hope.

Every detail seared into him. She didn't need polish or permission or the borrowed shine of anyone's name. She was the spark.

Little Fire.
And now she was walking into the night.
Not alone.
But not safe.
He would follow.
Of course he would.
And that smug bastard who thought he could contain her?
He didn't see the blaze coming.

CHAPTER 51

Where Shadows Gather

The sleek black car Gideon had arranged sliced through Manhattan's chaos like it didn't belong there—quiet, controlled, immune to the frenzy beyond its tinted windows. Inside, everything was smooth: the ride, the leather, the low hum of power beneath their feet.

Inside Arden, nothing felt calm.

The roses haunted her. Not as flowers anymore, but as evidence. A bloom on a counter. A stem by the door. A threat dressed in beauty and left where her life was supposed to feel untouched.

Gideon's presence had steadied her earlier. Anchoring. Silent. Sure.

But now, with only Penny's chatter and the blur of city lights streaking past, the night felt disjointed, as if she had slipped into a scene too glossy to trust.

Penny lounged across the seat like royalty, sparkling as headlights danced over her and scattered glints across the car's plush interior. Regal and rebellious, she looked like she belonged in a limo with a drink in one hand and chaos in the other.

"So," she drawled, flashing a grin that could spark a scandal, "what exactly did you do to get Gideon Blackwell to moonlight as your personal driver? Should I be expecting a horse-drawn carriage next time, or is that reserved for the engagement party?"

Arden rolled her eyes, but the warmth at her neck betrayed her. "He insisted. Something about the subway being unsafe."

Penny raised a brow, her grin sharpening. "Oh, he's insisting now, is he? Look at you, all kept and protected. Sounds serious."

"It's not," Arden said too quickly, turning toward the passing cityscape. "He's being...cautious."

"Cautious?" Penny's voice dipped with disbelief. "Honey, cautious is checking your locks and texting your location. This?" She waved a hand at the polished luxury surrounding them. "This is a man laying claim."

Arden didn't answer. Couldn't. The words snagged in her chest and stayed there.

She saw him again: his hands firm at her waist, the way he had looked at her like the world narrowed to the space she occupied. As if protection wasn't only a promise, but a need.

She exhaled, trying to shake it off as the car glided to a stop outside the bar.

Penny slid out first, silver platform heels striking the pavement with confidence, the sound echoing like the opening note of a show-stopping number. She turned with exaggerated flair, sequins catching the streetlights, and extended her hand like a queen granting an audience.

"Come on, Cinderella. Let's remind this city what royalty looks like."

Despite herself, Arden laughed—low, unguarded, bubbling up from someplace she hadn't touched in weeks. She reached for Penny's hand and stepped out into the chill.

The city greeted her like a dare, its pulse familiar, electric, and laced with the promise of something new.

AHEAD, the bar glowed like an oasis. Mismatched windows spilled warm light onto the cracked sidewalk, and laughter drifted out, tangled with the thrum of bass and conversation. It felt inviting. Safe. For one night, maybe, she could let the world soften around the edges. Here, the roses lost their grip. The shadows couldn't quite reach.

Rachel and Jade had already claimed a corner table, their greetings spilling out warmly beneath the bar's glow.

"Finally!" Rachel exclaimed, pulling Penny into a hug that sparkled with her characteristic exuberance. "We were starting to think your Gideon had you locked away somewhere."

She turned to Arden next, arms open wide. "Please tell me he at least lets you out for fresh air?"

Arden smiled, shaking her head as she slid into the booth. "Occasionally."

Jade leaned back, giving Arden a pointed look. "To be fair, you have been a little hard to track down lately. And Rachel's just mad she can't guilt you into more nights out now that you've got better things to do."

Rachel scoffed, flipping her blonde hair. "Excuse you, I prefer to think of myself as an excellent bad influence. And I am deeply offended that you've been choosing steamy billionaire romance over me."

Penny smirked, nudging Arden's shoulder. "Fair. But let's be so for real right now—Arden has always had main character energy. Now she has the swoony book boyfriend to match."

Rachel gasped, clutching her chest in mock horror. "Betrayal. You used to be fun."

"She still is," Penny said. "She just comes with security detail now."

Arden laughed, the tension in her chest loosening a little.

Their drinks landed without fuss, and the conversation picked up with the kind of rhythm only old friends shared: unforced, familiar, full of shortcuts that didn't need translating.

Jade pulled out her latest tattoo design, delicate and striking, each piece etched with a story Arden could almost hear. Her lean, toned arms moved with effortless precision as she flipped through the pages, dark eyes sparking with quiet intensity. "This one? I'm obsessed with it."

Rachel launched into the tale of a marketing pitch disaster that had them all in stitches, and Penny, as always, took the lead, her quick wit and infectious laugh keeping the momentum going, nudging them deeper into the night.

Then came the first notes of the next song, curling through the air like bait.

Penny's head snapped up, eyes gleaming.

Arden saw it instantly. "Don't even start."

Penny gave a long, dramatic sigh, her grin slow and dangerous. "Oh, babe... I thought you knew me better by now."

"Double rent for a month if you let me sit here."

"Bribery? From you? That's desperation, my love. And also? No." She grabbed Arden's hand and yanked. "Come on. You know the rules."

Arden groaned but didn't fight it. She had sung before. Several times, actually. And every single time, Penny behaved as if Arden had delivered a TEDx Talk set to music.

"This is a terrible idea," Arden muttered.

"This is an iconic idea."

She wasn't nervous, exactly, but the first step under the lights always felt heavy. The dim room wrapped itself in cozy anonymity, but the expectant buzz pressed in, steady and insistent.

Then the opening notes hit, a driving rhythm that slipped beneath her pulse and synced with the pounding of her heart.

Penny let out a gleeful squeak. "Oh, this is gonna be so good."

Arden drew in a breath, slow and steady, her fingers closing around the stand.

And then she released it.

The first note slipped free, and the room forgot how to move. Not gradually. Like someone had flipped a switch.

Her voice moved through the melody with an ease that belied the weight behind it. This wasn't only singing, wasn't only sound. Something unspoken rode every line. Each lyric loosened another knot; each note scraped at the quiet places where fear had settled and refused to leave.

The crowd felt it. The pulse of the room changed. They were no longer only an audience, half-drunk and half-listening over cheap beer and background noise. They were witnesses. Their silence wasn't passive.

It was captivated.

Eyes widened. Heads turned. Even the people who had come for distraction found themselves caught.

Arden's movements grew bolder. Her grip tightened. The power in her voice rose, then roared, filling the room with something too bright to ignore.

And then she saw him.

A figure near the back.

Motionless. Set apart.

The room moved around him, but he didn't. Everyone else leaned in, drawn closer by the force of her voice, but he only watched.

It wasn't wonder.

It was something else entirely.

Distant. Detached. Cold.

The chill hit her hard, slicing through the fire in her chest. Her voice caught, just for a second.

Then the fire came back.

Hotter.

Sharper.

She leaned in.

Let them watch.

The final notes soared, fierce and unrelenting, crashing through the room like a wave that refused to fall. Arden didn't back down. Didn't shrink. And when the song ended, it wasn't only applause that rose around her.

It was a shift in power.

Whoever was watching, they felt it too.

Penny grabbed Arden's arm, nearly spilling her drink. "Holy hell, what was that? You always crush it, but that? That was stop-the-world good."

Jade let out a breath like she had been holding it since the first note. "I've heard you sing before. But not like that."

Rachel crossed her arms, studying her. "That wasn't just singing. That hit different."

Arden reached for her drink. "It's something I used to do," she said quietly, as if naming it too loudly might break whatever spell had been cast.

"Used to?" Rachel echoed. "That wasn't some nostalgia act. That was a message."

The air shifted. The table quieted.

Only Arden knew what had really changed.

Because she could still sense it—that figure in the back, unmoved and watching.

But she hadn't shrunk.

She had answered it.

With fire.

Her glass was cool against her fingers, but it didn't help. The adrenaline still burned beneath her skin, that fire simmering low and bright, refusing to go out.

When she looked again, the spot in the back was empty.

As if he had never been there.

She was only half in the moment when Penny's phone buzzed and pulled her into a fit of laughter, the table coming alive again around her. But for Arden, the spark had twisted into something colder. Something coiled beneath her skin.

A chill.

Silent. Sure.

She needed air.

"Be right back," she said, standing.

Penny's head snapped up. "Where are you going?"

"I'm good." Arden raised a hand. "Just need a minute."

"I'll come with—"

"No." Too fast. She softened it with a breath. "Stay. Enjoy yourself. I need to clear my head."

Penny studied her. "You sure?"

"I promise."

Penny hesitated, then nodded. "Alright. But if you're gone too long, I'm sending a search party."

"Deal."

But it wasn't a deal. Not really. Not if Penny had known about the anonymous messages. Not if she knew about the man who used to wait for Arden after nursing shifts in West Virginia, never touching, never speaking, only watching.

If Penny hadn't been half a drink deep, and if Arden hadn't hidden the worst of it behind sarcasm and stubborn pride, she never would have let her walk out alone.

But Arden didn't tell her.

And Penny didn't ask.

She grabbed her jacket and slipped through the door.

———

THE BAR THROBBED BEHIND HER—GLASSES clinking, off-key verses, cheap laughter.

None of it touched Sebastian.

She was there.

Little Fire.

She stepped beneath the lights like she was walking into war, and he saw the way her fingers curled around the stand. Saw the spark beneath the surface. The part of her everyone else mistook for performance because they didn't know how to recognize a warning when it wore beauty.

Her voice was a match struck in the dark.

And when she sang, it wasn't performance.

It was combustion.

They didn't know it. None of them did.

But she was his.

Not yet.

Soon.

And when she slipped outside, the fire followed her.

She walked alone.

Little Fire, where are you going?

The cold air hit hard as Arden stepped onto the sidewalk, the hum of the city wrapping around her all at once.

Horns. Footsteps. A siren somewhere far away.

Normal sounds.

Except nothing felt normal.

The pressure returned, quiet and heavy, settling over her skin before her mind could name it. Arden scanned the street. Nothing. No figure in the mouth of the alley. No face turned too long in her direction. No shadow where one shouldn't be.

Still, the feeling stayed.

She rubbed her arms.

Breathe.

In. Out.

Footsteps sounded behind her.

Soft. Steady. Close.

She spun.

Nothing.

Her heart kicked hard against her ribs.

Then a hand clamped over her mouth.

The world snapped tight.

She was yanked back against solid heat, an unyielding grip locking around her as the city blurred at the edges.

Leather. Smoke. Metal.

Suffocating.

Panic ignited.
Then a voice came at her ear.
Low. Rough. Unforgiving.
"Don't scream."

For those who made it through the storm, thank you.

Stories like this aren't always easy to read. They ask you to sit with fear and longing, with tenderness and rupture, with the parts of yourself you may have learned to silence. But they also hold space for strength. For choice. For the fierce, fragile work of finding your way back to yourself.

The Storm and the Rose is a story about survival, belonging, and the spaces we fight to call home. It is about land taken in silence. About storms carried beneath the skin. About the invisible battles so many people fight alone.

It is also about what comes after: the messy, miraculous act of daring to heal. Of trusting again. Of letting yourself be loved, not because you are unbroken, but because you are beautifully, resiliently human.

If you carried your own shadows into these pages, I want you to know you are seen. You are not alone. Your story matters, even if it doesn't look like anyone else's.

Arden and Gideon's journey is fiction, but the truths beneath it are not.

Healing is not linear. Strength is not one-size-fits-all. And hope? Hope is one of the most rebellious things we have.

If you needed breaks, I honor that. If these pages echoed something real, I am grateful you stayed. If you are still healing, still finding your way forward, please know this: you are a miracle in motion.

This book was written for anyone who has had to rebuild themselves from the inside out. For the ones who learned how to speak again. How to trust again. How to rise.

You are the storm and the bloom.

Take care of your heart. You matter more than any story.

With gratitude,

T.L. Johnson

P.S. If you made it to this page, thank you. Whether you devoured every word or found your way here by moonlight and momentum, I am deeply grateful you spent time in this world I built.

If the story stirred something in you—if it made you feel, think, cry, ache, or curse—I would be so grateful if you considered leaving a review on Amazon. Even a few words help more than you know. As an indie author, your voice makes it possible for mine to keep going.

And if you read through Kindle Unlimited, yes, your review still matters. So much.

https://www.goodreads.com/tl-johnson
https://www.amazon.com/author/tl-johnson

Acknowledgments

This book was not built alone.

It is stitched together with the hands, the hope, and the fierce belief of so many people who carried me when I forgot how to carry myself.

To the advocates, educators, and quiet fighters who protect family land, and to those who fight for the healing of children and survivors: You are writing futures in places the world once abandoned.

To my husband and daughter: Thank you for giving me a safe, steady place to land. For loving me through every storm. For making room for this dream to grow.

To my early readers—you know who you are: Thank you for reading multiple versions, for offering your hearts and your encouragement when I needed it most. Your belief carried me farther than I can ever truly say.

To Sarah H., thank you for sparking the moment this story was born. One casual chat about BookTok led to the words, *"Hear me out... a guy walks into a bar,"* and everything changed. The rest, as they say, is fiction.

And to every person who stood in my corner:

To the coworkers and friends who kept asking, *"What happens next?"* and *"When's your book coming out?"* (Looking at you, Alesia.)

You didn't just believe in the story.

You believed in me.

To the ones who called me an author before I could even say the word out loud, you named the dream before I had the courage to claim it.

Every kind word and spark of belief.

Every whisper that said, *You are allowed to have this.*

You live in these pages too.

For anyone still finding your way toward healing, toward hope, toward a love you never thought you deserved:

This story is for you.

Your survival matters.

Your dreams matter.

Your heart matters.

This story is a hand reaching back across the dark, whispering:

You made it. And you are worthy.

If You Need It

Stories like this touch real wounds and real strength.
   If you or someone you love needs support,
   I've created a Resource Library with information
   on healing, advocacy, and hope.

Visit: midnighthaven.co/resources

If you or someone you love is in need of support,
   please don't hesitate to reach out.

The National Domestic Violence Hotline is available 24/7
   at 800-799-7233 or by text at 88788.

If you are struggling with thoughts of suicide or need
   immediate emotional support, the Suicide and Crisis Lifeline
   is available 24/7 by calling or texting 988.

About the Author

T.L. Johnson is a lifelong lover of stories that explore
resilience, strength, and the beauty found in life's storms.
A Mississippi native now calling West Virginia home for over a decade, she
draws inspiration from both her Southern roots and the mountainous
landscapes
she's come to love. A homebody with a love for travel, she enjoys spending
time with family and friends, savoring gray days, getting lost in a good book,
and writing short stories and poems during midnight meanderings.

facebook.com/thetljohnsonauthor

instagram.com/tljohnsonauthor

goodreads.com/tl-johnson

amazon.com/author/tl-johnson

threads.com/tljohnsonauthor